Jackie Ashenden writes dark, emotional stories with alpha heroes who've just got the world to their liking only to have it blown wide apart by their kick-ass heroines. She lives in Auckland, New Zealand, with her husband, the inimitable Dr Jax, two kids and two rats. When she's not torturing alpha males and their gutsy heroines, she can be found drinking chocolate martinis, reading anything she can lay her hands on, wasting time on social media or being forced to go mountain biking with her husband. To keep up to date with Jackie's new releases and other news, sign up to her newsletter at jackieashenden.com.

Stefanie London is the *USA TODAY* bestselling author of contemporary romances and romantic comedies. Her books have been called 'genuinely entertaining and memorable' by *Booklist,* and her writing praised as 'elegant, descriptive and delectable' by *RT Book Reviews.* Originally from Australia, she now lives in Toronto, with her very own hero, and is currently in the process of doing her best to travel the world. She frequently indulges in her passions for good coffee, lipstick, romance novels and anything zombie-related. For more information on Stefanie and her books check out her website at stefanie-london.com.

D0566666

If you liked *Dirty Devil* and *The Fling*
why not try

Sweet Temptation by Lauren Hawkeye
A Private Affair by A.C. Arthur

Also by Jackie Ashenden

Kings of Sydney

King's Price
King's Rule
King's Ransom

The Billionaires Club

The Debt

Also by Stefanie London

Melbourne After Dark

Unmasked
Hard Deal
Close Quarters
Faking It

Discover more at millsandboon.co.uk

DIRTY DEVIL

JACKIE ASHENDEN

THE FLING

STEFANIE LONDON

MILLS & BOON

First Published in Great Britain 2019
by Mills & Boon, an imprint of HarperCollins*Publishers*
1 London Bridge Street, London, SE1 9GF

Dirty Devil © 2019 Jackie Ashenden

The Fling © 2019 Stefanie London

ISBN-13: 978-0-263-27747-0

MIX
Paper from
responsible sources
FSC™ C007454

Printed and bound in Spain
by CPI, Barcelona

DIRTY DEVIL

JACKIE ASHENDEN

MILLS & BOON

For Veronica.

Hope you enjoy this one too!

CHAPTER ONE

Thea

I ALWAYS KNEW that breaking into the skyscraper apartment of Damian Blackwood, one of richest men in Hong Kong, would be a risky move. But he had something I wanted, so I had no choice.

His security was insane, though, and the only time I'd been able to get into his apartment unnoticed was during one of his infamous parties, when he himself would be distracted and there would be too many guests wandering around for security staff to discover that there was at least one person in attendance who shouldn't be there.

Privately, I was pleased with myself that I'd even managed it, since the parties were notoriously difficult to get into, even impossible, for those not in the know. Blackwood liked to keep his parties very, *very* private and very, *very* exclusive.

I was not exclusive. I was an unremarkable woman of indeterminate parentage, ordinary in every way. I was someone you wouldn't look at twice, which was what made me so good at what I did. You couldn't be a good thief if you were memorable. Or, at least, you didn't last long if you were.

Still, a lack of invitation hadn't stopped me from going where I wanted before, and it didn't stop me now. I'd managed to get hold of an ID and uniform for the catering company dealing with the event, and had distracted security from looking too closely at their staff lists by undoing an extra button on said uniform and bending to grab the pen I'd 'accidentally' dropped.

It had worked like a charm. Mr Chen had always told me to use whatever I could to my advantage when it came to jobs, so I did. Being a woman was sometimes a pain, but it came in handy every so often.

Especially because men were idiots.

Now I stood on the huge rooftop terrace of Blackwood's Central District apartment, trying to balance a tray of glasses and bottles of Cristal in my sweaty palms.

Music drifted in the air, a hard, driving beat, while beautiful and very famous people dressed in high-end couture talked, danced, drank and laughed. Through the heaving crowd partying on the terrace, wait staff like myself moved, dressed in black, distributing eye-wateringly expensive drinks and tiny, exquisite canapés that would satisfy exactly no one's appetite.

Over by the deep blue of the infinity pool came a splash as some idiot pushed another idiot in, followed by screams of laugher and shrieks. A third idiot—some famous actress in a white cocktail frock, probably worth more than my tiny Mongkok apartment—jumped in too. Then, after a lot of splashing, she held a ball of white fabric overhead to much cheering.

Clearly we'd reached the naked part of the evening.

I'd spent quite a bit of time researching Blackwood's parties beforehand and apparently anything went. Nakedness. Public sex. Blatant social climbing. Line dancing. It was all out there for anyone to see and join in.

Rich people... They were a whole thing.

Mr Chen, my mentor, had once told me to expect anything when dealing with the very wealthy; that the old saying about absolute power corrupting absolutely was true and that it applied to wealth as well; that you couldn't trust them as far as you could throw them. Which wasn't very far.

Not that I needed those lessons he'd drilled into me. There were only two people I trusted in the entire world and one was dead. The other was myself.

I might not be the world's most beautiful woman, but there was one thing about which I was confident: my ability to slip into a place unnoticed and steal whatever I found there. Though 'steal' was kind of a strong word to use for what I did.

Mr Chen called it 'reacquisition' and it was his 'reacquisition' business that he'd passed on to me after he'd died.

Basically, it involved 'reacquiring' stolen or missing items from people who shouldn't have them and returning them to their rightful owners. It wasn't technically stealing, as the items had been stolen to start with. You might say that was a job for the police rather than us. But some people didn't like to involve the law for one reason or another; they preferred a third party. Hence the nice little 'find and return' business Mr Chen had worked hard to build up and in which he had trained me.

His last wish before he'd died was for me to keep that business running, his legacy to the world, and as he was the one who'd pulled me off the streets, given me a home and a job, I felt I owed him.

So that was why I was here. On a job. A request had come through via the third party who acted as our intermediary for a necklace called the Red Queen. It had been stolen some twenty years ago and now had miraculously turned up in Damian Blackwood's possession. Its previous owners wanted it back and they didn't much care how that happened. Hence hiring me.

Ignoring the shenanigans beside the pool, I glanced once more at the man from whom I was to 'reacquire' the piece in order to make sure of his location.

The typical Hong Kong humidity was making me sweaty, my uniform prickling, but I'd learned to ignore all physical discomforts when on a job, and I didn't let it get to me. Instead, I adjusted my hold on the tray and took a moment to study Blackwood himself.

He was sitting in the corner of the terrace, where a number of couches had been arranged, in the centre of a group of stunningly beautiful, incredibly attentive women, all hanging on his every word.

I wrinkled my nose and tried to be my usual cynical self as I surveyed him. But it was difficult to be my usual cynical self. Because, despite my own good judgement—not to mention my common sense—and no matter that it was a *really* bad move professionally, I'd somehow developed a bit of a…crush on him.

Embarrassing, yes, and I didn't like to acknowledge it to myself. And maybe it wasn't any wonder, given what a very fine specimen of manhood he was—certainly there was a reason why all those women couldn't take their eyes off him. But still. I should know better than to get all starry-eyed over a good-looking man. Or indeed any man.

Mr Chen had been clear that involvement with anyone in our line of work was out of the question and that had never bothered me. Being an unwanted kid, I was used to being alone, and I'd never met anyone worth wanting to get to know better anyway. And as for sex, well… There was a reason humanity had invented vibrators.

Still, knowing all of that didn't stop me from being transfixed by the reality of Damian Blackwood himself.

I'd done my usual research, immersing myself in the history of Black and White Enterprises, and Blackwood's background in particular, studying news articles, looking at photos, watching interviews, the works.

He and his two co-owners, Ulysses White and Everett Calhoun, a Brit and an American respectively, had made huge amounts of money in crypto-currency speculation, initially starting Black and White as an online vault that boasted better security than the banks in Switzerland. They'd enjoyed phenomenal success with it and from there had gone on to build a billion-dollar empire that encompassed finance, import-export, luxury hotels, construction, security and God knew what else. They had their fingers in so many pies even they probably didn't know which was which.

The three of them were famous—or infamous, depending on how you looked at it—for being totally uncompromising both in business and in their private lives, for living however they wanted and not giving a damn.

Certainly Blackwood didn't.

He was a womaniser who spent millions on massive parties, his luxury lifestyle the stuff of legend. He was renowned not only for his love of beautiful women but for his love of fine jewels. He was a highly regarded collector and connoisseur of gems, and was constantly being talked about on every news platform and every social media channel there was. The man seemed to thrive on attention, a master of the perfect sound bite and the off-the-cuff witty comment, making much of his humble origins as the son of a Sydney burlesque dancer.

He had the kind of confidence and cocky charm that only a lot of money and extreme good looks could buy, and was pretty much my opposite in every possible way. Which I suppose made it strange that I was so fascinated by him. Then again, maybe that was kind of the point; opposites were supposed to attract, weren't they?

Not that he'd ever be attracted to me. With any luck he wouldn't notice me at all.

I stared at him from beneath my lashes, watching

his mesmerising smile along with all the other women around him. It was a thing of beauty, caught on the cusp between charming and wicked, promising all kinds of naughty, dirty things, and I found my heart beating a little faster than it had before.

He was dressed in an exquisitely tailored dark blue suit that showed off his long, tall, muscular frame to perfection, and he sat on the couch like a king holding court, the women his adoring courtiers.

His black hair was shaved on the sides of his head to leave a soft, spiky kind of Mohawk on top, highlighting the intensely masculine perfection of his face. He had a jawline so sharp you could cut yourself on it, high cheekbones that would do a Hollywood superstar proud and a long mouth that curled at the ends, pure sin and wickedness. His eyes were silver, the light colour emphasised by the thick black of his lashes, and were just as wicked as his mouth.

A pretty man. Maybe too pretty. At least he would have been if not for the piercing in his left eyebrow and the bright colours of the tattoos that peeked through the open neck of his black shirt.

But those things I already knew about. Those things only added an edge.

What I hadn't understood until now, what all the articles and the interviews hadn't told me, was that the real source of his power lay in his charisma. It radiated from him, an unholy mix of charm, confidence and focus, bathing people in its light. Rendering both men and women speechless with adoration.

I wasn't overstating. It was simply a fact.

Watching him was like watching the sun rise after a dark, cold night.

He was in the middle of telling some ridiculous story, his handsome face full of expression, his silver gaze making eye contact with his rapt audience as he made fluid gestures with his large, long-fingered hands.

I tried to resist him, tried to take refuge in my usual distrust, yet still I found myself edging closer, trying to listen, his charm like a tractor beam reeling me in.

His voice rolled over me, rich and deep. He didn't have that strange transatlantic accent that some ex-pats had, his Australian accent slight but there. He smiled as he told his story—some nonsense about a woman he'd once known back in Sydney, and her dog and her husband, Damian hiding in the closet.

His audience was enthralled, their eyes shining, laughing as he punctuated the story with jokes, some blatant, some dry.

He was a natural storyteller, weaving magic with his hands, and I nearly laughed myself at some ridiculous aside. Though I stopped the instant I realised what I was doing, appalled at myself.

Stupid.

I was letting myself be dazzled and I shouldn't. I had a job to do and that wasn't standing around watching him.

I was here to find the necklace he'd bought at a private auction three days earlier and take it back to its rightful owners, not get distracted by staring at his undeniably pretty face.

Making a few more adjustments to my tray, I kept an eye on Blackwood to make sure he stayed on that cripplingly expensive couch of his, only to freeze in place as he turned his head, the full force of his attention suddenly slamming into me.

The air seemed to thicken, the music fading, the rest of the party falling away, leaving only him, me and the incredible silver of his gaze. There was heat in those eyes, the promise of long, hot, decadent nights in silk sheets, the mysteries of sex revealed…

I couldn't breathe, abruptly aware of the movement of the air across my skin in the humid night and the scratchy feel of my uniform; of the fabric pulling tight across my breasts and the fast beat of my heart.

Of an ache right down low inside me that felt strangely like…longing.

A dim part of my mind told me that I was being stupid, that he was just a man, nothing special. A good-looking man, sure, but not one I should be losing my head over. And yet… I couldn't look away from him.

No one had ever looked at me the way he was looking right now. No one had ever even noticed me at all. I was ordinary. Unremarkable. Unmemorable.

I wasn't a woman a man like him would ever look at twice.

Then he gestured at me, making shock pulse hard in my veins. Oh, my God. What the hell did he want?

You're standing there dressed as a waitress, holding a tray of drinks. What do you think he wants?

Oh. Right. Yes. The uniform. He didn't want *me*, he only wanted a waitress.

Forcing away the effects of his gaze, not to mention the odd dip in my stomach that definitely wasn't disappointment, I concentrated on making sure my hands didn't shake as I made my way towards him and his entourage.

The women were all pleading with him to finish his story—he'd stopped at a very important part, apparently—and thank God he looked away from me as I approached, his mouth curling. 'Patience, ladies. Good things come to those who wait. Now, who else needs a drink?'

I came to a stop in front of him and held out the tray. He rose to his feet in one fluid, athletic movement, towering above me as he picked up the bottle, pouring liberal amounts into the glasses on the tray next to it. He didn't look at me, too busy talking and laughing with a couple of the women next to him.

The tension that had gathered across my shoulders relaxed a fraction, even as the dip in my stomach intensified. He'd definitely looked at me because I was a waitress and he wanted a drink. No other reason. And just as well, since anonymity was my number one weapon and the reason Mr Chen's business was so successful.

Go unnoticed. Stay under the radar. That was what he'd always told me and that was what I always did.

But you want to be noticed.

The thought slid through my brain like a snake.

No, that was ridiculous. Sure, being a reacquisition agent made for a lonely kind of existence, and sometimes I felt as though I was a ghost living in the walls of the city, passing by people unseen, leaving behind no trace of my presence. And, yes, there were times when I might have nursed a fantasy or two, late at night in my bed. Of having a lover. Someone to touch me and hold me when I was sad and lonely. Someone with whom to laugh and share the good times.

But Mr Chen had been very clear that it wasn't possible to have that and be in the business I was in. Draw too much attention from anyone, and there was the risk that I'd find myself in a jail cell.

I couldn't have that. I couldn't put Mr Chen's business and my livelihood in danger just because I was lonely. Which made the answer simple: I just wouldn't be lonely. And so far I hadn't been.

Shooting Blackwood a glance as he smiled at yet another adoring woman, I steadied my grip on the tray. It was slightly intimidating being this close to him after months of seeing him on a screen or in magazines. He was so much taller than I'd expected, even though the Internet had been very helpful as to his height and weight—six foot two, ninety kilos. He was a lot broader too. When he moved, his suit jacket pulled across his shoulders, highlighting the heavy muscle beneath it, and I could see by the way his trousers sat low on his lean hips that he probably didn't have an ounce of fat on him.

He laughed as one of the women made a joke, and I felt the vibration of that laugh settle right down low inside me, a deep, purring, sexy sound.

No wonder he was a terrific man-whore. Who could resist him?

You, for a start.

Yes, well, luckily for me, resisting him wasn't going to be an issue, as he hadn't looked at me again since I'd come over with the drinks.

Not once.

Which was good and definitely not in any way a disappointment.

I was still staring at him and silently judging the people around him for their open adoration, when he turned and looked at me again.

And, as it had before, the impact of his gaze moved through me like slow, sensual lightning.

Then his mouth curled and he winked.

Shock rooted me to the spot and I gaped, unable to stop myself, but he'd already looked away, turning that brilliant, sexy smile onto someone else.

It was as if I'd been under a spotlight and the beam had shifted, plunging me into darkness and leaving me blinded.

My heart raced and I struggled to get a breath.

Not good, fool. Not good at all.

No, it wasn't. I was staring at him like a rabbit in the headlights and if I didn't shift my butt he was going to notice me again. And not in a good way.

Because the one thing I *wasn't* supposed to do was gain his attention.

Damn it. I'd been so confident in my own ordinariness that I'd thought he'd never even look at me. Apparently, I was wrong.

It doesn't matter. Get moving.

No, it really didn't. After all, I wasn't here to get his attention. I was here to get in, find the Red Queen, take it and get out again. Simple.

On that bracing thought, I gripped my tray and turned away from sexy Damian Blackwood and his entourage.

And got on with the business of robbing him blind.

CHAPTER TWO

Damian

I SAT BACK on the couch with another glass of champagne and watched the sweet-faced little waitress who'd given me a pissy look disappear into the crowd with her now-empty tray.

It wasn't often that women looked at me as if they'd like to punch me in the face. Men, sure. Women, no.

She'd been standing there staring at me, a watchful, still point in the chaos of the party around her, which should have made my eyes slide right over her. Yet the opposite had happened. Almost as if her stillness was the reason my attention had been drawn to her.

Her eyes had been very dark and absolutely unreadable, like the surface of a deep lake I couldn't see the bottom of, and I'd found that interesting. So I'd winked at her, purely to see the surface of that lake ripple a little, and ripple it did; her shock at my attention had been loud and clear.

That she'd clearly not expected me to notice her was obvious, and I might have found that amusing if there hadn't also been something else about her that had bothered me. Something I hadn't been able to put my finger on. Something I should have been aware of…

But the ladies around me were begging me to finish the bullshit story I'd been telling them, and I couldn't be bothered figuring out what the issue with the waitress was. Not when my public was demanding a performance.

I took a sip of my champagne and put it down—fucking hate the stuff—and leaned forward, continuing with my story. The ladies were thoroughly enjoying it, and I was thoroughly enjoying pleasing them, especially when they all erupted into laughter as I punctuated the end with a very off-colour joke.

That laughter was music to my ears, making me smile. Because if there was one thing that made life on this shitty planet worth living it was making a woman laugh. It was almost as good as making a woman come, and since I was extremely skilled at doing both I indulged myself and them as often as humanly possible. Occasionally at the same time.

I sat back on the couch, watching the ladies around me, satisfied that they were all having a good time. Then I scanned the crowd in general, making sure everyone else was as well, as I took my parties very seriously.

They were a chance for guests to let their hair down without worrying about the press or whether their name would be plastered all over the Internet the next morning. A chance to cut loose and relax with no rules and no judgement.

Correction. There were two rules: nothing illegal and no one took advantage of anyone.

I policed those two things religiously, my security staff confiscating any illegal substances, not to mention phones or other recording devices, and kicking out any person stupid enough to think they could take advantage of anyone else.

Only people with a verified invite could attend, plus I personally vetted all staff working during the event so that…

Wait a second.

I narrowed my gaze in the direction the waitress had gone, going over her face in my memory. It was eidetic, so it was impossible for me to forget—both a blessing and a goddamn curse.

Small, with a sweet, heart-shaped face. Short, dark-brown hair in a straight glossy bob grazing a sharp, determined chin. Black almond-shaped eyes. Not pretty in the traditional sense but with a certain something.

I mentally compared her features to the list of staff photos I'd requested from the Black and White Enterprises catering company handling the party tonight.

No match.

If she wasn't on the staff list then that could only mean one thing: she was a fucking gate crasher.

Shit. That was the last thing I wanted to deal with, especially as she'd probably end up being a reporter, because there were always reporters trying to gate crash my goddamn parties.

Tonight was supposed to be about celebrating me finally getting my hands on the Red Queen, a necklace I'd been chasing down for the last three months and had managed to buy at a private auction a few days ago.

I'd seen a picture of it in an article on famous jewels about two years back and had decided that, as rubies had been my mother's favourite stone and I knew it was a piece she would have loved, I wanted to add it to my collection.

It would be the perfect advertisement for the jewellery auction that was to be part of the launch of the Black and White Foundation, a new non-profit organisation that Ulysses, Everett and I were hoping to get off the ground. I was putting up some of my more famous pieces as a fundraiser, and hopefully some of the proceeds would be going towards the new cancer research facility I'd set up back in Australia.

Yeah, jewellery might be a strange thing for a man like me to collect, but I liked a bit of glitter, especially against a woman's skin.

Call it a holdover from my childhood, watching my mother and her friends get ready for their performances at the burlesque club where they'd worked. I hadn't been allowed to see the show, but I'd loved watching them get ready. My always happy, always laughing mother, gossiping as she painted her face and did her hair, making herself look beautiful. The smell of greasepaint and hairspray in the air, the sparkle of jewelled and feathered costumes glittering in the light.

I had been a serious, quiet kid and she had taken her job of making the hand-to-mouth existence we led back then very seriously, trying to make it fun. Trying to get me to smile. It had mostly worked.

Until she'd died of cancer, of course.

But I didn't think about those days. Instead, I buried them under glitter, good times and the joy of hunting down the perfect jewel. And the Red Queen had led me on quite a hunt. I'd loved every fucking second of stalking that piece down, but now it was safe in the vault in my office, I was going to have to find something else to turn on my hunter's instincts…

That waitress, perhaps?

Ah, fuck. That's right. The damn waitress.

Pushing myself up and out of the couch, I excused myself to the ladies and made my way through the crowd towards Clarence, the head of my personal security team, checking on people as I went like the good host I was.

Everett was here—he'd been in Hong Kong for one of his hush-hush meetings—and he gave me a look from where he was standing by the pool, lifting a blond brow. If Ulysses had been here, he would have scowled, but Ulysses wasn't here. He was in London, where he always was, managing Black and White's money from his bank of computers, boring bastard that he was.

Not that Everett was any more exciting. He was a man of few words and fewer smiles, and took his role of being responsible for company-wide security far more seriously than he should have. The guy really needed to lighten up.

I shook my head to indicate everything was fine and

he gave a nod, turning his attention back to the action in the pool, where a famous actor and an equally famous musician had got rid of their clothing and were playing a game of naked tag.

Looked like fun. Sadly, I had business to attend to before I could join in.

I spoke to Clarence, gave him a description of the waitress and he assured me it would be dealt with. Then I stepped inside the penthouse—one of many I had around the world, though this one was my favourite—moving through the sleek, open-plan spaces full of people to my private office. I unlocked it and stepped inside, closing the door for some quiet, and took out my phone to give the catering company director a fucking piece of my mind.

I couldn't have people I didn't know and hadn't invited wandering around my party, not given the whole reason the parties worked was because of my stringent privacy rules. Not to mention the security concerns involved.

Still, Everett only hired the best, so it probably wouldn't take Clarence and his boys long to locate my little waitress and show her the door.

I hadn't bothered getting my office redone after I'd bought the apartment, and consequently it was all pale wood and pale carpet, a Swedish furniture designer's fucking wet dream. Not to my taste. Good thing I didn't spend much time in here—I didn't like to sit still, and preferred to dictate while I was doing something else rather than being tied to a desk.

Wandering over to the window, I paused beside it as I reached to grab my phone out of my pocket.

The room was sound-proofed, but I could still feel the heavy beat of the music through the thick, pale carpet on the floor. Neon-stained light from the city outside shone through the office's windows and over the pale wood of my desk.

Not quite hiding the tip of someone's foot sticking out from under it.

I went very, *very* still, the muscles in my shoulders tightening.

It had been years since I'd had to deal with a physical threat, not since money had taken me away from the clubs and the security jobs I'd once worked to pay for my sister's schooling. But, even if I hadn't had an eidetic memory, I'd still have remembered how to deal with said threat. It usually involved me picking up the person involved by the scruff of their neck and throwing them bodily out of the door. And making sure they didn't bother me or mine again.

Slowly, I got my phone out, making it look as if I was staring down at the screen and not at the tip of the foot sticking out from under my desk.

It was small and encased in plain black leather. So, not a guy, then.

I tilted my head, also spotting an edge of black fabric. It was as plain as the leather of the shoe and it looked cheap.

Who'd be wearing plain shoes and cheap fabric to one of my parties?

It wasn't hard to figure out, not when there were at least five or more people wearing exactly that combination, all of them circulating with trays of food and drink.

The catering staff.

'If you're looking for more Cristal,' I said calmly to my little waitress, because of course it was her, 'You won't find any under my desk.'

She didn't move.

Was she trying to pretend I hadn't seen her?

Irritation sat in my gut. Fucking security should have picked up on anyone reckless or stupid enough to try and get into one of my parties, but clearly they hadn't. And now it was my problem to deal with.

Everett was going to have some explaining to do, that was for sure, because not only had she somehow crashed my party, she'd also managed to get into my private goddamn office. My private *locked* goddamn office.

Which changed things. That lock should have kept out even the most professional criminal and yet some random waitress had managed to unlock it and slip inside.

No. That wasn't happening. And this woman wasn't a waitress. I'd bet my billions on it.

If she'd been a guy I'd have reached down, hauled him out and dragged that sorry motherfucker to Clarence myself. But she wasn't a guy. She was a woman; I'd never touched a woman in anger and never would.

Still, there were other methods.

'Don't bother hiding,' I said coolly. 'I can see your

foot. You've also got approximately five seconds to get the fuck out from under there before I call security.'

There was another moment of silence.

Then the little foot shifted, there was a rustling sound and a figure moved out from under the shelter of the desk, straightening up as she got to her feet.

Sure enough, it was the waitress.

The waitress who wasn't on the catering company's staff list.

I took another long look at her.

She was small, the top of her head just about equal to my shoulders, her figure in the catering company uniform lush and curvy. She smoothed the plain black dress nervously, the neon from the city outside shining directly on her face.

Her eyes were the colour of dark, bittersweet chocolate, tilted up slightly at the ends like a cat's. She also had a strong jaw, a determined chin and an adorably upturned nose. Her mouth was wide and generous, her skin smooth as old ivory, and her hair was the glossy brown of chestnuts.

Unconventional, that was for sure. Which from my point of view was far more intriguing than beautiful. When it came to jewels, flawless stones were supposed to be the finest and most expensive, but I preferred my gems to have irregularities. It made them much more interesting.

'Uh…hi,' she said, her voice low with a pleasant husk to it, her accent very definitely English. 'Guess you didn't expect me to be in here, right?'

I lifted a brow. 'What gave it away?'

A nervous-looking smile turned her full mouth. 'I'm so sorry. The door was open and I thought it was the kitchen and I—'

'No, it wasn't.'

She blinked. 'Excuse me?'

'The door.' I kept my voice calm. 'It wasn't open.'

Something flickered in her eyes, something that didn't fit with that uncertain smile or the way she was nervously smoothing her uniform. It was gone the next second, but I was good at reading people and I knew what it was. I'd seen it in her gaze out on the terrace.

She wasn't nervous. She was angry. And no doubt it was because she'd been discovered.

If she'd genuinely been a waitress, I'd have ushered her out, called her supervisor and had a few words.

Except she wasn't a waitress.

I didn't know what she was. But I sure as shit was going to find out.

Calling Clarence immediately and having him deal with it was the next logical step, but I didn't want to involve him. I didn't know what this woman was here for. She wasn't likely to be a reporter; I revised my earlier suspicion, because if she had been she would have been out there surreptitiously taking pictures of the famous naked people having fun around the pool; she wouldn't be in here, hiding under my desk. And, apart from anything else, reporters generally didn't have the skills required to get through the lock on my office door.

No, I wanted to deal with this personally.

'Oh, it really was,' she said, her forehead creasing. 'You must have forgotten to shut it or something.'

Which might have worked if I hadn't been the one person in a million who never forgot a single fucking thing.

Slowly, I shook my head. 'The door was shut. And secured with an extremely sophisticated electronic lock.'

Another flicker in her eyes—more anger, and this time the tiniest touch of what I thought was uncertainty. It was gone as quickly as it had come, to be replaced with something that looked calculating. Almost as if she was watching me and gauging my reaction.

Fuck, who was this woman?

There was a quality to her that held me like the light catching a particularly fine diamond. Except she didn't glitter like a diamond, not the way the women waiting for me on the terrace did, sparkly, showy and completely transparent. No, this woman didn't catch the light at all. Unlike them, she was opaque, like a black pearl. Just as beautiful and just as fine, but a whole shitload more mysterious.

Diamonds were showy stones, and there was a time and a place for showy. Right now, though, I was more interested in mysterious.

Especially the mysterious way she'd managed to get into my fucking office.

There was a time for charm and then there was a time for seriousness.

'Sugar,' I said gently. 'That five seconds? You've now got two to explain just what the fuck you're doing here.'

Her hands twisted in front of her. 'You really don't believe I was trying to find the kitchen?'

I smiled and this time I didn't bother making it pleasant. 'Try again.'

CHAPTER THREE

Thea

SUGAR. HE'D CALLED me *Sugar*. As if that wasn't patronising at all.

Him calling you Sugar is the least of your problems right now.

Controlling my instinctive bristle, I tried to slow the fight-or-flight adrenaline rush that had burst through my veins the minute I'd heard his deep voice tell me that he could see me as I hid under his desk.

I took a silent breath to get control of the anger and spike of fear, forcing my emotions down the way Mr Chen had taught me.

I'd never been caught, not once in all the years I'd been working with Mr Chen, and it was a point of pride. My ability to slip into a place unnoticed and slip out again, shadowy as a ghost, was what made me so good at what I did.

Getting caught so pathetically easily was a rookie mistake and I should be ashamed of myself. I just hadn't expected him to come in here. I'd thought he'd stay out on the terrace, entertaining his glorious public.

An error of judgment, clearly. I needed to be on my guard.

'Try again?' I repeated, attempting to sound like a confused member of staff who didn't realise what she'd done wrong. 'I don't know what you mean.'

He was standing not far away, his back to the windows and the magnificent view out over Hong Kong's financial district, neon outlining his tall, broad silhouette to perfection.

Damn him. Why had he come in here? I'd only just started to look for the safe before I'd heard the sounds of someone coming into the room. There hadn't been time for me to find somewhere decent to hide or check if there was another exit. The only place I'd been able to see had been under his desk, so that was where I'd bolted.

Not at all what I'd planned.

I struggled to pull myself together. Getting caught would put Mr Chen's whole business at risk, not to mention destroying the reputation for complete discretion he'd built over the years, and it would be all my fault. Which meant I had to fix it and fast.

'I think you do.' Blackwood tilted his head towards the light, neon sliding over his perfect features. 'And don't give me any more of that trying to find the kitchen bullshit.'

Damn. Damn. Damn.

There was no trace of his charming smile now, only

the hard gleam in his eyes. With the silver ring in his eyebrow and the tantalising glimpse of his tattoos from beneath his black shirt, he looked…dangerous as hell.

And sexier than the devil himself.

Even more irritated at myself, I shoved away that particular thought and reached into the pocket of my uniform, bringing out the staff ID I'd forged and waving it in the air. 'But I'm with the company. Check my ID.'

He didn't even look at it. 'I vet all the staff who come to these parties personally and you're not on the staff list.'

Shit. I hadn't known he was so hands-on with his ridiculous parties. I'd imagined he'd hire some kind of party planner.

'Who are you?' His voice had lost the lazy warmth I'd heard out on the terrace while he'd been telling his story. Now it had an edge creeping into it. 'You're not a reporter, not given how you managed to pick my lock. How *did* you do that, by the way?'

Quickly, I sorted through my options. I could brazen it out and insist on being with the company, but since he personally vetted his staff that probably wouldn't work. And, given the lock situation, as he'd already said, I couldn't pretend to be a reporter. Not when the lock had been heavy duty and somewhat difficult to open even for a person of my skills.

The only option I had left was…stalker fan desperate to catch a glimpse of her idol. Did billionaires have stalker fans? I guess there was only one way to find out.

I let out a breath, as if I was disappointed. 'Okay,' I

said. 'You win. I'm not actually with the catering company. But I'm not a reporter either.'

The gleam in his silver eyes was like a blade and something twisted deep inside me. This man was a different beast from the charming playboy out on the terrace. Honed and sharp as a dagger, and just as lethal.

It seemed at odds with the faint hint of his expensive, subtle cologne I could scent in the air, all warm spice and sunshine.

My heartbeat tripled, my breath catching. And it wasn't with fear.

There was something incredibly exciting about this—about him. About how different he was right now from the man I'd seen on the terrace, and I wasn't sure why I liked that. I just did.

Maybe it was the danger factor. It had been a while since I'd had a job quite as challenging as this one was turning out to be. Still, I couldn't afford to get too carried away. If I didn't get it together he'd go straight to the police and there would go Mr Chen's business. The business I'd promised him I'd take care of before he died.

'I'm waiting, Sugar.' Blackwood didn't sound impatient and yet that edge was sharpening in the air around him by the second.

I twisted my hands in front of me, trying to project nervousness, and to be honest I didn't have to try all that hard.

'Okay, so this is really embarrassing.' I shifted on my feet. 'I'm here because I… I wanted to see you.'

He lifted his pierced brow, the ring in it glinting. 'See me?'

Maybe billionaires didn't have stalker fans. Surely he would know what I was talking about?

'Yeah.' I cleared my throat, pushing on regardless. 'I…just think you're so amazing. I read everything about you, see all the interviews you've given. I mean, that interview you gave for *Vanity Fair* was just…' I injected as much breathlessness into my voice as I could, which for some reason didn't seem difficult. 'Anyway, my cousin was sick of hearing about it. She bet me a hundred bucks I couldn't get into your party and so I… Well…' I gave a nervous laugh and waved towards the door.

His expression didn't change, his silver gaze sliding over me, the pressure cool as metal on my skin. 'Is that a fact? And I suppose you just happened to be an excellent forger, not to mention an expert in breaking and entering?'

Oh, crap.

He's called you. Time for plan B.

That *was* plan B. I didn't have any other plans. Not when I hadn't expected to get caught.

Fear twisted inside me, but I fought it as I sorted through more options, forcing myself not to panic.

Hadn't Mr Chen always said to use anything and everything to your advantage when it came to difficult situations? Because there was one option I hadn't considered yet: using my femininity. Blackwood was, after all, a playboy who'd apparently never met a woman he didn't want to take to bed. And I'd done it before, with the security guy and the whole undoing the top button routine, and it had worked.

Yes, but he's not your standard security guy. He's a connoisseur and you're not exactly Scarlett Johansson.

This was sadly true. But I didn't have a choice. It was either try it or it was a jail cell for me.

So I took a couple of slow steps towards him, allowing my hips to sway, 'Does it matter?' Much to my annoyance, I didn't have to fake the husky sound in my voice as much as I'd thought I would. 'I'm an expert in other things too. Would you like to know what they are?'

He didn't move, watching me come closer. 'I feel certain you're about to tell me.'

I stopped inches away from him, my heart hammering in my chest. He was so very tall, that big, muscular body oh, so close. The black cotton of his shirt gave a hint at the hard musculature of his chest and I found my attention wandering, staring at him. He'd left the top couple of buttons undone, giving me a close-up glimpse of those tattoos, the colours bright reds, golds and blues.

Apparently that trick works on women too.

I gritted my teeth and tipped my head back to look up at him, making myself hold his gaze, listening to the beat of my heart get louder and louder in my ears.

I wasn't used to people looking at me. I wasn't used to people noticing I even existed. Yet now Damian Blackwood hadn't just noticed me; he was looking right at me with so much intense focus I could hardly breathe.

Being unseen and unnoticed had never bothered me

before—at least, I hadn't let it bother me. But it wasn't until now, with the gaze of the world's most beautiful man on me, that I realised actually I *was* bothered by it.

It made me feel cold. Because it was cold being a shadow. Cold and lonely. And he was like…the sun. Like summer. The promise of light, warmth and everything I hadn't known I was missing.

You're insane. Remember who he is and don't get carried away.

'Are you going to seduce me, Sugar?' His voice was soft and deep, and I could feel that heat in it now, the cold edge fading, leaving behind it something that sounded a hell of a lot like amusement. 'I mean, I assume that's why you're looking at me like that.'

Damn it. The bastard was seeing every play I made.

Shoving away my weird emotional reaction to him, I lifted a brow, consciously copying him, dropping the 'stalker fan' nonsense. 'I'm looking at you like what? You'll have to be clear, Mr Blackwood.'

And strangely, as if he'd simply been waiting for me to drop the act all along, he smiled that wonderful smile, slow and devastating. 'Oh, I can be clear, Sugar. I can be very clear. You want to give me a blow job. Or maybe a quick fuck on my desk. Anything to distract me, right?'

Electricity fizzed in my blood. I hadn't expected him to see through me. I hadn't expected any kind of challenge at all and I…liked it. But I had to be careful. He could steal control of the situation away from me so easily and I couldn't let him do that.

I took the last step so I was almost touching him, look-ing up from underneath my lashes. 'I could do any and all of those things,' I said huskily. 'If you think it'll work?'

That blinding, wicked smile deepened. 'It might. I guess the only way you'll know is to give it a try.'

He was goading me, I was certain of it, because that beautiful smile didn't quite reach his eyes. That hard gleam was still there. A challenge. And I knew I shouldn't respond to it, but what else could I do? My only other option was to turn and run, and I didn't think he'd let me get far.

If you play your cards right, you might have some time to search for the necklace later.

Good point. I could seduce him and that would at least mean he'd forget about calling security and throwing me out, wouldn't it? And, if I was *very* good, maybe I could even convince him to let me stay the night, which would then give me time to find and take that damn necklace.

You'd have to be very good, though. He's used to experience.

Which I didn't have. Then again, I was a quick learner. And I'd done my share of looking at sexy vid-eos on the Internet when Mr Chen hadn't been around. I had some idea of what to do.

Blackwood's scent filled the air, the heat of his body so close, and my palms itched with a very real desire to touch him.

It wouldn't be a hardship to seduce him. He was beautiful and, according to all the gossip columns, ex-traordinarily good in bed.

An unremarkable virgin seducing the billionaire playboy? Since when does that happen?

Cold fingers of doubt caught at me, but I forced them away. I couldn't hesitate—that was when mistakes were made, as Mr Chen used to say. Once you'd made a decision you had to fully commit to it.

So I took that final step, holding his gaze with mine. 'Let's find out, then, shall we?' I said and, putting my hands on his lean hips, I pushed him up against the windows.

I could feel his heat through the wool of his suit trousers and hard muscle too, a tensile strength that made my mouth go dry.

A silver flame burned bright in his eyes.

We stared at each other, the atmosphere around us getting denser and denser, more electric with every second that passed. As if a storm was gathering around us, full of lightning and thunder.

A storm about to break.

This is a mistake.

The thought was fleeting, but I ignored it. I was committed now, and the way he was looking at me, as if he really *saw* me, with that wicked smile and the gleam in his eyes...

It was addictive. It made me feel like I wasn't a ghost. That I was real.

'Are you sure you know what you're doing?' he drawled, the dark, hot thread winding through his voice making me shiver. 'Because it looks like you do. And I don't want there to be any misunderstandings.'

He was so hot. His heat glowed against my palms like the embers of a fire and suddenly, desperately, I wanted to press myself against him, have him warm me up.

'What kind of misunderstandings?' I tried to sound cool, but knew I was failing. 'I don't think blow jobs are all that confusing. At least not to a man like you.'

His laugh was a soft, deep rumble in his chest, as wicked as his smile. 'A man like me,' he echoed. 'And you know what that is?'

Of course I knew. He was a womaniser. A playboy. A party animal. He threw money around like it meant nothing at all and probably treated people the same way. Which was fine. In fact, it was perfect.

I could seduce him, spend the night with him. Get the necklace and then go. Besides, he must do this all the time. I would be just another woman to him; he probably wouldn't even remember my face come morning.

He smelled like heaven and the glitter in his eyes was making my mind go blank, a low throb starting up between my thighs.

My hands tightened on his hips as I leaned in close, meeting the challenge in his stare full on. 'Of course I know,' I murmured. 'But I'm always happy to have a few pointers.'

'Sugar, if you know already then what are you waiting for?' His smile set fire to something inside me, making it burst into flames. 'Get down on your knees and show me what you've got.'

CHAPTER FOUR

Damian

I WAS SURE the little gate-crasher-waitress-thief wouldn't take up my challenge. Not only was I a complete stranger to her, but I was also the one who'd interrupted her in the middle of whatever she was doing in my office.

And, despite the fire flickering in her dark eyes, I was pretty confident she'd stop short of actually giving me a goddamn blow job.

A pity. Because, despite how pissed off I was at the way she kept lying to me, the moment she'd pushed me up against the windows, her delicate hands on my hips, every rational fucking thought vanished from my brain.

I hadn't felt chemistry this strong in for ever.

There had always been women in my life and some I'd been really attracted to. But not like this.

I wasn't sure what it was, whether it was her lush figure and unconventional beauty, or whether it was more about that watchful stillness she had to her. That cool, quiet lake, tempting me to dive in as if it was a hot summer's day.

Or maybe it was just because I had no idea who she was or what she was doing here, and she wasn't giving anything away.

Possibly it was all three.

Whatever, I was fascinated. Absolutely bloody riveted.

I hadn't thought I liked complicated women, but apparently I was wrong, since I was certainly intrigued by this one.

I wanted to know who she was and why she was here. Why she was pretending to be someone she wasn't and why she'd been hiding under my desk in the first place.

I wanted to know what was going on behind those lovely, unreadable black eyes, because the glimpses I'd got so far had been of heat and, yeah, I was pretty fucking interested in that.

Then she dropped to her knees in front of me and every other thought vanished from my brain.

Okay, so I was wrong. She *would* take up my challenge.

My heart kicked, my dick hardening.

Her hands slid slowly from my hips to my thighs, and I could feel the heat of her palms through the wool of my suit trousers.

Holy shit.

I caught my breath. This was a problem.

Of course, I shouldn't have been baiting her the way I had, but hell, I hadn't been able to resist it. There was undeniable physical chemistry between us like a slow-burning fire, banked embers smouldering away, getting hotter the nearer she got to me. Until one breath of wind and the whole thing would go up in flames.

Fucking hot.

I liked the hungry way she looked at me and, unlike her nervous waitress and breathless fan acts, I was pretty sure that was real.

But what I didn't like was the fact that she probably wouldn't be getting ready to suck my dick right now if I hadn't caught her hiding out under my desk.

'Do this a lot, hmm?' I asked. 'Suck off complete strangers?'

Colour tinged her cheekbones, making her pretty eyes glow. Her ivory skin had the most incredible lustre, like the finest, most expensive of pearls. Did that go all the way down? If I took off that cheap uniform, uncovered the rest of her, would I find that lustre all over her lush little body?

My cock was all in, the dirty bastard.

'Oh, all the time.' She lifted her hands to the button of my trousers and they were trembling slightly.

So that was a fucking lie. She did *not* do this all the time. Which, sadly for me and my cock, meant I had to put a stop to it. Because I wasn't going to take advantage of some pretty little thing, no matter what she was doing in my office.

I reached down and put a hand over hers.

She blinked, genuine surprise flickering in her eyes, which was satisfying. Clearly she'd been expecting me to settle back and enjoy the ride, no questions asked.

'What?' Her surprise morphed into uncertainty.

I shook my head, keeping her hands trapped. 'Not tonight, Josephine.'

'What do you mean, not tonight?' She blinked. 'I thought you said—'

'I did. But I changed my mind.'

She didn't move, kneeling at my feet and studying me. Her hands were warm beneath my palms, the slight pressure of them against my stomach making me aware that my dick was not happy with me stopping her.

Too bad. It would live.

'Just to be clear,' she said, 'So we don't have any "misunderstandings". You don't want me to give you a blow job?'

'No. Like I said, I changed my mind.'

'Why?'

'I'm a lot of things, Sugar. But I'm not a man who takes advantage of women.' I gave the back of her hand a reassuring stroke with my thumb. 'Even women who break into my office and lie straight to my face.'

Another flicker in her eyes, and this time it was definitely fear.

It wasn't an emotion I liked to see in a woman's face.

'I'm not going to hurt you,' I said before she could reply, giving her another stroke to calm her. 'But you broke in here. And I can't have—'

She pulled one hand out from under mine and without hesitation laid her warm palm directly over my fly and squeezed.

I jerked as lightning shot through me in response,

jagged and sharp, igniting sparks in my blood and making my stupid dick very happy indeed.

Fucking hell.

'Naughty girl,' I said roughly. 'What do you think you're doing?'

Her lashes fluttered, thick, black and silky. 'Seems to me like some parts of you haven't changed their minds.'

Jesus. Determined little thing, wasn't she?

'Yeah, but those parts aren't in charge.' I pressed her palm against me so she couldn't move it. Which was probably a mistake, given how good the pressure felt. 'On your feet.'

But she stayed where she was. Again.

'Oh, come on,' she murmured. 'What kind of playboy says no to a blow job?' And she gave my dick another squeeze, as if to prove her point.

More lightning strikes of pleasure shot through me, bright and intense, making my breath catch.

Holy fuck. I'd never had a reaction like this to a woman handling my cock. What the hell was she doing to me? And why her?

I tried to pull myself together, pressing down hard on her hand so she couldn't move it. She was staring up at me, giving me a smoky look, yet I hadn't missed that shake in her fingers as she'd touched me. She might act as though she'd seduced thousands of men, but I'd bet all my billions that she hadn't.

'I know what you're doing,' I said. 'But I'm afraid that shit's not going to fly. I prefer a blow job where everyone's into it and no one has any ulterior motives except to get naked, understand?'

Her brows rose. 'And yet you're still standing here.'

Fuck.

She's got you.

I opened my mouth to respond—though Christ knew what I was going to say—when she leaned forward, pressing her tight, warm body against my legs. 'You don't know me. Getting naked might be exactly what I want to do.' She was soft against me, and hot, and then she leaned farther in, brushing her mouth over the back of my hand. 'Shall I get naked for you, Mr Blackwood? Is that what you'd like?'

Mr Blackwood.

It shouldn't have made any difference. I had women say that kind of shit to me all the time. But there was something about this particular woman... She'd gone from frightened waitress, to nervous stalker, to practised seductress in the space of five minutes and damn if that didn't make me even more fascinated than I already was.

Which one was the real her? Was *any* of them the real her? Or was she someone different? Was the real woman hiding deep inside, just waiting for the right man to come and find her?

Desire and fascination wound together, tightening their grip on me.

It had been a long time since I'd had a woman like this one. A woman I couldn't read and didn't know just by looking at her. A *very* long time...

Yeah, and you discovered her hiding under your desk, don't forget. Not only do you have no idea who she is, you also have no idea what she's doing here.

This was true. And security was an issue when you were as rich as I was. Which meant letting myself get side-tracked like this was the height of stupidity.

I stared down into her bittersweet chocolate eyes, saw the glaze of heat in them. Her pupils were dilated, the pulse at the base of her lovely throat fast, all the classic signs of physical arousal.

She wasn't faking this, that was for sure.

Keeping one hand over hers against my fly, I reached down with the other, taking her chin in my fingers and gripping her. 'I don't sleep with women who don't want me,' I said flatly, holding her gaze so she knew how serious I was. 'And I fucking hate being used.'

Her chin got a stubborn slant, the muscles in her jaw tightening. 'I'm not using you.'

'Sure you are. You're using me—or rather my cock— as a nice little distraction technique.'

For a second she said nothing. Then her face emptied of the flirty expression that had been there before, the mask of the practised seductress dropping. 'Okay, so maybe you're right. Maybe that's what I was planning on doing.' Her eyes were very dark in her pale face, but there was no mistaking the heat in them. 'Except, now, I just want you.'

I gritted my teeth because, shit, this wasn't a mask now. The truth was all laid out for me to see in her beautiful eyes and in the raw note in her voice.

She did want me. And my cock liked that far too much for its own good—or mine, for that matter.

You should be calling Clarence, not thinking about taking her up on her offer.

This was sadly true. She was a serious security breach and one I couldn't let slide.

I stroked my thumb over the line of her jaw, enjoying the warm, silky feeling of her skin, watching her eyes widen fractionally as I did so. 'That all sounds very convincing,' I said. 'And perhaps you're telling the truth. But I've got a lot of enemies. And you're here where you're not supposed to be, which can lead me to several conclusions, if you catch my drift.'

'What conclusions?'

'Oh, conclusions such as you being an assassin sent to kill me.'

'No.' Her throat moved as I touched her, a convulsive swallow, but she didn't pull away. 'I'm not here to kill you. If I was, you'd be dead already.'

I laughed at that. 'So sure of yourself. I like confidence in a woman. Okay, so if you're not here to kill me, maybe you're here to rob me instead. Is that it? Have I got something you want?'

She didn't answer, turning her head suddenly, and before I could move her lips had closed around my thumb.

My breath caught. Hard. Her mouth was hot and wet, her tongue tracing the tip of my thumb, her gaze on mine. Watching me. Gauging my response.

Little witch. She could see what she was doing to me

and, unfortunately, being a man meant I couldn't hide it. Not that I particularly wanted to hide it, because quite honestly, I was starting to get past caring.

I didn't often deny myself what I wanted and I couldn't see any reason to deny myself now. Or her, for that matter, given she'd made it very clear she wanted to do this.

And, really, how much could she get up to on her knees in front of me?

My brain was shutting down, all the blood in my body heading straight to my goddamn cock. And all I was conscious of was the heat of her mouth and the touch of her wicked tongue on my skin. Imagining how it would feel if she had that tongue touching my dick instead.

'Minx,' I drawled. 'You think I'm that easy?'

A stupid thing to say. Of course I was that easy.

She didn't speak, just tightened her lips around my thumb and began to suck. The gentle pressure felt fan-fucking-tastic and it was all I could do to keep my breathing under control.

So much for finding out who she is.

I almost smiled. Oh, I'd find out; no doubt about it. Afterwards.

This mysterious creature, creeping into my office to take whatever it was she was here to take, thinking she could distract me with a good old-fashioned blow job?

Yeah, not happening.

This was *my* territory, and seduction was *my* expertise, and she'd given away one vital advantage: she'd let me know that she wanted me.

Well, I was going to use that.

It was time to show her exactly who she was dealing with.

Gently, I pulled my hand from her mouth and undid the button on my trousers. 'You want to suck on something, Sugar? Then you know what to do.'

CHAPTER FIVE

Thea

MY HEART WAS jumping around behind my breastbone like a gymnast on a trampoline, a dim part of me wondering what the hell I was doing.

Seducing him hadn't seemed like that big a deal when I'd first decided on it, but now I was on my knees in front of him, with the salty taste of his skin in my mouth and the hard ridge behind his zip staring me in the face…

Well.

It seemed like kind of a big deal now.

I'd followed my gut when he'd started asking questions, dropping my act and giving him the truth—or at least a bit of it. Letting him see a piece of the real me: the woman who wanted the sun, not the shadow. Yet still he'd asked questions about whether I was there to kill him or to rob him, so I'd had to do something.

Taking his thumb into my mouth had seemed like a good idea at the time, giving me some control over what was happening. But somehow—and I still didn't know how he'd done it when I thought I'd been making progress—he'd taken charge of things again.

He was looking at me now, one pierced brow raised in arrogant challenge, a man supremely aware of his own beauty and his extensive sexual prowess.

Daring me to refuse. To say no and pull away.

But I couldn't. I was used to being unnoticed, yet he was noticing me, his focus so intense it was as if he was memorising every inch of me.

It was intoxicating. Addictive. And I wanted more.

You can't afford to have him notice you, not like that.

No, I couldn't. Then again, the chances of him ever actually remembering me were remote to non-existent. Not me, with a face you wouldn't look at twice in the street. Your average, every-day everywoman.

I could let myself have this moment, couldn't I, where I felt like the centre of the world instead of not even being part of it?

I took a slow breath, then another, trying to get my heartbeat under control, but he smelled so good, spice cut through with musk, and it made me ache. While the heat of his body made me want to stretch out and warm myself against him.

Yes, I could have it. I wanted it, so I was going to take it.

I lifted my hand and took hold of the tab of his zip. Then I drew it down.

The glitter of his eyes intensified, and as I spread the fabric of his trousers, I felt the tension in his muscles gather.

'Sugar…' he murmured as I leaned back slightly, looking at what I'd uncovered: the black cotton of his boxers stretched over the ridge of his very hard cock.

I certainly wasn't an expert but, whoa. He wasn't small, was he?

And it was me who'd got him like that. Pretty good for an unremarkable foundling whom no one had wanted.

Don't get ahead of yourself. He probably gets hard for any woman.

It was true, so I tried to ignore the satisfaction that filled me. Not that it mattered anyway.

His fingers brushed over my cheekbone, making me shiver, but I ignored the touch, refusing to let myself get derailed.

Turning my hand over, I stroked my knuckles down the length of his erection, feeling the heat of him through the fabric of his underwear. The muscles of his thighs tensed as I did so and my satisfaction deepened.

He might very well get hard for every woman, but right now that woman was me and, hell, I'd take it.

Dimly, the cool part of my brain tried to tell me that there had to be a better plan than kneeling in front of a complete stranger to give him a blow job just so I could steal a damn necklace.

But I didn't listen. It wasn't about the necklace any more. It wasn't even about distracting him so I could get away.

It was about the unfamiliar pulsing ache between my thighs and the hunger for something I hadn't even known I wanted.

Since Mr Chen had died six months earlier, I'd told myself I was fine with how isolating the business was. That I didn't mind being alone. Yet right now, with Blackwood hot and hard beneath my hand, I knew that I did mind. And that I wanted more than the shadows I currently lived in. I wanted some time in the sun.

My breathing was getting faster, louder. He could probably hear it.

I leaned forward and this time I brushed my mouth over the black cotton, inhaling his musky, masculine scent and the heat of his body.

'Jesus...' His voice sounded rough, stripped of its charm. His fingers slid beneath my jaw, gripping me firmly, and I just knew he was going to pull me away.

Well, that wasn't going to happen.

I lifted my hands and rested my palms on the steel of his thighs, nuzzling against him. His muscles went rigid and I heard his breath catch. So I did it again.

'Holy shit,' he said breathlessly. 'What the hell are you doing?'

I didn't answer. I couldn't. My whole body felt as if it was going to freeze and shatter into pieces if I moved away. I needed this. I needed him.

So I leaned farther into his heat, lifting one hand and hooking my fingers into the waistband of his boxers, tugging down the material.

Then it was my turn to catch my breath as I freed his cock.

Intellectually, I knew what a naked man looked like—I had a working Internet connection like most people—but looking something up online and seeing it in the flesh for the first time were two different things. And, as I was learning, that certainly applied to Damian Blackwood.

He was long, very thick and extremely hard.

He was also very pierced.

'Oh, my God.' I stared wide-eyed at the ring piercing the head of his cock. 'Didn't that hurt?' Fascinated, I reached out, sliding a finger along his shaft to where the silver ring pierced him.

'No.' He sounded strangled, the muscles of his thighs like iron beneath my other hand.

'But why?' His skin was very hot and silky too. I touched him again, stroking him with my fingertips, and he made a rough, deep sound, his hand coming down to cover mine.

'Because women like it. And so do I.' He guided my fingers to the head of his cock. 'It doesn't hurt when you touch it either.' The words were no longer smooth, but rough-edged.

He was liking what I was doing to him.

My mouth was dry and I swallowed, my own breathing coming faster as I stroked his velvety skin then cautiously touched the ring. Then, curious, I tugged gently on it.

He hissed, and I looked up sharply, worried for a second that I'd hurt him, despite what he'd told me.

Except it wasn't pain that I saw as his gaze slammed into mine. Only a raw heat that stole the remaining breath from my body.

'You want to suck me, then do it,' he said roughly. 'But you have to let me know now if you want the ring in or out.'

'You can take it out?'

'Yeah. If you want it in, don't worry. I'll be careful with your mouth. I know what I'm doing, okay?'

Of course. He'd probably done this a lot. But I didn't need to think about what I wanted. I knew already.

I eased my fingers around his shaft, running my thumb up the underside of it, loving how he hissed again, muttering a curse under his breath. 'Do you like it in?' I asked. 'Because I do.'

'Then do it.' His voice was harsh. 'Suck me, Sugar.'

I didn't need to be told. I wasn't sure how to do this, but for the moment that didn't matter. All that mattered was that I was hungry and I wanted to taste him. Wanted his heat inside me, chasing the shadows away.

So I tightened my grip and leaned in, touching my tongue to the head of his cock, licking him experimentally.

He made a deep sound of masculine approval, the tension in his body vibrating under my palms, so I did it again, tasting him. His flavour was rich and salty and suddenly I was starving for more.

I licked around the sensitive head, holding on tight, teasing the ring then playing a little with it, and he groaned.

It echoed through me, settling down between my thighs, making the hungry ache that pulsed there even worse. Because for once in my life I wasn't hiding. I wasn't passing by unnoticed.

I had his attention. I was right in the spotlight. And it made me feel brave.

So I lifted my gaze to his as I slid him deep into my mouth, sucking gently, wanting to see the expression on his face. It was tight, his features drawn in harsh lines, almost a snarl twisting his beautiful mouth. His gaze was electric and there was nothing of the charming storyteller I'd seen on the terrace in him at all now. This was nothing but raw, primal masculinity.

A shiver coursed through me, my sex throbbing.

If this was what a blow job was like every time, then I could get used it.

I held his gaze as I sucked him, watching pleasure blaze like a fire in his eyes, and he watched me in return, so intently it was as if he was trying to imprint me onto his memory.

A sliver of doubt crept under my skin, a bone-deep instinct murmuring that the way this man was looking at me could put my entire livelihood in danger.

But for once I couldn't bring myself to care. I didn't want to be like Mr Chen, dying alone, unnoticed and un-mourned by anyone except me. I wanted to have one person remember me, just one. To feel as though I'd been part of the world in some small way.

Blackwood lifted his hands. His long fingers were in my hair and I braced myself for him to hold on tight. But he didn't. He simply pulled his fingers gently through my hair over and over, his hips beginning to move as I sucked.

'Yes,' he murmured, his voice hot, dark and rich, like melted chocolate. 'Yes, Sugar. That's so good.'

All thoughts of Mr Chen vanished. The note of heat in the words stroked down my spine like a touch, the ache between my legs intensifying. I gripped him tighter, sucking harder.

'Fuck, yeah.' He spread his fingers out, cradling my head, massaging my skull. 'Love the way you're doing that. Fucking unbelievable.'

Something shifted inside me at the praise, something vulnerable and needy. I sucked even harder, teasing the ring with my teeth, and he groaned, his hips moving faster, sliding his cock deeper.

His features were twisted in agonised pleasure and he still didn't look away from me, his fingers firm on my scalp. He was looking at me as if he'd never seen anything like me before in his whole life. 'You're going to make me come, Sugar,' he growled. 'Is that what you want? Are you going to take everything I give you?'

I couldn't do anything but nod, because I did. I wanted to make him come; I wanted the hot taste of him to scare away the dark.

And he was as good as his word; he was careful of me as he began to thrust harder, holding me steady. I gripped him tight with one hand, the other spread on his rock-hard thigh for balance, sucking hard as he gave one last deep thrust then came, a growling curse escaping him, his head going back, his hips shuddering.

I swallowed him down, thick and hot and salty, watching the tension in his face, the cords of his neck tight, his jaw rigid.

Because, if I wanted him to remember me, I wanted to remember him too. Damian Blackwood in my power, brought to the edge by little old me.

Don't get too confident. Remember what you're here to do.

Realisation washed through me, cold and unwelcome.

Oh, yes, that's right. The necklace. No matter what I'd done to Blackwood, I still hadn't finished here.

The silence had deepened around us, punctuated only by the faint thump of the music outside and the sound of his harsh breathing. The salty, masculine scent of his body surrounded me, underlain by that warm spice.

The ache between my thighs was hot, demanding.

Get up and run. Now. While he's still recovering.

But my legs felt rubbery and his hand was still in my hair, stroking me, and I didn't want to move. Besides, if I ran now, I wouldn't get the necklace and not being able to fulfil a client's request wouldn't exactly help keep Mr Chen's business afloat.

No, I needed to stay. Occupy Blackwood's attention enough that he wouldn't ask me awkward questions, then wait until he eventually went to sleep so I could have some time to look around without being interrupted.

He was leaning back against the window now, his

eyes half-closed, his impressive chest rising and falling with his quickened breaths. His fingers were still moving in my hair, massaging my scalp gently, and it felt so good I didn't want to move away.

I shut my eyes, leaning my forehead against his taut stomach, the tension in my muscles relaxing under the pressure of his fingers, even as a different kind of tension—the one situated between my thighs—got even tighter.

'That was perfect,' Blackwood murmured into the silence. 'Fucking perfect. But I'm thinking I need to return the favour.'

Return the favour. Did that mean…?

Yes, of course that's what it means.

I broke out in a sweat, a surge of adrenaline stealing my breath and putting my pulse into overdrive. I couldn't tell if it was fear, excitement or a combination of the two. Probably a combo. Which shouldn't work but somehow it did.

'Well?' he purred, his fingers gently massaging down the back of my neck, making me want to sigh in pure, sensual pleasure. 'Would you like that, Sugar? Would you like me to put my mouth on you? Get you off the way you did for me?'

Another surge of adrenaline hit me, making me breathless. 'Yes,' I gasped out, before I had a chance to think twice. 'I would like it.'

The massaging fingers stopped and I nearly moaned in protest as he drew them away, quickly sorting out his own clothing before helping me up off the floor. Once again he was gentle, handling me carefully as he urged me over to his desk, but nervousness collected in my gut all the same.

To distract myself, I looked around at the pristine work surface of his desk. 'Is this really your office? Looks like you barely live in here, let alone work in here.'

'I don't work in here.' He eased me up onto the desktop, his grip firm, urging me to sit back on it. 'I'm not a fan of sitting still.'

My curiosity tightened, the instinct to get more information from him irresistible. 'So where do you work, then?'

He gave me one of those wicked smiles. 'In bed.'

Oh, yes, I could see him sitting in a massive bed heaped with pillows, wrapped in nothing but a crisp, white cotton sheet, all those colourful tattoos and hard muscles on show, tapping industriously on a laptop...

Warm hands wrapped around my ankles, easing them apart, and the image of him in bed working fractured then shattered. His fingers were so hot, painting fire on my bare skin, and he was watching me with that single-minded focus. As if I was the centre of his universe.

'Let your knees fall open,' he murmured, the look in his silver eyes making me dizzy.

I'd wanted to be in his spotlight and, now that I was, I could hardly breathe.

Slowly, I leaned back on my hands and let my knees fall wide, the fabric of my uniform sliding up, the subtle stretch of my inner thigh muscles a surprisingly erotic sensation.

'Perfect.' Blackwood pulled out the chair and seated himself at the desk, right between my thighs, as if he was sitting down for a meal.

And you're his meal.

My heartbeat was louder than the music outside, my world narrowing down to his palms wrapped around my ankles, his thumbs stroking the sensitive skin just beneath my ankle bone, striking sparks throughout my entire body.

'Now…' He ran those wicked hands up from my ankles to my calves, his fingertips hot on my skin, and then up farther to push my uniform even higher. 'Let's see you.'

I shuddered as he slid my uniform up to my waist, then shuddered again as his fingers moved to my inner thighs, stroking me as he eased them wide apart. My breath caught and I had to bite down on the low moan that threatened to break free, aware of every sensation: the burn of my muscles, the fire of his touch on my sensitive skin, the cool wood of the desk beneath me.

The throb of my sex and the wet press of the cotton of my knickers.

'You still with me, Sugar?' The words were as soft and dark as black velvet, his sharp, silver gaze searching my face as his fingers traced circles over my achingly sensitive skin.

I had to force the word out because my mouth had gone so dry. 'Yes.'

'You sure?'

My breathing had started to get out of control, the sound of it loud in the room. If I'd cared about it I would have been embarrassed. But I didn't care about it.

There was a pressure between my legs, getting more intense and harder to ignore, and every move he made, every touch, seemed to increase the weight of it.

'Yes, I'm sure,' I croaked, my voice sounding old, rusty and a little bit broken.

He nodded and then, still holding my gaze, he reached up and hooked the damp fabric of my knickers to the side, baring me.

I gasped, unable to help it as his attention dropped between my thighs, making me flush and tremble. No one had ever seen me *there* before. The only people who'd seen me naked were the nuns at St Paul's, the orphanage where I'd spent the first few years of my life. No one else.

But now *he* was looking at me. Damian Blackwood, womaniser extraordinaire, the biggest, most sought-after playboy and party animal in the western world, was looking at my bare sex and I was just about to go up in flames.

'Beautiful.' His gaze flicked up to mine and I could see heat in it, a hunger he didn't hide. 'Absolutely fucking sensational.'

My cheeks flamed. Feeling exposed, I wanted to close my legs and hide myself, but he must have picked up on my discomfort because his palms firmed on my knees, holding them where they were. Keeping me spread for him.

'I just want to look.' His quicksilver gaze was relentless. 'But I'm not going to do anything you don't want me to, so you need to be sure.'

I forced down my nervousness because, as much as this was confronting for me, I wanted it. And I wanted him looking at me. I wanted that spotlight.

I wanted to know that I existed. And his hands on my skin, his brilliant silver gaze... He was making me real with every touch.

'I am,' I whispered.

'Good. Because, I'll be honest, I'm going to do more than look. I fucking love eating pussy and you smell goddamn delicious.'

The frank words made me blush even hotter and I couldn't think of a word to say.

He smiled, charming and wicked, and something in my chest clenched tight. 'Don't worry, you don't have to say a thing. Just lie back and let me do all the work, hmm?'

I gave a shaky nod, my vocal cords momentarily escaping my conscious control. And that was all he needed.

He leaned forward, his hands sliding up to my hips, pulling me towards him, right to the edge of the desk. Then he put his palms on my inner thighs, holding me open as he bent his head, and his breath washed over my skin. I trembled at the sensation of warmth, and then again as his mouth brushed my inner thigh, a gasp escaping me. The kiss was like a hot coal pressed to my flesh, only without the pain, delivering delicious heat and intense pleasure instead.

I'd barely got used to his mouth when his fingers slid caressingly up my thighs to the slickness of my sex, and I shuddered, my breath catching hard as he touched me, gently spreading me open.

I found myself staring down at him, the sight of his dark head between my spread legs disturbingly erotic. The way he was touching me, opening me up with his fingers, was so careful, as if he was parting the petals of a flower. I'd never been touched like this before. So gently, as if I was something precious, and it made me feel oddly vulnerable, some part of me wanting him to stop, to tell him that I didn't like it. But I *did* like it. And I didn't want him to stop.

I shut my eyes and bit my lip, tensing as his finger circled around my clit, so close and yet not quite touching, teasing me, the vague friction scattering pleasure across my skin like sparks. Then he did it again and I couldn't stop the low moan that broke from me or still the jerk of my hips. 'Please…' I said, even though I hadn't meant to.

He made a rough sound that could have been either approval or denial, but either way I felt the vibration of it like a touch. And I was just shivering through that when he swept his tongue up the length of my sex, licking me as though I was his favourite ice cream.

I cried out as pleasure rippled the length of my body,

and then he licked me again, long and slow, turning the pleasure sharper, more intense.

I jerked in his grip, unable to keep still, wriggling on the desktop as his tongue swept over me again, trying to direct him, because he kept missing the place I desperately wanted him to touch.

But all he did was laugh, a low and sexy rumble, his hands shifting to my hips and gripping me, holding me in place. 'Oh, no, you don't.' His breath was warm against my skin. 'Not yet. You taste too fucking good for me to take this anything but slow.'

God, really? I didn't think I could survive slow.

My hands had reached down of their own accord somehow, finding the soft black spikes of his hair, my fingers twisting into them, trying to direct his teasing mouth. He only gave another rumbling laugh before pushing his tongue deep inside me.

My head went back, a hoarse cry escaping me as the pleasure burned brighter, hotter. I shuddered, pulling at his hair, trying to move my hips, searching for more pressure, more friction, but he held me still, not letting me move. He was clearly in no hurry, exploring me in a series of lazy licks, nips and soft kisses. The alternating pressures and sensations intensified the pleasure, making me pant, my whole body shaking.

I was so ready to come, *so* ready. And yet he didn't push me over, making the pleasure build higher and higher while he held the climax just out of reach.

I think I begged him. I know I pleaded with him. But either he didn't listen or he was enjoying playing with me, because he kept me hovering on the edge for what felt like an eternity. Giving me light licks and then some thrusts of his tongue, a tease on my clit, then strokes of his fingers on my inner thighs, gentle touches and caresses.

It was too much. It was not enough.

I felt as though I was coming apart at the seams when he finally tipped me over, sucking on my clit and sliding two fingers inside me, the pressure and friction enough to make me throw back my head and scream as the pleasure detonated like a bomb inside me.

Every thought in my head turned to ash and blew away.

I lay there, my brain empty, the aftershocks pulsing through me, utterly boneless and not thinking about anything in particular.

Blackwood trailed soft kisses up my inner thighs, nuzzling against my skin, the prickle of his jaw sending delicious shivers everywhere.

'Yeah, I called it. You did taste fucking amazing,' he murmured, his breath warm. 'I could have kept doing that all night.'

'I'm not sure I could,' I said with total honesty, my voice cracked. 'I think I'm pretty much dead as it is.'

He laughed that sexy laugh and I had the odd urge to wrap it around me and snuggle up in it. 'Tell me, Sugar,' he said after a moment, very conversationally, stroking my thighs with unhurried fingers. 'You're here for the Red Queen, aren't you?'

CHAPTER SIX

Damian

SHE LOOKED DELECTABLE, lying back on my desk in front of me with her legs spread, the black curls of her pussy all slick on her bare flesh, her inner thighs glistening from my mouth and her own arousal.

She was also totally unguarded, which made it the perfect time to get the truth out of her.

Because of course she was here for the Red Queen. Nothing else made sense. I had plenty of other jewels, but no one had tried to take them before, and I'd only just got my hands on this necklace. The timing was right.

Besides, no one but a thief would have had the skills to open the lock on my door. And I knew thieves. I'd met plenty of them back in Sydney while I'd been working security at various different clubs. The best knew how to deal with security systems and how to move around unnoticed. They were fast, patient and also incredibly observant.

Very much like this woman, in fact.

Because she was fast—she'd certainly disappeared

into my office fast enough—and she had the skills to by-pass my security systems. There was also that guarded, watchful quality to her. As if she was noticing things to file away in her memory for future reference.

Yeah, I'd lay money on her being a thief.

I stared at her, lying there on the desk, her breathing fast, echoing in the silence of the office. The scent of aroused woman and the salty-sweet taste of her in my mouth was making my cock start to get interested again. My cock didn't care that she was a thief. My cock just wanted that gorgeous pussy all spread out before me.

Too bad. She might have nearly made me lose it against the windows not ten minutes ago with that sweet mouth, but I had control of the situation now, and she wasn't getting it back.

I'd spent months tracking that necklace down and I wasn't about to let some sweet-faced pseudo-waitress take it from me, no matter how sexy she was.

You didn't get to be the head of a multi-billion-dollar company by being complacent, after all.

I felt her muscles tighten and I firmed my grip on her thighs, holding her there, because I wasn't going to let her get away.

Slowly, she sat up, her eyes dark and shocked in her flushed face. Strands of glossy brown hair stuck to her forehead and cheek, the mouth that had nearly made me lose my goddamn mind full and red and pouty.

My cock got even harder.

'What did you say?' she asked faintly.

'I think you heard me.'

'I don't know what you're—'

'Don't even try to deny it, Sugar. You might have blown my fucking mind with that gorgeous mouth and sweet little pussy of yours but my memory is fully intact.'

Her mouth opened then shut. She looked away, smoothing down her uniform and pulling her legs together to cover herself. Her hands trembled, the way they had as she'd undone my fly, but this time I didn't touch her.

The expression on her face gave nothing away, but that shake of her hands told me all I needed to know.

Of course she was here for the Red Queen.

The only question now was what to do about it.

She was good—she was *very* good; that was for sure—then again, she'd have had to be in order to get into my apartment.

But I couldn't have thieves thinking they could just waltz into my place and take whatever the fuck they liked. Everything I had I'd worked hard for, and what was mine stayed mine. It was something this pretty little thief needed a lesson in.

I stared at her, the taste of her lingering on my tongue and the scent of her in my nostrils. Sweet, musky and delicious.

What the hell made her think she could steal from me? And why did she want the necklace? She must have known this would be a dangerous job, that the risk of getting caught was high. Was this for herself or was she a contract thief, stealing on behalf of someone else? I had my share of enemies and there had been a fair few anonymous bids on the Red Queen at the private auction where I'd finally bought it.

Whatever her story was, there was an air of vulnerability to her. The thieves I'd come into contact with in my previous life were generally tough and harder than bulletproof glass. But she looked neither tough nor hard, not with her lashes lying all silky and black on the fragile curve of her cheekbone.

I hadn't thought I'd be into vulnerable, but right now I wanted to run my fingers along that curve, feel the fine grain of her skin.

Curiosity shifted inside me. Letting her leave wasn't an option, not now she knew the layout of my place and how to get into my office, not to mention how to bypass Everett's security measures. No, I had to keep her here, find out more about her before I did anything else.

Sure you do. You just want to fuck her.

That was true also, though that could wait. I needed a few answers first.

'I suppose there's no point in telling you I couldn't find the bathroom?' Her voice was cool and guarded.

'Like you couldn't find the kitchen?' I didn't move from where I sat, my hands resting on the desktop on either side of her hips, ready to grab her if she ran, because she sure as hell wasn't going anywhere, not now. 'No, we've been through that, and I didn't believe you the first time around. And a blow job, no matter how good it is, isn't going to make me change my mind.'

She gave an irritated sigh.

I pushed myself up out of the chair and reached forward, putting one finger beneath her pointed chin and tipping her head back, making her meet my gaze. 'I want answers.' I let a hint of authority edge my voice to show her I meant business. 'And I want them now.'

The look in her eyes was impossible to read. Normally I had no problems figuring someone out; the years spent in boardrooms across the globe had only sharpened those skills. But I couldn't get a bead on her, not one.

And that made me want to get beneath that dark, watchful gaze, see what lay beneath the surface.

'And if I don't give them to you?' Her tone was level and she sounded only mildly interested, not at all concerned.

Well, shit. Normally people fell over themselves to give me what I wanted. They certainly didn't argue or ask what would happen if they didn't, and I didn't like punishing people. Sure, I was firm when I had to be, I had no problems with that, but making threats to a pretty little thief? A *vulnerable* pretty little thief?

Yeah, I was reluctant. I preferred to make women feel good, not frighten them.

So I did what I always did when faced with a potential conflict of interest: I smiled my usual smile, the one that made both men and women blush and fall at my feet, ready to do my bidding. 'Let's just say I have ways of making you talk.' I released her chin and let my fingers trail lightly down her neck, enjoying the way her pupils dilated as I did so and noting the goose bumps that scattered all over her skin.

She swallowed and for a second I thought I had her. Then her straight dark brows lowered and I caught a glimpse of something steely and stubborn in the depths of her eyes. 'I don't have to tell you a thing. You'll get rid of me either way.'

Damn it.

She shouldn't push me, not when she had no idea what I was capable of when I was pushed.

I took my hand away then put both palms flat on the desk top and leaned forward, my face inches from hers. She didn't flinch, not even a flicker, staring back at me as if daring me to do something.

Beautiful little witch.

Clearly the ball was in my court.

'What's your fee?' I asked casually. 'For the necklace.'

'You're assuming a lot.'

'I have to when I have a thief in my office, sitting on my desk, not giving me a straight answer.'

She only stared and didn't say a word.

Heat began to gather in my gut, along with a healthy dose of adrenaline, making my cock even harder, and my heart beat like a fucking drum. It was my hunter's instincts kicking in again.

Except this time it wasn't a jewel I wanted to hunt.

It was a woman.

'What?' I raised a brow. 'Got nothing to say?'

She didn't even blink. 'If you're going to call the police, then do it. Don't keep me waiting, hotshot.'

Ah, so she was going to go down the full-on challenge route. Excellent. My dick fucking loved that and
so did I.

'Who said anything about the police?' I searched
her face, looking deep into her dark eyes, trying to see
what was going on behind them.

And just for a second I saw surprise flicker through
them.

So, she'd expected me to call the cops on her, which
was a fair enough assumption. That was what most
people catching an intruder in their house would do.

Not me, though. I hadn't finished with her yet.

The surprise had vanished as if it had never been,
her gaze as reflective as it had been before. Then she
suddenly leaned forward, closing the small gap between
us, her fingers threading into my hair and her mouth
pressed against mine.

Now it was my turn to be surprised. So much so that
for a second I couldn't move. Her tongue touched my
lower lip and pushed gently, demanding entry, and I
didn't even think about denying her, opening my mouth
and allowing her to explore. She did so, hesitantly at
first then with more confidence. She tasted sweet, as
if she'd been eating strawberries, and I bet she could
taste herself on me because she gave a little shudder, a
soft moan escaping with it.

There was desperation in the sound, her fingers tightening in my hair, and I was rock-hard. My hands were
on her thighs, sliding beneath the hem of her uniform,
stroking her silky skin, the kiss getting deeper, hotter.

I knew this was another of her distraction techniques, but I didn't care. If this was the kind of distraction she was offering, then fuck, I'd take it. I needed another challenge anyway, and she was providing it.

But if she thought sex was going to make me forget what she was doing here she'd picked the wrong man.

My bedroom wasn't very far away. I could take her there, stretch her out over my bed, bury myself inside her, take us both to heaven and back and then… Well, there was no rush for answers. I could take my time, spend the night undoing her. By morning, I'd have her secrets, that was for certain.

She'd eased closer to me, sitting on the edge of the desk with her thighs slightly wide to allow me to stand between them. I could feel the heat of her pussy through my trousers and it was making me breathless.

Christ, how long had it been since a woman had made me breathless like this? With only a kiss?

I slid my fingers over the curves of her butt and gripped her, pulling her more firmly against me, her hot sex pressing against my aching dick. 'Your distraction techniques are getting predictable,' I murmured against her mouth. 'Are you sure this is the game you want to play?'

'Yes,' she whispered back, her voice thick, her hips pressing against mine in blatant invitation. 'If you can't handle it, then let me go.'

I didn't laugh, even though I wanted to. Handle her? She clearly had no idea with whom she was dealing.

'My bedroom,' I said. 'Now.'

CHAPTER SEVEN

Thea

HIS HANDS SLID under my butt and he picked me up as though I weighed nothing. I wrapped my legs around his lean waist, pressing my throbbing clit against the hard ridge of his cock. The friction sent glittering sparks of pleasure scattering through me, making me shiver.

His mouth was hot and insistent on mine as he carried me to the door, his tongue exploring me unhurriedly, as if he had all the time in the world.

I couldn't believe how desperate I was for him yet again.

I'd only kissed him to shut him up, so he wouldn't keep asking me questions. Because I'd run out of answers to give him.

He'd guessed why I was here, which had shocked me more than it should have. I suppose I hadn't thought he'd be interested enough to think about why I'd been in his office and what I was doing, but it seemed I was wrong.

He'd also said he wasn't going to call the police,

and that had surprised me too, though I'd decided not to question it too closely, going in for a kiss instead.

I'd still been intent on seducing the hell out of him, and maybe escaping once he'd fallen asleep, but the way he was kissing me now, it was clear I was the one being seduced.

His mouth on mine was hot, his kiss rich and dark, decadent as chocolate cake. And it was difficult to process anything while I was plastered against his rock-hard body, the heat of it burning me alive in the most delicious way.

He didn't break the kiss, not even to lock the office door behind us as he stepped out into the hallway.

The beat of the music was loud out here and I heard someone shout his name. He ignored it, kissing me deeper, nipping on my bottom lip as he strode down the hall with me.

I wound my arms around his neck, arching against him, everything fading away under the heat of his mouth and the feel of his hands beneath me, his spicy masculine scent and the hard body I was wrapped around.

The hard body I wanted to run my fingers all over, kiss and lick, rub myself against.

I'd never wanted to touch a man before. Now I literally couldn't think of wanting to do anything else.

He came to a door and opened it, kicking it shut behind him.

Another large room, the sound of the party falling away as the door closed. I didn't pay any attention, too busy kissing him back as he strode over to the massive

bed situated beneath huge windows that looked out over
the cityscape. He put me down on the edge of the mattress and stepped back. That big, muscular body was
inches away, the black cotton of his shirt giving a hint
of the hard musculature beneath it. He'd left the top
couple of buttons undone, giving me a close-up glimpse
of those tattoos, the colours bright.

I lifted my hands, desperate to touch him, but he
gently circled my wrists with long, strong fingers, holding me away.

'Uh-huh,' he murmured. 'I need to lay a few ground
rules first.'

'Ground rules?' I echoed blankly. 'What ground
rules?'

His eyes glinted in the darkness. 'Like I told you before, I'm not into misunderstandings, and I'm not into
reading a woman's mind. You tell me what you want,
what you like, and you tell me straight.'

I flushed. I wasn't used to frank discussions about
anything, let alone sex. And that wasn't even going into
the fact that I had no idea what I liked and what I didn't.

Couldn't he just screw me like a normal man?

I pulled against his hold. 'Do we really have to have
this discussion right now?'

His fingers tightened, keeping me still, but he smiled,
warm and intimate. 'Yeah, we really do.'

'Why? It's none of your business.'

'Sure it's my business.' His mouth quirked and I
found myself watching it. God, it really was the most
perfect I'd ever seen. Full lower lip, beautifully carved

top lip. And the way it curved at the ends... 'If you have a crappy time, it screws with my reputation, and I can't have that.'

Damn it. I had been hoping for less conversation, not more, because I didn't want to make myself memorable to him in any way, and I'd bet that the presence of my virginity might end up doing just that. He probably didn't encounter many virgins at his parties and that would make me stand out.

He's going to guess. He's not stupid.

Pity. And, even worse, he was observant too; while that felt good, it also presented a difficulty I hadn't anticipated. Because it meant he could read me. Most people ignored me, but not him.

I forced down my irritation. Perhaps a few half-truths would be enough. 'Well, we can't have your reputation being screwed with, can we?' I said, trying and failing to hide my sarcasm.

His eyes narrowed and he let go one of my wrists, his warm hand cupping my jaw instead, his fingers hot against my skin. 'This isn't a joke, Sugar. I'm serious. When I fuck a woman, I want her to enjoy it, and if she doesn't enjoy it then I don't either, understand me? I don't waste my time on crappy sex.'

'You didn't seem to want to have a conversation before.' I tried not to lean into the warmth of his hand.

'Yeah, but you had your mouth wrapped around my dick.' Wickedness glinted in his eyes. 'So I was thinking of other things.'

I put my hand on his chest, feeling the solid strength

and heat of him. 'Well, I liked everything you did back in your office.'

He watched me, trying to read me. 'You ever fuck a man you didn't know before?'

A flush crept up my neck, making my cheeks burn. Clearly nothing was going to happen until we'd discussed his 'ground rules'.

'No,' I said, attempting not to sound sulky.

'Didn't think so.' His thumb found the line of my jaw, stroking gently. 'Which makes talking about it even more important. Because you don't know me, and I don't know you.'

What he was saying made sense. Good sense. But I didn't want to talk. I didn't want to have to tell him a single thing if I didn't have to and, now I'd got a sense for this physical chemistry between us, I was starting to think that I didn't have to. Not if I played this right.

I turned my head, nuzzling into his palm, brushing my mouth over it. He stilled, so I kept going, kissing his wrist, his strong, steady pulse against my lips. And then I leaned forward until I'd closed the distance, pressing my mouth to his.

His fingers tangled in my hair, gripping me and pulling me back. 'Sugar—'

'I'd like it if you took off your clothes,' I interrupted breathlessly, hoping that would shut him up.

For a second I thought it wasn't going to work, danger glittering in his eyes as he studied me. Then abruptly the sharp glitter faded, a slow-burning smile curving his mouth. 'There, that wasn't hard, was it?' He let me go and stood back, shrugging out of his jacket and tossing it over a nearby armchair, before taking off his shoes too. Then he began to undo the buttons of his black shirt.

My breath caught, relief mixing with my building hunger, unable to take my eyes off him.

He took it slow, as though this was a strip show he was putting on just for me, undoing each button, the fabric of his shirt parting little by little to reveal skin and ink in a gradual tease.

My mouth went dry and I had to curl my fingers into my palms to stop myself from reaching for him.

By the time he got to the last few buttons, I could hardly contain myself.

And then there were no more buttons and he was shrugging off the shirt, leaving him in only the suit trousers that sat low on his lean hips.

Light from the city outside painted his skin, drawing attention to the chiselled lines of his pecs and abs, and the Japanese-style tattoo that covered his chest, left shoulder and crawled down his left arm. Against a background of ornate fish scales in beautifully shaded blacks and greys, a brilliantly coloured dragon coiled amongst delicate flowers. The piece was as glorious as he was.

He dropped a hand to the waistband of his trousers, flicking open the button and then easing down the zip. Then he was shoving the fabric down along with his boxers, getting rid of them so he was finally, gloriously naked.

I shivered, my gaze falling to his lean hips and powerful thighs, to the proud jut of his long, thick cock.

He was so very beautiful I couldn't stand it.

Desperate to touch, I moved to the end of the bed, kneeling upright on the mattress, reaching out to brush my fingertips over his chest, feeling the hardness of his muscles and the burning heat of his skin. He didn't move, letting me explore, letting me brush one of his nipples with my fingertip.

Him being naked while I was dressed should have made me feel more in control, but it didn't. His nakedness only highlighted his raw sexuality, sheer physical strength and power and the mega-watt burn of his charisma. And how much all those things made me his slave.

'Don't think I'm going to forget that you didn't answer me properly.' His voice was a low purr as I stroked him with a shaking finger, liquid honey and black velvet all rolled into one. 'Which means you have two choices. One, you let me take charge. Two, you have to ask me for everything you want.'

I didn't want to have to ask him. I didn't want to have to give anything away. Which left me with only one choice.

'The…first one,' I murmured, tracing the head of the dragon over his pec, not wanting to look at him.

But he pressed my palm flat to his chest while his other hand slid along my jaw, his fingers in my hair as he tugged my head back until I met his tarnished-silver gaze.

'Say it,' he ordered softly. 'I want the words so we both know what's happening here.'

I swallowed. 'I want you to be in charge.'

The expression on his beautiful face didn't change. 'You know what that means, don't you? That you're going to have to trust me.'

Something inside me yawned wide. Trust? Seriously? How could I do that? The only person I'd ever trusted in my life was Mr Chen and he was dead.

But he must have seen my uncertainty, because he added, 'Just with your body and your pleasure. That's all.'

Oh. Well. That I could do. He'd given me so much pleasure already, it was an easy choice to make. 'Yes, I trust you,' I said thickly.

'Okay, then.' The tension around his beautiful mouth eased and one corner of it curled wickedly. 'Time for you to get naked.'

He released me and reached for my uniform before I could move, pulling it up and over my head, leaving me kneeling on the mattress in nothing but my underwear. Then he slid one hand behind me and flicked open the catch of my bra in an easy, practised movement. I caught my breath as the fabric fell away, and then again as he crouched in front of me, his hands going to my hips to ease my knickers off. The fabric slid down and I moved so he could pull it off me, and then he stepped back, leaving me naked on the bed.

For a second neither of us moved and I could hear my own accelerated breathing, loud and fast. His gaze ran over me, the heat climbing, becoming molten.

Then he got onto the bed with all the lithe grace of

a panther, picking me up as if I weighed nothing and taking me back down onto the mattress, pinning me beneath him, his body hot as a furnace.

Shivering, I wrapped my legs around his waist, arching into him, desperate to get close. I'd forgotten about the necklace, about my client, about Mr Chen. About staying unnoticed and unseen. About keeping him from asking questions I didn't want to answer.

All that was important was the contact of his body against mine and how, the more he touched me, the less like a ghost I felt. As if he was drawing me into the world and making me a part of it.

Perhaps I should have found that scary, but I didn't. Right now, right here, I craved it.

He kissed me, lightly at first, teasing and seductive, biting and nipping, before deepening the kiss, his tongue delving into my mouth as his body pressed me down onto the cool sheets.

He'd taken control completely, and I didn't care as I slid my hands down his back, glorying in the steel beneath his skin, the lithe power of his body and all that leashed, coiled strength.

God, he was so *hot*.

I tightened my legs around him, rubbing up against the hard ridge that pressed between my thighs, feeling the metal of the ring in his cock scrape deliciously over my sensitive skin. I groaned at the sensation while he gave a low, breathless laugh. 'Greedy girl,' he murmured against my neck. 'Stop that.'

'Why?' I tried to do it again, but he held me down.

'Because if you don't stop rubbing that gorgeous pussy all over me this'll be over before we even get started.' He gripped me then rolled us both over, so he was lying on his back and I was on top of him. Then he pushed himself up the bed until he was leaning against the headboard, long and muscular, bronze skin and coloured ink. A big, powerful sexy man, tattooed and gorgeous.

I leaned forward, my palms on his hot chest, tilting my hips against the steel bar of his cock pressed between us. 'Come on,' I ordered, unable to contain my frustration. 'I want you.'

His smile ignited something demanding deep inside me. 'I love that you're so into me, Sugar. But I'm in charge remember? And right now, I just want to look at you.'

'What? Again?'

He laughed and a flush of pleasure rose the length of my body, making my growing frustration even worse. 'Yes, again.'

It was weird, feeling this impatient, given patience was one of the things I'd learned early on in my line of work. Watching and waiting was part of a successful mission.

Yet I didn't want to watch and wait now. I wanted him to get on with it.

'Please,' I murmured, brushing my lips against his.

'Patience.' Keeping one hand on my hip, he leaned over to the bedside table, rummaging around in it. Drawing out a handful of small colourful packets, he straightened up and held them out in his palm. 'Pick a colour.'

They were condoms. Obviously.

My hand shook as I picked out a blue one at random and he dumped the rest on the bed beside us. Then he made me sit down across his thighs as he lay back, ripping open the packet and taking out the condom.

I watched, fascinated, as he deftly rolled the latex over his cock and the piercing, and my half-formed fears of it somehow tearing the condom died a death. He knew what he was doing; of course he did.

Once that was done, he stared at me and this time he didn't smile. His eyes were molten and there was a tightness to his jaw.

Something gathered in the air between us, a tense, burning thing.

'Ready?' Threads of darkness ran through his beautiful voice, quicksilver glinting in his gaze.

'Yes,' I said aloud, my voice so thick, it didn't even sound like mine.

He urged me close, gripping his cock in one hand, and then he was nudging the entrance to my body. I shivered, my breath catching. His face was inches from mine, the look in his eyes shockingly intense.

I trembled, my body tensing despite my best intentions, waiting for the thrust. But it didn't come. Instead, he rubbed the head of his dick through the folds of my sex, a gentle sliding sensation that made me gasp. I could feel the metal of the ring pressing lightly against my clit, the hardness of it striking sparks of intense pleasure along every nerve-ending I had.

'Oh… God…' I breathed shakily, curling my fingers into the firm muscle of his chest. 'What…are you doing?'

He put a hand on my hip, holding me down. 'Getting you off.'

'I know but…' The ring pressed lightly on my clit again and I jerked, gasping, electric pleasure searing me. 'I want… I want…'

'What do you want?' He growled the words, demanding. 'Tell me.'

I was panting again, unable to stop, my hips moving against his hold as he tormented me, the heat of his body and the musky scent of fully aroused male like a drug. 'You,' I gasped. 'I want you.'

'Then take me.' The molten silver of his eyes held me fast. 'Put my dick inside you.'

I didn't think about how I hadn't done this before. I didn't even think about how I was going to hide my inexperience from him. Operating entirely on instinct, I reached down, sliding my fingers around his thick shaft, then I positioned myself and guided him into me without any hesitation at all.

It didn't hurt. It didn't even sting. There was just an intense stretching sensation and an unfamiliar feeling of fullness that had me panting and trembling uncontrollably. Were all men this big or was it just him?

His jaw was tight, the glitter of his eyes like silver flames. 'You okay?'

'Uh…yeah…' I managed to force out.

'Good.' His hand on my hip gentled and he slid his other hand to the small of my back, pressing lightly, encouraging me to arch my spine. 'Take me deeper, Sugar.'

And I did, groaning at the intensity of the sensation. When I was finally sitting down on him, his cock deep inside me, all I could do was sit there shaking, my hands pressed to his chest, trying to breathe through the pressure.

His body was tense and I knew he was holding himself back. But he didn't move. Instead, he stroked my back with one of his warm hands, up and down, while with the other he cupped my breast, circling his thumb over my nipple, gently teasing it.

The combination of soothing strokes and white-hot bursts of pleasure was confusing yet erotic as hell. And I found myself forgetting about the pressure of him inside me, leaning back and arching into his hand.

He pinched my nipple lightly and I gasped, flexing my hips, wanting to move, but he remained still, stroking my back unhurriedly as he toyed with my breast.

'You…c-can move now,' I stuttered breathlessly. 'Please.'

'Not yet.' His voice was full of lazy heat, as if he could sit there doing this all night. 'Remember who's in charge.'

'But I—'

'I know. I want to get you off again first.'

'You already did before.'

'So?' He pinched my nipple again, harder, making me groan. 'One orgasm doesn't make an orgy. A woman gets to come as many times as she likes; that's your super-power. And it's a fucking crime to waste it.'

I stared up at him, exquisitely conscious of him stretched long and thick inside me. Of his body like a furnace against me, smooth skin, hard muscle and iron strength. His gaze searched mine, looking at me as though I was a new language he wanted to learn or a puzzle he wanted to solve.

I liked that, even though I knew I shouldn't.

Still staring at me, he dropped his hand from my breast down to where we were joined, stroking my clit lightly with one finger. I shook as the pleasure of it licked up my spine, and the hand he had in the small of my back firmed, keeping me there. Then he took one of my hands from his chest and drew it down between us. 'Put my fingers on your clit. Show me how you like it.'

I was shaking now, unable to think. All I wanted was more of what he'd already given me, so I took his hand and put those warm fingers on my sex, the pres-sure against my clit. And I showed him, rubbing up and down lightly, tantalisingly, letting the pleasure flood through me.

He didn't take his gaze from mine as I used his fin-gers, watching me with such focus it felt as though I was at the centre of his universe. That nothing was more important for him right now than what I was showing him.

'Fuck, you're hot,' he murmured in that dark, purring voice. 'Keep your eyes on me. I want to watch you come again.'

I could feel his body beneath mine tensing up, but he didn't move, continuing to hold himself back. And I wanted to push him, drive him as crazy as he was driving me, so I pressed his fingers to my slippery flesh, showing him how I liked it, hard then soft, light then firm, drawing it out until I was gasping and trembling.

'Come all over my fingers, Sugar,' he whispered. 'Do it.'

And I did, my control slipping away, the pleasure washing over me, a deep, strong wave that had me moaning, holding his fingers hard against me as the orgasm caught me up and held me fast.

I was still shuddering through it when he wrapped an arm around my waist and turned us over, so I was lying beneath him and he was still buried deep inside me.

'I'm going to fuck you now.' He leaned over me. 'If it gets too much, tell me to stop.'

'Okay,' I croaked, the breath going out of my lungs as his weight settled on me. But, God, he felt good. He was big and hot inside me, and over me too.

Putting one hand on my hip to keep me in place, he reached up with the other and gripped the ornate wooden headboard. Then he drew his hips back in a long, slow glide before pushing forward, again long and slow, using the headboard as leverage.

I gasped and shuddered at the sensation, the aftershocks I was already feeling intensifying, spilling over into yet more, almost unbearable, pleasure.

He thrust again, looking down at me as he moved, his biceps flexing as he gripped the headboard. Going deeper, harder.

'Yes,' I whispered raggedly. 'Yes… *God*…'

His eyes were pure silver and he wasn't smiling now, his jaw tight, the expression on his face burning.

I stared back, unable to look away as the pleasure rolled over me, irresistible, unstoppable. The pressure in combination with the intense way he was looking at me was agonising, yet I didn't want him to stop.

I never wanted him to stop.

I put my hands on his lean hips, his skin hot under my palms, and arched my spine, moving with him, watching the pleasure burn in his eyes.

'Look at you,' he purred like a big, lazy cat. 'Look at you, all beautiful and perfect.' He drove inside me harder, deeper, searching my face, looking at me as if I was a fabulous new piece of jewellery he wanted to acquire. 'Who *are* you? Give me your name.'

I groaned, arching beneath him as another climax threatened. Another one; God! What was this man doing to me?

He adjusted his angle slightly, as if he knew exactly what was going through my head, and suddenly I was shaking and gasping as the pleasure exploded through my body without warning.

He let go of the headboard and gathered me up in his arms, holding me as I shuddered, my face turned into his neck. 'Thea,' I said hoarsely against his skin, giving him a gift for all the pleasure he'd given me. 'My name is Thea.'

His arms around me tightened and he thrust once more, hard and deep, and groaned into my hair, his big body shuddering as the orgasm came for him too. 'Hi, Thea,' he whispered after a moment, his voice ragged. 'I'm Damian.'

CHAPTER EIGHT

Damian

'ANY SECURITY ISSUES from last night? Clarence mentioned something about a waitress.' Everett sounded impatient. 'Quickly. I gotta flight to catch.'

I was standing on the terrace, scowling at the detritus from last night's party: empty glasses and plates strewn everywhere, a glittery high heel on top of the pool diving board, someone's boxers shoved under one of the outdoor couches and various other clothes lying discarded on the tiles. There seemed to be a spray of glitter with a balloon lying in the middle of it near the pool. Fuck, if any had got in the water, there'd be hell to pay.

'I dealt with it.' I gripped my phone and turned around, staring at the view of Kowloon stretched out before me instead, the scents of rain and pollution, flowers and garbage hanging in the sticky, humid air. 'And if you have a flight to catch, why the hell are you calling me?'

'Because it's important,' Everett growled. 'In fact, you of all people should know how important it is.'

Yeah, I did. Coming from the backgrounds we did—none of us had had easy childhoods—security was always going to be vital and any breach had to be taken seriously. So, why I was getting pissed off with him, I had no idea.

Black and White had its share of enemies—the bigger we got, the more we had—and anything that put either our business or our staff at risk needed to be dealt with and fast. Especially with the launch of the new non-profit coming up.

We all wanted this to be a success and even minor issues, such as a thief who'd managed to get herself where she didn't belong, needed to be contained.

Thea.

She'd given her name to me so unexpectedly, like a gift, and that was how I was treating it. Because a woman like her, all guarded and watchful, wouldn't simply give a piece of herself up to just anyone. Yet she'd given it to me. I didn't know whether that meant anything or not—I certainly didn't want it to mean anything—but, whatever, it certainly fucking changed things.

Last night, I'd been intending to tell Everett all about her but now some protective and territorial instinct had me not liking that idea one bit.

She was mine to deal with, and if either of those two bastards found out she'd breached Everett's security, especially considering the launch, they would not be happy. They might want to contact the authorities and that would not be happening.

If anyone wanted to question Thea about how she'd got in and what she was doing, *I* would be the one to ask her, not the cops. And certainly not my fucking friends.

Since when have you got territorial about a woman before?

Pretty much never. I didn't get territorial about people because getting territorial implied that they mattered and I didn't want anyone mattering to me.

I already had my little sister, Morgan, to worry about and I didn't need anyone else. She worked for Black and White, managing our PR, but I'd made sure she based herself in London rather than anywhere near me.

It was just easier that way. For both of us.

And anyway she worked with Ulysses, whom I trusted like I'd trust family, and he was there to look out for her.

Ulysses and Everett might not be my blood, but they were my brothers just the same.

'Yeah, I know how important it is.' I forced down my irritation and tried to keep it casual. 'But, like I said, I dealt with the issue. Would you like me to repeat it again in American so you can understand?'

Everett ignored that. 'You disappeared for a long time last night.'

'Because I was busy fucking an extremely beautiful woman. If you want the details, I'm more than happy to supply them. Hell, I've even got the video if you want to check up on me.' Not that I'd ever send him a video even if I had one—too easy for that shit to fall into the wrong hands.

'Someone mentioned an issue with one of the catering staff,' he went on, as if I hadn't spoken, being the usual Everett bulldozer that he so often was. 'A last minute replacement.'

Christ, the guy could be relentless. He was ex-military, systems-oriented and detail-obsessed, which made his security expertise legendary. It also made him a pain in the arse to deal with. I honestly didn't know how Freya, his best friend other than Ulysses and me, managed to deal with him without wanting to punch him in the face.

Maybe she did want to punch him in the face. I certainly wanted to on a regular basis. But it wouldn't do to get irritated with him. He'd just want to know what the problem was and that might lead to other questions I didn't want him to ask.

'And I checked out all the staff,' I said easily. 'You know how anal I am about making sure only people who are actually cleared to be there are there.'

Everett grunted again. 'There were—'

'Yeah, Ev… I don't care what there fucking were.' I tried to keep the growl out of my voice. 'Everything was roses as far as I'm concerned. Now, I have a very naked woman in my bed who I'm very keen to get back to, so if you don't have any other bullshit to talk to me about, why don't you go get on that goddamn flight of yours?'

There was a long silence.

'Fine,' Everett said expressionlessly. 'But if I hear anything different I'll be calling you back.'

I opened my mouth to tell him what he could do with

his damned call, but he disconnected before I could get a word out.

Shit, this was a problem. If Everett had had reports of a security breach, he wouldn't stop sniffing round until he'd discovered the truth. Which meant I needed to deal with Thea, and fast, starting with getting some answers out of her.

And then what?

That would all depend on what answers she gave me. Still, I wasn't going to lie to myself and pretend that all I was concerned about was security. No, last night I'd had enough of a taste of her to know that I wanted more. Our chemistry was through the roof and I wasn't letting that go in a hurry.

Jamming my phone in the back pocket of my jeans— the first item of clothing that had come to hand when I'd got up to answer Ev's call—I turned around and stalked back into the apartment, heading for my bedroom.

Getting answers out of Thea might be a problem, given she hadn't been keen on giving them to me the night before; then again, one thing I'd discovered about her was that she was passionate. She'd been into everything I'd done to her and everything I'd showed her how to do to me. Fuck, she'd been incredible. The way she'd looked at me, the way she'd touched me, as if all of this had been new and exciting to her…

She'd been a virgin, if I wasn't much mistaken.

I was normally pretty good at judging when a woman was experienced or not, but I had been too busy getting hot for her last night to notice. In fact, it had only been after she'd snuggled down into my arms after our fourth round and fallen fast asleep that I'd had a chance to think about it and her behaviour. To go over in my head the moment I'd first pushed inside her and to see that what had flickered through her eyes had been uncertainty. And a bit of fear.

My memory was good for some things; I'd give it that.

But that was another thing I'd have to ask her about, because she really should have told me. Especially when I'd given her every opportunity.

Feeling not a little pissed about it, I got to the bedroom and pushed the door open, expecting to see her where I'd left her, all curled up in my bed and wrapped in the white high-thread-count cotton sheets I preferred.

Except the bed was empty.

Okay. Where the hell had she gone?

Acting on a hunch, I turned and went back down the hall, heading to my office. And sure enough, when I pushed open the unlocked door, there she was, standing in front of a painting I had on the wall, her hand already on the frame.

Looking for my safe and the Red Queen, clearly.

She must have heard the door open because she whirled around as soon I came in, her dark eyes clashing with mine. She wore nothing but the shirt I'd had on the night before, the black cotton making her eyes look even darker and highlighting the flawless, deep ivory of her skin.

Christ, the more time I spent with her, the more beautiful she became. Especially wearing my shirt and nothing else.

A possessive streak I didn't realise I had woke up and suddenly I wanted the shirt gone and her naked so I could see again all those luscious curves she'd showed me the night before. Rounded hips and thighs, full tits, small waist. Classic hourglass; fucking perfection.

I could drape her in the black-pearl jewellery I'd bought from a destitute British aristocrat, ropes of baroque pearls, rich and glossy and unique, lying against her glowing skin.

Yeah, black pearls. She'd look gorgeous in black pearls.

Leaning against the doorframe, I folded my arms. 'Am I interrupting anything?'

Her expression was instantly guarded, but her chin lifted in unconscious challenge. She dropped her hand from the frame. 'No. I was just having a look around.'

Little liar.

'Sure you were.' I grinned. 'If you want the safe, it's behind that picture and, yes, the necklace is inside.'

'I wasn't—'

'Yeah, we went through that last night.' Pushing myself away from the doorframe, I strolled calmly over to where she stood and pulled the picture away from the wall to reveal the safe. The lock was biometric so I put my thumb on the pad and the lock flashed green as it disengaged. I pulled open the door and reached inside for the sleek black jewellery case that held the necklace.

She watched me, her expression opaque, but I could tell by the way she blinked that she was surprised. That was a mannerism I remembered from last night, just as I remembered everything about last night—from the way she'd moaned when I'd licked her, to the sob of release when I'd made her come all over my cock.

The way I was going to make her come again. Maybe soon. And all I could think about was how that guarded gaze of hers had splintered under my touch like a cheap paste jewel, revealing heat and passion hot as lava. She was like my safe. Only the right touch could open her up.

I held out the box to her. 'This what you're looking for?'

She blinked again, rapidly, glancing at the box then back at me, but made no move to take it. So I flicked it open so she could see the intricate loops and coils of diamonds that formed the neck piece and the rubies that fell from it like red rain on silver chains. The Red Queen, finally.

Her eyes widened as she glanced at it, then back at me.

'Beautiful, isn't it?' I took the necklace out, discarding the box onto the floor, and held it up, the weight heavy in my hands. 'It was made for a queen, which is what gave it its name.' The light caught the rubies, sending them burning, glittering in the fascinating way jewels did, but she didn't stare at it.

She looked at me instead. Which told me something else about her: it wasn't jewels per se that she was interested in, not the way some people were. I'd seen enough of that to recognise the glint some people got in their eyes when confronted with a piece they wanted. Greedy. Possessive.

No, my little thief wasn't looking at the jewel like that at all.

That greedy, possessive glint in her eyes right now was all for me.

Something hot clenched tight in my chest.

I always gave a lover diamonds as a goodbye gift and I'd never had any complaints. In fact, once the diamonds were in their hands, they never looked at me again, which I was completely happy with. I didn't want anyone getting close. I was in it for a good time, not a long time.

But apparently not Thea. I had the Red Queen glittering in my hand, all brilliant rubies and diamonds, and she was ignoring it as if it didn't even exist.

She was greedy for me, not the necklace.

Fuck, it turned me on. And it shouldn't, because I didn't actually want a woman to be greedy for me. But that didn't change the fact that the way she looked at me just about stole my fucking breath.

And it told me something else too: she wasn't here to get the necklace for herself.

'You're supposed to be looking at the necklace, Sugar,' I said gently. 'Not at me.'

Colour rose in her cheeks. 'But I—'

'The Red Queen isn't for you, is it? It's for someone else.' I took a step towards her, then another, stalking slowly closer. 'Is that what you do? Steal to order?'

She didn't move, didn't back away, just watched me advance, her chin lifted. And she didn't look at the necklace in my hands either; her gaze stayed glued to mine. 'You seem to know everything already. Do I even need to answer?'

'I do know everything, it's true.' I circled round behind her. 'I even know that last night you were a virgin and you didn't tell me.'

She was silent.

'In fact, there are a lot of things you haven't told me, Thea.' I could hear her breathing getting faster and, when I leaned forward to brush my mouth over the delicate shell of her ear, the sweet, musky scent of her arousal caught me, making my already hard cock twitch in response. 'Any particular reason for that?'

'No,' she whispered.

'Well, you can't just break into my apartment to steal something of mine then seduce me into bed without telling me vital things about yourself that I might have liked to know in order to enhance your experience.' I lifted the Red Queen over her head and draped it around her slender neck. 'Not if you don't want consequences.'

She went still as the jewels settled on her skin. 'What…are you doing?'

I fastened the catch, letting my fingers graze against her nape. 'You wanted the Red Queen. So here it is.'

'But I—'

'But you what?' I brushed my mouth over the sensitive spot just beneath her ear, inhaling her scent. 'This is what you're here for, isn't it?'

She shivered. 'You said something about consequences.'

'So I did.' I reached around to the buttons on the
front of her shirt and began to undo them as I kissed
my way down the side of her neck, because there was
only one way this particular scene was going to play
out. 'You answer every single one of my questions, or…'

'Or…?' Her breath hitched as I pulled apart the cotton.

'Or you don't get to come.'

CHAPTER NINE

Thea

THE JEWELS AROUND my neck were heavy and cold compared with the man standing at my back. He felt like the sun blazing away behind me, bathing me in heat.

His hands deftly got rid of the shirt I'd pulled on when I'd woken up that morning, slipping it from my shoulders so it fell onto the floor, leaving me standing there naked but for the necklace.

I shivered, and not because I was cold. I could never be cold with Damian Blackwood around.

His hands settled on my hips, his touch blazing through me like sunlight, his warm mouth nuzzling against my neck.

I should never have risked coming into his office like this, but when I'd woken up that morning and found him gone, it had seemed like the perfect opportunity. I'd been planning to stay awake, to wait until he'd fallen asleep and then go back for the necklace, but some time after that fourth orgasm he'd put his arms around me, bringing me up against his hot, hard body, and I'd just...

fallen asleep. I'd slept like the dead, something I never did, which wasn't the best when I was here for a reason.

It was only that he'd been so…dirty, pushing my boundaries, making me want things I'd never thought I would. Try things I'd never thought I'd try. And, more than that, he'd made me feel so good, like a goddess. Beautiful. *Special*.

I shuddered against him as his mouth found the sensitive place where my shoulder met my neck, trying to get my stupid brain into gear. Of course he'd figured out I was a virgin—I'd been stupid to forget about that—but it was difficult to think when he kissed me.

It had been difficult to think from the moment I'd laid eyes on him, lounging in the doorway watching me.

He hadn't been in a suit this morning, but a grey T-shirt and a pair of faded jeans that had holes in the knees. Simple clothes that fitted him like a second skin, highlighting a muscular chest and shoulders, lean hips and powerful thighs. His black hair had been spiked up, the ring in his eyebrow shining, his silver eyes burning with an intensity that stole my breath.

He'd been so damned hot all I could do was stand there and stare at him as he'd sauntered over to where I'd stood, pulling aside the painting and accessing his safe. He'd watched me all the while, electricity crackling in the space between us, twice as intense as it had been last night.

And then he'd brought out the Red Queen and held it up.

But it hadn't been the necklace that had held my

attention. It had been him and his gaze and the heat blazing in it.

I'd expected him to act there and then, put me in a room and lock the door, keep me safely contained until the police arrived. Because of course he would have called the police. I was a thief come to steal his precious jewels, after all.

Except he hadn't done any of those things.

He'd taken the necklace out and draped it around my neck, stripped me bare and pulled me against him, kissing me as if he wanted more.

And of course asking me questions. I hadn't forgotten that.

If you don't answer my questions, you don't get to come.

His large, warm palms burned against my skin, his mouth an ember against my shoulder. I closed my eyes, unable to help leaning back into him. He was so much bigger than I was, so much stronger, and I could feel that strength in the hard muscle I was leaning against.

He could hurt me if he wanted and there would be nothing I could do about it. I'd learned some rudimentary self-defence moves from Mr Chen but nothing that would help me against this man.

It should have scared me, but it didn't. He'd been nothing but gentle with me the night before, and he was nothing but gentle now, and I didn't feel afraid.

It was almost as if he was a wall at my back, standing between me and the rest of the world, and instead of feeling afraid I felt almost…protected, somehow.

A dangerous thing to feel. I could never let my guard down, not now Mr Chen was gone. It was his legacy I was protecting and that was something I took very seriously. I couldn't let anyone threaten it, most especially not the powerful, sexy man standing behind me.

'The rubies are pretty on you,' he murmured, one hand sliding up from my bare hip to touch the jewels hanging between my breasts. 'But I'd love to see you in pearls.'

My mouth had gone dry. I knew I should be doing something to save myself, but all I could think of was seducing him the way I had last night. And I couldn't tell if that was something I wanted for myself or so I could get out of the situation.

'P-pearls?' I stuttered, trying to grab my flailing thoughts.

'Yeah, you'd look perfect in them. I love sparkle; don't get me wrong. Sometimes I'm in the mood for showy and that means a diamond.' His finger slid off the ruby and onto my skin, tracing the underside of my left breast, making another delicious shiver move over my skin. 'But other times I'm in the mood for subtle and mysterious, in which case it's pearls.'

I swallowed, trying to breathe properly. 'Are you saying I'm subtle and mysterious?'

'You're definitely mysterious.' His mouth brushed behind my ear once more, heat washing over me. 'Thea.' It sounded as if he was tasting my name, turning it into something sensual rather than just the first name the nun who'd found me on her doorstep had given me.

My head fell back against his shoulder, my eyelids feeling heavy. They wanted to close, and my body wanted to lean into his heat and strength, let him touch me any way he wanted. Take as much pleasure from him before the hard slap of reality came again—because it did; it always did.

You'll go back to being a ghost in the walls again.

'What are you doing here?' Damian's fingers spread out, cupping my breast gently in his palm. His thumb teased my already hard nipple, making me gasp. 'Who are you?'

Why not tell him?

So many reasons, not the least being Mr Chen's business. He'd treated me like a daughter and that required that I protect what he'd built. Even though he'd decided against formally adopting me in the end.

'You're not my blood, Thea,' he'd told me. 'And, anyway, you're too unstable. Too wild.'

It had been hard to hear that, to know that no matter how hard I'd tried to force my feelings down to take on the lessons of calm and silence that he'd taught me, I still hadn't been good enough for him. But that was okay.

He'd left me his business and that was a pretty major gesture of trust all on its own. And if looking after that legacy meant I remained alone, well, so be it.

I'd always thought I was okay with it, but now, with Damian's arms around me, I wasn't so sure. Would it be so bad to share a few things about myself with another person? I'd already given him my name, after all.

His thumb brushed steadily back and forth over my aching nipple and I shut my eyes. 'I'm Thea Smith.' My surname another name the English nuns had given me. 'And, yes, I'm here to steal the Red Queen. But it's not for me. It's for someone else.'

'Who?'

That teasing thumb brushed over me again, pleasure an electric shock through my system. I sighed and leaned back into him. 'I don't know. Everything is done through a middle man. I never know who I'm reacquiring for.'

'Reacquiring?'

Another electric touch, firmer. A soft pinch that made my breath catch. 'That's what I do. I reacquire items that have been stolen.'

Are you sure telling him this is a good idea? You don't know what he might do with the information.

No, of course it wasn't a good idea. But I was sick of being in the shadows, sick of not being seen. Sick of not being known.

Sick of not existing.

The sun was against my closed lids and Damian's fingers on my breast were light, teasing. 'Reacquisition,' he echoed. 'Interesting thing to call it. But there's no record of the Red Queen being stolen.'

'It must have been at some stage in its history otherwise I wouldn't have been asked to reacquire it.'

'Hmm.' His hand spread out, cupping me, while his other hand slid down over my stomach, his fingers tangling in the curls between my thighs. 'I guess I need to look into that.' He pulled on the curls very gently, then his finger moved, finding my clit and grazing it lightly. I stiffened, pleasure lancing through me sharp and bright. 'You need to tell me more about this reacquisition business.'

'Do I…have to do it now?' My hips lifted against his touch, restlessness and need filling me.

His laugh vibrated against my back, a deep, soft rumble that somehow made everything hotter. 'Getting desperate, hmm?'

I shifted again, pressing back against him, the hard ridge of his cock digging into me. 'Can you stop talking for once?'

Another sexy laugh and then I felt his teeth against the side of my neck, the sensation making me shudder in delight. 'Can you blame me for being interested? I like a mystery.' His finger slid around my clit and then over it, and I sucked in a ragged breath as the fierce pleasure of the sensation gripped me tight. 'And I've never met a mystery like you.'

He might feel differently when he finds out how very un-mysterious you are.

The thought drifted through my head like smoke, but I let it dissipate. Of course he would, but I couldn't think about that now. Not with his hands on me and the pleasure that was gradually building.

'Why didn't you tell me you were a virgin?' The finger between my legs was stroking slowly, sliding over my slippery flesh and finding the entrance to my body, teasing me. 'I would have been more careful with you.'

'Because...' I gasped as he slid his finger inside me, making me arch against his hand.

'Because?'

'I thought...you might stop. And I didn't want you to.' It wasn't the entire truth, but it was all my brain was capable of.

'Bad girl.' The hand on my breast tightened, his fingers pinching my nipple harder, scattering bright sparks of pleasure through me. 'You need to tell me about this stuff. I want it to be good for you, understand?'

But my brain was starting to lose the capacity to listen, let alone understand.

'Damian.' His name escaped on a ragged breath as I shuddered against him.

'What? You want more?' His teeth closed around the cords of my neck, biting down gently, making me gasp. 'You want me to fuck you, is that what you're trying to say?'

'Yes.' The word escaped on a hiss as he bit me again, his finger sliding out then into me in a long, slow glide. I didn't even have to think about it, my body was aching for him. 'Oh, please...'

'But that's not the real question. The real question you should be asking is whether you've answered all the questions to my satisfaction.' He worked me with his finger and then added another, stretching me lightly as he kissed and nipped my neck and shoulder. 'And I'm not sure that you have.'

'Stop.' I groaned as his other hand tortured my aching nipple. 'Talking.'

He laughed again, his hands reducing me to a trembling, gasping mess. 'I said you couldn't come until you answered my questions.'

But I could feel the demand rising in me and I didn't fight it, grinding my butt against his hard groin in response, turning his laugh into a curse then a growl. He propelled me forward to the huge windows that looked out over office towers and apartment blocks, the teeming traffic and crowds far below, and I shook as he gently pressed me face-first against the window, the glass cool against my burning skin.

'But I want to see you,' I protested as I looked out over Kowloon, suddenly feeling exposed. When I'd realised I wanted to be seen, I hadn't meant pressed up against a window naked in full view of all of Hong Kong.

But then he was behind me, a wall of heat as he pressed his body up against the length of mine. 'The window is reflective. No one can see in, I promise.' His hands ran lightly down my sides, making goose bumps rise all over me, and I groaned, shifting against him. 'Restless, Sugar? You're so watchful and still, but you're not really, are you? Not when you want me.'

No, I wasn't still now. I was hot, desperate, needy. All the things that I couldn't be in the kind of business I was in. All the things I wasn't allowed to be.

And right now I didn't care. The only thing that mattered was him and his hands on my body.

'Damian…' I gasped, squirming against the window, the heat of my skin causing condensation to bead against the glass. 'Turn me around. I want to look at you.'

'Demanding, too.' He pressed harder against me. 'Why? Have you forgotten what I look like?' His teeth scraped gently over the sensitive part of my neck where it met my shoulder and I shuddered. 'Do you want me to remind you?'

He was teasing me, the bastard, and part of me liked it. 'Please…' I groaned as he bit me, arching. 'Please, Damian…'

'Fuck,' he muttered as my butt came into contact with his hard cock. 'You do present a powerful argument, I have to admit.'

His hands firmed and I was spun around, the glass against my back and him in front of me. He was over six foot of pure muscle, the silver ring in his eyebrow echoing the gleam of his eyes, which had gone molten with desire.

I reached for him, wanting to see the bright inks on his skin, wanting all the colour and life and heat that he represented. Wanting to touch it, get it on me somehow. Wanting to take it for myself.

And he seemed to understand because his hand dropped to his fly and he was undoing the button and zip of his jeans, getting that magnificent cock of his out. I touched him, traced the ink of his tattoo as he got a condom out and sheathed himself, his skin so hot he burned.

He'd gone quiet, the way he had last night, the lines of his face hard, no amusement there now. Only pure masculine desire.

He reached for me, gripping me as he lifted me

against the window with pathetic ease, and then he was pushing inside me, the stretch of his cock making me shudder and both of us groan.

But he didn't move, not quite yet. Instead, his gaze dropped to the jewels around my neck before rising again to my face, looking deeply into my eyes. And the sense of exposure returned. Only it wasn't the city and the stares of unknown strangers that I was afraid of.

It was him and his silver gaze scanning the contents of my soul.

He wasn't going to forget me the way I'd hoped; I could feel it in my bones. Yet it wasn't that which made me feel afraid.

No, it's the opposite. You're afraid he'll discover that he was wrong; that there's nothing so very remarkable about you after all.

But I shoved the thought away, reaching for him, burying my hands in his black hair and pulling his head down, kissing him hungrily.

And he let me. He knew I was hiding, I was sure of it, but he didn't protest. He only kissed me back, just as hungry and desperate as I was.

Then his hips flexed and he was moving inside me, hard, deep. Driving me back against the glass, every thrust sending brilliant, electric shocks of pleasure through me. I gripped his hair tight, groaning as he kept me pinned against the glass before reaching down and hauling one of my legs around his waist, opening me up so he could slide deeper.

God, it felt so good.

I might not have been anything very special, but right now, in his arms, I felt as though I was. I felt brilliant and beautiful. Sexy. Interesting. All the things I'd never thought about myself, but somehow still secretly wished I was.

He made me feel these things. It was all him.

That should have been a warning then and there and I should have stopped it. But I didn't. I wanted to take what he was giving me, so I did.

And he gave me more, his mouth finding my nipple, sucking and biting it gently, teasing it with his tongue, making me pant and moan as he thrust steadily into me. Making me glitter and sparkle with pleasure, blazing as bright as the jewels around my neck.

Until I shattered, turning my face against his warm neck and sobbing.

CHAPTER TEN

Damian

THEA SAT AT the breakfast bar in the kitchen of my apartment, dressed once more in my black shirt, the Red Queen glittering around her neck.

It was possibly a mistake to let her keep wearing the necklace, but I liked the red glitter of the rubies on her skin. She could of course disappear on me, taking the necklace with her, but I was taking the chance that she wouldn't.

Not after the way she'd come apart against the glass in my office so spectacularly. And probably not after she'd answered all my questions with what I thought was the truth.

The real issue right now though was that the answers should have satisfied my curiosity. Should certainly have helped me make a decision about where to go from here. But they hadn't. If anything, they'd only made me more curious, which I really didn't want to be. Not to mention more possessive, which was another thing I didn't want to be.

It was more comfortable not to be interested, and way more comfortable not to give a shit, and yet here I was, standing in my kitchen with her dressed in my shirt, wearing my jewels, and all ready to eat the breakfast my housekeeper had prepared. Again, potentially concerning.

Or at least it would have been if it was possible for a pretty little thief to be a threat to my emotional wellbeing. And, as it wasn't possible, I shouldn't be concerned.

So I wasn't. But curious? Oh, yeah, still fucking curious.

How had she got into the 'reacquisition business' or whatever the hell she'd called it? And why? It sounded shady as shit to me, yet I didn't sense anything shady about her.

No, the only thing I'd got from her was hunger. For me.

When I'd turned her around against the glass in my office, she'd looked at me as if she was starving and only I could feed her. And I had the sense that her hunger went beyond physical need. That it was something deeper, though I wasn't sure what.

Dangerous fucking territory, bro.

No, it wasn't, not if I didn't want it to be, and I sure as hell didn't. If she was hungry for something more than sex then she was shit out of luck, because sex was all I had to give anyone. A bit of pleasure, fun and a bit of luxury; that was it.

Anyway, even if I'd had something more to give, I

wouldn't. Not when I'd only just met her and knew exactly zero about her.

The breakfast my housekeeper had left me on the counter consisted of bowls of fruit and yoghurt, bacon and my favourite, scrambled eggs and toast.

I put some food on a plate for Thea, spooning out some scrambled eggs, and she watched me with those beautiful dark eyes as I did so, not saying a word. For some reason, I didn't feel the need to say anything either.

A silence fell and it wasn't uncomfortable. It was… restful, which I hadn't expected. Every day I was surrounded by people and noise, bright colours and sparkle, the frenetic pace that was doing business at Black and White, and normally I preferred it that way.

I'd always liked the sense of moving forward, away from the memories of my happy, pretty mother slowly wasting away from her battle with cancer, taking all the joy and sparkle from my life with her.

So many clear, vivid memories. Memories that would never fade.

Of her laughter disappearing. Her smiles vanishing. Of Morgan, who'd been such a happy little thing, getting more and more anxious. More and more frightened. And Mum telling me it was up to me now to look after her, to be the light in her life. Up to me to make things less terrible, less awful.

Because I was the serious one. The dependable one.

So I'd helped her; I'd saved her from pain. And I'd done my best to look after Morgan. Tried not to be so serious, to make her laugh, to make her believe that there were good things left in the world.

Never again, though. I was *never* going to be responsible for another person's happiness, another person's entire life, ever again.

So I avoided silence, because silence only made me think, and I didn't fucking want to think. Parties, music, talking and laughing. And sex. Yeah, bring that shit on.

Yet right now, in my kitchen, there was no noise, only silence and calm, and it seemed to radiate from her. And, weirdly, it didn't make me think about the past. It only made me focus on her instead.

I pushed the plate in her direction. 'Eat, Sugar. You probably need it.'

She stared at me a second then picked up a fork and pulled the plate close, taking a bite of the eggs. Something tightened in my chest—the protectiveness that I tried to keep locked away.

Don't let it get to you, dickhead.

I wouldn't. I might have those feelings, but they didn't have to mean anything if I didn't want them to. And I didn't want them to.

Picking up a bowl of fruit, I leaned against the counter and stuck a fork into a piece of mango.

The silence deepened and I let it rest for a while, trying to ignore my nagging curiosity. But I was too impatient to let it go on for long.

'You said the Red Queen was stolen?' I asked eventually.

'Yes, but, like I told you, I operate through an intermediary and we don't get any of the details or reasons, or even the name of the person who requests it. We just get the request for acquisition.'

So, I wasn't going to be able to follow up on that. How annoying.

I shifted against the counter. 'So, this reacquisition business…how does it actually work?'

Thea chewed slowly on her mouthful then swallowed. 'It was my mentor's business. The police aren't so much concerned with retrieving stolen items as they are with putting those responsible in prison, which means the owners of the items often don't get them back. Also, there are some people who don't want the police involved at all, they simply want their items returned.' She speared more eggs with her fork. 'We don't have anything to do with the client and they don't have anything to do with us. That way, everyone remains safe.'

'Sounds like a useful kind of business. At least until you get caught.'

Thea swallowed her eggs. 'I've never been caught.'

I lifted a brow, surprised. 'Never?'

'No.' Her dark eyes gave absolutely nothing away. 'It wouldn't be good for business if I was.'

'True.' I stared back at her, fascinated. 'You must be very good at it.'

'I am,' she said simply. 'I've been doing it for nearly eight years.'

Holy shit.

This small, curvy little woman, sitting there naked apart from the jewels around her neck and the black

cotton of my shirt, her skin glowing in the light coming through the windows and looking like some kind of
angel, had apparently been slipping in and out of people's houses and vaults, 'reacquiring' various items, and
all without being caught. For eight years.

'Except I caught you,' I couldn't help pointing out,
feeling vaguely triumphant about it, though I wasn't
sure why.

Her mouth firmed. 'I was careless.'

'Or maybe you wanted to be caught.'

'Why would I want that?'

'Because you saw me.' I grinned, flirting with her,
wanting to see her smile. 'I am, after all, pretty fucking amazing.'

Sure enough, her mouth twitched, which I counted
a victory. 'That's not arrogant at all.'

'Kind of comes with the billionaire territory.' I ate
another piece of mango, not missing the way her gaze
dropped to my mouth. The chemistry between us flared,
but as much as I wanted to spread her out over the
breakfast bar and feast on her naked body, I needed
answers more.

'Sugar,' I said, 'you're going to have to stop looking
at me like that. Especially since I think we both need
some recovery time.'

Colour stained her cheekbones, her lashes fluttering
as she looked away. 'Sorry,' she muttered.

'I'm not. But, since I'm guessing you didn't have any
dinner last night, and as we've done a lot of physical
activity since then, you need to eat.'

She didn't protest, dutifully finishing up her eggs then the bacon, then reaching for a bowl of fruit and yoghurt.

Satisfied she'd had something, I went back to my questions. 'So how did you get into this business, then? You mentioned a mentor...'

The corners of her eyes tightened minutely; if I hadn't been watching her, I'd have missed it.

'Why do you want to know?'

I tried to figure out the undercurrents in her voice, because they were there—I could hear them. And that tightness around her eyes...

She didn't like the question. But why not? Was it painful for her?

Why the fuck do you want to know? You've got the answers that matter already. Time to get rid of her before Everett figures out there's been a security breach and goes after her.

That would have been the smart thing to do. Yet I didn't want to do it.

There was something about her that reached out and gripped me by the throat. Something to do with her physical hunger for me, plus the odd sense of vulnerability I got from her. Whatever it was, it made the latent protective instincts, that I thought I'd managed to get rid of the day I'd sent Morgan away, sit up and take notice.

Which was a complication I didn't need.

I shifted against the counter, ignoring the logical part of my brain nagging at me to call Everett.

'Why do I want to know?' I echoed. 'Because I'm interested.'

'Why? So you can shut my business down?'

'Your business? What about this mentor that you mentioned?'

Something flickered through her eyes. 'He's gone,' she said flatly. 'It's my business now and I'm not putting it at risk simply because you're "interested".'

I studied her for a moment. Looked as though I'd hit a nerve. And maybe more than a nerve. That had been pain in her eyes; I was sure of it.

'I'm not going to go to the authorities, Thea,' I said. Hell, I'd already made the decision that I wouldn't even before I'd taken her to bed the night before. 'No matter what you tell me.'

Her gaze narrowed. 'So what are you going to do with me, then?'

That was the sixty-four-million-dollar question, wasn't it? I could let her go, but that wouldn't change the fact that she'd got past my security systems and knew the layout of my place. Plus, I had the suspicion that if I did let her out of my sight I wouldn't see her again.

That's probably a good thing.

But was it? Our chemistry still hummed in the air between us and I wasn't done exploring that. What could keeping her a few days hurt, if she was willing? It would satisfy us both, and with the upcoming launch of the Black and White Foundation, and the fact that I was going to have to go to London and see Morgan in a few days, I was certainly in need of some distraction.

And Thea would make for one hell of a distraction. She was like a mysterious present I wanted to unwrap slowly, uncovering her a bit at a time to tantalise myself. And then, once my curiosity about her was satisfied and our physical hunger for each other dealt with, we could both move on.

Yeah, why not?

I held her gaze. 'I know what I want to do with you and it's got nothing to do with a jail cell.'

She flushed, the colour moving down her neck deepening in the reflection from the rubies at her throat, her skin lustrous as a pearl in the morning sun, her eyes glowing with desire as they looked into mine.

'Damian...' She stopped.

Was that reluctance I could see in her face? Was she going to tell me no?

It was surprising how badly I didn't want her to.

I put my bowl down on the counter and moved around the breakfast bar, coming to stand behind her. Then I reached to spin the stool she was sitting on so she faced me, and put my hands on the counter on either side of her, leaning in close.

She didn't move, only stared at me, watchful and wary.

'I should have been clear,' I said. 'I'll let you go back to your business; that's safe with me, I promise. But, before I do, I want to keep you for a little while. A few days maybe.'

Her expression didn't change, but I could see the pulse at her throat beating fast. 'Are you saying that I have to sleep with you again before you—?'

'No,' I interrupted, because the day I had to blackmail a woman into bed would be the day hell froze over. 'I'm not saying that. You can go now if you want—minus the necklace, of course, but you can. Shit, I'll even call a car to take you home if that's your preference. But what I am saying is that I'd like it if you wanted to stay here with me for a few days before you go.'

It probably wasn't a good idea, not if Everett was still sniffing around about the security breach, but I could handle him if push came to shove. I'd make sure Thea stayed hidden and safe and her little 'reacquisition' business would too. Because neither she nor her business was a threat, and I didn't waste my time threatening people who weren't dangerous to start with.

She might end up being dangerous.

To my fucking cock, maybe. But not to anything else. I'd make sure of it.

She watched me silently and I thought I saw surprise flicker in her eyes. Then her gaze dropped to my mouth and the darkness lit with something else: hunger.

Satisfaction burned low in my gut. She wanted to stay; oh, yes, she really did.

'I'm not sure that's a good idea,' she said quietly.

I didn't move and I didn't look away. 'Why not? It's just sex and fun, all good stuff.'

'Because…' Her gaze lifted to mine before dropping to my mouth again, as if she couldn't stop herself from looking.

'Because?' I wanted to kiss her, close the distance between us, but I didn't. She had to make the choice for herself, no matter how much I wanted to make it for her. And I did want to make it for her. I didn't want her to say no.

'I have a business to run. Jobs I need to take.'

Did she want me to convince her? If she did, she was shit out of luck. This was her decision and I wasn't going to make it for her.

I could be quiet when I wanted to be and I was quiet now.

A crease deepened between her straight, dark brows. 'You're not even going to try to convince me?'

'You either do or you don't, Sugar. I wouldn't have asked you to stay if I didn't want you to, but whether you do or not is up to you.'

'Is this how you do all your business deals? Makes me wonder how you're so successful if you're not even going to try a little persuasion.'

'This isn't a business deal. And if you need persuading then perhaps you'd better leave right now.'

A spark glittered in her eyes and her throat moved as she swallowed. 'Tell me you want me.'

Ah, okay. If it was reassurance she needed, then I could do that.

'You really need me to say it?' I asked. 'After last night and this morning?'

Her gaze was steady and unapologetic. 'Yes.'

So I filed that little discovery away for future reference, liking that finally she was being straight with me. And this was something I could give her that didn't cost me anything, and was true into the bargain.

You know that once you start giving shit to people, they only want more.

I shoved that unhelpful thought away, staring into Thea's dark eyes instead and letting her see the truth. Without the smile this time. 'I want you, Thea. In fact, I don't think I've wanted anyone as much as I want you right now.'

She stared at me for a beat. Then her hands came out, her fingers burying themselves in my hair, and she pulled my mouth down on hers.

Giving me her answer.

CHAPTER ELEVEN

Thea

HOURS LATER, FRESHLY showered and changed into a pair of soft cotton yoga pants and a T-shirt that Damian had produced from somewhere, I lay on the couch on his terrace, curled up on the cushions, the thick heat of the Hong Kong early evening lying like a warm blanket around me. The usual tropical rain that passed over the city every afternoon had gone, leaving the night clear and full of the scents of flowers, mixed in with hints of spices and trash, plus the faint smell of salt from the harbour.

I couldn't believe how relaxed I felt, as if a constant, low-level hum that had been buzzing in the background of my life was now gone.

I wasn't sure quite why that was, whether it had to do with the intense physical workout Damian had given me or whether it was simply having another person around. It seemed as though I hadn't realised until now how tough the last few months without Mr Chen had been, or how lonely. I'd had a bird I'd bought at the Bird Market once, thinking that it would be good to have something other than my mentor to keep me company. But I'd had to get rid of it in the end. It had sung too loudly and Mr Chen had thought it would draw attention.

I'd never got another, and I'd convinced myself that I didn't need anything but the job; that knowing it was Mr Chen's legacy I was carrying on would be enough to sustain me.

But it wasn't. And it seemed as though only now I was here, lying on Damian's couch with his touch still echoing through my body, could I admit it at last.

I had a lonely life and perhaps I wasn't as suited to it as I'd always thought. Mr Chen hadn't needed anyone else and, after he'd refused my adoption request, I'd convinced myself that I didn't need anyone else either.

Except, maybe I did. Perhaps not Damian in particular, but just…someone.

Which makes staying here risky.

It did and doing so was probably a mistake. Wanting things never worked out well for me and there was no reason to think that this would turn out any differently. But… Damian had asked me to stay and he'd told me he wanted me. I couldn't resist that or the way I felt in his arms.

Temptation was a bad thing and it turned out I wasn't immune. But for the first time in years I was going to allow myself to want something and let myself have it. Because, after all, it was only a couple of days of pleasure. A couple of days when I could feel less like a ghost and more like an actual woman. When I didn't have to remain unseen and unnoticed, or be someone else. Where I could bask in the sun and not skulk in the shadows.

That wasn't too much to ask, was it?

And what will happen when you have to leave?

Stupid question. Nothing would happen. I'd vanish like I always did and that would be the end of it. This was like…a holiday fling. Nothing more.

Damian's deep, rich voice rolled over me and, God, the sound of it… It made me want to purr like a cat. I watched him from the couch as he paced around the terrace, talking on his phone. He'd been like that for the past half an hour, taking call after call, always in constant motion, making fluid, emphatic gestures with one hand as he talked. Sometimes his voice was hard and businesslike and sometimes it was warm and cajoling. Sometimes he laughed and, every time he did, I closed my eyes and basked in the sound.

I hadn't had much laughter in my life, not when Mr Chen hadn't had a sense of humour and disapproved of levity. Listening to Damian laugh was like a drug. It was deep and sexy and made me shiver every time I heard it.

You could get used to listening to that every day.

I opened my eyes again, watching Damian's face as he smiled at something someone had said on the phone, and my chest ached. That smile was dazzling, making him even more gorgeous than he was already, intensifying his charisma to megawatt proportions.

Okay, so he had a sexy laugh and his smile made me want something I hadn't even realised I wanted. But that wasn't *his* laugh or *his* smile. It could be anyone's. It was nothing to do with him specifically. Not when I only knew him as a public figure rather than a person.

Damian turned around, his tarnished-silver eyes met mine and that smile was suddenly focused in my direction, hot and wicked, and I had to catch my breath as my sex throbbed.

We'd already spent hours in bed. Surely I couldn't want more, could I?

Oh, yes. I could.

Damian finished up his call then shoved his phone into his jeans and came over to where I lay. He was back in that soft grey T-shirt, which was a pity, as I preferred him naked with all that glorious muscle and bright ink on full display.

'Sorry. Had to take some work calls.' He stopped in front of the couch, eyes glittering as he surveyed me. 'Hungry for something in particular, Sugar?'

'Yes.' I didn't even bother to pretend. 'You. Naked.'

His smile deepened. 'Are you trying to get me into bed by any chance?'

'Of course.' I gave a lazy, sensual stretch, pleased by how his gaze followed my movement hungrily. 'Is it working?'

His hand dropped to the front of his jeans, the outline of his hardening cock already obvious. 'What do you think?'

I looked up from underneath my lashes, pleased with myself and enjoying flirting with him. 'So what are you waiting for?'

He laughed, which made me shiver with delight. 'You've got no idea how much I love an insatiable woman. But dinner won't just happen by itself, even for super-powerful billionaires. And you need to eat.'

I pouted a little. 'You're always trying to feed me.'

'Hey, it's all pure self-interest. I want to make sure you've got enough energy for all the things I've got planned for you.'

Well, he wasn't wrong. We'd missed lunch because we'd been too busy screwing each other senseless and I was hungry. Plus, I kind of liked being waited on. Made a nice change from having to do everything myself.

'Fine.' I gave him a mock-stern look. 'But you owe me, okay?'

He grinned and sketched a cross on his chest. 'Cross my heart and hope to die. Now, you need a drink?'

Five minutes later, I was sitting in his lap, a gin and tonic in my hand while he nursed a beer. And it felt natural to be there, leaning back against his hard chest, as if we'd been lovers for years instead of merely a night and a day.

'So,' he said after a moment's comfortable silence. 'Are you going to tell me how you got into the "reacquisition" business or do I have to guess?'

Oh. That.

I'd been hoping that if I didn't answer and distracted him with sex he might forget about his questions. Sadly, that didn't appear to be the case.

I still felt reluctant to talk about it, to give him any more details of my life, my guardedness by now instinctual. Then again, he'd promised he'd let me go after a couple of days, and that my livelihood wouldn't be at risk. I probably shouldn't have believed him, not when I didn't know him, but I did anyway.

Or maybe it was more that I simply wanted to talk to someone.

He'll remember you. He can't meet that many women who do what you do.

Well, maybe I didn't care that he wouldn't forget me. Maybe I didn't want him to.

'Why do you want to know?' I took a sip of my G&T, relaxing against his heat. 'It's not very interesting.'

'Says the jewel thief who somehow got past my security, sneaked into my party and unlocked my securely locked office door,' Damian purred. 'Yeah, that's definitely boring shit right there.'

I didn't consider what I did exciting, but the way he said it made it sound as if it was.

My mouth twitched as a smile threatened. 'I'm not technically a jewel thief. And most of that "boring shit" *is* actually quite boring.'

His fingers tangled in my hair, giving it a gentle tug. 'Boring for you, maybe. But not for me. Come on, don't leave me in suspense.'

'You're really interested?'

'Is the Pope Catholic?'

I smiled up at him this time, and he grinned along with me. 'That's right,' he said. 'Give your uncle Damian a smile.'

I laughed. 'Now you sound like a pervert.'

'Never pretended to be anything different.' He gave my hair another gentle tug. 'Gimme the news, Sugar, come on.'

'What's to tell? Mr Chen—that's my mentor—picked me up off the streets when I was seventeen.'

'What do you mean, picked you up off the streets?'

'Well, you know the stories of kids left on the steps of the church for the nuns to find? I was one of those kids. I was left in a cardboard box on the steps of the local Catholic church when I was a baby.'

He frowned. 'You're shitting me. People actually do that?'

It was years ago and I didn't blame my parents. They'd obviously had some crap choices to make and I was just glad they'd given me to people who'd cared what happened to me.

'Sure,' I said easily. 'It happened to me.'

'Jesus,' he muttered, his expression darkening further. 'That's fucking appalling.'

His response scraped up against something unexpectedly painful. 'It might be, but maybe my parents were desperate.'

'Plenty of other options.' There was a thread of tension in his voice that hadn't been there before and suddenly I wished I hadn't given him the truth. 'You don't have to leave a kid on the fucking steps of a building, for Christ's sake.'

The painful thing dug deeper, and I shifted, leaning forward. 'You don't want to hear the rest.'

'Yes.' The hand in my hair tightened, pulling me

back against him. 'I do.' His breath was warm on the side of my neck as he pressed a kiss there. 'I'm not angry at you, Thea. And, sure, your parents might have been desperate, but that's still no excuse. Like I said, there are other options.'

The heat of his body should have been too much, given the hot night, but it wasn't. And I found myself leaning back against him, arching my neck for more kisses, the feel of his mouth soothing that painful thing inside me. 'Maybe,' I murmured, still not sure why I was defending my birth parents, not when I didn't know anything about them. 'But at least they left me somewhere that could take care of me.'

Damian only made a noncommittal noise, giving me another kiss before settling me back against his shoulder. 'Go on. Let me hear the rest.'

'Okay.' I sighed and tried to relax, taking another sip of my drink. 'Anyway, I ended up being fostered out to different families, and when I was sixteen I got sick of being sent from pillar to post and ran away. No one bothered looking for me and I ended up living on the streets for a year or so.' Those had been hard times and I didn't like to think about them too much. 'Mr Chen caught me trying to steal some money from him and he liked my guts. Thought I had talent. He didn't have any kids and wanted someone to pass his business on to so he took me in and taught me all he knew.' I took yet another sip of the cool liquid, my throat feeling dry. 'He was like a father in many ways.'

Except he never took that final step. He never adopted you.

No, but he'd been clear about his reasons. Yes, I'd been hurt and upset when he'd refused—I'd been just shy of eighteen and desperate to feel connected to someone—but I'd understood. He'd always wanted his own children and I would never be that for him. I was too different. I wanted things that he didn't and, even though I tried to pretend, I could never quite manage to replicate his brand of cold dignity.

Nothing at all to do with the fact that it felt like you weren't good enough for him and never would be.

Damian's fingers had strayed to the back of my neck and began to massage some of the little knots I hadn't realised had gathered in my muscles.

It felt so good that I nearly groaned, leaning into his hand.

'You lost him, you said?' he asked, a gruff edge to his rich voice.

I shut my eyes. 'He died six months ago. His business is all I have left of him.'

'So you're carrying on his legacy?'

That he understood this without me having to say surprised me.

I twisted slightly to look up at him. 'What makes you say that?'

'My mother died when I was sixteen.' His smile had disappeared and, without it blinding me, I saw what I hadn't before: the lines of grief around his mouth and eyes. 'Cancer. Basically everything I have now is her legacy.'

The honesty of the admission caught me off-guard, my throat tightening at the bleak look in his eyes. Clearly time hadn't healed things for him, and I knew that feeling all too well.

Responding instinctively, I reached up and touched his cheekbone. 'Your company, you mean?'

'Yeah. She told me to make something of myself, so I did.' His gaze turned distant. 'She was a burlesque dancer, loved jewels and feathers and all that sparkly shit. And I promised her once that when I was rich I'd buy her the real thing.' Abruptly, he looked down at me. 'So I did.'

All those jewels he collected…they were for his mother?

'She liked rubies,' he went on softly. 'So I bought the Red Queen. Ulysses, Everett and I are going to be launching a new non-profit in a week or so in London, and some of my jewel collection is going to be auctioned off, proceeds to go to the foundation and to a cancer research facility I started up. The Red Queen is the centrepiece.' Something fierce glittered in his eyes and for once it wasn't desire. 'So, yeah, I know a little about wanting to carry on a legacy.'

I pressed my fingertips against his warm cheek, my throat too tight to speak. I hadn't expected him to be so honest with me. Somehow we'd gone from lightly flirting to deeply emotional, and I wasn't sure how to deal with that. Deep emotions weren't things that Mr Chen had liked to talk about.

'I'm sorry,' I said huskily, the words sounding ineffectual even as I said them. 'I didn't know that about the necklace.'

'Why would you?' He put his hand over mine where it rested on his cheek. 'I haven't told anyone else.' His fingers curled around my hand and he brought it down to his mouth, kissing my palm. Then his smile came out again, brilliant and bright, and the grief disappeared as if it had never been. 'Not too bad a legacy for Mum, though. Could have been worse.'

I wanted to smile with him, but I didn't. Because for the first time I realised that his smile was a deflection. A mask. A beautiful, stunning mask, but a mask all the same.

And who was the man behind it? Was this glitzy lifestyle he led really him? And, if so, why? What did he get out of it? Or was there something else behind that too?

'How?' I asked. 'How did you do it?'

'Hard fucking work.' That smile flashed again, hiding something. 'Plus I met a couple of guys online who were in the same dire straits I was in. One of them just happened to be great with computers and had a way with crypto-currency.'

'Ulysses White,' I murmured. 'And Everett Calhoun.'

'That's right. Everett's the security guy. Ulysses is the money man.'

'So what does that make you?' The details on his

role within Black and White were hazy. I'd kind of assumed, given his looks and his ease with people, that it was the PR side of things.

His mouth took on a sly curve. 'I'm the glue that holds it together.'

'But how?' I persisted. 'What is it that you do?'

'I collect jewels and beautiful women. I throw parties and live the lifestyle.' He said the words casually, a throwaway, practised line. 'I make sure everyone's nice to each other.'

'No, you don't,' I said. 'And stop smiling. I can see right through it.'

The smile on his face froze, the tarnished silver of his eyes taking on a sharp edge. 'You're an observant woman. Okay, then, tell me what you see.'

I studied him for a long moment and he didn't look away. 'I see a beautiful man who dazzles people into thinking that's all he is. But there's more to you than that, isn't there? Something you don't want anyone else to know.'

His gaze was absolutely unreadable. Then his mouth twisted and he gave a mirthless laugh, shaking his head. 'Jesus, that's the last time I ask that question, then.'

'Well, you did ask.'

'I know.' His fingers tunnelled into my hair at the back of my head, his fingertips pressing lightly against my skull, as if he couldn't stop touching me. He was an intensely physical man, as I was beginning to understand.

'I'm right, aren't I?' I wasn't sure why I was pushing him, since I hadn't expected deep and meaningful when I'd said yes to staying with him, nor did I particularly want it. But that curious part of me wouldn't let go. 'You're hiding something.'

He tilted his head slightly. 'We're all hiding something.'

It came to me then in a kind of rush that, though we might on the surface be quite different, we were also quite similar. Both of us were guarded, except while I stayed in the shadows, using them to hide me, he hid in plain sight. Using his looks and his charisma to deflect people.

'I really wanted Mr Chen to adopt me,' I said before I had a chance to think better of it, almost throwing the words at him, a gesture of trust. 'But he'd always wanted his own kids. He didn't want an adopted one. Especially not one like me.'

Damian stared at me, his fingers drifting from my hair down to the back of my neck again, massaging gently. 'Why not one like you?'

Such a casual sounding question, yet it was loaded. Full of sharp edges like a handful of broken glass.

Perhaps I shouldn't have told him about my reckless adoption request, not when Mr Chen's refusal didn't exactly reflect well on me. Still, it was too late now.

I swallowed. 'He thought I needed to be calmer, quieter. That I was too needy. Too emotional. I tried to be calm and quiet, all those things, I really tried, but—' I stopped.

Damian was silent, his fingers on my skull moving

in that gentle, massaging motion. Then at last he said, almost reluctantly, 'I have an eidetic memory. It makes me very, very good at remembering things.'

I blinked at the change of subject then found myself holding my breath. Because he'd given me something, hadn't he?

'I...see,' was all I managed.

'No, you don't.' He let out a breath. 'The problem with remembering everything is that you end up forgetting nothing.'

I wasn't sure why but a chill collected in my gut. 'You don't forget anything? Ever?'

There was no smile this time. 'No. Not a single fucking thing.'

CHAPTER TWELVE

Damian

FROM THE EXPRESSION on Thea's face, I knew she didn't understand. Why would she? No one did. Memories ate away at you, sank their teeth into you, and for most people it was time that made them let go. But not for me.

Time did nothing for me. Those memories remained as real and as sharp as the day they'd been laid down.

The sight of my mother's beautiful face gone gaunt, hollowed out by her illness. The sound of her voice, ragged and uneven, asking me to make something of myself. Asking me to look after Morgan and make sure she was happy.

Thea's eyes darkened slowly and the crease between her brows deepened. 'Why don't you forget things?'

I didn't like talking about it. When I was a kid, I'd used my memory to impress other kids, like a dog doing tricks. But then as I'd got older, and realised what a fucking curse it was, I'd kept it quiet. Sure, it had helped me build the empire I had now, but it was a double-edged sword all the same.

Thea's hair was silky against my fingers, the delicate curve of her skull fragile. It was soothing to touch her, though I wasn't sure why. Luckily she didn't seem to mind.

'My memory is eidetic,' I said reluctantly. 'And I have perfect recall. I remember everything.'

I probably shouldn't have told her and I don't know why I did. Our conversation had turned quickly into something I hadn't been expecting and what I should have done was to turn it back to flirty and fun.

But, given what she'd told me about her past and her mentor, about how she'd wanted him to adopt her and how he'd refused, changing the subject had seemed... wrong. And, more importantly, dismissive.

She was so guarded, yet she'd told me things that were intensely private, not to mention painful. And I had no idea why she wanted to trust me with those things, but I couldn't repay a confidence like that by pretending they meant nothing.

I'd had to give her something in return.

'That's amazing.' The crease between her brows deepened as she searched my face. 'It's not amazing?'

'No.' It was only one word, but it was the only one I could say.

She was silent a moment, studying me. 'No,' she echoed. 'I guess it wouldn't be. Especially, I imagine, when you have things you want to forget.'

I didn't say anything because I didn't want to go into it. And she seemed to understand, because she lifted her hand and touched me again, her cool fingertips brushing over my mouth. 'I suppose most people forget the bad stuff over time.' Her fingers trailed down to my jaw. 'You don't?'

'No,' I repeated, the word far too short and far too hard. 'But, hey, that doesn't stop me from trying.' I forced out my usual smile, not wanting to think about why it was suddenly difficult when it had never been difficult before. A smile covered everything, even the cracks in a person's soul.

But Thea ignored it, her expression serious. 'What are you trying to forget?'

'Careful, Sugar.' I kept my tone light, because I didn't want to talk about this any more. 'Not sure you know me well enough to ask that question.'

She looked contrite. 'Sorry. You don't have to tell me if you don't want to.'

'Good. Because that's not why you're here, okay?' I curled my fingers into a fist, her hair silky and soft against my skin as I drew her head back a little, baring her throat. 'You're here so we can both make each other feel good, and talking about the past is not part of that.' I leaned forward and brushed my mouth over her throat, inhaling the familiar scent of my shower gel and the sweet smell of her body underlying it.

She sighed, relaxing against me, the warm weight of her in my lap both arousing and calming at the same time, which I'd had no idea was even possible.

'Okay,' she murmured. 'So, tell me the good things you remember, then.'

That surprised me. I lifted my head and stared down at her. 'Good things?' I repeated blankly.

'Yes. You must have some good memories.'

Did I? Did I have any? For a second I couldn't even think.

I could tell her about the different pieces I'd collected or the women I'd fucked. The fine wines I'd drunk or the parties I'd attended. But all those suddenly felt empty. Meaningless crap I'd cluttered my head with so I didn't have to think about the bad stuff.

But the problem with meaningless crap was that it hid the good stuff too.

'Good memories,' I murmured, looking past her, thinking. 'Yeah, there are a few. Hanging out with my mother in her dressing room, watching her get ready for a show.' I smiled, remembering. 'She loved dancing. Got all excited about it. And she always looked so pretty and glittery, laughing with the other dancers.' I glanced down at Thea. 'I was a serious kid, kind of boring, but she always made me smile. Made things fun. Sometimes she let me choose which costume she wore and all the accessories that went with it.'

A ghost of a smile turned Thea's mouth, faint but definitely there. 'You? Serious?'

'Yeah, I know. Impossible to believe, right? It's true, though.' Before the weight of all those responsibilities crushed me. Before I'd sent Morgan away, getting rid of the last burden. A selfish move; I knew that. But I'd had to protect myself somehow, because no one else was going to do the job.

'So what changed?' Thea asked. 'What made you not so serious?'

The conversation was starting to go in directions I wasn't comfortable with again, so I lifted a shoulder and said carelessly, 'Oh, you know, the usual bullshit. Life.' I grinned. 'But, about those memories, it wasn't about the costumes or even the jewellery. It was about spending time with Mum, I guess. She was a happy person and she liked making people feel good.'

If Thea recognised the subject change for what it was—avoidance—she gave no sign. 'You like making people feel good too,' she pointed out.

She wasn't wrong. I *did* like making people feel good—just as long as I wasn't ultimately responsible for them.

'It's a shit job, but someone has to do it,' I said, turning it into a joke and shrugging.

But Thea didn't smile. 'You're lucky to have had those times with your mother. And to be able to remember that.'

I'd never thought it was lucky. Not when those memories only reminded me of what I'd lost. Then again, Thea had never had the memories of a mother at all, had she?

'Yeah, I suppose I was lucky,' I said slowly, something heavy shifting in my chest. 'Funny how it's always the bad stuff that sticks in your head.'

'It always is.' Another smile flickered over her face, brief and fleeting, but there. 'What about your father? Do you remember him?'

I could hear the hungry note in her voice and I found myself cradling the back of her head in my palm, my thumb stroking up and down the silky skin of her neck, as if my touch could ease that hunger.

Christ, I didn't know why I wanted to do that for her, share these memories with her, not when I preferred all my interactions with women to be on the surface or not at all. But she was getting something out of this, so what the hell?

'I never knew my dad,' I said. 'Mum never told me who he was.'

'But you have a little sister?'

'Yeah. She's technically my half-sister since she's the result of a one-night stand Mum had when I was about five.'

'And does she live here in Hong Kong?'

'No, she's in London.' Another change of subject seemed like a good idea, so I went with it. 'What about you? You have a boyfriend or something anywhere that I should know about? Because if you do you really should have told me way before this.'

Thea looked away, her lashes sweeping down and veiling her gaze. 'No. I don't have a boyfriend.'

'Well, not one you've slept with, I guess.'

'I don't have one at all.' Her voice was steady and calm, and if I hadn't been listening I wouldn't have heard the edge in it. 'I've never had one.'

'Never?' I asked, surprised despite myself.

'Mr Chen was very clear. We couldn't have…attachments. It was too risky for the business.'

Shit, that sounded terrible. Especially for a passionate woman like her.

'Even friends?' Part of me didn't want to ask because I had a feeling I already knew the answer. 'Anyone at all?'

She didn't look at me, her gaze on my chest. 'Not really. I had a pet once. A bird. But he sang too loudly and it drew attention. Mr Chen didn't like attention.'

Christ. My past was pretty crap, but at least I'd had Morgan, Ulysses and Everett. But poor Thea had had no one. No one at all.

No wonder she's hungry. She needs contact.

I kept on stroking her, her skin warm beneath my fingers. 'And since his death?'

Her shoulder lifted. 'I had to protect his legacy and he was very clear how it had to be done. I've never been caught and there's a reason for that.' She paused, then added, 'I never thought I was lonely. Not until…' She stopped again, clearly reluctant.

The heavy thing in my chest shifted, and even though I knew what was coming and dreaded it I put a finger beneath her chin and tilted her head up so I could see her face anyway. 'Until?'

Her gaze was very dark. 'Until I met you.'

That latent protectiveness inside me tightened and I wanted to shove it away hard, pretend it didn't exist. Because I didn't want vulnerability. I didn't want her to look at me the way she was looking at me right now, as if I could give her what she needed, because I couldn't.

But I couldn't ignore what she'd said either. Or at

least, I could, but that would hurt her and I didn't want to hurt her. So I tried some distraction instead, stroking her with my other hand, my fingers finding the little knots of tension at the nape of her neck and massaging gently. 'I'm sorry, Sugar. That can't have been easy.'

She leaned back, arching her neck, her eyes half-closed once more, clearly enjoying my touch. 'No, it wasn't. What about your sister, then? Tell me about her.'

It was a change of subject I was more than ready to let her have, even though I didn't particularly want to talk about my sister.

'Morgan?' I said. 'She's about five or so years younger than me and probably ten times smarter. She manages Black and White's PR, and somehow also manages to keep Ulysses in line, which requires some massive fucking patience.'

Thea's mouth softened and her lashes lifted slightly, the darkness of her eyes gleaming from underneath them. 'You care about her, don't you?'

The question caught me off-guard and the words slipped before I could stop them. 'She's my sister,' I said simply. 'I'd move heaven and earth for her if I could.'

And yet you haven't been to London in years. You haven't seen her since you sent her away.

Yeah, because it was easier to be here in Hong Kong, away from her. Where she wasn't in my face, asking me questions I didn't want to answer, reminding me of a responsibility I never asked for and didn't want.

'She's lucky to have you for a brother,' Thea said

and there was a huskiness to her tone, the faint edge of longing.

I wanted to tell her that Morgan was far from lucky to have me for a brother. That I'd had to make some shitty choices and those choices had ended up hurting her, no matter how many times I'd smiled at her, hoping to make the bad things go away.

That caring about people was nothing but a god damned burden and I didn't want it any more.

But I didn't tell Thea any of that.

Instead, I smiled the same empty smile that I knew she could see right through, because that was all I knew how to do when it came to handling this type of bullshit.

Her gaze narrowed slightly, but all she said was, 'You must be looking forward to seeing her, then.'

'What? For the non-profit launch?' I tried to stay relaxed, tried not to tense up at the thought of having to face Morgan in the flesh after so long. Going to London hadn't been my choice but there was no way to avoid it. The launch was too important and I had to be there.

I figured I'd just pretend that five years hadn't passed since I'd seen her. That everything was fine and nothing was wrong, nothing at all.

Yeah, that'll work out just fine.

The thought was snide so I ignored it, smiling at Thea yet again, conscious of just how much of a mask it was. 'Of course I am,' I said blithely. 'I can't fucking wait.'

She didn't say anything, but then she didn't have to.

I could see the knowledge in her dark eyes reflected back at me.

She knew I was lying as much as I did.

'You want another drink?' I changed the subject without any grace at all, shifting her so I could move. 'Our dinner will be here soon.'

Thea caught my hand, her fingers threading through mine as I got up, stopping me. Her expression was open and I could see the concern in her eyes. 'I know it's weird to say, since we haven't known each other long. But…you can trust me, okay?'

That hit me like a damned bullet right in the centre of my chest and I didn't know why. Trust her with what? With my past? With my memories?

Either way, I didn't want to ask, because I didn't want to know. I wasn't going to tell her anything more, that was for certain.

I smiled again, even though I knew she wasn't fooled, then raised our joined hands and kissed the back of hers. 'Of course. Wait here; I won't be long.'

I let her go and went inside, my heart beating like a fucking drum, and for a second I just stood in the living area, the tinted windows giving me some protection from Thea's knowing black eyes.

She was still looking towards where I stood, still looking concerned.

You're letting her get to you.

Was I? Shit, if I felt this way after only one conversation, then yes, I definitely was. And it had to stop. Both for her sake and mine.

My phone vibrated suddenly in my pocket and I reached down, pulling it out to check the screen.

Morgan.

She was pretty much the last person I wanted to speak to right now, but I could never deny her anything, so I hit the answer button.

'Hey, kiddo,' I said as if nothing was wrong and never had been. 'What's the news?'

'The news is that you're still expected in London in two days.' That was Morgan. Cool and calm and blunt as a brick to the head. 'I need to know you'll be there.'

I closed my eyes, gritting my teeth. 'Of course I'm going to be there. Are you calling to remind me? Because you know you don't have to do that.'

'No. I'm calling you because I've decided on another change for the launch party.'

I prayed for strength. Having to go to London was already bad enough; what the hell was Morgan going to ask me to do now? 'Anything, kiddo.' I tried to make my voice easy and relaxed. 'Just name it.'

Morgan wasn't fooled. 'Don't bother pretending you're okay with this, Damian,' she said bluntly. 'I know you're not. And, for the record, I'm not either. But you boys wanted to start up this non-profit and so it's going to require some work. Image is everything in the charity business, understand?'

I sighed. 'What do you want, then?'

'You need to bring a date.'

'A date?' I repeated blankly.

'Yes. And not one of your usual models.'

'Hey, I date scientists too; don't be sexist.'

'You know what I mean.' Morgan's voice was cool. 'This isn't one of your parties and it can't be some random pick-up or one-night stand.'

Shit. That was my sister. She always asked the impossible.

'That makes for a really short list,' I said.

'That's not my problem. Find someone. I'm already going with Ulysses and Everett's bringing Freya. You need to—'

'Wait, what?' I interrupted, frowning. 'You're going as Ulysses's date?'

'Bring someone who's going to impress potential sponsors,' Morgan said, completely ignoring me. 'Because I'm sorry to have to say it but you're not enough to impress them on your own, Damian.'

'But I—'

'See you in two days.'

I didn't have time to protest. Morgan disconnected the call.

CHAPTER THIRTEEN

Thea

LIGHT FELL ACROSS my face and I groaned, turning over and burrowing my face into the soft pillow. My body felt heavy, my muscles aching along with other, more sensitive parts of me. It was a delightfully sensual feeling.

Finally I stretched and cracked open an eye, pleased to find that I hadn't materialised in my crappy Mongkok apartment and that apparently I was still in heaven.

The sun was coming through the huge windows of Damian's large, roomy bedroom, lighting up the dark walls and the polished dark wood covering the floor. A thick black rug covered the middle of the room, the huge white bed I was lying in a pale contrast. There was a soft-looking modular sofa near the bed, covered in dark, silvery velvet. The whole effect was one of richness and decadence, and I loved it.

I rolled over, luxuriating in Damian's expensive sheets and soft mattress.

You need to go tonight. Two days, remember?

A tight feeling sat behind my breastbone, as if a part

of me felt sad at the thought. Which was stupid. This was a fling, a fantasy. A wonderful holiday in a luxurious setting with a sexy man.

I was Cinderella and when the clock struck midnight I'd be going back to my place beside the fire. Or, rather, back to my life and the business Mr Chen had left for me. And that wasn't bad. It was a living and it was better than being on the streets, right?

Ignoring the sudden doubt, I shoved back the sheets and slipped out of bed, pausing to grab Damian's grey T-shirt from where it lay on the floor and pull it on over my head.

Then I went in search of him, heading down the hallway to the living area, following the sound of his rich, deep voice.

He was standing near the windows, on the phone yet again. Dressed only in a pair of worn jeans, the morning light fell over the contours of his broad shoulders and muscled chest, making the coloured ink of his tattoos stand out. As I watched, he ran a hand through his black hair, lifting it into soft inky spikes. The sun glinted off the ring in his eyebrow and turned his eyes molten, gleaming silver from underneath his black lashes, and my heart caught a little.

He was a beautiful man and yet there was something else going on underneath all that beauty. Something I'd caught a glimpse of last night as he'd told me about his memory; about his mother and sister too. Something painful. It shouldn't matter to me and I shouldn't want to know it—I'd been with him only two days after all—

but his pain scraped at the edges of my own heart and I couldn't ignore it. I'd always been too soft, as Mr Chen had liked to say.

Damian looked at me and I moved instinctively, going to him and wrapping my arms around his lean waist, pressing myself against his hard, hot body, hungry to be close to him even though I'd been sleeping next to him all night.

He finished up his phone call and put his arms around me, holding me without speaking, as if he enjoyed the contact as much as I did. Then he lifted me up, carrying me over to the breakfast bar and setting me down on top of it. Putting his palms down on either side of my thighs, he leaned in, giving me one of his focused looks. 'I have a question for you, Sugar.'

'Oh?' I touched his mouth, loving the softness of it under my finger, given it was pretty much the only thing about him that was soft, following the line of his bottom lip as it curved into a smile.

'Naughty girl. This is serious.'

'Uh-huh.' I leaned forward and kissed him, indulging myself shamelessly. 'So is kissing you.'

His smile this time was natural and full of heat. 'Seducing me again?'

'Just practising my skills.' I grinned then kissed him once more, nipping at his bottom lip.

He laughed and tangled a hand in my hair, pulling me back a little. 'Hold that thought. At least until after you've answered my question.'

I narrowly missed a pout. 'More questions?'

'Remember the launch of the non-profit I was talking about last night? And how I have to go to London for it? Well, Morgan is managing the PR, and she called me yesterday to tell me that I need to bring a date.'

I blinked. 'A date?'

'Yeah, that was my response.' He twined my hair around his fingers. 'It has to be someone who is going to impress potential sponsors so apparently I'm not allowed to bring my "usual random pick-ups or one-night stands".' There was a wry note in his voice that made me want to smile. 'It seems I'm not impressive enough on my own, which I get. My reputation is not…stellar, let's just say. Or, at least, not from a charity perspective. Too many parties and shit.'

'Do you care about your reputation?'

'Not really. But Morgan does. And so does Ulysses. Which means I have to too.' His eyes glinted. 'Fancy a trip to London, Sugar?'

A pulse of shock went through me. 'You mean you want…me to be your date?'

That sexy smile played around his mouth. 'Yeah, I do.'

'But…' I stopped, a thousand insecurities that I'd been trying not to think of suddenly bubbling to the surface.

He raised a brow. 'But what?'

'But I'm not…' I stopped again, feeling my cheeks heat. *You're not pretty enough, you mean?* 'I mean, I'm kind of your usual random pick-up, aren't I? Or a one-night stand?'

'Technically you're a two-night stand,' he corrected. 'But, seriously, you're the perfect woman to have on my arm for this. Not only are you beautiful, but you're smart. And observant.' He grinned. 'You can take a look at our potential sponsors and tell me which ones to trust.'

Being at an important function. On his arm. There would be lots of media covering it, no doubt, and lots of cameras. Lots of people wanting to know who I was and why I was there. Why I was with him.

I would lose my anonymity completely.

My expression must have given me away, because his black brows twitched in sudden concern. 'Hey, what's up? You don't want to go?'

'There'll be media there,' I said. 'They'll all want to know who I am. My face will be known and...' I took a breath. 'That will put Mr Chen's business at risk.'

Damian frowned. 'Okay, that's a legit concern. But we don't have to give the media your real name. We can make up any story we want for you. And as for your face...' He lifted one of his long-fingered hands, his fingertips brushing my cheek. 'You'll have your fifteen minutes, Sugar. But then everyone will forget because everyone always does. The public's memory has about the span of a goldfish's.'

'But you won't forget.' I wasn't sure what made me say it. Maybe it was simply because I wanted the reassurance. 'Will you?'

'No.' One finger drifted along my jaw. 'Everyone will forget but me.'

It was true what he said about the public's memory. I could go with him, be in the spotlight for a little then disappear. The next scandal would hit and no one would even remember I existed.

No one except him.

You don't care about the party or even the anonymity. You just want more time with him.

It was true, I did. And that was probably a warning for me not to go, because I couldn't let myself get attached to him. Couldn't allow him to become important to me. But… I knew I was going to go all the same. Because I wasn't ready for this to end. I wanted more time with him, more memories of heat, pleasure and laughter to last me for when I had to go back to my real life.

I had a feeling this chance would never come again, so how could I say no?

'In that case…' I tried not to let my voice get too emotional. 'I'd love to come.'

A bright, quicksilver spark ignited in Damian's eyes, making my heartbeat accelerate and my breath catch; he was pleased, I could tell.

'Are you sure, though?' I went on, unable to help myself. 'You haven't got someone else who's more…' I wanted to say beautiful but couldn't bring myself to voice it. 'I don't know, more suitable?'

His fingers moved from my mouth down to my chin, gripping me gently. 'Why wouldn't you be suitable?'

'Well, I'm…just kind of…' I stopped again, feeling stupid.

'Kind of what?'

You're going to have to tell him.

Especially as I'd now made it into a big deal.

'Ordinary,' I said, forcing the word out. 'I'm just kind of ordinary.'

His gaze narrowed. 'Did you miss the bit where I said you were beautiful?'

'I know, but I—'

'I don't say shit I don't mean, Sugar.' His thumb brushed over my bottom lip caressingly. 'And you *are* beautiful. And passionate. And, given how you've managed to stay one step ahead of the authorities for so long, incredibly smart. All of which makes you very far from ordinary.'

My stomach did a long, slow somersault and I couldn't think of a single word to say except, 'Oh.'

I knew I shouldn't let his opinion matter to me. But it did.

'I guess the real question, though,' he went on, studying me, 'is why would you think that?'

I let out a breath and glanced away from him. 'I wasn't fishing or—'

'I know you're not. But seriously, Thea. Why the hell would you think you're ordinary?'

Telling him the truth would make me feel vulnerable, but I couldn't think of a decent excuse. And, besides, I'd already told him most of it.

'I don't really,' I muttered. 'It's just… Mr Chen didn't think I was good enough for him. Or at least not good enough to adopt me. I know he said it was because I wasn't his blood but…' I stopped, my throat tightening, and then a whole lot of words I hadn't meant to say came tumbling out. 'My parents just left me on the stairs of the orphanage. They didn't even leave a note. And sometimes I wonder why they didn't name me or leave any sign that they cared about me. And sometimes I think it was because there was nothing about me that made them care.'

A silence fell.

Oh, God, why had I said all that? It sounded so pathetic and needy—attention-seeking, even—all things that Mr Chen had told me I needed to overcome if I wanted to make a success of this job.

So much for overcoming...

I forced my mouth shut, focusing on the bright inks of the dragon on Damian's chest instead, given it was better than looking into his face.

Then a finger was beneath my chin, he was tilting my head back with irresistible strength and I met his gaze, dreading what I was going to see there.

But there was none of Mr Chen's cold disapproval, only an oddly fierce expression that I didn't understand. 'You are not ordinary, Thea,' he said quietly, forcefully. 'I don't know why your parents gave you up, but it wasn't about you, I'd stake my entire fucking corporation on it. You are rare and precious. Priceless, even.' Conviction burned in his eyes, his thumb moving caressingly over my bottom lip. 'That's why I'm asking you to go to London with me. Because I'm not ready for you to disappear on me. I want more of you, understand?'

There was a hot feeling inside me, an ache that I didn't want to examine too closely, afraid of what it might mean. So I didn't examine it. I looked at him instead, seeing the belief in his gaze.

He thought I was rare and precious. He thought I was priceless.

Careful. You have to be so careful, Thea.

Oh, yes, I did. Mr Chen had been very clear: no husband or children. No friends, as they couldn't know anything that could compromise client discretion. He'd told me that it was easier to have no one, to get used to being alone, because that had worked for him. So I had got used to it, telling myself that it was easy not to want anything if you tried hard enough.

Except now I'd taken a step over that line and allowed myself to want something: more of Damian Blackwood.

It's going to blow up in your face; you know that, right?

Maybe it would. But right now I didn't much care.

I didn't know what to say—anything was going to sound way too emotional and I had the sense he didn't want that. So I settled for nipping playfully on his thumb instead.

He smiled and took his hand away, leaning forward and kissing me, long and slow. 'Leave everything to me. I'll arrange it.'

Damian was as good as his word.

Over the next few days, he dealt with everything, including the issue of a passport, because I didn't have

one—I'd never needed one before now. I didn't know
how he managed to get it through so fast—connections,
in all likelihood—but a passport was soon produced,
and the problematic issue of clothing was resolved.

I was all set to go home and grab some things, but
Damian wouldn't hear of it, handling the ordering of
some clothes for me himself. Which was fine. I was
more than happy to let him order and pay for things
for me. After all, what was the point of a having billionaire lover if he didn't buy you stuff? I wasn't all
that interested in clothes anyway, but it sure was nice
to be taken care of.

However, when the small mountain of clothing arrived by delivery that afternoon and it was all in my
size, and all fitting perfectly, I could suddenly see why
he'd called himself the glue that held his corporation
together.

He remembered everything, from fluctuating stock
prices and employee wages, to the names of everyone
in his massive company. He could recall spreadsheets
and reports, money going in and out, as well as what
was happening in all the different markets and indus-
tries in which his company was involved.

He was a walking, talking database and it also soon
became clear why he was on the phone all the time; people were constantly calling him to request information,
ask his opinion or to solve problems. And he dealt with
it all with a combination of easy charm and firmness
that I found insanely attractive as well as a little scary.

Because his formidable memory, combined with the

razor-sharp intelligence that went along with it, was incredibly intimidating. And when the fierce intensity of his will shone through at the same time... Well, he was a force of nature. But he kept that well hidden behind the charm he cultivated. Behind the mask of that smile.

Personally, I found his intensity incredibly exciting, especially at night, in bed.

He always remembered what I liked and how I liked it and he'd watch me intently, using my reactions as cues either to push my boundaries or pull back if it got too much. It was amazing having all that attention focused on me.

It was also like a rollercoaster you couldn't get off, careening around corners and looping the loop, going too fast for control and wondering if you were going to crash and burn, yet loving the wind in your hair anyway.

I could get off that rollercoaster, though, and I knew it. I could tell him that I didn't want to go anywhere and slip away back to Mongkok and my existence in the shadows.

It wouldn't take much to leave.

But I didn't want to. The part of me that ached for the sun wanted to keep basking in it while it lasted. And if leaving ended up being harder than I thought it would be, then what of it?

I'd survived everything else life had thrown at me— what was a little more pain?

CHAPTER FOURTEEN

Damian

WE TOUCHED DOWN in London a few days later and, although I'd done my best to hide my growing tension, I knew Thea had picked up on it.

She kept throwing me concerned looks as we disembarked from the corporate jet, apparently not bothered by the grey and gloomy day London had produced to welcome us.

Perhaps asking her to come with me hadn't been the best decision. Maybe I should have asked someone else, someone less interested in me and less perceptive. Someone less vulnerable. Someone who didn't look at me with those big, dark eyes and tell me that there had been times when she'd wondered why her parents hadn't left her any sign that they'd cared about her. And if that reason was her.

I shouldn't have said anything that day. I should have smiled and kissed her, distracted her. But I hadn't. My chest had gone tight and every single one of my protective instincts had woken up and taken notice, as if a part of me knew exactly what she was talking about and ached that no had cared for her the way she ached.

I hadn't been able to stop myself telling her what she needed to hear: the truth. That she wasn't ordinary in the slightest, that she was rare and precious—priceless. Because she was all those things. Even I could see that and I'd only been with her a handful of nights.

I hadn't thought it would cost me anything to say it, that the words would be easy because they were just words. But saying them had cost me. They'd reminded me of what it was like to have someone in my care, which was everything I'd been trying to avoid.

They also reminded you of how good it is to be important to someone.

Ah, fuck. I didn't want that either. I was important to all the people who worked for me, and I was important to Everett and Ulysses. That was all I needed, nothing else.

What I did *not* need was Thea being concerned about me, that was for sure. Which made it a good thing that Morgan wasn't waiting for us once all the customs formalities had been taken care of.

Perhaps she was as uncomfortable about my presence here as I was.

Considering it had been five years, it was no wonder.

Thea and I went straight to the penthouse apartment of a building I owned on a bank of the Thames which had a great view of Tower Bridge. Not that I was planning on looking at the view. The launch of the Black and White Foundation was in a couple of days and I was hoping to spend as much of that time as possible naked with Thea.

I'd worked for most of the flight from Hong Kong, leaving her to her own devices, but I'd been achingly conscious of her, curled up in her seat, flicking through a magazine. I'd totally gone to town on choosing clothing for her—including a fucking magnificent gown for the launch that I couldn't wait to see her in—but she seemed to prefer comfort over style; the past couple of days she'd worn nothing but stretchy black yoga pants and a T-shirt, today's being red. I didn't mind. She looked incredibly sexy in it, though all things being equal I preferred her wearing nothing at all.

In fact, the whole goddamn flight I wanted to strip the clothing from her and eat her up there and then, especially because the closer to London I got the more the tension inside me gathered. But work needed to be done, so I busied myself with that instead and pretended the tension didn't exist.

I was pretending it didn't exist now as I stood in the living area of the apartment, my hands in fists in the pockets of my suit trousers as Thea walked over to the windows, gazing out at the view of the Thames and Tower Bridge, one of her rare smiles lighting her lovely face.

I'd had the same interior designer who'd done my place in Hong Kong do something similar here, though they'd kept all the furniture here white, the floors hardwood and covered in thick, colourful and no doubt insanely expensive silk Persian rugs.

Restlessness filled me, and my cock was already getting hard, wanting to push Thea up against those big windows and tear her clothes off. But that was the tension talking, and I wasn't going to let it get to me, so I stayed where I was and asked instead, 'You haven't been to London before?'

'No. Mr Chen did all the international work. And since he died all the jobs I've had have been in Hong Kong.'

I moved over to where she stood, took a look out at the view and then turned around, stalking back to where I'd been standing. 'Do you enjoy what you do? I guess you must if you're still doing it.'

She turned towards me. 'Most of it involves lots of research—which can be interesting—and then planning. Then lots of waiting around for the right opportunity.' Her gaze narrowed. 'What's wrong?'

'What do you mean, what's wrong?'

'You're…' she gestured '…pacing.'

I could feel my mouth curving in its usual bullshit smile. 'Nothing. Just a little restless.'

'It's more than that. You're incredibly tense.'

Fuck. I'd hoped she wouldn't notice, but of course she had. As I'd already discovered, she was incredibly observant.

Realising I'd paced over to the windows again, I forced myself to stop, giving her a smoky look. 'Of course I'm tense. It's been hours since I was last inside you.'

'It's not that. The whole way to London you almost didn't sit down once and, ever since we got here, you're all…tight.' She came over to me and put her hands on my chest as if she'd been doing it all her life, pressing lightly against me, concern in her eyes. 'What is it? The launch?'

But I didn't want to have this discussion so I leaned down and kissed her, taking her bottom lip between my teeth and biting down gently, hoping some distraction would work instead.

Except she didn't move and didn't kiss me back. She merely stood there, as if she was waiting until I was done.

Irritated, I lifted my head. Colour had risen to her cheeks and I caught the familiar glint of hunger in her eyes—she definitely wasn't immune to a good kiss, that was for sure. Yet she clearly wasn't going to be distracted either.

Fuck.

I let her go. 'I need to get some work done.'

But her hands were settled in the middle of my chest and they stayed there, her steady gaze meeting mine. 'Damian.'

'What?' I tried to keep the impatience out of my voice and failed.

She didn't move and she said nothing, letting her calm silence speak for her.

I could have walked away at that point. I should have. I didn't have to stand there and tell her what was going on, because I certainly didn't fucking want to. I could have gone and worked out my tension in the penthouse gym or covered her mouth and used one of the tricks I knew she liked to make her forget her own name, let alone the question she'd asked me.

But her hands on me were warm, and they felt good.

And the expression in her eyes wasn't demanding. Only patient. As if she was happy to stand there all day, waiting until I was ready to talk to her.

There was a gentleness to her that I couldn't resist, and a genuine concern that I hadn't seen in anyone else's face for a very long time.

No, because you make sure you keep everyone at a distance.

Yeah, I did. And I'd thought I was happy with that. More than happy with it. I didn't need anyone, didn't want anyone, and that was good, because then no one would need or want me.

Yet right now, with her looking at me, that excuse felt hollow, leaving an emptiness inside me that felt almost…painful.

Would it really be so bad to talk to her? To let her in just a little? It didn't have to be far and, after all, I'd already told her a few things about my past and about myself. What could a few more hurt?

'Look,' she said softly, breaking the silence. 'You don't have to tell me if you don't want to. I'm not trying to pressure you and I don't want to make whatever it is worse.'

'What do you want to know?' I wasn't sure why I asked. It wasn't as though I particularly wanted to hear the answer.

'Because…well…' She glanced down at her hands on my chest. And there was a long silence. Then she said, 'Because I want to help. Because you matter, Damian.'

Something inside me clenched tight at the same

time as something else relaxed, which made no fucking sense.

I didn't want to matter. Not to her or anyone else.

Yes, you do. Why else have you kept her with you?

Because I wanted to fuck her. Because I needed a date and couldn't get anyone else. That was it. End of goddamn story.

Liar. You've already fucked her, numerous times. And you could have found yourself a different date.

I ignored the thought, sullen anger beginning to burn in my gut. At myself for bringing her here when I should have just got rid of her; for dragging this out unnecessarily and potentially opening her up to hurt. And at her, too. And, yes, I knew it wasn't fair, but I was angry at her anyway. For letting me matter when she shouldn't have.

'Don't do that.' I tried to keep the harsh edge out of my voice, laying my hand over hers where it rested on my shirt to soften the words. 'Mattering to each other is not what we're here for, remember?'

This time she didn't look away. 'No, but you said this was about making each other feel good. And you're definitely not feeling good right now.'

I could feel my jaw get tight. 'I was talking about sex, Thea. Not anything else.'

'Right.' Her dark eyes flickered, thick, black lashes coming down to conceal her expression. 'Sorry.' She made as if to pull away, but I could hear the pain in that carefully neutral word. I'd hurt her. Fuck.

Instinctively I held her hands against my chest, preventing her from moving. Because hurting her had never been my intention.

Jesus, next you'll be thinking she matters.

I gritted my teeth, shoving the thought away. Shit, all I'd wanted was some good times, some fun and pleasure for both of us, nothing too deep, nothing too heavy. But this was turning into something I hadn't expected and I didn't like my reaction to it.

Perhaps if she knew the truth she'd understand.

Yeah, well, maybe it was time to be straight with her. I couldn't have her getting any more involved than she was already.

She was looking up at me, a question in her eyes, and suddenly her touching me was too much so I stepped back, letting her hands drop away.

'It's not you,' I said before she could say anything.

She clasped her hands together as if she didn't know what to do with them. 'So I'm going to get the "it's not you, it's me" speech?'

Shit. I should have been clear right from the beginning, shouldn't I? I should have told her exactly what she was getting into with me, and now I'd left it too late.

Because you're a selfish prick, remember?

'You want to know why I'm tense?' I said harshly, shoving the thought out of my head. 'It's because I haven't been to London for years.'

'Oh? Why?'

There was something heavy in my chest, like a big fucking rock that just sat there, unmoving. 'Because Morgan lives here.'

CHAPTER FIFTEEN

Thea

DAMIAN STOOD THERE with the grey London light falling over him, in a tailored charcoal suit with a white shirt. The neck of his shirt was open, exposing his bright tattoos, and he had his hands in his pockets. It was supposed to be a casual pose, but he looked anything but casual.

Tension poured off him, in the lines of his powerful shoulders and arms and in his beautiful face. I could see that his hands were curled into fists in his pockets and there was sharp grief in his silver eyes as he looked at me, grief he was trying to hide.

Grief I didn't understand.

'So…you avoided coming to London because of your sister?' I asked tentatively. 'But why?'

He tried to smile, tried to put on that mask again, but it was more of a snarl than anything else, and I found myself taking a couple of instinctive steps towards him, wanting to do something for him.

But he gave a sharp shake of his head, freezing me in place. 'Don't.'

So I stayed where I was, my throat tight, my heart beginning to ache, because whatever he was going to tell me hurt him.

'It's the usual sad story,' he went on. 'Mum's illness was terminal, and her pain was getting worse, and nothing I did helped.' His beautiful voice got rougher. 'I couldn't save her. I knew I couldn't. I knew there was nothing to be done. But...' A muscle flicked in his hard jaw. 'The helplessness of it. Knowing there was nothing, fucking *nothing*, that I could do. She sent me out before the end. She didn't want me to see it—not me or Morgan.'

My heart felt as if it had grown sharp edges and was cutting me deep inside. I could only imagine what it must have been like for him, a sixteen-year-old boy having to shoulder the burden of his dying mother. Alone. Because he had been alone, hadn't he? Like he still was.

'The nurses told me she died peacefully.' Damian's voice was ragged around the edges. 'And in no pain, so there was that.' His gaze lifted abruptly. 'But Morgan didn't understand. She changed after Mum died. She became scared and anxious... It was like Mum took all the joy out of her when she died. I tried to make life fun again for her.' The muscle in his jaw jumped again. 'But it was hard and I was only fucking sixteen. What did I know about what little girls liked? I couldn't help her, so I sent her to boarding school for some stability and to be with other kids her age, working my arse off to cover the fees. And then when she was done with school, and our company was doing well, I sent her to Ulysses.'

His eyes glittered. 'And I haven't seen her since, because she doesn't need to be reminded of the past and what I couldn't do for her. And, besides, my responsibility to her is done. I'm not getting sucked into doing any more.'

He was silent a moment, staring at me, something fierce burning in his expression. 'I'm telling you all of this, Thea, because caring for Mum while she was dying, and then having to care for Morgan…it took everything I had.' The lines of his face were drawn tight. 'I don't have anything left for anyone else. And I don't want to matter to anyone, because then they don't have to matter to me. It's not personal, it's just the way it is. If you want fun and sex from me, fine, I can give you that. But nothing else, understand?'

The sharp edges of my heart were rubbing me raw and I had to take a silent breath. I could only imagine what he'd gone through, the bravery it would have taken to help his mother and then take on the responsibility of caring for his sister too. It would have taken both courage and compassion.

And who would he have had to turn to? Had he had anyone? Oh, but I knew the answer to that already. No, he hadn't.

Somewhere inside me another sharp pain caught, but I ignored it.

It wasn't about me. And, if there was a part of me that secretly wanted to be the person he could turn to, then that was my own fault. He hadn't promised me anything but a few days, and I was already on borrowed time.

My vision blurred, grief for him making tears start behind my eyes. But I blinked them away hard. He didn't need me being all emotional on him.

'It's okay,' I said, trying to sound calm and steady. 'I get it. I'm so sorry you had to go through all of that, Damian. I'm just…so sorry.'

It sounded so inadequate and trite, and I wanted to close the distance between us and put my arms around him. But that was about me and what I needed, not him. So I stayed where I was.

'You don't need to worry,' I went on instead. 'I won't ask any more questions, I promise. Just sex and good times from now on.'

His silver gaze had settled on me, the look on his face completely unreadable. And, no matter how hard I tried to tell it not to, my heart still ached.

'I mean, I know it's not the same,' I continued, wanting to reassure him and maybe convince myself too. 'But I don't want more either. Mr Chen wasn't my father, but I cared about him and his legacy. And I want to continue it, which means doing a job where I'll always have to remain alone. It was a choice I made years ago and I'm not changing my mind just for you, okay?'

Damian stared at me for a long time and I didn't understand all the emotions that crossed his face. And he didn't smile. It was as though the mask had dropped and what I was seeing was the raw, unvarnished man.

Serious. Intense. But something fierce blazed in his eyes.

Then quite suddenly it was he who crossed the distance, taking my face between his hands, his palms hot against my skin.

'Why tell me that?' he demanded, staring down at me. 'Is it supposed to make me care that you're alone?'

He was angry; I could see that now. 'Why?' I shot back, staring up at him, something fierce rising inside me too. 'Has it made you change your mind?'

'No.' His fingers tightened on my jaw. 'I'm a selfish prick and I don't give a shit about you or anyone else.'

And then, before I could move, he bent his head and kissed me fierce and hard, his tongue pushing inside, exploring. Demanding. Taking.

There was no finesse this time, none of his practised charm. None of his usual focus or care. The kiss was rough, raw and totally uncompromising. The kiss of a man who had a point to prove and was going to use me to prove it.

I shuddered as he ravaged my mouth, desire gathering tight and hot inside me, because although he'd been angry it wasn't anger I tasted in the kiss. It was desperation. Hunger. He wanted to prove that he didn't want anything from me, or from anyone, but the desperate way he was kissing me told me otherwise.

And instantly all my own anger drained away.

No wonder he was desperate. No wonder he was hungry. He'd given everything he had to the people he cared about, and because his mother had died and his sister had been too young he hadn't got anything back.

No one had given him what he needed.

Except for now. Now he had me. And I had plenty to give.

I tore my mouth from his, staring up into his blazing eyes. 'Tell me what you want,' I said fiercely. 'Tell me and I'll give it to you.'

He took a moment, as if he didn't understand at first. And then the silver light in his eyes seemed to grow brighter.

'Strip,' he ordered roughly. 'I want everything off. Now.'

I didn't hesitate. My hands shook as I pulled at my clothes, discarding them quickly onto the floor, Damian's gaze burning as he watched me.

Once I was naked, the air moving over my skin, he pointed to the floor in front of him. 'Down. Now.'

I dropped to my knees, the wooden floor hard beneath me, my pulse getting louder and louder in my head.

His hands dropped to his fly and he undid the button, jerking down the zip. With one hand he pulled out his cock while with the other he reached for me, his fingers tangling in my hair. 'Open your mouth,' he demanded, and when I did he shoved his cock into it, stretching my lips wide around him.

'Now suck it.' His voice was hardly recognisable, a deep, rough growl, and I responded, closing my mouth around him and taking him in deep. So deep he brushed the back of my throat.

He made a harsh sound, his handsome features tightening with pleasure, and I liked it. Liked that he was taking from me and that I could give him what he wanted.

But I wanted to give him more, so I began to suck him hard, licking around the sensitive head in the way I knew he liked, teasing the ring in his dick with my tongue, letting my teeth graze him. He tasted good, musky, salty and male, so I took him deeper, tasting him harder.

Another growl escaped him, the look in his eyes burning me alive as he stared down at me. God, he was incredible. His jaw was hard, the intensity he always kept masked suddenly blazing.

His fingers tightened in my hair, his hips flexing as he thrust into my mouth. I wanted to shut my eyes, give myself over to the experience and to him, but I couldn't drag my gaze from his face.

He hit the back of my throat, making me groan, and then abruptly he pulled out of my mouth, his fists in my hair. 'Lie down.' His voice was rough, breathless, and he released me. 'On your back.'

And I did, my breathing fast and short, the nagging ache between my thighs getting stronger. I was wet and I wanted his hands on me, wanted his mouth, but I wasn't going to ask. He'd done nothing but give me pleasure for the past week and now it was my turn to give. He could take me, use me however he wanted. This was for him.

The floor was hard against my bare back, the wood cool, and it made me shiver.

'Spread your legs,' Damian growled, staring down at me.

And I did, spreading them wide, my thighs shaking.

His gaze dropped to my bare sex and stayed there, making me catch my breath. Then he dropped to his knees between my legs, still staring at me, reaching into his back pocket and pulling out his wallet. He took out a condom packet and ripped it open, and there was something incredibly erotic about the deliberateness of his movements that had me shifting restlessly on the floor.

My breathing was embarrassingly loud, but I could hear his too and it was just as fast, just as ragged. But he didn't move any faster, taking out the condom and slowly rolling it down over his cock, still glistening from my mouth.

Then he looked down at me and put his hand out, his palm settling on my stomach, the heel of his hand pressing lightly on my clit. Bolts of fire ignited as he pressed down, pleasure licking up inside me. I gasped, my hips lifting automatically into his hand, wanting more, wanting harder.

But he took his hand away. 'Roll over.'

I sucked in a shaky breath and did as I was told, the wooden floor pressing against my hard, achingly sensitive nipples. But the rest of my senses were completely focused on the demanding man behind me, breathless with excitement about what he was going to ask of me next.

I jumped when his hands settled on my hips and he

hauled me up onto my knees, leaving my face pressed to the floor.

'Legs apart,' he ordered, one knee nudging the inside of mine and forcing them wider.

I couldn't stop shaking and I started to pant, his heat behind me a tease and a temptation.

Then his hands were between my legs, spreading apart the folds of my sex, and I felt his cock push against me. There was no delicious teasing now. He thrust in hard, penetrating me deep before sliding out, then thrusting in again.

Pleasure spread out in a sharp wave and I shut my eyes as it washed over me, rolling me over and over, swamping me.

He thrust deeper, harder, the slap of his flesh against mine combining with my ragged breathing and the rough, masculine sounds of his own pleasure echoing off the walls.

My hands had spread out onto the floor, my nails digging into the wood as if I could hold on to it, stop myself from being washed away in the flood of sensation. But it was futile. He moved faster, my body shuddering against the wood, rubbing against my nipples and my knees. It was painful and yet somehow incredibly erotic at the same time.

I gasped as he shoved himself deeper, his hands gripping my hips so hard they were going to leave bruises. But I didn't care. I wanted bruises. I wanted all the evidence I could get that he'd taken what he needed from me.

I hadn't been able to give to anyone before, but now I could and I wanted to give him everything.

And he took it with both hands, shoving himself into me, his fingers digging into my flesh, bruising my knees and setting free my heart.

But it wasn't all for him and I should have known that even now, even while he was taking, he still couldn't stop himself from giving. Because, just when I thought I was going to have finish myself off, he reached around and found my clit, his finger pressing down hard.

'Come, Thea,' he growled.

And because I was his to command I did, sobbing against the floor, barely aware of his own roar of release as he followed me.

CHAPTER SIXTEEN

Damian

MY HEAD WAS RINGING, the blood pumping hard in my veins, and it took me a couple of moments to realise I'd slumped forward over Thea's naked body and that she was pressed to the floor beneath me.

Fuck, what had I done?

I'd never just taken what I wanted from a woman the way I had from Thea. I'd never just taken what I wanted from *anyone*.

All I'd meant to do was tell her why I couldn't give her anything more than the sex and good times we'd agreed on. And I'd been honest about it because I hadn't wanted her to think that it was all her fault.

Yet as soon as the words had come out of my mouth all the grief and anger had come rushing back. Yes, anger. Because I hadn't wanted to think about it, let alone say all those words out loud. And they all fucking hurt.

But then she'd stood there looking at me, her beautiful eyes full of tears, telling me exactly what I wanted to hear. That she wasn't going to ask for more. Wasn't going to ask me questions. Wasn't going to push me into caring.

Then she'd mentioned Mr Chen and the legacy she was carrying on, and the choice she'd made to remain alone, and something inside me had clenched so goddamn tight. Almost as if the thought of her being alone hurt. And that had made me angry because I didn't want to care.

Yet somehow I hadn't been able to get rid of the tight feeling in my chest, so I'd kissed her, because I was a giant fucking cliché who thought sex would make things easier.

But it hadn't. All I'd felt was hungry. As though I needed something for which I didn't have any words. Something to do with her. And then she'd said she'd give me whatever I wanted…

I didn't know why that had made me so hard. Why the sight of her doing everything I told her was so fucking erotic. She hadn't stopped me, hadn't told me no. And I knew she would have kept on giving me what I asked for, no matter what it was, because that was who she was. A natural giver.

Unlike you.

It was true. Because of course I didn't give to people. But I made sure I didn't take either, so it was a winwin situation.

Except right now it didn't feel very win-win.

She was trembling beneath me and all I felt was shitty, like the biggest prick alive. Like I'd taken advantage of her generosity and her passion and used her in the worst way possible to work out my own selfish anger.

Hating myself, I quickly pulled out of her and shifted so I wasn't lying directly on top of her. I probably should have walked away from her at that point, just left her there. Either that or taken her to the bedroom to ensure there was no more talking.

But I didn't. Instead, I dealt with the condom before gently scooping her up in my arms, carrying her over to the couch and sitting down on it, gathering her close in my lap.

'I'm sorry,' I said roughly, stroking her silky dark hair. 'Thea, I shouldn't have—'

She put a delicate finger on my mouth, silencing me. 'Yes, you should. You don't have to give all the time, Damian. It's okay to take and it's okay to take from me.' A blush stained her lovely skin, going all the way down her neck and across her chest. 'Besides...' Her dark eyes glowed. 'It was hot.'

Hot? She'd thought me being a giant, selfish arsehole was hot?

Fuck.

I gently took her finger from my mouth, held her hand in mine. 'No. Don't do that. Don't make it okay.'

'Why not?' She lifted a brow. 'It *was* okay. It was more than okay.'

'Me being a selfish dickhead is okay? No, Thea. Because you're wrong. I never give anything to anyone.' My heartbeat was racing and I couldn't seem to slow

it down. It was important that she understood this—
no, shit, it was vital. 'And I never take, either, because
that's the whole fucking point.'

She was silent, her silence filling the room, and
somehow it felt suffocating, like pressure tightening
around me on all sides. And I wanted to push her aside
and leave, just get the fuck out there, but she was soft
and naked and warm. And I couldn't do that to her.

You're screwed, mate.

Yeah, I was. Because once you started not wanting
to hurt someone you were already on the slippery slope
that led down towards caring about them. And, once
you cared, that was it. You were fucked.

'You do give,' Thea said quietly. 'What do you think
you've been doing for me all this time? You didn't call
the authorities on me the night you found me. No, you
let me talk you into a blow job and then you took me
to bed. And then you fed me breakfast and bought me
clothes. And you let me talk about Mr Chen and you
told me I was rare and precious. You didn't have to do
any of those things. You didn't have to make me feel
good.' Her gaze searched my face. 'But you did. Isn't
that all giving?'

'No,' I said, because I had to. 'Sex is easy. The rest
is just money.'

'Don't be so ridiculous,' she said calmly, settling
against my shoulder, completely unconcerned about
being naked in my arms. 'You could have kicked me
out onto the street and got me locked up. But you didn't.
You let me lie around your apartment, plied me with gin

and gave me the most incredible neck massage because you could feel I was tense. You might not think that's any big deal, but it is to me.' Her mouth softened. 'In fact, it's a massive deal to me, Damian. I've never had anyone look after me like that. I've never had anyone look after me at all.'

I had to stop her. I had to. 'Thea—'

'No. I know what it means to me and you don't get to tell me otherwise.'

My heartbeat was raging out of control, tension coiling through every muscle. I wanted to do something to relieve it, something violent, but she was so delicate and soft, like a precious jewel in a bed of velvet, and I couldn't bear to move her.

'Don't make me into something I'm not,' I said hoarsely. 'I'm a selfish fucking guy and I've never pretended to be anything different.'

Something flickered in her eyes and it looked horribly like sympathy. 'I think that's what you tell yourself, Damian. But that doesn't make it true.'

My jaw was so tight it ached and I didn't know why she was telling me this stuff. I didn't know why I was simply sitting here listening to it either. 'Then what's the truth?' I demanded, more forcefully than I'd intended. 'What do you think I am?'

'I think you're lonely,' Thea said, her dark eyes never leaving mine. 'I think you're lonely just like me.'

I didn't know what I'd expected. But it wasn't that. And what was even worse was, as soon as she said it, a deep pit opened up inside me, the black hole of need that I'd told myself time and time again wasn't there. That I'd covered up with jewels and money, parties and noise. So I could pretend it didn't exist.

But she knew. This little woman with her dark eyes and her silence. With her passion and her soft touch. She'd seen it—she'd reached inside me and somehow opened it up as easily as the lock on my fucking office door.

'No,' I said, because what else could I say? I didn't want that pit to be there. I didn't want anything to do with it. 'No. How can I be fucking lonely? I'm constantly surrounded by goddamn people.'

But Thea only smiled, and it broke me a little, because her smiles were as rare and precious as she was. 'Because you don't let anyone in. You hold them at a distance. And that's okay, I get it. After what you went through, I understand completely. But cutting yourself off kills something inside you. I should know—it happened to me.' She lifted a hand to my jaw, her fingertips brushing my skin. 'But meeting you brought it back to life again. And I saw what I'd been missing all this time.'

Everything in me wanted to deny it and to deny her. She was going to drag me down that slippery slope into caring if I let her. Into pain, hurt and grief. Back into worrying about people and wanting to save them, into being helpless because I couldn't do a fucking thing.

I didn't want it. What I wanted was to let her go, walk away. Never come back.

Except that black hole inside me wouldn't let me do it. She was too warm and her touch felt so good.

And it felt weirdly as though I'd been dead too all this time, thinking that I was alive and enjoying life. Thinking that I was fine, that I didn't need anyone. Until she'd turned up, standing on my terrace in Hong Kong, watching me with her too-perceptive gaze. Seeing straight through me and into my soul.

'It's okay,' she went on quietly, still watching my face as if it fascinated her. 'We can give and take from each other. Just a little bit. It doesn't have to mean anything if we don't want it to.'

I didn't know what to say to that, except, 'Thea.'

And she only smiled more deeply, as if I'd said something profound. Then she reached up and pulled my head down so her hot mouth was under mine, stealing my breath and any other words that I'd been going to say.

Then that black hole opened up inside me, all the need flooded out and I'd pushed her back down onto the couch cushions before I'd had a chance to think about it, her warm, soft curves beneath me.

She gave a little moan of delight, arching up into me, and I knew that, just like before, she'd give me anything and everything I wanted.

So I didn't think. I stripped my clothes away so we were skin to skin and I took everything I wanted from her, everything she had to give.

Then I gave it all right back to her.

Perhaps we could do this after all. Give and take. Just a little bit.

Just for a while.

CHAPTER SEVENTEEN

Thea

I REACHED FOR Damian's hand as the limo pulled up in front of the grand columned entrance of the British Museum. There were crowds of people standing outside, assembled media and interested tourists gawking at the procession of beautifully dressed people going through the museum doors.

It was the night of the launch for the Black and White Foundation, an event Damian and I had both been anticipating and dreading in equal measure.

He'd seemed to take what I'd said about give and take to heart, and over the past couple of days had talked to me about his sister.

I thought he felt that he'd failed her somehow, though I wasn't sure how, not when he'd told me how many years he'd spent working hard to give her the life his mother would have wanted her to have. I thought he felt he'd failed his mother too, though again I wasn't sure why, not when he'd done everything he could for her.

I didn't talk about that to him, though. There were

only so many deep and meaningful conversations you could have in an affair that was supposed to be about pleasure and fun, so for the past couple of days that was exactly what we'd been concentrating on.

Damian had taken me sightseeing around London and then had let me help him prepare his jewellery collection for the auction that would be taking place tonight, both of which I'd enjoyed hugely. Sightseeing with him was fun because, thanks to his memory, he knew all kinds of odd facts that were either amusing, strange or both, and would bring them out either to pique my interest or to make me laugh. Mostly laugh, which was something I needed more of.

Helping him with his collection was unexpectedly fun too, because he knew jewels and knew all the histories of the pieces he'd collected. I found it unexpectedly fascinating. In my line of work, I'd never known anything about the things I'd 'reacquired' and I hadn't realised I'd find it so interesting. But I did. I enjoyed hearing about where a piece came from, how it was made and what had gone into its creation.

We didn't talk about what had happened between us the night we'd arrived in London, and I was fine with that.

But now I could feel his tension as he sat beside me in the limo, and I knew what it was about: he would be face to face with his sister for the first time in years and that was always going to be tough.

I reached out to where his hand rested on one powerful thigh and I threaded my fingers through his, letting him know without words that I was there for him.

He glanced at me, the lines of tension around his eyes and mouth obvious. Then his expression relaxed and he gave me a faint smile, his grip on my hand tightening.

My own tension eased at that smile and I gave him one back.

He was even more beautiful tonight than he normally was, dressed in an insanely expensive tux, the black fabric highlighting his incredible silver eyes and the exquisite tailoring around his broad, muscled shoulders.

'You okay?' he asked, because he knew I was going to have a bit of difficulty being the object of so many people's attention. 'Remember, you're the daughter of a diplomat who grew up in Hong Kong and you have ties to the jewel industry. Keep it simple, yes?'

It was the story of my background that we'd agreed on to protect my anonymity. There would be interest in me because I was showing up on the arm of an infamous playboy, someone new and unknown, and therefore fascinating.

Of course any cursory search would find out my story wasn't true, so Damian had got one of his staff members to concoct a few Internet records here and there, none serious enough to prompt investigations by authorities, but real enough to satisfy any reporters wanting to research me.

'Yes,' I said. 'What about you? Are you okay?' I didn't mention Morgan's name but we both knew that was what I meant.

His smile became a little grim. 'Don't worry about me, Sugar. I can handle myself.'

But I did worry about him. That was the problem with all of this.

And you know why, don't you?

But I didn't want to think about that, so I didn't.

The limo stopped, but Damian didn't get out straight away. Instead, he held up his hand for me to wait and he shifted, moving to pull something out of one of the limo compartments in the door beside him and holding it out to me.

It was a long black box.

I stared at it, not understanding. 'What's this?'

'It's a present.' He wasn't smiling at all now, his silver gaze intense. 'Open it.'

A present. He'd got me a present.

Warmth spread through me, my heart getting tight in my chest, and my hands shook as I took the box from him and flicked it open.

Lying on black velvet, gleaming in the light coming through the limo windows, was a long rope of dusky, irregularly shaped pearls. My breath caught. They were simple and beautiful, glossy and lustrous, and looked very, very old. They were also probably worth thousands.

'Oh...' I breathed, unable to say anything else.

Damian reached for the pearls and drew them out of the box, then he leaned over and draped the long necklace around my neck, looping the pearls into a knot that hung between my breasts.

'I knew it,' he said softly. 'I knew you'd look beautiful in it.'

The necklace felt heavy, the pearls warm and silky against my skin. I lifted a hand to touch them, feeling slightly shaky. 'Damian, this is…amazing.'

'They're black pearls. I bought them from a Brit a few years back.' He touched the knot between my breasts. 'The pearls are irregular because they're baroque. I think they're beautiful. Rare and precious.' His gaze lifted to mine, burning. 'Like you.'

I swallowed. 'I shouldn't accept it. It must be worth—'

'It doesn't matter what it's worth. I want you to have them.'

My mouth had gone dry. 'Why?'

'Because I want to give you something.' He wasn't smiling at all now, his expression deadly serious. 'For what you've given me.'

The warmth in my chest spread out further, a bittersweet ache in my heart. 'You don't have to give me anything.'

'I know. But I wanted to.' He gently touched my cheek. 'Keep them, okay? Now, it's time to face the crowd. Are you ready?'

I couldn't speak, could only nod.

The limo door swung open, light and the clicks of a thousand camera shutters flooding into the silent interior, and Damian fluidly slid out. I could hear the reporters shouting and hurling questions at him, and the rich sound of his voice replying, easy, charming and quick.

Then he turned from the crowds and held his hand out, giving me the smile he saved for me, reassuring me.

My heartbeat was thumping hard and it wasn't just because of the prospect of the attention of the media and the people gathered outside.

It was him. It would always be him.

I took his hand, feeling his warm fingers wrap around mine, and he drew me out of the limo, the deep red silk of the gown he'd bought for me falling around my ankles. It had a plunging neckline and wrapped around my figure before flaring out in a mermaid-tail hem, the pearls Damian had given me complementing the dark red silk. I felt beautiful and mysterious in it, no longer an unnoticed shadow or an unseen ghost. No longer the unwanted girl that someone had left on the steps of a church.

Damian moved at my side, smiling at the crowds and lifting a hand to people here and there. He was used to being in the spotlight and it loved him, his smile electric, his silver eyes glittering.

A prince. *My* prince.

And you're falling for him.

I didn't smile, didn't think about the fact that, yes, I probably was falling for him. I kept my attention on what was happening around me instead as he led me inside and into the Egyptian Sculpture Gallery where the launch event and auction was being held.

It was a beautiful space, all lit up with glass cases full of ancient Egyptian antiquities, sculptures scattered throughout the gallery while music played and staff swirled through the designer crowd with drinks.

People gave way to us as we entered, a thrill of excitement moving through the crowd as they realised that Damian was here. And then a small group of people materialised in front of us—two very tall, good-looking men in tuxes, one blond and built like a gladiator, the other dark-haired, dark-eyed and built like a heavyweight boxer. The blond man had a tall redhead on his arm, and she was dressed in a green gown. He was unsmiling, while she grinned as though she was having the time of her life.

I knew him, of course, having seen his picture in my research: Everett Calhoun. I didn't know the woman, though.

The dark-haired man had a petite brunette holding his arm. She was stunningly gorgeous, with long black hair and deep blue eyes, and the moment she saw us she froze. I saw her hand on the man's arm, saw how white her knuckles were, and I knew immediately who she must be.

The man was Ulysses White and the woman was Damian's sister, Morgan.

The one he'd sent away. The one he hadn't seen for years.

Silence settled around us, the chatter of the crowd becoming muffled, the tension pulling tight.

'Hi, kiddo,' Damian said softly.

'Damian,' Morgan replied, her voice clear as a bell and slightly edged. 'So glad you could make it.'

Ulysses said nothing, frowning at his friend, while Everett just nodded.

Men of few words, clearly.

Damian's grim expression relented as he looked at the redhead. 'Hey, Freya, nice to see you too.'

'Same.' Freya's green eyes slid to me and suddenly I was the object of four people's intense gaze.

It was uncomfortable, but I lifted my chin and stared back. I might be ordinary, but on Damian's arm, with his pearls around my neck, I felt anything but.

If he was the prince, then tonight I would be his princess.

As if he could feel my sudden tension, he slid an arm around my waist and drew me close, the movement protective and not a little possessive.

The ache inside me deepened.

'This is Thea Smith,' Damian said. 'I asked her if she would be my date for the evening and she graciously accepted.'

The others all looked at me with varying degrees of interest, Everett with outright suspicion.

'Thea,' Damian went on, ignoring his friends. 'This is Ulysses White and Everett Calhoun, my partners in crime; and this is Everett's friend, Freya Thompson; and of course my sister, Morgan.'

They all greeted me courteously enough, though Everett's disapproval was palpable and Ulysses only gave me a cursory greeting and a curt nod before he turned and abruptly disappeared off into the crowd. Everett murmured something to Damian, then he and Freya went in Ulysses's direction.

Only Morgan remained, standing there staring at her brother.

The tension between the two of them gathered and I could feel the muscles in Damian's arm tighten. 'I need to talk to you,' he said quietly to Morgan, his voice devoid of its usual charm. 'But now is not the time.'

'Talk?' Morgan's blue eyes widened. 'Will wonders never cease?'

He ignored that. 'After this is done, okay? There are a few things I need to tell you.'

'Only a few? I was thinking more.' She lifted a careless shoulder, as if it didn't matter. 'But, fine, I'm sure I can spare some time at some point. Right now, though, I need to talk to you about this auction. There've been a couple of issues.'

This was clearly going to take some time, so Damian suggested I go and get a drink and he'd join me once he'd finished with Morgan.

I left them to it, moving through the crowd towards the bar.

It was strange being on my own again after nearly a week in Damian's company, weird to be surrounded by other people too.

I'd thought that once I was out of the range of Damian's spotlight no one would even look at me, but I could feel their attention as I made my way to the bar, dozens of eyes watching me curiously.

I had expected it—being on the arm of one of the

most notorious playboys in the world was hardly going to render me invisible—but the reality was still…odd.

Then two men suddenly appeared out of the crowd in front of me.

Everett and Ulysses.

I stopped dead, my heart thumping, because the expressions on their faces were anything but friendly.

Everett's blue eyes blazed with suspicion while Ulysses's dark ones were cold as ice.

'I've been investigating the security breach at Damian's last party,' Everett said without any preamble at all, his voice a deep Texan drawl. 'And I've been looking at the security camera footage. You're there, Miss Smith. Except you're in a catering company uniform.' His gaze narrowed. 'Want to tell me why that was when you weren't on the staff list?'

Oh, hell.

My mouth went dry.

'I should warn you not to lie,' Ulysses said, his voice deep and hoarse. 'I can spot a liar a mile off.'

'I'm sorry,' I began.

'Apologies won't help you,' Ulysses snapped before I could add anything else, his gaze like black frost. 'This is an important event, and if you're using Damian to interfere with it in any way we will be very, *very* angry.'

No need to look for the warning in that. It was loud and clear.

'I'm not here to sabotage your launch, I promise,' I said shakily. 'I'm here for Damian. Yes, I crashed his party, but I'm not a journalist or anything. I was there to—'

'She was a last-minute replacement for one of the catering company staff.' Damian's smooth voice cut me off, his arm sliding around my waist and pulling me up against his hard, hot body. 'And I asked her to stay on after the party.'

There was silence as Everett's and Ulysses's attention switched from me to Damian, while Damian stared back, his hold on me tight and possessive.

'You're fucking her,' Everett said flatly and it wasn't a question.

'Say that again and I'll rip your head off,' Damian growled.

'You are. Jesus.' Ulysses frowned as he glanced at me. 'Why?'

Something turned over in my gut, because it was clear that to him I was just a plain waitress who'd suddenly turned up on the arm of his friend, decked in red silk and pearls, pretending to be someone she wasn't.

Can you blame him? You're no one's princess. Even Mr Chen didn't want you in the end.

No. That wasn't true. Damian had asked me to be here. He'd bought me pearls and a dress, and he thought I was beautiful. He thought I was mysterious. He thought I was very far from ordinary and, right now, that was exactly what I felt.

I could feel Damian's sudden surge of protective anger and, even though I appreciated it, I didn't need it.

'Do you have a problem with me, Mr White?' I asked

before Damian could get a word in. 'Because, if you do, I suggest you say it to my face.'

You could have cut the air with a knife.

Ulysses's eyes widened. 'Excuse me?'

'You heard me.' I gave him a disdainful look then glanced at Everett. 'What about you, Mr Calhoun? Are you often this rude to women you've never met before or is it just me?'

Ulysses opened his mouth to say something, but I didn't miss Everett elbowing him hard in the side, making him shut his mouth with a snap.

Beside me, Damian was silent, letting me have my moment.

'If you must know,' I went on, taking advantage of the silence, 'I'm not a waitress. I'm a reacquisition agent, and if you don't know what that is then I suggest you educate yourselves before making any ridiculous assumptions.' I lifted my chin, looking both Ulysses and Everett in the eye. 'I'm not here to sabotage anything. I'm here because this event is important to Damian and I wanted to be here for him. So take your rude insinuations elsewhere, please.'

Both Ulysses and Everett were silent, staring at me as if I'd suddenly grown another head.

I stared back, daring them to say another word.

'Don't waste your time on these bastards, Sugar,' Damian said, his voice warm with approval. 'Neither of them has any social skills to speak of and no one likes them anyway.'

Then his hold on me tightened and, without another

word to his gaping friends, he pulled me away through the crowd to the side of the gallery, near a big piece of sculpture.

His expression was full of admiration as he turned me to face him. 'Congratulations, Sugar. I don't think I've ever seen anyone speak to either of those two pricks like that before.'

I flushed. 'I was rude.'

'And they were ruder. I would have punched their faces in, but you saved me the trouble.' The respect in his eyes made my chest ache. 'Look, I know you can handle yourself, but I honestly wouldn't mind going and punching their faces in if you like anyway. Just say the word.'

Maybe it was the adrenaline, maybe it was triumph. Or maybe it was simply the way he was looking at me, full of warmth, approval and respect, but a rush of feeling suddenly swept over me, so hot, raw and intense that I didn't know what to do with myself.

It felt too big to keep inside me and I was up on my toes before I could stop the urge, brushing my mouth with his. 'Thank you,' I murmured against his lips. 'Thank you for the dress and the pearls. Thank you for making me feel like a princess instead of a nobody.'

Damian's silver eyes glinted and he smiled. Not the fake smile, the real one he saved just for me. And the hot feeling inside me intensified.

I knew what it was. I'd always known. It had been lying there inside me, like a seed waiting for the sun to make it bloom. And I don't know why I told him, when

I knew it wasn't what he wanted to hear. But I said it all the same, because I couldn't help myself.

'I love you,' I whispered.

And everything smashed to pieces like a glass bauble falling off a Christmas tree onto the floor.

Shock rippled over Damian's face, his smile vanishing, the warmth draining from his eyes. 'No.' His voice had gone harsh. 'No, Thea.'

Of course he'd say no. He'd been very clear from the outset that all of this was sex and fun. Nothing deep. Nothing meaningful. And I'd just turned that inside out.

No, I shouldn't have said it. Yet, now it was out, I didn't want to take it back. So I stayed where I was, my hands on his chest, looking up into his tarnished-silver eyes, letting him see what was in my heart. 'Yes, Damian,' I said simply. 'I love you.'

He lifted his hands, gripping my shoulders, his fingers digging into me. 'You can't,' he said flatly, as if just by saying it it would be true. 'You barely fucking know me.'

'I can and I know you well enough. Well enough to fall in love with you anyway.'

His mouth twisted in a kind of snarl and he let me go, stepping back at the same time, putting distance between us. 'That's not what we agreed.'

I felt cold now he wasn't near, but I didn't make any attempt to get close. 'I know it's not what we agreed. But it happened anyway.'

'So what do you want?' he demanded, anger suddenly glowing bright in his eyes. 'You want me to love you back? Is that it?'

My heart was a hot, tight knot in my chest and a dull kind of pain was echoing through me. I wasn't sure why it hurt so much. This was always going to have been his reaction and he'd warned me right from the start.

'No, I don't want anything from you.' I swallowed back the ache, lifting my chin and meeting his gaze head on. 'I told you that already.'

'Then why did you say it?' He looked at me as if I'd betrayed him. 'Fuck, Thea. Don't you know this changes everything?'

He was right, it did. And maybe if I'd been the Thea of a week or so ago I would have told him that it didn't change anything; that he could pretend I hadn't said it, that it didn't mean a thing.

But I wasn't that Thea any more. I wasn't the poor little ghost happy with some sex and fun and a few smiles. With a nice gown and some pearls. Who would tell him that it didn't matter, that I was happy with whatever he wanted to give me.

Because the truth was, I wasn't happy with that. I wanted more. I *needed* more. And he was the one who'd showed me that.

'You're right.' I tried to keep my voice steady, tried to stay calm. 'It does change things. But perhaps things need to change.'

'Thea—'

'I'm tired, Damian,' I went on, needing to say it. 'I'm tired of not wanting more than what people are prepared to give me. I'm tired of pretending that I'm not lonely. That I don't need someone to laugh with or someone to hold me when I'm sad. Tired of pretending I don't want a family or friends.' I stopped, my heartbeat thundering, a gritty feeling behind my eyes. 'I'm tired of pretending I don't need someone to love me, because I do. I really do.'

A fleeting look of anguish crossed his handsome face and then it was gone. He smiled, but it was a fake one this time, the one that didn't reach his eyes. That didn't make my heart feel like a flower blooming in the sun. 'Then I'm sorry, Sugar,' he said casually, 'but you've got the wrong man. You can't have any of that with me.'

My throat was so tight I could barely swallow, the dull pain throbbing in my chest. 'No,' I said thickly. 'But I could. If you weren't so afraid.'

He went very still at that and I knew I'd hit the mark.

Of course he was afraid and I knew why. Love for him had been all about demand, never about giving. I'd tried to give him what I could, but it clearly hadn't been enough. And maybe it never would be.

Maybe in the end, I just wasn't enough for him as I hadn't been enough for Mr Chen.

'Thea,' he began, a harsh note in his voice.

But I was done. 'Don't,' I said shortly. 'Don't say anything else.' I could feel the weight of the pearls around my neck and suddenly it was unbearable. A reminder of what he'd given me and how it paled in comparison to what I really wanted. I reached for them and

dragged them off, coiling the necklace around my hand
and holding it out to him. 'Here, take them.'

His gaze darkened as he glanced at the necklace,
then back at me. 'The pearls are yours. I don't want
them back.'

'I don't want jewels, Damian.' I stared right into his
eyes. 'I only want you.'

His mouth opened, but he didn't speak.

So I dropped the pearls in a heap at his feet.

Then I turned and walked away, leaving him standing there.

My heart breaking into tiny pieces as I went.

CHAPTER EIGHTEEN

Damian

I WATCHED THEA'S figure disappear into the crowd, the red silk of her gown fading, feeling as if something was trying to claw its way out of my chest from the inside, tearing and biting at me.

But I ignored it. Because letting her walk away from me was easier. Simpler.

For you, maybe. Not for her.

Yeah, well, she shouldn't have told me that she loved me, should she? She should have kept pretending that she didn't care. I'd never promised her anything different. Sex, fun and pleasure. That was it.

Yet as I bent to pick up the necklace she'd left at my feet, the pearls silky, smooth and still warm from her skin, I felt the pain echo through me. It was sharp, blinding. As if she'd stabbed me before she'd walked away.

But, fuck, what else could I have done? I'd *had* to let her go.

Love was a demanding master and I didn't want to deal with it any more.

She's right—you're afraid.

Jesus, no, I wasn't afraid. I just knew I'd fail her in the end, like I'd failed my mother and Morgan. Mum had died, despite what I'd done to try and save her, and Morgan's life had been turned upside down. I hadn't been able to save her either. So in the end it was better not even to try.

No, it was good I'd let Thea leave. Her apparent love for me would fade over time, just like her memories. She would find another man who'd give her what she needed. That man just wouldn't be me.

Forcing away the terrible sense that I'd just made a catastrophic mistake, I shoved the pearls in my pocket and re-joined the party, pasting my usual bullshit smile on my face and acting as if nothing was wrong. And, hey, if I pretended hard enough it would be, right?

Everett asked me at one point what had happened to Thea and I told him she'd gone home with a headache. He just looked at me as if I'd gone mad, which I didn't understand. Ulysses didn't seem to notice, which was par for the course with him, given he was socially challenged at the best of times, and this wasn't even the best of times.

The launch ended up being a huge success, the auction raising shitloads of money for the foundation and the cancer research facility, and after it was over I stayed on to drink champagne and laugh like I didn't give a fuck, the way I always did. Using alcohol to blot out the memory of Thea's retreating figure vanishing into the crowds.

It wasn't till much later that I finally made my way outside, to where the limo was sitting waiting for me. Only to find Morgan leaning against the side of it, her arms crossed.

Ah, shit. I'd been going to talk to her and had psyched myself up to do it at the beginning of the evening. But now Thea was gone, all I could think about was avoiding Morgan too.

Coward.

I wanted to deny the thought, but this time I couldn't seem to find the energy. Thea had said that I was afraid. Maybe she was right.

I slowed as I came down to the steps towards the limo. 'Can we have this discussion tomorrow?' I asked shortly. 'I'm too drunk for it now.'

'No.' Morgan stared at me, her blue eyes sharp as knives. 'You're not drunk.'

I wasn't either. The haze of alcohol had all burned off the moment I'd seen her. 'Okay, no, I'm not drunk,' I admitted. 'I just don't want to talk to you right now.'

Morgan ignored me. 'Where's Thea?'

I shrugged, as if it didn't matter. 'She's gone.'

'Ah.' Morgan's blue gaze had narrowed. 'So that's the problem.'

'What problem?'

'Don't be stupid, Damian. I saw the way you were looking at her at the beginning of the evening.' She gave me yet another searching look that I didn't much like. 'You sent her away, didn't you?'

I gave her my usual smile, even knowing how empty

it was. 'No, actually. It was her decision. She decided to leave.'

But Morgan wasn't fooled, which was typical. I'd never been able to fool her.

'I'd forgotten how bad you are at hiding things,' she said, staring at me. 'She means something to you, doesn't she?'

'Morgan, I'd really rather—'

'And you meant something to her. I could tell. I saw the way she looked at you, too.'

Everything in me tightened, and I wanted to walk away. Or to smile, tease her, distract her the way I used to do when she'd been small. When she used to put her arms around me and beg me to make it better.

But I couldn't make it better then and I couldn't make it better now.

'Sometimes it's easier not to care, Morgan,' I said before I could stop myself. 'Sometimes it's better just to let someone go.'

'Oh? Like you let me go?'

Clearly she wasn't pulling any punches tonight.

I gritted my teeth and made myself look her in the eye. 'I couldn't make it better for you. I couldn't help you.'

'So, what? You sent me away?'

'Yes.' My hands were in fists in my pockets, tension crawling between my shoulder blades. 'If that's what you want to know, yes. I sent you away. Because there was nothing I could do for you. Just like there wasn't anything I could do for Mum.'

Morgan glanced away abruptly, her mouth tight. 'You didn't have to do anything, Damian. Just being there was enough.'

There was an open hole where my heart was, a great, gaping wound.

And then suddenly, out of nowhere, I could feel Thea's fingers squeezing my hand, a ghost of her presence beside me letting me know she was there.

'Mum died, Morgan,' I said hoarsely, not knowing I was going to say it until then. 'I couldn't save her. She was in pain and I couldn't do anything. And then I couldn't do anything for you either…'

Morgan slowly turned to look at me, her face white. Then abruptly she pushed herself away from the limo and, before I could move, she was there, flinging her arms around me the way she used to and holding me tight.

She didn't say anything. Just hugged me.

'I failed you,' I heard myself say, the hole in my chest getting deeper and wider. 'I failed you and I failed Mum. And I let Thea go because I'll only end up failing her too.'

Morgan looked up at me, her blue eyes full of tears. 'You didn't fail,' she said fiercely. 'You were always there for me. And you were there for Mum too.'

'I couldn't make it better, Morgan. It's there in my head, all the time. The memories of you crying, of Mum hurting. They don't go away and they never fade.' My jaw ached, everything raw. 'Sometimes it's all I can think about.'

Morgan blinked, her gaze dark. 'Then you need different memories, Damian. Better ones.'

'You mean money isn't the answer?' It was a flippant, stupid response, but I couldn't think of anything better to say.

She scowled, treating my answer with the contempt it deserved. 'Don't be a dick. Honestly, you don't get better memories with money. It's with people, Damian.'

People like Thea.

I could still feel the clasp of her hand around mine, still see her smile. I remembered completely the first time I'd seen her, standing on the terrace in Hong Kong, frowning at me, my beautiful, dark-eyed mystery woman. And then the way she'd felt in my arms, warm and silky.

But there were more memories, too. Of her rare smiles and her fierce passion. And her generosity. Her honesty and her sympathy.

Her love.

I could feel that love. In the ghost of her hand around mine, in the warmth of the pearls in my pocket. In the strength of her demand that I give her more. In her refusal to settle for less.

She wasn't afraid to ask for what she deserved and she hadn't been afraid to call me out on my own cowardice.

She hadn't been afraid to tell me she loved me, even knowing that I had nothing to give her.

If she's not afraid, why are you?

I closed my eyes, my chest aching, everything aching. And I knew there was only one way I could stop the pain.

'Damian?' Morgan's voice was soft. 'Are you okay?'

'No.' I didn't open my eyes. 'I think I'm in love.'

'Oh,' Morgan said.

'Yeah. It fucking sucks.'

There was a silence and I let myself enjoy my little sister's hug for one moment longer. Then I released her and stood back. 'I'll talk to you again, kiddo. I promise. But there's a woman whose forgiveness I have to beg first.'

Morgan gave me a long, measured look. 'Better make it good, Damian.'

'Oh, don't worry, I will.' I turned towards the limo. 'I'll even get down on my knees if I have to.'

And I would.

Because I wasn't planning to come back without her.

CHAPTER NINETEEN

Thea

IT WAS EASY to find myself a cab and go back to the apartment on the Thames. Easy to slip out of my beautiful gown and change my clothes. Easy to pack a single backpack—I'd decided to travel light—and call a cab to take me to Heathrow.

I hadn't really thought through the whole getting back to Hong Kong thing, but with any luck there would be some standby seats on the next flight in that direction.

Going back home was the hard part. Now I knew what I was missing, knew who I was leaving. I wasn't sure what I was going to do about the business, given I hadn't got the Red Queen, and that would be the first request I hadn't been able to fulfil. But that was a worry for later, when the pain of leaving had faded.

When my broken heart wasn't lying shattered in my chest.

Heathrow was full of people even this late at night, the lights of the departures hall too bright, the sounds of people talking and the blare of the public announcement system too loud. And all of a sudden the thought of going back to the darkness seemed like a good thing. At least as a ghost, though I'd been lonely, I hadn't been in any pain.

I stood in line for a ticket, and I was lucky—there was a seat on the next flight out. It would be quite a come down from the trip over in Damian's corporate jet, but being safely anonymous in cattle class was exactly what I wanted right now.

There wasn't any point in waiting around in the departures area so I turned and began to walk towards Security.

And then someone from behind me said, 'Thea.'

The voice was deep and rich, the sound every fantasy I'd ever had.

I stopped in my tracks, my heartbeat thundering in my head. I didn't turn around. I couldn't. Because I knew who it was and I knew if I looked at him, if I saw his beautiful face, looked into his silver eyes, I'd be lost.

I'd forget everything I'd told him and fling myself into his arms. And then what would have been the point of walking away?

'You have every right to walk away from me,' Damian said quietly, his voice sounding much closer. 'And I'm not going to stop you. But I wanted to tell you something before you left.'

My heart was so loud I could barely hear him and I was shaking.

I should have just kept on walking, but I couldn't move my feet.

'I want you to know that you were right,' he said, his voice soft. 'Right to demand everything from me. Right to tell me that I was afraid. And you were right to walk away when I didn't give it to you.'

I shut my eyes, felt the tears prick.

'I *am* afraid. I failed to save my mother. I failed to give my sister the childhood she deserved. And I'm afraid I'll fail you, too. I'm afraid that I'll disappoint you, hurt you. That my love won't be enough.' He let out a breath. 'Because that's the problem, Thea. I love you. And I've loved you since the moment you turned up on my terrace at that stupid party. The moment I set eyes on you, standing there all quiet and still, watching me. I didn't know it then, but every second I've spent with you over the past week has only made it clearer.'

My chest was tight and so painful. I couldn't breathe. I didn't know what to do, whether to turn around or keep on going. Because all these things he was saying... I wanted to believe them so much.

'And I thought, if you had the courage to tell me you loved me, I should have the courage to tell you that I loved you back.' A fierce note entered his voice. 'So here I am, not being a fucking coward. Telling you that I love you. And I don't expect you to stay. I don't expect anything at all. I just thought you should know before you leave.'

He must have been close, because I could hear him just behind me, but he didn't touch me.

A tear slid down my cheek.

'It's wrong of me to ask this,' he whispered. 'Especially considering what I said to you at the museum. But… I don't want you to go. So please don't disappear on me, Sugar. Please stay.'

I stood there rigid, tears falling, my heart a hard ball in my chest. 'I don't want just a few days, Damian. You know that, don't you?'

His breath was warm on the back of my neck, and I shivered. 'I'm not offering you a few days. I'm offering you for ever.'

I trembled, my face wet. 'I don't want to force you into anything.'

And then his arms slid around me and he was gathering me close against his big, powerful body. 'No one can make me do anything I don't want to do,' he murmured in my ear. 'Except maybe you. But you're not forcing me into this. I want it. I want it more than I've ever wanted anything in my entire life.'

So I turned around in his arms and buried my face against his chest, in his heat and the delicious, familiar scent of him.

The handsome prince in his tux.

My handsome prince.

'Are you sure?' I asked. 'Are you really, positively, absolutely—?'

He didn't let me finish. Cupping my face between his palms, he tilted my head back and kissed me sweetly, softly, silencing me. And then, when an aeon had passed, he said, 'Tell me what you want. Tell me and I'll give it to you. Anything.'

'Take me home,' I whispered, my heart slowly knitting itself back together, the ache not so painful this time, but sweet. So very sweet. 'Take me home and love me.'

He smiled the smile he saved just for me. 'How about I take you home and marry you instead?'

What could I say but yes?

I might have broken into his apartment to steal a necklace, but I'd ended up stealing his heart instead.

And one thing was for sure: he wasn't getting it back.

EPILOGUE

Damian

I TOOK HER back to Hong Kong and we eloped to Italy the week after that.

She didn't want a big wedding and neither did I.

Our honeymoon was spent in a villa on the Amalfi coast and it was perfect. All Thea wore for at least a week was the black pearls I'd given her and nothing else.

And, when I wasn't making her feel special in every way that counted, I helped her figure out the fabulous new business she was going to manage herself. I'd decided to provide her with some capital to make Mr Chen's reacquisition business a little more legitimate, a little more legal. I had the contacts and the staff to help her out and, though she might lose out on some shadier clients, she'd make up for it in terms of legitimate ones.

More importantly, she could carry out Mr Chen's legacy but do it her way. On her own terms. And definitely not alone.

But it wasn't all on me. At night, by the pool in our villa, she got me to share stories about my mother and

Morgan, going over my memories of the good times, not the bad. Turned out there were a lot of good times.

There were going to be a lot of good times in the future too, lots of wonderful memories to be created, though I wasn't naive enough to think that meant there wouldn't be bad ones as well.

But this time I had her.

We had each other and that made all the difference.

* * * * *

THE FLING

STEFANIE LONDON

MILLS & BOON

To all the siblings, take care of one another.

CHAPTER ONE

Drew

"Wait, you're serious about having a *rehearsal* for the hen's night?" I stare at my sister's bridesmaids, each more tanned and manicured than the last. Annaleigh, Sherilee and…crap, what was the third one's name again? I'll call her Merrily in my head until I have a chance to ask my sister.

Not that there's anything merry about her, mind you. She's staring at me like I'm patient zero. Is it my fishnets? Maybe it's the fact that I was a little heavy-handed with the eyeliner today and ended up looking less Brigitte Bardot and more stripper-at-the-end-of-a-long-shift.

"Yes. We're *very* serious about having a rehearsal for the hen's night." Annaleigh exchanges a look with the other two, as though mentally questioning how my twin sister and I share DNA.

Thankfully, Presley isn't here tonight.

I swear I'd intended to play nice. My twin and I might be chalk and cheese, as my mum always likes to say, but I love Presley. I really do…just not her taste in clothing, men, food, music, home decor or life interests.

Nor her taste in friends, either, it seems.

"This wedding is going to be perfect." Sherilee tucks a strand of hair behind her ears, revealing a winking stone that's so big it must be putting strain on her earlobe. It pales in comparison to the one on her finger, however. "Capital *P* Perfect. That means every event before the wedding will be perfect, too. The bridal shower, the kitchen tea, the dress fittings, the makeup and hair trials, the rehearsal dinner, the Jack and Jill party *and* the hen's night."

"The Jack and what?" My head is spinning.

"The Jack and Jill party." Merrily sighs as if she thinks I'm a small, dumb animal. "It's a combined hen's and buck's party."

"In additional to the *actual* hen's and buck's party?"

"Yes," all three of them say at once with identical, exasperated tones.

"And *you're* organising it, along with the best man," Annaleigh says. "I've passed on your email address, so you should hear from him soon. All the events have been divided up. You've got the Jack and Jill, and the presentation for the rehearsal dinner. I've got…"

Oh, boy. I've already tuned out the droning list of tasks that lie ahead of me.

I look longingly at my beer, which sits untouched, condensation gathering on the glass, next to three flutes of prosecco. I feel like being the first to reach for the booze will be seen as a sign of weakness, like flinching in a fight. But *man*, I could use a drink right now.

I picture my sister's sweet face, with her silvery-blue eyes so similar to mine—sans stripper makeup, of course—and tell myself to get my shit together. Do it for Presley! I'm an adult and I deal with snotty people all the time at work. I'm a flight attendant, after all. I can totally manage this.

When Annaleigh pauses to take a breath, I put on my brightest smile. It doesn't crack any of the icy facades in front of me. "How do you all know Presley?"

"We work together," Merrily replies.

"Oh, right." I nod. Finally, something I know. "At the Wentworth Department Store."

"Head office," Sherilee adds. "I'm in the communications team, Annaleigh works with Presley in training and Pauline is in recruitment."

Pauline. I make a mental note to remember Merrily's real name this time.

"Sounds fun," I say benignly. There's a beat of silence and I shift in my seat.

"Presley told us that you go by your middle name, right?" Annaleigh asks, as though she's trying to keep the conversation from stalling completely. "We're having T-shirts printed for the hen's night. Would you prefer Melanie or Drew?"

"Drew."

Melanie might be the name on my birth certificate and passport, but I've always been Drew to my family and friends. I got my middle name from my Uncle

Andrew. It's a weird quirk of our family. Presley is the same; her real first name is Anne, but no one calls her that.

"Why don't you use your real name?" Pauline asks.

I shrug. "It's kind of…basic."

She frowns. "My sister's name is Melanie."

An awkward silence descends over the group, burrowing under my skin. But the moment Sherilee opens her mouth and begins to discuss the best type of napkin origami for rehearsal dinner table settings, I question my stance on silence.

An hour later, things have not improved. I'm learning that weddings are serious business, with Google spreadsheets and accountabilities and brainstorming sessions and rehearsals and *dress* rehearsals. I wouldn't be shocked if one of them asked me to set a SMART goal for how I want the wedding to go.

And it's not even my damn wedding!

Better live vicariously while you can, Little Miss Not-Marriage-Material.

I shake off my snarky inner voice and concentrate on my second beer. Not only did I cave and reach for my drink before any of them even glanced at their prosecco, but I'm currently entering the stage of the evening where my verbal filter clocks out.

And unfiltered Drew is *not* for the faint of heart.

"So, games for the hen's night. We're thinking something fun, like a quiz on how well we know Presley." Pauline taps a Montblanc pen against her chin. "Maybe some wedding-related trivia."

"And pass the parcel." Annaleigh claps her hands together. "We could include fun wedding things, like a garter and a pen for signing the guest book."

"Or condoms." The comment slips out before I can check in with my brain. See? Unfiltered. "You know, for the…wedding night."

Sherilee laughs awkwardly and moves her pen as if she's writing it down, but I can see that no ink is being wasted on my suggestion.

"I saw this cute take on pin the tail on the donkey," Pauline says. "But you had to pin the kiss marks on a picture of Ryan Gosling. Fun, right?"

This suggestion is met with a round of appreciative *oohs*. I went to a hen party once where we had to pin something on a poster of a hot, half-naked guy…and it wasn't a kiss. But I get the impression that games involving photorealistic male appendages *also* wouldn't make the cut for Presley's capital *P* Perfect hen's night.

Stop snarking. Now.

"What about a goodbye singleton treasure hunt?" I suggest. "A friend of mine did that last year and it was really fun."

"Sounds interesting." Annaleigh drums her nails against the tabletop. "How does it work?"

"It's kind of like *The Amazing Race* but for all the things you would do when you were single. You get a point for each item—get a guy's phone number, dance on a table, do a shot with a dirty name."

"Actually, that sounds *super* fun." Annaleigh looks at me, surprised.

Phew. Maybe I won't disappoint Presley after all.

"We could have a scaling point system. The more difficult the item, the higher the point value. And we could have tie-breaker activities in case two people have the same amount of points." Sherilee's eyes widen. "I'll make a spreadsheet."

I decide it's a good idea to end on a high note. I've provided one useful suggestion—which *did* get written down, thank you very much—so that means I can now make a graceful-ish exit. Well, as graceful as is possible after a couple of beers while wearing platforms.

"Ladies, as much as I am *thoroughly* enjoying myself right now, I've got an early start tomorrow," I announce. "Can we wrap this up?"

"Sure." Annaleigh looks as relieved as I feel. "Sherilee is our resident note taker, so she'll send the minutes out. If you could review them and respond within twenty-four hours, that would be great."

I nod, swallowing my growing desire to murder my sister. "Absolutely. I will definitely read every single word. Even the footnotes."

At this, Sherilee perks up. "Usually *nobody* reads my footnotes."

Sarcasm is a foreign language, I see. Lord help me. I down the remainder of my beer and rest the empty pint glass on the bar with a *thunk*. "Happy to be the first."

"And the best man will email you tomorrow," Annaleigh reminds me. "If you don't hear from him, let me know."

I climb down from my bar stool and bid them a good

night. The bar's clientele mirrors my sister's friends—suits and pencil skirts, perfectly highlighted hair. Pearls, diamonds, Louboutins. Presley would fit right in. I decide to text her as I walk.

DREW: I love you more than anyone else on earth.

PRES: Wow. That bad, huh?

DREW: Where do you find these people?

PRES: They're my friends, D. Be nice. I know they're a little intense.

DREW: Ya think?

PRES: They mean well.

Debatable. I got some hella strong Regina George vibes tonight, but I vowed I would not let my personal shit interfere with my sister's big day. That means no snarking at her friends.

DREW: How long til this is all over? ;)

PRES: Three weeks. And trust me, I want this done as much as you do.

Unlikely, but I'll let her have it. I might look like the lovechild of Debbie Harry and Wednesday Addams, but inside I'm a big ball of mush when it comes to my sis-

ter. Nothing will get between us. Not even email minutes with footnotes.

PRES: And don't do that thing where you shut everyone out before they have a chance to get to know you.
You might make a friend!

Three hearts punctuate my sister's text. If ever there
was physical evidence of the difference between us,
this is it. Shaking my head, I continue down Clarendon
Street toward my temporary residence in South Melbourne. 21 Love Street is the most ridiculous name for
an apartment building, even one as swanky as this. But
I'm grateful to have the cushy place to stay until the
wedding is over.

And truthfully, the people here *do* seem nice. It's
been so long since I lived in Melbourne that I don't
have many contacts in this city—and the one friend I
do have is away and letting me crash in her apartment.
My friends are scattered all over the world, a product
of working as a flight attendant all my adult life. Do a
stint in Dubai and another in Singapore and one more
in London and you'll end up with a globally fragmented
social circle.

But that suits me fine. I make do wherever I go,
and my colleagues are always up for some fun when
they're in town.

I enter the building, marvelling as I usually do at the
foyer's softly glowing chandelier that manages to somehow *not* be tacky. A couple of velvet chairs are dotted
around and some pretty art hangs on the main wall.

Capital P *Perfect!*

I stifle a laugh and head to the elevators. The concierge desk is empty, with a sign stating they're currently "on patrol." That's been happening a lot ever since they found out a crime ring was operating out of this building last week. Yeah, *that* happened. Doesn't bother me, though. I enjoy a little excitement in my life.

I tap my foot, waiting while the elevator does its thing. But it's taking forever. Five minutes pass. Then ten. The concierge still hasn't returned to his post. Grumbling, I head toward the service stairwell and start making my way up.

CHAPTER TWO

Flynn

"FLYNN ANDREW LEWIS, what are you *still* doing here?"

I drag my eyes up from my screen to look at my assistant, Francis, standing in the doorway to my office—arms folded, lips pursed. She's the only person who can get away with using my full name because she's *also* the only assistant who's lasted more than five minutes working for me.

Still, I won't let her get too big for her boots.

"How do you do that?" I wave my pen in her direction.

"What?"

"Channel my mother so effectively."

She narrows her eyes at me. "Are you calling me old?"

The ironic thing is that if my mother were still alive, she would actually be *younger* than Francis by a good decade. And while I might be known as "that jerk in the navy suit" to most people who work in this industry, even *I* know not to call a woman old.

"I would say more…draconian." This gets the result I predict—intensified lip pursing.

"It's nine p.m."

"I know how to tell the time." I turn back to my screen, trying to make the numbers spin a different story. It's futile, but still more productive than looking at my inbox—which resembles the aftermath of a toddler toy-flinging rampage.

"Flynn." This time my name is softer.

I know she means business when she talks like that—because to everybody else in this company Francis is a stony-faced, rule-spouting gatekeeper. She's all: *you shall not pass.* It's why she's so good at her job. But *I* know she's actually a lovely woman with a heart of gold—a fact she prefers to keep hidden.

Generally, I prefer it when she keeps it hidden, too.

"You haven't left this place before midnight in over a month. It's not healthy." She sighs. "I know you care about these trials. I do, too. Everybody does."

My niece, Zoe, stares at me from a photo on the side of my desk. She's like a laser burning into my skin, reminding me over and over. Pushing me. Driving me to stay one more hour. "Then we have to keep working."

"If you don't start taking care of yourself, I'm going to walk in here one day and find you dead on your desk from a heart attack." When I don't take my eyes off my screen, she claps. The sound is a bullet through the room.

"Did you just *clap* at me?" I gape. "You know I sign off on your bonus, right?"

She folds her arms. "Trust me, I don't work solely for the money."

"Then why am I paying you more than most people here?"

"Because you're trying to convince me not to retire so you don't have to churn through twenty more assistants before you find another one who will put up with you."

Damn, she got me there. "I did not enjoy that."

"Neither did they, I'm betting." Her face is full of concern. "It's one night. You won't solve the world's problems today. Go home, eat some crappy takeaway food and watch television like a normal person."

I want to tell her that I don't own a television, just to wind her up…but I feel like she might explode from frustration. And she's right, I *don't* want her to retire. Not yet.

"If you don't leave now, I'm going to shred every document in the office and then set it all on fire." She stares pointedly at me.

"You know our servers have a triple-redundancy that backs up to a secure off-site location, right?" I can't keep my face straight and she shakes her head at me. "See, you're doing it again. Better stop or I'll start calling you Mum."

"Get. Out. Of. Here. Right. Now." She punctuates each word with a clap.

"All right, all right." I shove my chair back and smooth my hands down the front of my suit pants. "No need for the aural abuse."

Francis watches as I grab my trench coat and look longing at my laptop—my inbox exploded past two thousand emails earlier this afternoon and I could use a night of digital filing.

If only Mum could see you now.

My mother, who believed wholeheartedly that life was a party, would be appalled by my lack of social life.

Good.

Besides, I go to charity balls and cocktail parties on the regular—it's part and parcel of being a CEO. Though I have to admit, even when I'm there in body, my mind is always on work. The picture of my niece continues to watch me from the desk and I make her a silent promise, as I do every day, that I will help her.

"Come on, out with you." Francis herds me into the common area, which is mostly empty. I spy my head of IT bent over someone's desk and the CFO talking on his phone. I have a great team—built from scratch with my own bare hands. I've met a lot of top dogs who surround themselves with sycophants, but I always promised myself I wouldn't do that. I want people who are renowned in their fields. People who challenge me.

Maybe not as much as Francis challenges me, mind you.

On the way down on the elevator, my mind spins.

Go home, eat some crappy takeaway food and watch television like a normal person.

Is that what normal people do? I can't remember the last time I did anything in my apartment that wasn't changing my clothes, sleeping or taking a shower. It's basically a hotel room at this point. I don't eat there. I don't entertain. The closest thing I get to free time is the hour I spend at the gym every morning running on the treadmill and lifting weights while I listen to the notes that Francis voice-recorded the evening before.

I *live* for my job.

How many people can say that? I threw in a seven-figure salary as the youngest equity partner with a boutique consulting agency to start my own company. A company with a purpose that is more than raking in zeroes. I wanted to do something important with my life, not be another thoughtless corporate drone whose only care in the world is whether to holiday in Europe or the Maldives.

My frustration builds as I walk the short block to my apartment. Francis can get on her high horse about the way I live my life, but I'm doing *exactly* what I want to be doing. And that's not being some money-chasing egomaniac like my mother, a woman who was only ever capable of giving a shit about herself.

I enter my apartment building, trying to shrug off the bad memories along with my coat. A night without the distraction of filing emails seems like a daunting task. Quiet moments are the worst. Maybe that's another reason working 24/7 appeals to me—easier to avoid the stuff I don't want to deal with.

"Mr. Lewis." The concierge waves me over as I enter. The poor man looks like he's run through a tornado—his tie is skewed, his hair mussed. "We've had some issues with the elevators today, but they're working now.

Just wanted to let you know in case they take a bit longer than normal while we get everyone up to their apartments."

I nod and continue on. I don't know my neighbours. Hell, I couldn't even tell you who lived next door. I'm not one of those people who feels the need for community connection. Nor do I want to attend the various social events the building puts on for its residents. Frankly, if I had to stand around making small talk with people I don't know or care about, then I'd rather be doing it where I might find an investor for my business.

When the elevator arrives, it's crammed. So, I wait for the next one. It's not like I've got to rush upstairs for anything, after all. My cupboards are spartan, and my fridge is worse. The only thing ingestible in the whole place is the protein powder I take after my morning workout and a bottle of cognac my brother gave me for Christmas.

Not exactly the ingredients for an enticing dinner.

When I reach my floor, I step into the hallway and approach my apartment with an increasing sense of dread. This is ridiculous. It's the same damn place I come home to every night. But now it's ominous, like something I've built up to mammoth proportions. A representation of how little my life contains.

"Hello?"

A voice startles me and I turn, my gaze swinging across the empty hallway. There's not a soul around. Great. Now on top of this unwanted and unappreciated trip down "existential crisis" lane, I'm losing my mind, too. Francis is going to pay for this tomorrow.

"Is someone there?" A loud thump draws my eyes to the service stairwell. "Hello? I need help."

The voice is definitely female, but I don't recognise it. I pull on the door. It's locked. That's when I notice an electronic keypad flashing: *Error. Enter code.*

"The door is locked," I say.

"No shit," the voice snaps. "Why else would I be in here?"

"Self-reflection?" The comeback slips out before I can think better of it.

"You're a regular smartass, aren't you?"

I'm tempted to leave the woman in the stairwell. It's not my problem and I've had enough abuse for one day. But the second I start to walk away, my conscience kicks in and I almost growl in frustration. I can't leave a person stranded.

"Hello?" she tries again.

"I'm still here."

"Look, buddy. I've had the day from hell and all I want is to get into my apartment so I can faceplant in a tub of ice cream and eat my emotions. Think you can help me out?"

"I'll see what I can do."

"Try *really* hard."

Shaking my head, I bend down to look more closely at the keypad. It has a thin layer of plastic covering it and I notice some dust and paint shavings on the floor. Then everything clicks into place—I'd bet my last ten bucks they installed these things today and blew a fuse while testing them out. That probably tripped the security system and shut the elevators down.

Which could mean… I punch 1234 into the electronic pad and the screen flashes once, twice and then displays the word: *open*. Yep, they haven't set up the passcodes yet.

I yank the door open. For a moment, my brain stutters like a lawnmower failing to start. The woman in the stairwell looks like she's stepped out of my wildest, dirtiest fantasies—endless legs in fishnet stockings, waist-length hair that's so pale it's almost white, and a leather miniskirt and lace-up boots. Not to mention the black eyeliner that rims her eyes, making the silvery-blue irises seem otherworldly.

Looking at her is like being shocked with jumper cables.

I have definitely *not* seen her around before. Suddenly, I'm acutely aware of how long it's been since I was with someone. Every woman I've dated has been a strategic decision, because I don't waste time with short-term flings and one-night stands. I only do what gets me closer to my goals—and casual sex doesn't.

But work has taken over everything. My personal life is a husk and…well, I've been flying solo in the bedroom for a while. My sex life is a wasteland. A ghost town. And this is the first sign of life I've felt in over a year. Sensation rockets through me, blanking out the worries that usually clog my mind and filling me with a strong, pleasurable hum. Maybe denying myself for

so long wasn't a smart move—because I'm feeling like
a man crawling through the desert, with water shimmering on the horizon.

I hold the door open for her, tamping down the un-
characteristic surge of attraction. "You're welcome,"
I quip.

"I didn't say thank you," she replies, a wicked curve
pulling at her lips. "Yet."

CHAPTER THREE

Drew

I DUST MYSELF off and roll my shoulders back, trying not to wince at the pain in my feet. These boots were *not* made for climbing four flights of stairs. Mr. Suit is watching my every move like his life depends on it—though I don't mind. He's gorgeous. If I had to make a quick guess I'd say mid-thirties, a lawyer/banker/insert mind-numbing profession here. But his suit fits like a dream, nipping in a trim waist and accenting broad shoulders. He might be desk-bound, but he works out. His eyes are the colour of the sky and his hair has an attractive reddish sheen to it, with warm-toned stubble on his sharp jaw to match.

Who would have known I'd be hot for a ginger?

"Were you stuck in there long?" He steps back so I can escape the concrete column of doom.

"How long is too long without phone reception? I was starting to worry I'd have to forage for food." I cock my head. "Why don't I know you? Do you live on this floor?"

He nods. "405."

"We're neighbours, then. I'm in 406." I have a sudden urge to do something bold—to shake off the critical voice that's been nagging me ever since I packed my bags and flew home to Melbourne. Each night has been an exercise in distraction—Netflix binges until I fall asleep, trying not to wish the weeks away so I can get on with my next adventure. Being home makes me antsy.

But tonight just got a whole lot more interesting.

"Want to come in for a drink?" I tilt my head, studying my smart-mouthed rescuer. The guy looks serious, like he's got a gold medal in frowning. But I sense something beneath the surface—a simmering heat, like he's stripping me back. I've had a lot of guys look at me over the years…but nothing like this.

It's like I'm something precious behind glass.

"Is that your way of saying thank you?" he asks. There's a slight crinkle to the edge of his eyes—like a delightful chink in his armour. "With liquor."

"It only seems fair. After all, if you hadn't come along, the poor concierge guy might have found a pile of bones at the top of the stairs. It would have traumatised him for life." I nod, a mock sincere expression on my face. "You're basically a national hero."

He laughs, but still hasn't accepted my offer. There's no ring on his finger—no tan lines, either. That doesn't mean he's single, however, and for a moment my heart drops like a stone off a cliff. It's stupid. I've recently come out of the biggest heartbreak of my life and I am *not* looking for anything.

In fact, when I'd hastily thrown everything I owned into two suitcases, tears streaming down my face, I'd promised myself I was done with trying to live up to other people's expectations. And I was certainly done with men in suits. Men with money. Men who had more power and more value than me.

Mr. Suit is clearly one of those guys. Wrong for me. Bad for me. And so tempting my body is throwing a party. Which should be the biggest red flag of all—because the more I want a guy, the bigger a jerk he usually turns out to be.

I open my mouth to rescind my offer, but he nods. "Sure, why not?"

What happened to turning over a new leaf, huh? Learning from your mistakes?

Sadly, my brain is out of there so fast only a brain-shaped cloud of dust remains.

I can't find the willpower to turn him away, because this guy's magnetism is so strong, my body is almost vibrating with want. There's something about him—something mysterious and enticing that's like a hand pulling me closer so he can whisper naughty things in my ear.

I head toward my temporary apartment and pull the key out of my bag. "I didn't think you'd say yes for a minute."

"Neither did I."

The way he says it sends a delicious shiver through me. Maybe this is exactly what I need right now—a little instant gratification to smooth the edges of the

gaping hole where my heart used to be. A meaningless make-out session with a random guy to boost my
confidence. Possibly a hookup. Quick, dirty, with no
tomorrows. With no talking and no plans and no worrying about what happens next.

Yeah, psychologists would have a field day with me.
But I'm reaching deep into the bag of fucks I have to
give and I'm coming up empty.

*Aren't you getting ahead of yourself? You only in-
vited him in for a drink.*

Everyone knows what that means, right? Sure, he's
my neighbour and I probably wouldn't go there under
normal circumstances. But I'm only here until the wedding, and then I'm taking off for some sunshine and
sand while I sort my life out. This situation is temporary, so who cares if I have to avoid him in the elevators for a little while afterward?

"Nice place," he says as we walk into the apartment.

"It's not mine." I glance at the chic decor, with the
eclectic art making up the gallery wall next to the dining table, and unique trinkets from all over the world
adding life and personality to the room. "I'm only here
for a few weeks."

Mr. Suit raises an eyebrow. "Why's that?"

"I don't like staying in one place." I shrug out of my
jacket and toss it over the back of a chair. "Life's too
short to set down roots."

Mr. Suit snorts. "Ah, so you hate responsibility."

I bristle, more because it's true than because it's a
rude thing to say. I don't like being easy to read—it

makes me vulnerable. I decide then and there not to tell this guy *anything* real. Nothing about my life, about my job, about my family. If this goes somewhere, it'll be all about the pleasure. The physical. I can tuck the real me away into a little box and let my alter ego out to play.

"Let me guess." I walk straight to the vintage bar cart and wriggle my fingers over the generous selection of liquors Charlotte thoughtfully told me to "go *ham*" on. "You're pro-responsibility."

"I am."

I sense him behind me, the chemistry snapping like an electric fence around us. I don't think I've been so attracted to someone this quickly before—usually I like to suss a guy out. Dig a little deeper. But I don't want to do that with Mr. Suit, because I know it'll be bad, bad, bad, all the way down.

Better to go by the ignorance-is-bliss principle.

I pull the lid off a bottle of Glenfiddich and pour two glasses. The heavy cut-crystal tumblers are like weights in my hand, and I turn to Mr. Suit, offering one to him. "And you're a workaholic, which is why I haven't seen you around before."

"Perceptive." As he takes a sip of his drink, I notice the way the amber liquid mimics the reddish tones in his hair. "But not exactly an out-of-the-box guess. You could do better."

Oh, really? Challenge most definitely accepted.

"You're a hardass. You've lost employees because they hated working for you." The words shoot out of me. Yep, Unfiltered Drew is in fine form tonight. "You don't need to fire people, because they leave of their own accord."

Instead of being insulted, he smirks. "Better, but not great."

He's goading me. Trying to get me to say something horrible. Is he looking for a reason to walk away?

Too bad, Mr. Suit... I've got you right where I want you.

Need flows through my body like sparkling champagne, fizzy and light. For the past three months I've felt nothing but self-loathing, heartache and resentment. It's like my ex hollowed me out with a rusty spoon. But now I'm alive—and the hurt is quiet. The shame is quiet. I'm in control and it feels amazing.

You deserve this.

Just one night of pleasure for the sake of pleasure. Like cheating on your diet with greasy pizza and beer—tomorrow I can get back on the horse. Tomorrow I can go back to trying to sort my shit out. But right now...

"People think you're uptight, but underneath you're a little wild." I sip my Scotch, enjoying the way it warms me. "You've got a bad streak."

"And?" His blue eyes are locked on mine—unwavering and unafraid. This is a man who's used to having the upper hand, who expects others to bend to him. I've dealt with his type before—the key is to meet them at their level.

"And you're here because the second you opened that door to the stairwell, you knew you wanted to sleep with me." I drain the rest of my Scotch and set the glass down. There's no beating around the bush—we both know what this is. Why sugar-coat it? I'd seen the flare of heat in his eyes and I knew what it meant.

Mr. Suit laughs and the sound is like gravel and shadows and darkness. It's the sexiest thing to ever grace my ears. "You're bold."

"I'm honest."

"And that's a rare quality." He sets his glass down. It's not empty. "But I only came for a drink."

"Bullshit."

He smooths his hand down the front of his suit, strong fingers caressing the wool in a way that has my mind conjuring all kinds of sexy mental images. They're white-collar hands—uncalloused, smooth.

And I would bet the last cent in my bank account that he knows how to use them.

"Am I not your type?" I tilt my face up to his. I'm tall, especially in these boots, but he's still got half a head on me.

The corner of his lips twitch. But it's not cruel, more…amused. "You're so far from my type I'm not even sure how to categorise it."

Well, he certainly doesn't pull any punches. "Should I clutch my pearls and tell you I have a wardrobe of twinsets and flat shoes in my bedroom? Would that make a difference?"

"I don't do casual sex."

Despite what people assume based on my choice of outfits—and believe me, they do—I don't usually indulge in casual sex, either. I've had a few boyfriends, and a few flings. A lone one-night stand in my twenty-seven years. But I've always been a relationship girl, secretly. Which is why I was ready to give it all to Vas... until he made it clear that forever had never been his intention.

"That doesn't mean I'm not attracted to you..." Mr. Suit frowns. "Is it weird if I ask for your name now?"

"While you're in the middle of turning me down?" I laugh. "Why bother?"

He nods. "Right. Anyway, it's not you. It's me."

"Unoriginal." I shake my head. "I'm so disappointed."

Despite the fact that he's walking away, I'm feeling more like myself than I have in weeks. I'm going after something I want, setting my own rules. I'm not shrinking into my sadness anymore. That sounds like progress, right?

"Trust me when I say it's not you. Because I could happily tear those stockings off with my teeth and make a meal of you." His gaze rakes over me, leaving fire in its wake. "And it *is* me, because I don't have time for anything besides my work."

"I'm not asking for anything beyond tonight."

"Neither am I." He looks as though he might offer further explanation, but then he walks across the room and grabs his coat. "Now, I'm going to head home and get myself off in the shower while thinking about your incredible legs."

I'm left standing open-mouthed as he disappears into the hallway. A second later I hear his door slam shut.

CHAPTER FOUR

Drew

IT'S PAST MIDNIGHT and I can't sleep. I've got a head full of bad memories and images of my sexy next-door neighbour, which is a potent and annoying cocktail. So I'm restless, tossing and turning until the bed-sheets wind around my legs like a python going in for the kill.

If only I didn't have to come home for Presley's wedding. If only I hadn't let myself fall for a guy who was destined to break my heart. But oh, no, I had to go and think that I could be the only woman he *wasn't* lying to when he told me he loved me. Even though I knew his reputation, I fooled myself into thinking that I was different. That I was special.

What could be further from the truth?

Huffing, I untangle myself and get out of bed. My bare feet hit the cool floorboards and I realise I'm burning up. Tossing and turning is quite the workout.

The apartment is quiet and unfamiliar. I've only been back in Melbourne for three weeks and already it's reminding me of all the reasons why I left—how far I've fallen behind my sister. How much more lovable she is.

I pad out to the main room where the window looks out over South Melbourne. The view is awash with glimmering lights, and in the far corner of the view, I can see the occasional car gliding along Clarendon Street. It's Wednesday night, so the traffic isn't too heavy. I've always found the noise comforting—because total quiet unsettles me. It means I have to focus on what's in my head, instead of something easier. Something more tangible.

Pulling open the sliding door to the balcony, I almost sigh in relief when the cool air hits my skin. The rain has stopped and it smells glorious—like springtime and wet grass and jasmine and life. This apartment is on the corner of the building, with the balcony facing the back of the property. The garden below is lush and beautiful, and I can totally see why my friend bought this place.

I lean my forearms against the railing and suck in a big breath. I'm wearing an oversized white T-shirt, which the breeze flutters around my body. I have no idea how long I stand there, leaning and trying not to think. Just feeling. Eventually I'll need to get back to bed, but as I turn, I catch a glimpse of something. A warm light emanating from the apartment next to me.

I can only see into Mr. Suit's place because of the angle of the corner apartment, and even then it's not a full view. Only a sliver. But it's enough for me to see the glow of a room inside the otherwise dark apartment. A door is open, and light spills from what looks like a bedroom. A shadowy figure emerges, momentarily blotting the light with its broad frame.

My breath catches in my throat as the figure stills. Can he see me peering in? For a second I freeze, mortified at being caught looking like some peeping Tom. What the hell am I thinking? It's a total invasion of his privacy, especially after he said no to me.

He also said he was going to go home and get off while thinking about you.

Images swirl of him in the shower, water streaming over what I know will be a rock-hard body, while he reaches one of those strong, long-fingered hands down between his legs…

I shiver.

The figure is still standing there. Unmoving. Waiting.

Waiting for me?

It's a silent standoff. I should go inside before I embarrass myself further in front of this guy…but something keeps my feet rooted to the ground. Desperate desire winds through my system, slow and steady like the drip of condensation down a glass on a summer's day. I want him. I want the feeling of hot, confident hands roaming my body and stubble-roughened kisses on my neck.

When the shadow disappears into the darkened apartment, I think the show might be over. Disappointment stabs me in the gut. I'm *definitely* going to have to avoid this guy in the elevator until I skip town. Lord, what am I going to tell my friend when she comes back?

Hey, sorry if things are a little weird between you and the guy next door. I unsuccessfully propositioned him for sex and then stared into his window in the middle of the night.

But then a lamp flicks on inside the apartment. The warm glow grows enough that I can see more detail—the white towel around his waist, the shadow of definition in his muscular torso, the brooding expression on his face. In the dim light, his hair looks like burning embers, matching the intensity of how he watches me, watching him.

I swallow and find my mouth dry, waiting for him to wave me away. Or mouth an appropriate "what the fuck?" while glaring at me. But nothing like that happens. He takes a step forward, more fully into the light. I can see more detail now—the smattering of hair on his chest and the trail that winds from his bellybutton down to where the towel is knotted, riding low on his hips. Any lower down and I'd be able to tell whether the bulge there is from the material of the towel or something else.

Show him what he missed by walking out on you tonight.

There's that dark little voice again. The one that urges me to make bad decisions and get into trouble.

I skim my hand along the edge of the T-shirt, fingertips dancing across my bare thigh. The hem barely covers the bottom of my cotton underwear—tonight it's pink and red stripes—and I gently brush the T-shirt up enough to expose it.

Mr. Suit's chest moves sharply, as though he's sucked in a quick breath. The guy is so cut I second-guess my assumption that he works in an office. His shoulders are strong and round, his biceps deliciously curved, but it's the flex in his jaw that does me in. Like he's grinding his teeth, trying to hold his reaction back…and failing.

Emboldened by the fact that he's still watching, I draw the hem of my T-shirt up higher. Cool air grazes my bare stomach, and I hold the material just over my breasts—teasing at what might be beneath without actually showing him.

Mr. Suit stalks toward the glass. Oh, yes, there's definitely a bulge under that towel. His eyes are so strikingly blue that I'm captured for a moment. He's much closer now, his face still shadowed by the dim light inside. There's no balcony outside his bedroom—they stagger the rooms here, and his bedroom shares a wall with my living room. That means the balconies are spaced apart—probably so the residents don't feel in each other's pockets if they're both outside. But it means I can't hear him. The double-glazed windows keep all the sound inside. His mouth moves, but I'm too dazed to lip-read.

But then I catch one word: *more*.

He wants more? Am I really going to do this? Give a stranger a peep show while anyone else could come outside and see?

It's late. Everyone is getting up early for work tomorrow. Nobody else will see you.

Won't they? I swallow.

Mr. Suit nods. *More.*

Biting down on my lip, I drag the T-shirt higher up, exposing my naked breasts to the night air and to Mr. Suit's hungry gaze. My nipples peak at the shock of the cool breeze and my sex clenches when I see his reaction—that single flame sparking and catching alight. Creating an inferno.

Holding the fabric with one hand, I let my other hand roam over my stomach and up to my breasts, squeezing and pinching. It sends arrows of excitement through me, heating up my blood and creating a dull pulse in my sex. I feel powerful like this—in charge and beautiful and naughty and brave.

Mr. Suit's lips part and I imagine the sound coming out of him, letting my mind fill in the blanks so I get the whole experience. I've never done anything like this before—so brazen and bad. But it feels good. *So* good.

"More," he mouths.

I dip my hand over my stomach and toy with the waistband of my underwear. There's a little bow right below my navel, and I dance my fingers over it before snapping the elastic against my skin. But I don't want to be the only one playing this game—if he wants more, then I need a show of faith. I need to know I'm not the only vulnerable party.

I nod toward him, to where he's holding the knot at his waist. His eyes darken and he reaches down, squeezing himself through the fluffy fabric. I almost go weak at the knees; the sight of him handling himself is insanely hot. Not to mention it looks like he's got *quite* the handful there.

I dip my fingers under the elastic of my underwear, finding myself wet and ready. A sigh slips out as I brush over my clit—the tight bundle of nerves sending a jolt of pleasure through me.

Oh, God, am I really doing this?

For a moment, doubt roars in my head. What would Perfect Presley think if she knew I was giving a stranger a peep show? What about the Stepford bridesmaids? What would Vas think? My thoughts darken for a second. Vas wouldn't think anything because I was nothing but a toy to him anyway. A plaything. A disposable pleasure.

Fuck Vas. And fuck what other people think, too. I'm done with that. This is for me, because right now I feel good and I'm a grown woman who can make her own bloody decisions.

I touch myself again, circling my fingers over my most sensitive part and letting out a soft groan. Not too loud—because I don't want anyone else but Mr. Suit to come outside and see the show. It feels so good, with his eyes on me, his mouth slack and his hand palming himself through the towel. I wish it was his hands on me. I let myself imagine what would have happened if he'd stayed and stripped me out of my fishnets and my leather skirt.

If he'd taken me to bed and laid me down, peeling the underwear from my body and sliding his hands back up my thighs, thumbs tracing circles on my skin. Getting higher, higher, higher…so close.

My eyes flutter shut and I'm lost. I imagine his big body covering me, knees pushing my legs apart as he presses his lips to mine. The fantasy plays out in vivid colour and a tremor rips through me. Everything is wound tight like a coil. I'm so close…so close.

I apply the right pressure and my orgasm breaks. Release is sweet and swift and I steady myself with one hand against the balcony railing. When I open my eyes, Mr. Suit is standing there—eyes wild and cheeks flushed, and he's looking like a caged animal.

"This is what you missed," I say, having no idea if he understands. But I'll take that as my cue to leave— showtime is over and I'm feeling the warm burn of pleasure knowing he's going to bed with me on his mind. Let him regret walking out.

I drop my T-shirt back down over my stomach and wink at him before scampering back inside, my heart pounding and my head swirling. I can't believe I did that.

But there's no denying I feel better than I have in weeks. Maybe I needed to act out a little after twelve months of minding my p's and q's and trying to be wife material. After twelve months of pretending to be someone I wasn't.

I crawl back into bed with a big smile on my face and instantly fall into a deep slumber.

CHAPTER FIVE

Flynn

WHEN I WALKED into the office at 7:00 a.m. with a spring in my step, Francis had assumed it was because I'd done exactly what she told me to do: rest, television, and take-away food. Ha! The truth couldn't be further from that.

After watching Blondie touch herself brazenly on the balcony of her borrowed apartment, that beautiful face screwed up with pleasure, I'd needed *another* cold shower to shake the desire creeping through my body. But even with the most monumental of teases, I still went to bed happy. When was the last time I slept soundly, fully engaged by dreams that had me not wanting it to end? That had me waking with a wicked smile? So long, I can't even remember.

I've been thinking about it all day. For once in my life, *I* was the space cadet in meetings. I was the one staring into nothingness, my mind miles away from work. But the fantasy will have to keep me going, because I've got a full plate and a fuller head. When I go home shortly, I'll have to force myself not to knock on her door. I can't afford any distractions—no matter how tempting—to derail my plans.

And speaking of unwanted distractions…

I scrub a hand over my face and let out a frustrated groan when yet *another* email appears from the maid of honour about the Jack and Jill party we're supposed to be organising. One, the idea of a Jack and Jill party is stupid. Two, I'd already asked Francis to take care of it so I didn't have to waste time on party planning. But oh, no, Little Miss Warpath is nixing every single thing I say, and she wants to have…a costume party.

I shudder. Costume parties are the seventh circle of hell. I can't think of anything worse than going to a party dressed in some crappy polyester version of what someone else wore. It's tacky and I'm duty-bound to ensure my cousin isn't photographed looking like an idiot. I'm not sure why he chose me to be best man, to be honest. We've never been close, not even growing up. But family is the single most important thing in my life, so I wasn't about to decline when he asked, even if I had *zero* interest in the job.

But after the tenth email from Melanie D. Richardson, I'm about to throw my laptop out the window. Never mind that the windows in this office tower don't open, I'll *make* an opening.

Apparently, I'm being "overbearing" and "uptight" because I don't want to go ahead with the costume party. Okay, and maybe it's also because I told her she should step back and let me handle it all since I know what I'm doing (and by me, I mean Francis.) I disagree that costume parties are "fun" (they're not) and "creative" (double nope) and "perfect for such a happy couple" (of course they seem happy, they're spending an exorbitant amount of money to announce to the world that they're in love…they *have* to seem happy).

Call me cynical—many do. But I've never understood the over-the-top nature of weddings. If you're really in love with someone, why do you need all the fanfare? Why do you need the audience?

But I'll keep that opinion to myself.

I fire back an email that shuts the discussion down. I'm happy to compromise on other things, but it feels like she's being purposefully difficult.

A second later, Francis pops her head into my office. She's wearing that lip-pursed, motherly face again. "That was a bit harsh, Flynn."

"What? I told her it's not happening and she's wasting my time by being argumentative," I reply, leaning back in my chair. "I've tried to compromise on something else, maybe the menu or colour scheme, but she's stomping her feet like an angry toddler."

"You're used to people bending to your will." My assistant smirks, like she's got grudging respect for the other woman. "And she's not."

"She'll run out of hot air eventually. This wedding is going to be enough of a circus as it is." My cousin is a *more is more* kinda guy—as was evident by the enormous rock he gave his fiancée. And the fact that he proposed to her in the most outlandish way possible, with multiple hot air balloons custom printed with their names and "will you marry me?" on the side. "I keep thinking how much my mother would have loved it."

"Is that why you seem so prickly about the whole thing?"

"No, I'm more worried about stuff ending up in the papers. He's got a habit of making a fanfare and getting bad press for it." I rake a hand through my hair. "And with everything hinging on these trials…"

"Ah," she said. "So that's what it's about."

I look at the picture of my niece. Zoe is seven and she was diagnosed with Batten disease two years ago. It's extremely rare. Most people with Batten disease die in their teens or early twenties. There's no cure. *This* is why I work as hard as I do. *This* is why I worry about things like my stupid cousin drawing attention to our family name for all the wrong reasons. I can't risk people not wanting to donate money to our cause because they think we're a pack of idiots.

Call me a bastard. Call me selfish and a killjoy. I don't care, if it means my company might find some way to help people like Zoe. To help her dad, who's already starting to grieve for all the time he likely won't have with her.

"Let me take care of it," Francis says. "I'll sort it out so you don't have to deal with it anymore."

"What would I do without you?"

"Lord knows," she mutters as she walks away, her low, sensible heels clacking against the hardwood floor.

Outside, the city is bathed in inky darkness. It's almost midnight and we're the last two left, like always.

I tell Francis to go home every night around seven, but she's as much of a workaholic as I am. I let her take every Friday afternoon off to pick up her grandson from school so they can spend time together, but that doesn't make up for the hours she puts in. I make a mental note to write her a cheque this week as a thank-you.

Sighing, I pack up my laptop. I'll spend another hour on the computer sifting through emails when I go home. I'm on pins and needles while we wait for results of a gene therapy trial that's running currently, so it's not like I'm going to sleep properly anyway. I head out of the office and stand by Francis's desk, making sure she packs up, too.

Outside, I walk as though my body is being drawn by some magnetic force. The second I think about setting foot in my apartment, my mind drifts to Blondie. Knowing she's on the other side of the wall is the purest of tortures.

I've never met a woman like her before—not one who was so daring and who didn't give a crap what I thought about her. It's refreshing, frankly, because most people are putting on a front, playing a role, trying to seem more important than they are. But Blondie is who she is.

I walk into 21 Love Street and nod at the security guy behind the desk. The building is quiet and my footsteps echo. I'm the lone passenger in the elevator. As I walk down the hall, my eyes linger on the apartment at the end—number 406. How easy it would be to keep walking past my door to hers, and knock.

I'm already imaging her answering in that flimsy, threadbare white T-shirt and pink underwear that had me salivating last night. I'd love to see that wild, white-blond hair tumbling over her shoulders and all around her body.

I shake off the feeling and head straight to my door, determined not to let the images distract me. But just as I'm about to reach for my keys I notice a little piece of paper. It's been carefully folded in half and wedged between the door and the frame.

I pull it out.

Tonight it's your turn. Call me when it's late. D.

D. I wonder what her name is.

I push my front door open and stand in the middle of my apartment, my eyes still locked onto the note and the number scrawled at the bottom. Her handwriting is loopy and a little erratic, the *g*'s and *l*'s taking up more space than they should. There's nothing efficient about her style. It's wild and free, probably scrawled quickly and without much consideration.

I crumple the note, toss it into the wastepaper basket by my bookshelf and continue toward my bedroom. I shower quickly, intending to get into something comfortable and then open up my laptop. But when I come back out to the lounge room, my eyes immediately go to the wastepaper basket.

I won't go to her apartment and I won't invite her to mine.

No casual sex. That's the rule.

But what about phone calls? It's a loophole and my

brain loves a flaw in a carefully formed plan. I dig out the crumpled paper and reach for my phone. And for the second night in a row, I ignore my instincts.

Blondie picks up on the third ring.

brutal low was a flaw as I carefully formed the plan. I dug out the crumpled paper and reach for my phone, wait for the second ring, in a sweat, press my finger to ... Hanging up, I carried to with ease ...

CHAPTER SIX

Drew

"You said to call when it was late."

I'm hazy and still within slumber's firm grip, but the sound of a gravelly voice that's rich like dark chocolate and sinful as a forbidden tryst has me stretching my body. Waking myself. I'm a little shocked he called.

"What time *is* it?" I'm on the couch, wearing the T-shirt from last night under a blanket that's cosy and warm.

"Twelve thirty," he says.

"Did you just get home?"

"I did."

"Why do you work so late?" I snuggle into the corner of the couch and pull the blanket up to my chin. There's something nostalgic about this—a late-night call when I know I should be asleep. I feel like a naughty teenager, sneaking time away with her crush.

"I'm a busy man."

"Not so busy that you don't have time to watch a little live entertainment." I bite down on my bottom lip, stifling a smile at the appreciative grunt on the other end of the line. I try to picture him. Is he standing by his window hoping I'll be there again? Or is he in his bed, in boxer briefs and with his chest bare? Or maybe he's in a towel.

"You put on one hell of a show," he says. There's a darkness to his voice and it's making my heart flutter.

"It felt a little one-sided," I admit. "I showed you mine, but you didn't show me yours."

"Is it so bad to watch?"

The question sends a delicious shiver through me. "No, I like watching. I like listening, too."

When he chuckles it's like someone is running a razorblade over my nerve endings. How can a laugh make me feel so much?

"I like knowing the women I have sex with," he replies.

"Who said we're having sex?"

"I assume you didn't slip your number into my door so I could give you a wakeup call for nothing."

I grin. "I did not."

"Then why did you do it, Blondie?"

I laugh. "I've been calling you Mr. Suit in my head all day long. Seems we've both got nicknames for one another."

"I was trying to figure out what *D* stood for," he said. "I've already crossed off Danielle, Debbie and Diana."

"You would be correct, so far." Not that I have any intention of telling him my name—I made that promise to myself last night. Nothing real. This is just for fun. A necessary diversion while the rest of my life is smoking ruins. "I'll tell you it's not Deanna, Deirdre or Dominique, either."

"What about Dallas?"

I laugh. "Do I look like a cowgirl to you?"

I could talk to him all night long. There's something soothing about his voice—the deep bass and dry wit—that makes me forget about all my problems.

"I guess this is the point where I'm supposed to make a dirty joke about how hard you ride." There's noise in the background, like he's moving around. "But you deserve more than a cliché, Blondie."

"What are you doing right now?"

"Getting ready for bed." Something clicks, maybe a light switch. "It's late."

"And dark."

"And it's my turn, according to your note."

This is it—the open door. He's willing to play. A shiver runs the length of my spine and I burrow further down into the couch, keeping the blanket up over me. I feel like we're playing a game of cat and mouse. Teasing one another.

Playing with fire.

"I believe in equality for the sexes," I say. "Orgasms for everyone."

"That's very noble." There's that dry humour again. "What made you do it on the balcony last night? Revenge for me saying no?"

"There was a little of that," I admit. "You left me

hanging. I had pent-up energy to expel, and I wanted to show you what you were missing."

"I couldn't get you out of my head. I've been trying to concentrate on work all day and I could only think about your pink underwear and incredible legs."

"And you're thinking about them again now."

There's a soft releasing of breath. "How could I not?"

"I'm wearing blue tonight. With little white stripes and lace around the edges." I bite down on my lip as there's a muffled moan from his end. "Same T-shirt."

"Take if off."

I pretend to. I'm not going to defile my friend's couch—there's girl code about that kind thing. But Mr. Suit doesn't need to know. And besides, I like the fantasy. I like controlling what he thinks is happening because it makes me feel powerful to be in charge of his pleasure.

"No bra tonight, either," I say.

"Just the blue stripes, huh?" He lets out a jagged curse. "Are you in your bed?"

"On the couch. Just where I would have been last night in you hadn't walked out on me. I bet you're regretting that now."

"I don't know what would have happened if I'd stayed."

"You want storytime, huh?" I cluck my tongue. "That's naughty."

"Not as naughty as what I'm doing right now."

My sex clenches at the thought of it. I know his body is made for pleasure—all broad shoulders and strong arms. I know he was packing something hefty behind that towel last night. I imagine him on top of the covers looking every bit like something I'd hope to find waiting for me at the end of a long day—hooded eyes and a wicked smile and a hard cock.

"Well, my plan was to have a drink and a chat and a kiss." I close my eyes and let myself sink into the fantasy. "I wanted to see how you kiss, because that's a sure-fire way to tell if a guy's good in bed."

"Did you have concerns that I don't know how to use my tongue? If so, you'd be wrong."

Ah, so he's cocky. I'm not surprised and I kind of like it—he's a man who doesn't mince words. He's firm in his opinions and beliefs. He's a man of conviction, especially in himself.

"That's for me to decide, Mr. Suit. Not for you to tell me."

The dark chuckle that vibrates through the line sends goose bumps skittering across my skin.

"Now, if I'd decided you were a good kisser, I was going to lead you into the shower."

"The shower, huh?"

"Not my apartment, remember? I can't bring a guy into my friend's bed. And truth be told… I love being fucked in the shower." When he moans, I squeeze my thighs together. "I love the water running over my skin, and the way the tiles feel cold against my palms as I brace myself. I love being clean and dirty at the same time."

"I think you're dirty to the bone, Blondie. No shower

is going to fix you up." He grunts. "And bloody hell it's sexier than anything."

I'm warm now and I push the blanket back, letting the cool air prickle over my skin. I wish he was here, hands on my thighs while he lowered those full lips to the pulsing spot between my legs. "I would have invited you into the shower, stripped down while you watched and climbed in to give you a show."

"Like on the balcony." His breath comes a little quicker now.

"Just like that, but with no T-shirt and no underwear so you could see every part of me." I pause, making him wait for one heartbeat. Then two. Three. I've got him hooked. "I'd give you a show and get myself all warmed up for you. Then I would have told you to strip down and join me."

"What then?"

"I'd tell you to get on your knees and show me how you use that tongue."

"Fuck," he grunts. "I bet you taste sweet as honey. I would have loved feeling those beautiful thighs clamp around my head."

Now it's my turn to stifle a moan. Having a big, strong man on his knees for me is my personal catnip. I love a guy who enjoys oral sex—both giving and receiving. Like I said, orgasms for everyone.

"Do you like to be taken from behind?" he asks, his breath sharp and quick.

"Yes," I hiss, fighting the urge to touch myself.

I'm going to need one hell of a cold shower after this is all done.

"You want to feel my hands on your hips as I push my hard cock into you? I bet you'd look like a goddess with all that gorgeous hair tangled and running down your back."

"I'd ask you to pull it, Mr. Suit. I like it a little rough." I can hear that he's close now. Just like I was last night as I touched myself in front of him. So close. "I'd want to feel that last hard thrust before you came, calling my name so loud the whole building could hear."

"Blondie."

There's a groan and I feel the pleasure of it all the way down to my toes. He curses again and the sound is pure. Raw. I wish for a second that I'd gone to knock on his door instead of leaving a note—so that I could be wrapped in his arms. So that I could feel the hot press of his body and the warmth of his lips against my skin. The fullness of him inside me.

There's a keening sound on the other end of the line and I know it's over. For him, at least. Frustrated energy makes me squirm on the couch and I have to force myself not to go to him. He had his chance—this is simply fun and games.

"Was it good, Mr. Suit?" My voice is rough with desire and my body is coiled tighter than a spring.

"Not as good as if you were here." His breath is starting to even out. "Not even close."

"You had your chance," I tease. "Good night, Mr. Suit."

"Good night, Blondie."

CHAPTER SEVEN

Drew

SATURDAY MORNING IS the final fitting for the brides-maid dresses, and I am living my worst nightmare. I promised myself that I wouldn't say one negative thing today—not about the other bridesmaids, not about the fanfare, not about the fact I feel like I've stepped out of a Barbie display.

The dresses are pink, of course. With these off-the-shoulder sleeves and delicate line of beading at the waist, floor-length skirts and bodices fit for Grecian princesses. Apparently, I was supposed to bring a pair of high heels to wear with the dress, but I must have missed that memo. Maybe it was in one of Sherilee's forty-five footnotes.

Ha. Foot*notes...get it?*

My guess is they wouldn't, so I keep my mouth shut.

"How's everything going with the Jack and Jill party?" Annaleigh asks as we stand around while the dressmaker pins the hems. I get a grunt of disapproval from the older woman when she spies my Doc Martens peeking out from under the frothy pink fabric.

"Just peachy. Everything is fine."

It's a total lie and Presley shoots me a look across the room. She'll try on her dress after the bridesmaids are done, so she's still wearing her blue skinny jeans and a cream silk blouse. I'd told her all about the GPITA—Giant Pain in the Ass—who is the best man.

"Why do I not feel confident about that?" Annaleigh asks with a crease between her perfectly plucked brows. "What's going on?"

"Nothing." I wave a hand and get a slap on the thigh from the dressmaker, who tells me to stand still. "We're currently…aligning our approach for the party."

"He's being a disagreeable bastard," Presley chimes in, and I snort. It's funny hearing my sister swear in public, since she always seems so prim and proper unless it's only the two of us.

"I'll work it out," I reassure the other women. "I don't care if I have to track the guy down personally and beat him over the head. We're *going* to have the costume party."

"I thought it was such a fun idea," Sherilee says. I'm surprised I have her support. Something told me the Stepford bridesmaids wouldn't be into dress-up parties, but Presley and I *lived* for them as kids. It's a nostalgic thing. "The wedding itself will be very formal and we can all get our party dresses out for the hen's night. This is a chance to do something different. It's a good idea, Drew."

My heart warms for a second at Sherilee's firm nod of approval, her expression serious as always. "Thanks."

"Ugh, men. I swear to God, they're terrible at organising anything until we do something they don't like and then all of a sudden they want to be hands-on." Pauline snorts. "Typical."

"Who *is* the best man, anyway?" I ask. "One of Mike's friends?"

"His cousin, actually. Some corporate bigwig." Presley shrugs. "I've never met him."

"You've never met him?" I blink. "Does he live in another country?"

"No." My sister shifts her position, turning away ever so slightly so I can't see her whole expression. A bad feeling settles in my gut—we've never been the kind of twins who had that whole "twintuition" thing, but I *know* her. Better than anyone. Something is off. "He lives in Melbourne."

"How come you've never met him?" I ask.

There's an awkward silence in the room now—so thick it's like soup. Hot, awkward, gross soup. "Mike's family has a lot of drama. I've never met his stepbrother, either. They're…estranged, I guess you could say."

I raise a brow. "I had no idea."

"Yeah. His parents had a nasty split years ago and it made things super uncomfortable for the family business—Mike works so hard but he's constantly stressed that his stepbrother is going to come home one day and take the company from him, because he's the 'real' son." She shakes her head. "And I think he asked his cousin to be his best man because he wanted *someone* from the family to stand next to him, but he doesn't want his stepbrother there."

"That's sad," Sherilee murmurs.

I have to agree. My family is *far* from perfect. It was just Presley and me and our mum growing up because our dad was never in the picture. Who has twins off a random one-night stand? Talk about bad luck. So our mum was young and she probably wasn't very well equipped, and our grandparents didn't speak to her for a long time after it happened. They only came back into our lives when we were in high school. There's still tension and hurt there. But we make do. They're *all* coming to the wedding, because our family rallies, even if it takes them a while.

"Yeah. I guess it's that whole thing about money not buying happiness." She sighs. Her fiancé's family are rich—proper rich. And we grew up aspiring for middle class. But Presley has worked hard in her career, as I've done in mine. We take care of our mum as best we can and we're happy. Mostly. "They seemed so perfect the first time I met them, but it was like an onion of drama. Every time you peeled back another layer there were more family secrets. More scandals or affairs or feuds."

I don't like the sound of that. Presley is a lover, not a fighter—she's sweet and liked by all and I can't see her being happy in a family like that. But I bite back the urge to say so, because ultimately who she marries is her decision. Maybe she won't end up having much to do with his family.

"All right." The brusque dressmaker gets slowly to her feet. "It's the bride's turn."

She whisks Presley into a change room, and I stare at myself in the big section of curved mirrors that frames the room. Objectively, the dresses are pretty. And on the other women with their beautiful hair and tanned complexions, the design is perfection. But on me...hmm.

I'm sure it'll be fine on the day. Having a pair of high heels on instead of Docs will do wonders.

"You're very different, you and Presley," Sherilee says as we stand around, waiting for the bride's big reveal. "Especially for identical twins."

"Maybe that's exactly *why* we we're different." I shrug. "At some point after years of comparison, it's appealing to stand out as an individual."

She nods. "I can see that. My parents always compared me to my older brother—nothing I did was ever good enough."

"I find that hard to believe."

"Seriously. I felt like I was the dud child until I married my husband and then suddenly I was legitimate in their eyes." She shoots me a rueful smile. "And that's only because they want me to start popping out kids. They're desperate to be grandparents."

"And you're not ready?"

She shakes her head. "I love my job and I want to see how far I can go in this career...at least for now."

I feel an unlikely kindship with Sherilee. What women want is always open for criticism, and even when we try to conform, when we try our damnedest to be what someone wants…it's never enough. "But isn't your biological clock ticking?" I say with a healthy dose of sarcasm.

"Don't even get me started!" She snorts. "And seriously, I think the dress-up Jack and Jill party will be super fun. Don't let the best man bully you into doing something else."

At that moment, the curtain parts and Presley walks out of the dressing room and into the middle of the couture dress shop. It's all I can do not to let my jaw hit the floor. Presley and I have exactly the same body—tall and slim, all arms and legs without much to speak of in the boobage area. Yet this dress has transformed her into curves and sweeping lines. The strapless bodice moulds to her figure, drawing her waist in and flaring out over her hips so she looks like a perfect hourglass.

She's so beautiful I know our mother will cry buckets on the day. But then I'm struck by something deeper, something intense and…painful.

The dress looks identical to the one I tried on three months ago. I did it on a whim, while shopping in London. Vas and I were due to have dinner that night at some hoity-toity place in Mayfair and I had a feeling he might propose. So I'd ducked into a bridal shop and slipped myself into a dress exactly like this—giddy with excitement and so in love I couldn't see the red flags through my thick rose-tinted glasses.

Suddenly, it all comes crashing down. The breakup and my heartache, the fact that I have no idea what I'm doing with my life and seeing Presley—which is like looking at myself—all dressed up for her wedding…

There's a lump in my throat. Tears prick the backs of my eyes and when Presley sees me, her face crumples. But I will *not* let any of my shit ruin her day. So I pretend it's nothing more than sisterly admiration.

"You look *so* beautiful, Pres," I say. And it's true—she's majestic. So perfect I wonder how she even exists. "Mike is going to be bowled over when he sees you."

She rushes over and wraps her arms around me, despite the cries from the dressmaker about crushing the fabric. Presley smells like vanilla cupcakes and a spring garden, as she always does. I hold her tight, blinking back tears and pressing a kiss to her cheek.

"You okay?" she whispers. "It's not like you to get all emotional."

"Yeah, I'm fine. I was…taken aback. The dress is perfect."

"I'm so glad you're here."

"Me too."

We hold each other tight for another minute, and when we break apart there isn't a dry eye in the room. No matter what happens in my life, I'm grateful to have Presley. Even if she manages to be everything I desperately want to be.

An hour later we all bundle outside to go for cocktails and make important decisions around bridal accessories and hairstyles. I pull away for a moment and bring up my email on my phone. There's another email from Giant Pain in the Ass. Or rather, his assistant.

To: Melanie D. Richardson
From: Francis Albright on behalf of Flynn Lewis
Subject: Lewis-Richardson wedding: Jack and Jill Party

Dear Ms. Richardson,
My name is Francis Albright, and I'm Mr. Lewis's executive assistant. I've stepped in to assist with the organisation of this event. To save further delays, I have gone ahead and booked the venue for the Jack and Jill party (please see a record of the booking with all pertinent details attached).

A theme of "black and white with a touch of gold" has been selected and the venue will be decorated accordingly. Email invites are currently being designed and will be distributed next week according to the list you compiled. A sample menu, music list and schedule are attached. At this stage, nothing further is required on your end.

If you have any questions, please contact me rather than Mr. Lewis.
Kind regards,
Francis Albright

That motherfucker! Not only did he palm me off on his assistant, but they went and organised the whole event without me. *And* ignored everything that I put forward to ensure the event was what Presley would want it to be.

If I were a cartoon character, steam would be shooting out of my ears right now. I'm livid. Beyond livid.

But here's the thing *Mr. Lewis* doesn't know about me: when someone decides to play dirty, I'm more than happy to change my tactics and respond in kind. This is no longer event organisation: it's war.

CHAPTER EIGHT

Flynn

THE DAY IS surprisingly warm. I leave the office around four and head to my brother's place for a beer. It's Saturday, so Zoe has been to ballet class and she's refusing to get out of her uniform. If Gabe let her, she'd eat, sleep and shower in pink tights, matching legwarmers and her black leotard with the dance school's logo.

Even now as we sit out back, shaded by the veranda and big, sweeping jacaranda that's in the early stages of blooming with purple flowers, Zoe is diligently practising her *pirouettes*. She flies around with abandon, her thick-framed glasses sliding down her nose. I know her vision is getting worse, and it breaks my heart.

"Don't say a word." Gabe takes a long swig of his beer. "I can't talk about it today."

I nod. My brother wants to pretend we're a normal family with normal problems. That's hard for me— because I'm like a dog with a bone when it comes to this stuff. I want to tell him about every aspect of the trials, about the experts I'm hiring and all the hope I'm pouring into this work. But some days it's too much for him and I have to respect that.

"Tell me something good," Gabe says. He pulls a pair of sunglasses over his eyes as the clouds shift and bright light filters under the veranda's edge. "What have you been up to?"

"You told me not to talk about it." I sip my beer. I let the relaxation filter through my muscles.

"I mean besides work."

"There's nothing besides work." Though that's not entirely true. There's Blondie—the sexy anomaly in my otherwise perfectly structured life.

I had phone sex like a horny teenage boy. I don't know what I was expecting when I dialled her number, but hearing that sleepy, gravelly voice was so utterly intoxicating. I've never experienced anything like it. It took all my willpower not to go to her apartment and bang on her door so she'd let me inside to bang her.

Fuck. I need to get her out of my head. Even today— Saturdays are quiet, so it's my most productive day—I couldn't concentrate. Blondie is occupying way more of my brain than I want her to. That she's occupying anything at all is a problem.

"You need something besides work, man."

"Like what? A relationship?"

"It wouldn't be so bad. Don't use me as a yardstick for what it's like." Gabe is self-deprecating like that, but he has no idea how much pain his words cause. "My failure of a marriage shouldn't deter you."

His failure of a marriage might be my fault. Here's

the thing—Gabe and I have been best buds since the second I was born. He's older and he looked after me, showed me the ropes, and I've always looked up to him. Idolised him, even. It killed me when he married Monique, a woman who didn't deserve someone *half* as good as Gabe.

He was steady and she was irresponsible. He was strong and she was weak. And selfish. And judgmental. She undermined him, manipulated him—spewed her negativity into him until he was a husk of the man I knew. Things started to change when Zoe came along... until they figured out something was wrong.

Then Monique started partying. Sleeping around, from all accounts. She was killing my brother and neglecting her child.

I couldn't take seeing Gabe like that anymore, so I decided to lay it all out for her. Help her have a "come to Jesus" moment about what she was doing to her family. I told her straight—no bullshit—that she was lucky to have Gabe and Zoe, and she was throwing it all away. I thought I'd gotten through to her, helped her to see the error of her ways.

The following morning, she packed her bags and took off, leaving behind a note that said she didn't have it in her to be the wife and mother that Gabe and Zoe needed. They haven't seen her since.

And I've never told Gabe about that conversation.

"I don't have time for a relationship," I say flippantly, shoving down the shameful memories. "I certainly don't have the headspace to deal with another person's baggage."

"For someone who's so intent on making himself out to be a selfish bastard, you sure do visit us a lot. Baggage and all." Gabe smirks. He knows I'd take a bullet for my family. "You could cut that time in half and find a woman. Be happy."

"That's not going to make me happy."

"Then go out and get laid, at least. Christ. One of us has to live."

I glance over and see the crinkle between Gabe's reddish brows. We've got the same colouring: red-toned hair, blue eyes. None of that got passed onto Zoe. She's her mother through and through—chestnut hair, hazel eyes and skin that tans at the drop of a hat.

"Fucking around isn't living," I reply. "Despite what pop culture would have us believe."

"So you don't want a relationship but you don't believe in casual sex. What's left?"

I grin, though it's hollow. But I don't want to bring Gabe down. "A peaceful, drama-free life of solitude and meaningful work."

"That's sad."

"It's freeing." I shrug. "I don't need someone else to make me happy. I've got all I need right here."

"I don't buy it." Gabe shakes his head. "You were the guy in university who had all the women flocking to you."

"I was young and stupid."

"You weren't bogged down."

"You think I'm bogged down?" I raise a brow. "By what, trying to do something with my life?"

"By living your life for other people."

I let his comment stew for a minute. "Even if that person is your daughter?"

"Yes." He rakes a hand through his hair. "Zoe is the one who's got it all figured out. She tries everything and fails often and doesn't miss a beat before trying again. She makes new friends every day."

She's at the age where Gabe is starting to talk to her about her disease, to help her understand why she's a little different from the kids at school. But they haven't had *the* conversation yet…that probably won't happen until she's a little older.

"Some days I swear she knows what's going on." Gabe's voice is a little choked up. "It's like she's trying to cram a whole life's worth of experience into every day. Don't you think we could learn from that?"

I don't want to disagree with him, because it seems cruel. I *love* that Zoe is living each day like it's a whole life—and she should. But that life isn't for me. Because I've seen the darker side of that lifestyle. People like my mother and Monique put their own pleasures before responsibility—they're hedonists who neglect the people they should love so they can be "free." So they can "find themselves."

Whatever the fuck that means.

So no, I don't subscribe to the "live every day like it's your last" theory. I'm building my life on stability and responsibility and future-focus, because that's what Zoe and Gabe need from me.

"I should get going." I push up from my chair. The amber dregs swish around the bottom of the glass as I set it on a table.

"More work?" Gabe asks drily.

"Self-preservation. Little Miss Ballerina mentioned something about a movie night involving *Frozen* and I can practically sing 'Let It Go' in my sleep at this point." I shudder. "That one's on you, buddy."

Gabe chuckles and his expression softens again. "Thank you. I know I don't say it enough—"

I hold up a hand. "Don't give me an emotional declaration. I don't do it for you."

Both our gazes slide over to the little girl who's dancing, tinny classical music belting out from a pink speaker that Gabe bought her so she could practise in the backyard. When she notices me standing, she rushes over and throws her arms around me, burying her sweet little face against my leg. I stroke her hair and pack everything I feel down into a small lump so I can swallow it all.

This is why I can't afford to get distracted. Not by Blondie, not by this stupid Jack and Jill party. Not by anything.

CHAPTER NINE

Drew

I WAKE WITH a start. It's late—lights glimmer against an inky backdrop outside the window and I'm lying on the couch doing my best impression of a pretzel. What happened?

Cocktails. *Lots* of cocktails.

I'd started out with the bridal squad and when they left, it was Presley and me. My sister might look like little miss perfect, but she can pound tequila like nobody's business. I groan and push myself up into a sitting position.

I couldn't have come home *that* late, since we started drinking around 3:00 p.m. It's coming back to me— Presley bailed around nine when her fiancé picked her up. Then on the way home I'd made a phone call…to who? I search my memory.

Oh, no. The venue for the Jack and Jill party. I'd called them to confirm we'd had a change of plans—the bride wanted a new theme. It would now be a dress-up party—come as your hero. And I'd asked them to direct all future queries about the event to me, instead of to the Giant Pain in the Ass's assistant.

Presley is going to kill you if you start a war with her in-laws.

Then I came home and...yep, greasy pizza and bad reality TV. The television screen is black with an "are you still watching?" message displayed.

"Don't judge me, Netflix," I grumble as I pick a piece of salami from my leggings.

Although maybe Netflix *should* judge me. I've clearly fallen asleep mid-drunk snacking and now I have grease stains on my pants. I peel them off, immediately dropping them into the washing machine tucked away behind a neat little door next to the bathroom.

I glance around the room. The pizza box sits open, illuminated only by the glow of the TV and the city lights filtering in. The view is magnificent. In the dark, Melbourne is splashed across the window like a masterpiece. My mind flickers to the night on the balcony when I'd given Mr. Suit a show.

I don't think I'll ever look at balconies the same way again.

For a moment, I consider leaving the pizza and dragging my tired, slightly still-drunk butt to bed. But I'm a guest in this house. Scooping up the box, I head to the front door and scout the hallway. It's a little after midnight and dead silent—I guess that's too late for the older residents and too early for younger ones to be coming home.

I dart across the hallway to the door marked "trash chute" and open it.

"What the hell are you doing?"

The gravelly, male voice startles me and the chute lever slips out of my fingers, the metal banging against my other hand. I'm ready to chew the ear off the person who's appeared behind me like some creepy-ass stalker. But my gaze collides with a steely expression and a shock of reddish hair. Mr. Suit.

Never one to waste an opportunity to pay back a man who's rejected me, I glare at him with all the fake anger I can muster. "You usually sneak up on vulnerable women like that?"

He cocks a brow, his eyes roaming up and down my body. Is he thinking about our naughty phone call? Or the night on the balcony? Then I remember I ditched my grease-stained pants into the washing machine. My jumper is oversized, so my underwear is covered. Barely.

That's twice now he's seen me without pants.

"You usually break the rules while staying in someone else's apartment?" He folds his arms across his chest.

I was aware of the garbage chute curfew, but in the moment I forgot. I am not surprised, however, that Mr. Suit is a stickler for the rules. "Do you usually get your knickers in a knot over other people's behaviour?" I fire back.

"That's rich coming from a woman who doesn't seem to own any pants."

Touché. "I'm not disturbing anyone by getting rid of my pizza box." I wink, knowing it will grate on him. Maybe I should change his name to Mr. Stick Up His Butt.

"The cut-off is 10:00 p.m." His jaw ticks. "There's a reason for that."

"Oh, really? Please tell me about it. Was it The Great Garbage Chute Incident of 2006? I heard quite a few people lost their lives over it."

I want to know what Mr. Suit's deal is. He's got this weird mix of blistering heat and uptight, almost stuffy rigidity about him. I've never met anyone like him before. Most guys seem to fall into only one camp, but he's got a foot squarely in both.

Tonight he's not in suit, however. He's wearing a soft crew-neck jumper with a shirt underneath and jeans with boots. Faded denim clings to his muscular thighs and makes his long legs look even longer. It's a damn sight, let me tell you.

"I would think that you'd be on your best behaviour considering this isn't *your* apartment," he says drily. For some guys, there might've been a hint of threat in a statement like that. But Mr. Suit is grouchy, not menacing.

"Good behaviour isn't my forte." I place a hand against his chest, giving him the gentlest shove so I can exit the chute room. "As you well know."

Mistake. His jumper is soft and snuggly, covering a hard wall of muscle. My mind spins off into a fantasy, but I have to remain strong. I will *not* let Mr. Suit best me in a verbal beatdown.

"And what exactly is your forte?" He steps back, freeing himself of my greedy hands. "Semi-goth makeup? Getting stuck in stairwells? Not wearing pants?"

He wants to judge me? Fine, it's not like I give a shit what he—or any other man—thinks of me. "Very perceptive. I'm a two-time gold medallist in going pantsless."

He shakes his head. "You're like a stubborn teenager."

"You didn't seem to have a problem with me when you called the other night," I purr. "In fact, why don't we add that to my list of fortes. Dirty talk. What can I say? I'm a woman of many talents."

Unfortunately, none of those talents count for much. I've got a PhD in emotional self-defence, a black belt in pushing people away, and several medals for snark, sarcasm, profanity and beer drinking. Useless skills, except for when it comes to keeping my heart protected... or so I'd thought.

But I'm not going to lay those weapons down ever again.

Mr. Suit's gaze burns right through me, like he sees past my trolling. Past my smudgy eye makeup and the hard stare that tells people to stay away. Like he's drilling through all of that to the stuff I don't want anyone to see.

Ever.

"That's usually my job," he says with a smirk. "It was interesting to be on the receiving end for a change."

"Well, Mr. Suit, consider yourself lucky. Try to get some rest, if you can. I know it'll be hard with all the irresponsible people throwing out their trash at such an inconvenient hour." I turn on my heel, heading back to the apartment with an exaggerated swing of my hips.

My whole body prickles with the sensation of being watched—it's like fire in my blood. Like jumper leads have been attached to my nervous system. I like being watched by him. Being consumed by his eyes.

I reach for the handle of the front door and turn. Nothing. I try again, rattling it slightly. Still nothing. A dark chuckle comes from behind me and I sigh, letting my forehead bump against the wood as I sag in defeat.

I've locked myself out.

CHAPTER TEN

Flynn

I DON'T SAY a word. I don't even breathe. Instead I lean against the wall and watch as Blondie realises she's locked herself out of her apartment. I'm guessing a rule-breaker like her didn't bother to bring her keys with her—after all, where would she put them if she's not wearing pants?

I can tell by the style of the lock that there's an automatic dead bolt installed. The desire to laugh bubbles up inside me.

Blondie turns, barely able to raise her ethereal blue eyes to mine. "Don't laugh at me."

"Wouldn't dream of it." It's a total lie and I can barely choke the words out without snorting. After her high-and-mighty display a second ago, it's more than a little fun to see her toppled from her pedestal.

"Someone has a master key, right?" Her eyes are pleading.

"Yes, the office manager starts work at ten a.m. on Sunday mornings."

"Of course you would know that," she grumbles. "What about security?"

"They don't have access to it, because they're usually contracted through a third party. It's too risky to give them the master." I cross my arms. "Your options are to ask security to call the office manager and wake them up. They'll probably charge a penalty to the person who owns the apartment, *if* you can get a hold of them. Otherwise you can call a locksmith and have the locks changed."

"I can't do that." Blondie bites her lip.

"Midnight emergency callout won't be cheap."

"It's not even my apartment. Will they let me do it without the owner here?" She swears and scrubs a hand over her face.

"You don't have a great track record with locked doors, do you?" I can't help it, the jab is wide open and I take it. To my surprise, Blondie isn't pissed. Instead, she laughs so hard that tears form in her eyes.

"I really don't." She sags back against the door and shoots me a black, sooty stare. "I don't suppose you'd mind having a misbehaving, anti-responsibility, pottymouthed guest on your couch tonight?"

The universe is determined to test me, I'm sure of it. But I'm not about to let her sleep in the hallway.

"Come on." I motion for her to follow. "Let's get inside before you give the guys watching the security cameras too much of an eyeful."

"What were you doing out here so late, anyway?" she asks. "Or did you really come out here to tell me off?"

"You think I'm some cave troll who waits around for people to break a rule so I can yell at them?" When I glance at her mischievous grin, I shake my head. "Don't answer that."

Actually, I was about to go for a walk—I do that sometimes when I'm feeling cagey and stuck. On a Saturday night, South Melbourne is bustling. I like to wander along Clarendon Street, enjoying the lights and the sounds of life around me. As much as I say I want a quiet, work-focused existence, sometimes the silence becomes too much.

I open the door to my apartment and hold it for Blondie. I try not to look at her incredible bare legs as she pads into my space—a space where no woman has come since my last failed attempt at a long-term relationship two years ago. My place is spare—less "design-y" than the apartment she's staying in. It's like me—functional, to the point.

Gabe would probably say it needed a bit more personality, but frankly I don't spend enough time here to warrant finding a designer I would trust enough.

"It's very…white." Blondie bobs her head. "Minimalist."

"I'm sure you'll find my couch more comfortable that the hallway floor," I say drily.

"I'm afraid to touch anything." Her laugh sounds a little tight—like she's nervous being here. It's a far cry from the feisty woman I've encountered thus far. But I guess there's a difference—here, she's on my turf. Under my roof. "It's so pristine. Do you really live here?"

"Of course I live here."

She turns to me, subtly tugging down the hem of her jumper but all it does is draw my attention to her slender thighs. Her white-blond hair is piled into a messy bun on top of her head and a few tendrils have escaped around her face and down the back of her neck. I'm struck by how beautiful she is—even while looking like sin and smelling like cocktails.

I *shouldn't* be attracted to someone like her. She screams party girl, wild child. She's a sexy hot mess of a woman and fucking hell, it's got me all knotted up.

"Don't most people have a book on the coffee table or a cup of cold tea discarded somewhere? Maybe a jacket slung over the back of a chair?" There's that nervous laugh again. "You know, normal people things. I bet if we sent the Mars Rover through here it would come back reporting no signs of life."

I roll my eyes. "Excuse me for not living in a pigsty. Do you want to stay here or not?"

"Sure, thank you." She nods. "I, uh…"

"Spit it out."

"I was about to have a shower. I smell like pizza and I really don't want to ruin that pretty white couch."

Christ. How am I supposed to function with the thought of her naked in my shower? What the hell did I do wrong to be saddled with this temptation?

I clear my throat. "Of course. I'll get you some towels."

"I guess I already know where the bathroom is." She bites her lip again. "When I saw into—"

"I know."

The vision of her on her balcony, her hand down the front of those ridiculous pink undies, is etched into my memory in permanent ink. A fleeting thought dashes through my brain—I wonder what colour she's wearing right now. My muscles are wooden as I head to the linen cupboard and pull out some fresh towels.

"Here." I shove them toward her, averting my eyes.

"They're white. What a surprise," she teases softly.

I ignore the dig. "I'll leave a blanket and some pillows on the couch when you're done."

And then I will make sure I am in my bedroom with the door closed so that I don't have any more sexy images of her to add to my growing collection.

Instead of heading straight to my room, I decide to pour myself a drink. I reason that it'll help me sleep. Okay, fine. Seems legit. But then I walk to my balcony and pull the sliding glass door open.

The air outside is heavy, warning of a late-spring storm. It's cool but not cold, the scent of grass and flowers and lemons wafting up from the big garden below. Although I don't spend much time at home, I enjoy the view of the property, which is far greener and more lush than most places around here. There's a communal vegetable patch and a barbeque area and a big indoor swimming pool surrounded by glass.

I sip my drink, listening to the sound of water running in my bathroom. My throat is tight, but the drink relaxes me. I'm still stinging from my brother's assessment earlier today—mostly because I know he's right.

Every decision I make, everything I do, is for Zoe. It's part of the reason I don't do casual dating, because my niece gets attached to people easily, and she's desperate for a mother figure. The first time it happened was about six months after Monique left. I brought a woman to a barbeque and Zoe was smitten. A month later we were over, but Zoe asked about her constantly.

It's exactly why Gabe hasn't dated since the split. We might not have long with Zoe—and neither of us wants to waste that time.

I swish my drink around in the heavy glass. It clings a little to the edges, glowing like an ember in the glittering city lights. I've not once regretted sacrificing my old job, my old ways of partying and dating and hookups. The past few years have changed me. I've thrown everything into my company, I've poured all my money into hiring the best and brightest medical researchers.

What if it's not enough?

It's the thought that keeps me awake at night and no matter how hard I try to shove it away, it haunts me.

"Mr. Suit?" Blondie's husky voice calls me back to the present, luring me with the perfect way to forget about my worries. "I don't suppose I could borrow a T-shirt to sleep in."

When I turn, she's standing in the door of the bathroom, backlit so the edges of her hair glow like they've been touched by God. She's an angel. Surreal and so perfect I wonder if it's all a figment of my imagination. It's the first time I've seen her without makeup—well, there are slight traces of it around her eyes. But otherwise she's fresh-faced, her full lips bare and parted, her pale eyes wide.

I swallow and down the rest of my drink. "Sure."

It takes every bit of willpower to walk into my bedroom, instead of what I want to do—which is tug at the towel until it slips from her body. But as I stand at my chest of drawers, hunting out a T-shirt, I feel her presence behind me. It's like flames licking at my back.

"Aren't you even a little bit tempted?" she asks. There's a curiosity to her voice, and I'm certain she's never been short on men finding her attractive. Maybe my reasons don't make sense to anyone else—hell, I'm not even sure they make sense to me anymore.

What if your work isn't enough?

Today has worn me out. The stress of dealing with my idiot cousin and the wedding, and waiting impatiently for progress on our trials and then seeing Zoe and my brother today, seeing just how in pain he is…

I reach down deep for the strength I need, but I'm empty.

"Blondie, *tempted* doesn't even begin to cover it." I shake my head. "I wouldn't have called the other night if I wasn't tempted out of my fucking mind."

"But you have your rule."

I turn. She's leaning against the door frame, water droplets dotting her shoulders and chest. Her hair is damp. My towel swamps her, covering her sexy thighs and trim waist and small perky breasts.

"I guess you're used to men falling at your feet, huh?" I say.

To my surprise, she laughs. "I'm a novelty. They might fall at my feet but the second they've got what they wanted, they're out of there. So I figured, why not set the terms myself? Not all women need to be looking for a husband."

"And not all guys need to be looking for a quick fuck."

"I'm happy to take my time with you."

I bite back a moan. "You didn't lock yourself out on purpose, did you?"

"Nope. I really was trying to dispose of a pizza box." She draws her fingertip across her chest. "Cross my heart."

Would it really hurt to break my own rules just one time? She's not staying for long so there's no chance of it getting messy. I want her. There's absolutely no denying that—my cock's been like a soldier snapping to attention since the night I rescued her from that stairwell. Every time I think about her—think about the peep show and the dirty phone call…bam!

That's what you get from self-imposing celibacy for so long. When *was* the last time I had sex? I can't even remember. And now my body is starved. Desperate. Coiled like a hungry animal with a big, tasty deer in its path.

Only this deer wants to be caught.

"I don't know anything about you," I say in a last-ditch attempt to put some distance between us.

Her lip quirks and she steps into my room, one hand at the knot holding the towel closed. "I'm a Pisces who enjoys long walks on the beach and candlelit dinners."

"Liar."

"See, you *do* know something about me." Her grin is wicked. "Doesn't that sound a whole lot better than jaded rebel who doesn't believe in relationships and only wears black?"

"The second woman sounds a whole lot more real to me."

She's close now, and I trace my finger along the top edge of her towel, skirting the knot and soft skin behind it.

"And that's exactly why I've stayed away," I add. "You're not my type."

"How's your 'type' working out for you, then?" She tilts her face up to mine.

"Horribly."

"Exactly what I thought." Her hands slide up my chest.

"Why do you keep chasing a guy who's doing his best to push you away?" I close my hands over hers, halting her. My bedroom is dim, the only light coming from the hallway. It's intimate here, in the shadows, and I feel like a different man. Looser, less inhibited. Like the old me. "Why put in that much work?"

"Ah, you think I'm a glutton for punishment." She ducks her head. "Maybe I am. But here's what I figure— you want long-term, but not with a girl like me. So I'm safe, and things won't get awkward. We can have some fun, then I'll take off and you won't ever see me again. I need a palate cleanser and you're also not *my* type."

"Then how the fuck is this chemistry so hot?" It

doesn't make sense—we both know we're wrong for one another on a visceral level. I want a serious woman, a career-driven, family-oriented, long-term woman. The total opposite of her. She probably wants a man who's light and fun and makes her laugh.

And yet…she has me salivating like one of Pavlov's dogs. She has me thinking about her, reaching for my harder than steel cock every damn night.

"I honestly don't know," she says with a shrug. "But you feel it, right?"

"I wish I didn't." I let out a breath. "But there's something about you, Blondie. Something crazy sexy. You're like a thorn."

"Is that a good thing?"

"I don't know, but I've lost the ability to care." I lean down, still holding her hands against my chest. She tilts her head back and opens her lips, inviting me in.

The kiss is sweeter than I thought it would be—tentative and soft. Like she's testing me. I'm sure this prickly woman isn't so hard on the inside; she's tender and delicate and clearly trying to protect herself.

Aren't we all?

I reach for the towel and I tug it until the fabric falls open and slips to the ground. Her naked body is pressed hard against me and I slide my hands down her back, delighting in her smooth skin and the pert, round curve of her butt. When I pull her toward me, she sighs into my kiss. My tongue is dancing with hers, lips firm and willing.

"Hmm, smooth," she whispers. "What is that?"

"Cognac."

"I like it."

I pull back to take her all in. My God, she's magnificent. Pale as anything, but her breasts are tipped with dark pink nipples and there's a small black tattoo on her hip. I drop to my knees and trace it with my finger, pressing my lips to the delicate yet intricate design.

"My sister and I have matching ones," she says, her fingers playing with my hair. "It's a wattle flower, because we had a huge tree in our backyard growing up and my mother would always find the yellow flowers in our hair."

I think this might be the only truth she's told me so far.

CHAPTER ELEVEN

Drew

So MUCH FOR not letting Mr. Suit see the real me. I'd been doing so well, keeping the truth of who I am locked away and letting my alter ego take the wheel. But the way he'd lowered to his knees, touching me in a place that's so personal, and doing it with such reverence… I'm slayed.

Vas had teased me about the tattoo—calling it "tacky"—saying he liked it because it made me look a little bit slutty. I'd almost walked out on him then. I *should* have walked out on him because that one comment said more about his opinion of me than anything else. To me, my tattoo is art, a representation of something I care about deeply. I'd drawn the image on a napkin before dragging a nervous Presley into the tattoo shop on our eighteenth birthday, and we'd gotten them in exactly the same spot on our hips.

It was a symbol of our bond, of the life we'd shared and the thing that mattered to us most: family.

There wasn't anything slutty about it.

"It's beautiful." Mr. Suit presses his lips to my skin, peppering my hip with kisses as his hands slide up my thighs. "Did you draw it?"

"Why would you guess that?" My voice is shaky because it's like he can see me clearly and that's not what I want—yet it feels like sunshine on my face. To be seen. Understood. Isn't that all anyone craves deep down?

"You seem creative."

"Goes with my rule-breaker tendencies, I guess." I rake my fingernails along his scalp, and he growls, burring his face against my leg and nipping my skin. The sharp flash of pain is instantly soothed by a swipe of his tongue and I almost melt. His hands are working my muscles, thumbs kneading circles into my skin. "I'm not going to be able to stand up much longer if this is going where I think it is."

"It is *definitely* going where you think it is." He gets up and reaches for the hem of his jumper, tearing it and the layer beneath it over his head.

I back up and sit on the edge of the bed, determined to enjoy the show. Mr. Suit moves with the sleekness of a tiger, his body fit for a museum. He's muscular, but the thing I love most is the dusting of fire-tinged hair on his chest. Just a smattering. I curl my hands over the edge of the bed as he pulls his jeans down past his hips.

"Black boxer briefs, huh? That's a little boring," I tease. He's straight as an arrow, right down to his underwear.

He raises an eyebrow. "What were you expecting? *Looney Tunes* boxer shorts?"

I snort. "That would be a sight."

"Well, this will have to do." His shoes and socks and jeans and belt lay in a pile on the floor. When he hooks his thumbs into the waistband of his underwear and slides the stretchy fabric down, I find it hard to breathe.

"It'll more than do." I'm in sensory overload, barely able to vocalise the words dancing in my head.

His cock is long and hard, and it curves up toward his stomach. There's no hesitation in Mr. Suit's step as he comes toward me; he's a man totally confident and comfortable in his body. And why wouldn't he be? The guy could put the statue of David to shame.

"Like what you see?" He asks it in that self-assured way of a man who's never been turned down. He kneels at the foot of the bed, spreading my legs and planting a soft kiss to the inside of my knee.

I'm suddenly feeling self-conscious—his confidence is overwhelming. I've always wished I could be like that, but I've only ever managed to fake it. But as his lips work over my skin, getting higher and higher, the thought slips from my mind. Hell, *all* thoughts slip from my mind. Soon there's only teeth and tongue and lips and warm breath drifting over my skin.

"Lie back," he says, gently pushing me down.

I let my eyes shut, my body cradled by the silky-soft bed covers. He draws my thighs over his shoulders and slides his hands under my butt—lifting me to his mouth. The sensation is so intense, so sharply beautiful, that I cry out. He's an expert on me already—finding my sweet spots with ease. Playing me like a musical instrument.

It's almost embarrassing how quickly I come. But maybe that's because I've been so hollow these past few weeks, and this is the first drop of something good.

Mr. Suit rests his cheek against my thigh, his stubble a pleasant scratch against my tender skin. But he doesn't come up, instead kissing me again. Softly at first so I shudder and squirm, but as he builds up the pressure that too-sensitive feeling starts to shatter into something power and desperate. He swipes his tongue over my clit, flicking and teasing while his finger presses against my entrance.

"I didn't think I was ready yet," I pant. "But my God that feels good."

It's strange, a sensation of too-much and not-enough and everything in between. He works me like a master, making my body go liquid and my pussy pulse. "You want me to keep going?" The words are muffled against my sex and the movement of his lips sends pleasure flaring through me.

"Yes." I arch into him, flinging one arm over my eyes to blot out the senses that don't matter right now. I only care about touch—his lips against my most private part, the feel of his finger working in and out of me, curling in a way that hits me deep and right. "Don't stop. Please."

Satisfied, he feasts on me. Bright bursts of light shatter behind my lids, and release rushes up from deep inside. I cry out, because it's all I can do. The feeling is intense and I come harder than I've ever come before. I'm grinding against his face, taking everything from him. Taking it all.

When I sag back against the bed, my limbs heavy and my heart racing, the world slowly filters back. There's a thump from the apartment above us, and the sound of a door closing somewhere. The scent of Mr. Suit's aftershave dances in my nostrils and the bed shifts as he comes up beside me. I'm feeling everything now—feeling it with a sensitivity that's new. Even the gentlest brush of cool air ripples across my heated skin in a way that feels foreign and exciting.

It's like he's turned up the dial so I feel as though I'm experiencing it all for the first time.

"I don't know if I can move," I admit, grinning and trying to turn away to hide it.

But Mr. Suit isn't having it, and he draws my back to him. I feel the hard press of his cock against my butt and it's impossible, but I'm so turned on I don't even want a minute more to rest. I rock back against him, eliciting a moan. His strong arms wrap around me and his lips come down by my ear.

"You're good to keep going?" he asks. His voice is roughened and darkly sexy.

"That's like asking a girl if she wants to keep eating a piece of cheesecake after she's only had one bite." I catch the quirk of a smile on his lips. "Yes. I'm good to keep going."

He chuckles and pulls away for a moment. There's

the sound of rummaging and when I roll over, I see him going through his drawer. "I swear I had some in here."

"Been a while?"

He shoots me a look over his shoulder that tells me not to prod, but I'm a little warmed by the idea that we're both dipping our toes back into the waters together. For some reason, it makes me feel comforted. Safe. I admire his ass until he finally produces a foil packet from the depths of his sock drawer.

"Are you worried I'm out of practice?" He rolls the condom down his length. Watching a guy handle himself has always gotten me hot—there's something so primal about it. So...animalistic.

"No." I resist the urge to tell him that it makes me feel less intimidated, but I decide to keep that information to myself. This is *not* about being vulnerable. "With a mouth like that, I'm sure I have nothing to worry about."

A wicked smile lights up his face and he comes down to the bed, dragging me beneath him. Mr. Suit brushes the hair from my face and hovers over me for a second—not rushing. Not racing toward the finish line. He seems like the kind of guy who likes to enjoy the anticipation.

"You were right about something that first night," he says, scraping his teeth along my neck and grazing my skin with his stubble-coated jaw.

"What's that?"

"I *did* want to fuck you the second I opened the door to the stairwell."

"I knew it," I reply smugly. "I could see it in your eyes."

"You're hot. That's no secret." He kisses down my chest and draws one nipple into his mouth. The pressure makes my sex pulse and I suck in a moan. "Wearing that tiny little skirt and those high-heeled boots... fuck. There was no way I was going to get that image out of my head."

The comment sets off a little warning bell inside me, but I brush it aside. That's why I'm here—mutual attraction. Nothing more. If he sees me as a piece of ass, then that's fine. This is just sex. I don't even know his real name and that's *exactly* how I want it.

But the damned voice in the back of my mind whispers its disagreement.

"And then none of that mattered the second you opened your smartass mouth." He nips at my breast, then soothes the mark with his tongue. He's driving me mad—giving me enough to keep the pleasurable feeling swirling, but going no further.

I rock my hips up, trying to encourage him to push into me. But instead he rubs back and forth, the tip of his cock bumping against my clit in a way that makes me ache. He's teasing me, getting me so wound up I know I'm going to burst the second he enters me.

"There's nothing sexier than a woman who doesn't take any shit." He works his way back up to my face.

"I thought I wasn't your type." I reach down between us and wrap my hand around his cock, squeezing. The little power play that's been going on between us since day one is addictive—it's a sexy game of cat and mouse, only I have no idea who's the predator and who's the prey.

"I didn't think you were." He lowers his head to mine and kisses me hard. I taste traces of myself on him, the scent of sex and power and lust drawing me deeper into the moment. I guide his cock to my entrance, showing him what I want. "But no other woman has ever tempted me to break my own rules."

It makes me feel strong and beautiful and desired, things that have eluded me for some time now. But the thing is, I can't afford to be fooled into thinking this means something. "You don't have to sweet-talk me, Mr. Suit. I'm already here."

"I'm not sweet-talking you, Blondie. I don't say something if I don't mean it."

I loop my arms around his neck and pull his face down to mine, because I need to distract myself. I will *not* fall for him. I don't even know his name, for crying out loud.

"I'd prefer it if you stopped talking all together," I whisper into his ear.

"Bossy," he teases.

"Shut up and fuck me."

His gravelly laugh lights my body up. Flipping on every damn switch I have.

He pushes into me with one smooth thrust and the feeling of fullness consumes me. I'm dripping, aching and needy. I rock my hips up to meet his as we create a rhythm that's wholly ours—he's big and thick and my body takes a moment to adjust. But it's perfect, dirty and sexy and a little rough. A little wild. I tug his hair and rake my nails down his back, and in kind, he pulls out for the briefest second to flip me around.

"That's how you want to play this?" he growls.

I'm on all fours at the edge of the bed, with him behind me, and I'm so desperate to come again I'm almost weeping. "Yes."

He pushes into me and wraps my hair around his hand, giving it enough tension that my head is pulled back slightly. It doesn't hurt and I know I could stop it if I wanted to, but the fact that he can read me so well is making my legs tremble. He's still buried to the hilt and I squirm back against him.

"Tell me what you want," he demands.

"I want you to fuck me hard." I'm breathless, wanton. Wanting.

"What else?"

"Pull my hair."

"You a dirty girl, Blondie?"

"Yes," I whimper.

"You're a dirty girl who does peep shows and phone sex and likes to be fucked from behind."

Oh, God. I'm so wet I'm sure he's totally coated in me. "Yes. I am."

"I fucking love it."

His fingers bite into my hip as he thrusts into me, the sounds of our sex echoing through his apartment. All that teasing we've done has been nothing but a path leading to this moment. I gasp as the tremors begin, my orgasm building and building and building…

"Oh, my God," I gasp, squeezing my eyes shut.

The end is frantic and sharp, like a thousand bubbles bursting. I shake and tremble as release washes through me and Mr. Suit drives into me one last time with a sound that's going to be etched onto my memory forever.

He pulls me down to the bed, wrapping his arms around my body and cradling me. Warm breath puffs against the back of my neck and I feel totally and utterly sated.

CHAPTER TWELVE

Flynn

BLONDIE DIDN'T LEAVE my bed all night—well, except for the brief interlude we took to shower and rehydrate. Then it was back to bed, more sex. More teasing. More laughing. I don't remember the last time I woke up feeling so exhausted and yet so satisfied.

I stand at the foot of the bed, stifling a chuckle. Blondie sleeps like I imagined she would—messily. The sheets are totally ripped from her side of the mattress and bunched around her body. Her mass of platinum hair is spread out around her, gleaming in the pale morning light. One arm is flung over her face and her bare breasts are exposed to my hungry eyes. Her other hand is stretched across the bed and is resting below my pillow as if she's reaching for me. She takes up as much space as possible, stretching out like a misshapen star-fish.

It's adorable, and more than a little sexy.

She has this air of chaos about her that I'm finding unnervingly addictive. Perhaps it's the antidote to my heavily regimented lifestyle—opposites attract and all that. Even though I know it's not going anywhere, I don't regret breaking my "no casual sex" rule. That's not a night I'll forget in a long time.

I dress quietly, so as not to wake her, then head downstairs to chat with the building manager about getting her back into her apartment. Next, I duck into my favourite café and order us some breakfast—two coffees, bagels and those sweet Danishes with the strawberry jam in the middle.

By the time I make it back, I find Blondie sitting upright in my bed. Her hair is a fluffy, tangled cloud.

I set the coffee cup next to her. "There's breakfast out here, if you're hungry. Security is going to come up with the building manager in an hour to help you into your apartment."

Blondie eyes me with a whole lot of suspicion. Then she wraps the sheet around her and gets out of bed. "Thank you."

"Why are you looking at me like you've caught me snooping in your drawers?"

"Because I'm confused." She comes closer, her pale eyes narrowed. "Why are you being nice?"

Christ. What kind of losers has she dated in the past that a coffee and pastry is considered a big deal?

"I thought you might be hungry. I know I am." I shrug. I'm not going to turn this into a thing—Blondie has walls higher than I'm willing to climb. But that doesn't mean I'm going to screw her and then shove her out of my apartment. "It's nothing."

She picks up the coffee and pads out of my bedroom, still wearing the sheet and letting it trail behind her. I shake my head. I was going to wash it anyway, but it still makes me laugh.

"So you're a genuine nice guy, Mr. Suit."

"It's not self-proclaimed, so it must be true." I follow her and reach for the double-shot latte sitting on my kitchen table. I rarely eat at home, but there's something nice about sitting here with her, enjoying the sunshine streaming in and taking a moment to relax. "And I really don't like the whole Mr. Suit thing. Makes me sound stuffy."

"You *are* stuffy." She smirks. "Remember the whole rubbish chute conversation?"

"I'm considerate of my fellow residents."

"Stuffy," she repeats as she rummages through the white paper bag stamped with the Wooden Llama cafe's logo. "Ooh, what flavour pastry?"

"Strawberry."

She plucks one out and bites into it with a blissed-out expression. "My favourite."

Somehow, I'd known that when I ordered them. Which is crazy, since I don't know a damn thing about her—not her name, nor her profession. Only that when she cried out in the throes of sex, it was the best sound I've ever heard.

"I want to know your name."

Blondie stiffens on the other side of the table. "I thought we weren't doing names."

"A name now isn't going to change anything, but

two people who've had sex are past the point of using pseudonyms," I point out. "At least, that's how it's always been in my experience."

"You really don't know how this whole casual sex thing works, do you?" She wrinkles her brows. "The rules don't include pastries and names."

"Then what *are* the rules? Enlighten me since you think I enjoy them so much." I roll my eyes and fish out a pastry for myself. It's heaven on my tongue, and a rare treat. I don't usually eat things that are quite so nutritionally devoid.

You really are *stuffy.*

"No follow-up calls unless it's booty related. No deep and meaningful conversations. No romantic dates." She ticks the items off her fingers. "No introductions to friends or family. And definitely no commitments."

"Who made these rules?"

"Me." Her stare is direct and unwavering. "It's for both our protection."

"Ah, like an emotional condom."

In spite of herself, she snorts. "I like that."

"Look, Blondie. I'm not trying to drag you into something you're not comfortable with. But I didn't want you passing out on my floor because there's literally nothing to eat in this apartment, hence me buying breakfast. And I stopped by the concierge desk because I was walking past it and you were sleeping pretty heavy."

Never in my life have I needed to justify a kind deed.

She's an enigma…a damaged one. I shouldn't be intrigued, but I definitely am.

"You make it sound like I'm being irrational," she says, taking a sip of her coffee. When I don't respond, she huffs. "I'm *not* being irrational."

"Whatever you say, Blondie."

She looks at me for a long minute. I could drown in those strange, almost colourless eyes—they're beautiful and different and a little unnerving. It's like being picked apart, layer by layer.

"My name is Drew."

"Is that your real name?" Call me cynical, but I feel like I can't take her first answer as the truth.

"Sort of." Her lips quirk up.

In other words, no. Maybe it's a nickname or perhaps it's a short form of her real name, but whatever the reason…she's not letting me in. "Do you want to know my name?"

"No. I think Mr. Suit is a good fit. It keeps you very sexy and mysterious in my mind."

I shake my head, but decide to drop it. She's set her boundaries and that's her prerogative. It's not like I didn't know she had walls up. But despite the clash in our desires to get to know one another—or *not*, in her case—I'm enjoying her company.

She eats her breakfast, quietly sipping her coffee and watching me as if waiting for my next move. No deep and meaningful conversations, no commitments and no follow-up calls.

Before I've figured out how to handle this morning-

after situation, there's noise outside. A knock. Must be
the building manager coming to unlock Drew's door.
Before I have the chance to say anything, she stands
and grabs her coffee.

"Thanks for breakfast." She makes her way to the
door as I watch, dumbstruck. Sure enough, she leaves
my apartment still wearing my bedsheet and the second
the door slams shut I burst out laughing.

CHAPTER THIRTEEN

Drew

I HAVE BEEN thinking about Mr. Suit for days. Thinking about the incredible night we spent together, about how sweet and yet blunt he was the next morning. Who would have thought *that* was an appealing combination? Not me.

In the early days of dating my ex, he'd done similar things—coffee and pastries in bed. He'd even cooked for me one time. On reflection, I see those actions as a means to the "goal" he was trying to achieve. Wowing me enough so I'd keep fucking him, even though he undermined me in so many ways. I think he got off on that—making me fall for him while disrespecting me. I'm ashamed I didn't see it sooner. It makes me feel… vulnerable. Dumb.

Used.

But there's an honesty in Mr. Suit's actions. It wasn't for an outcome or for manipulation. It was something he did without thinking. And I know there was a level of trust there…because I told him my name is Drew.

Not Melanie, my legal, for-official-purposes-only name. Drew. The name I've gone by with my closest friends and family. The *real* me.

"She's gone off in fairy-land again," Presley announces as she waves a hand in front of my face. "Earth to Drew. Now, *what* has gotten you so distracted?"

We're sitting at the kitchen table in the house we grew up in. It's cramped and well-loved, as I remember. The round table is tucked into a corner and we've got mugs of steaming Earl Grey in front of us. There's Iced VoVos and Tim Tams, as well. All the things I love about being home.

"I've got a lot on my plate, you know. It's not easy being 'project managed' by Sherilee all the time." I take a Tim Tam and dip it into my tea until the chocolate starts to melt and then I take a glorious bite. "She's like a pretty drill sergeant."

Presley laughs. Today she's dressed down—happy to officially be off from work until after her honeymoon—wearing yoga pants and a T-shirt that says "I like my puns intended." I'm also dressed for comfort—no makeup and shredded jeans with a black hoodie. I catch a glimpse of our reflection in the glass door that leads out to the backyard. Without our usual "outside world" armour on, we're mirror images of one another. Same pale blond hair and light silvery blue eyes, same fair skin. We've even got dimples in exactly the same spots on our left cheeks.

It's been so long since we were home together.

"I've missed you," I say suddenly. The words leap

out without getting my brain's permission, and Presley immediately tears up. She gets up and throws her arms around me.

"I've missed you, too."

It's like being squeezed to death by a Care Bear.

"You don't have to go back to London, do you?" she asks as Mum comes to the table, a tray of mini meat pies steaming in her hands. "You quit your job. Why not stay here?"

I wait for my mother to chime in, but she doesn't. She's never once objected to my life of travel and being away from home—not like I imagine she would if Presley did the same thing. They're close—always have been ever since Presley got sick when we were little. I was left to fend for myself a lot and that made me a little rebellious. A little difficult in my unmet demands for attention.

I became convinced at one point that my mother only had enough love for one child—and I drew the short straw.

"I've done this country," I say flippantly. "I need something new."

A new chance to find somewhere to belong. After all these years, I keep chasing it.

"You've practically been everywhere already," Presley objects. "What's wrong with staying here?"

"I don't want the white picket fence and the two point three kids and the big backyard," I lie. "That's your dream, not mine."

"You can stay here without settling down, you know.

There's plenty of airline work to keep you travelling, but you could have a home base here." She frowns and reaches for a biscuit.

"Your sister is a free spirit," Mum chimes in. "Always has been."

I'm not, I want to scream. I just want to find the place where I'm supposed to be. For a moment I was sure that was with Vas—living by the water and eating fresh figs and learning his language. But I was wrong.

And here…here I'm shivering in the eternal shade of Presley's perfection.

"I'm being selfish," my sister says with a sigh. "I feel like part of me is missing when you're away all the time. I know I'm not supposed to say that, but it's true."

I take a long gulp of tea, hoping it will ease the lump in my throat. It's hard for people not to compare siblings, and it's doubly worse for twins. I can't blame anyone, because I do it, too.

It's why I left in the first place.

"You know I'll always visit," I say.

"It's not the same."

My mother reaches for Presley's arm and gives her a quick squeeze. Do I get any similar comfort from her? Nope.

You don't need it. You've been looking after yourself for years. Why stop now?

"Anyway," I say. "Enough about that. The Jack and Jill invites are going out tomorrow. I know it's late, but thanks to the best man, we've had some trouble getting on the same page."

"I'll talk to Mike about him."

"Don't bother. It's almost done now and it's not like I'm going to be around much after the wedding to cause problems." I'd decided not to tell Presley about the old switcheroo I pulled on the party theme because I figure the less she knows, the less chance of her fighting with her fiancé. Plausible deniability and all that. I can take the heat so Presley gets what she wants.

Story of my life.

"You don't cause problems." She rolls her eyes.

Maybe not. But sometimes I feel like the best thing for my relationship with my sister is for me to keep my distance—it's a safeguard against my jealousy of her perfect life. Against my bitterness over how my mother has always preferred her. Against the fact that no matter what I do, she will always be ahead of me.

And I love my sister more than anything, so I'll do what's necessary to protect our relationship.

"So tell me about Greece," Presley says. "Weren't you with some guy?"

I've been dreading this ever since I came home. I've kept purposefully quiet about the breakup in the hopes Presley might have forgotten about that one excited email I wrote her right before it all fell apart.

"Yeah." I stare into the depths of my tea, my reflection shifting in the milky surface. "It was a bit of fun."

"It sounded like you really liked him."

I steel myself. I can't tell Perfect Presley that I got dumped because a guy couldn't fathom committing to me—not when she got her first proposal at age four.

She'd been engaged properly once in her early twenties, and though it didn't work out, it was *her* decision to end things. Not his. People don't have problems seeing Presley as a long-term option.

"He was great." I paste on my best Fun Time Gal smile. "For a while."

My mother snorts. "You change boyfriends more often than you change your knickers."

"And like knickers, frequent changing keeps me feeling fresh." I wink at Presley and she shakes her head, laughing. "Vas was fun, but it was a fling. Nothing more."

I never should have assumed it was anything else.

"And what about now? Are you seeing anyone?" she asks.

My mind immediately drifts to Mr. Suit. The somehow uptight yet dirty, hot man of my fantasies. Ever since I walked out of his apartment wearing only a bedsheet, I've been on pins and needles waiting to see if he'll call. Yesterday, I dropped the sheet by his door with nothing but a Post-it note marked with a red lipstick kiss.

Then this morning, I found a bag containing the hoodie and underwear that I'd left at his place, which he'd washed. Along with that, he'd left a note saying he was busy with work for the next few days but asked if I wanted to come over next weekend for a "repeat."

It was a booty call…which is exactly where I'd drawn the line with him. For some reason, a handwritten note felt a little less sleazy than a text. Or maybe I'm justify-

STEFANIE LONDON   105

ing it to myself because I *want* to see him again. He's compromising to meet my requirements, which I get the impression he doesn't do often.

"I'd say that sly smile says you *are* seeing someone!" Presley leans forward. "Tell me everything."

"It's nothing," I say, but I can barely wipe the grin off my lips. As soon as the Jack and Jill party is done with on Saturday night, I'll be paying Mr. Suit a visit.

CHAPTER FOURTEEN

Flynn

I STARE BLANKLY into space with my hands behind my head as I swing on my office chair. Anyone observing me might assume I was in a meditative state of calm. Or perhaps contemplating a complex problem.

On the inside, however, I am a blazing inferno. Furious, indignant, desperate and sad. Two families have pulled out of our gene therapy study, including one group that I flew over from New Zealand, paying for their accommodation out of my personal bank account. They've left us short and now we're scrambling trying to find new test subjects.

None of the research matters unless we can test it on real people with real diseases.

Of course I understand the parents' fears—they know they might not have a long time with their kids, and they're worried about "wasting it" in clinics and hotel rooms. Perhaps this is the reason there's still no cure for Batten disease. Not enough time to test out theories and not enough willing test subjects.

I won't lie down and admit defeat. Drawing in a long breath, I bring my hands to my thighs and swivel back to my desk. Francis is standing in my doorway, a big crease between her brows.

"I don't want to talk about it," I say, holding up a hand. She knows every part of the business here, because she sees all my emails and fields my calls. And she loves Zoe, too. Dotes on her every time she comes to visit.

"Okay." Francis nods and comes into my office, closing the door behind her. "Maybe I can distract you with some wedding drama then?"

"Again?" I groan. "Is it this fucking Jack and Jill party?"

"I'm afraid so." Francis settles into one of the plush leather seats on the other side of the desk and smooths her hands over her tweed skirt. "I thought everything was sorted after I made the booking, but I have a friend who works at the venue and she caught a glimpse of the event plan. Apparently it's now a costume party and the key contact is your favourite maid of honour."

"She called them behind our backs and changed all the plans?" The balls on this chick.

"It appears so." Francis purses her lips.

"Change it back." I feel an ache in the back of my jaw and realise I've been grinding my teeth. This is not the best moment for party problems to surface. I'm in one of those "burn it all to the ground" moods. "Change it back to what we talked about and make sure you're the key contact. Explain that we're having some issues with a very enthusiastic maid of honour who wants to stick her nose into everything. Should they get any calls from her, the venue can advise that it's all been handled, but they should not give her any further information."

Francis looks at me for a second. "And the invitations?"

"Send them out today. We're doing them by email anyway and my understanding is the bridesmaids sent a 'schedule of events' with all the dates several weeks back, anyway. So this is simply a formality."

"What are you going to do when she sees the invite? She'll know you've reverted to the other theme without informing her."

I shrug. "Then it's done, isn't it? Too late for her to change it back."

Francis gives me that stern mother look. "Are you stirring up trouble between your cousin and his fiancée?"

"No." I shake my head. "From what Mike told me, his fiancée's sister is never around anyway. She flits in and out as she pleases and she's kind of the black sheep of the family. Mike doesn't seem to like her too much, so I doubt it's going to cause any more of a rift than there already is."

"Okay." Francis nods and pushes up from her chair. "I'll make sure we're locked in for the black, white and gold theme."

As my office door clicks shut and I'm alone again, I tilt my face toward the ceiling. In all this chaos and stress, the only happy part of my day is when I think about Blondie. *Drew.* I'm still chuckling days later after she walked out of my apartment wearing my bedsheet. The note she left me, sealed with a red-lipped kiss, is stuck on my monitor. Even now, with all this other crap going on, seeing it makes me smile.

There's something unique about that woman that drives me totally and insatiably wild. It's been torture not to go home early and knock on her door. Not to call her in the middle of the night.

You're not getting attached to a woman who's that emotionally unavailable.

True. But it doesn't stop me wanting her like crazy. I'm counting down to this weekend—Sunday. The day after the Jack and Jill party, when I'm going to need to relax and unwind. I'll let myself see her then.

In the back of my mind, warning bells are ringing. She's not right for me. I don't do casual sex.

And if I'm being totally honest, there's something very *un*-casual about this. I like the woman, even though I know nothing about her. But she's like an antidote to the hardest parts of me. To the uptight, unable-to-slow-down, unwilling-to-compromise parts of me.

And right now, I'm craving her more than anything.

CHAPTER FIFTEEN

Drew

IT'S THE DAY of the Jack and Jill party. Thank the freaking lord! I can't wait for this to be over so I don't have to exchange any more angry emails with Flynn Lewis. Ugh. Flynn. What kind of name is that anyway?

I'd thought about looking up his company and doing some snooping, but why give him the internet traffic? Frankly, I don't want to do a damn thing that might benefit him.

Fun little piece of Richardson family history: Presley and I are *super* competitive with costumes.

It was our favourite thing as kids—we'd cobble together costumes out of almost anything for birthday parties, special days at school and fake Halloween. I say fake, because we don't formally celebrate Halloween in Australia, but my sister and I were determined to bring it to our neighbourhood after watching too many re-runs of *Hocus Pocus*. We'd round up support from the other kids and convince Mum to let us host a spooky party. One time I turned myself into a stegosaurus entirely using hand-painted egg cartons.

So this is a big deal—my sister's pre-wedding party. Well, one of. We've got the Hen's party *and* a kitchen tea which includes the mothers and all the aunts and older relatives. But tonight is only for the bridal party and friends of Presley and Mike. The theme is "dress as your hero" so I'm going as Gene Simmons from KISS. Obviously. He's an icon. Plus, I thought it would be fun to wear a faux-leather catsuit with studded bat wings.

As one does.

I called the venue today to confirm the time, because I never got my email invite. When I checked over the list I'd provided the best man and his assistant, I realised I'd forgotten to put my own name on the list. Rookie mistake. It's no big deal, however, and I can't *wait* to see what Presley has pulled together for her costume.

After spending a good hour doing my makeup in the traditional black-and-white KISS style, I slip a coat over my costume to ward against the chill. Then I stride out of my apartment building in the patent leather over-the-knee books that I've decorated with silver studs, which gets a thumbs-up from my Uber driver. He blares "Mr. Speed" as we head to the Jack and Jill party.

I'm late, which isn't much of a surprise. Punctuality was never my strong suit, but Flynn's assistant told me she would be there early to fix up payment for the party.

Plus, I like to make a grand entrance. Most people slip on a kitty headband and call it a day—so Presley and I get a lot of attention for our creative outfits.

The Uber rolls to a stop and I take my time navigating the uneven cobblestone entrance in my platform boots. The old mansion was originally owned by a super-wealthy family who lost the house during the recession, and it lay abandoned for years. Eventually someone purchased it and turned it into an event venue, restoring it to its former glory. It's a cool spot, and the perfect place for a party.

I head through the main doors, where a table is set up. There's printed papers and a list, along with a few pens and bottles of water. A gold sign tells me to "please wait here" but nobody is manning the desk. I scan the area and hear classical music floating in from one of the rooms off to one side. Following the sound, I reach the door and poke my head in. There are lots of people around, but all are dressed in suits and cocktail attire. Little black dresses as far as the eye can see.

Perhaps they have another event on at the same time. Before anyone can see me, I walk back through the foyer and check out the other side of the venue. Empty. So Presley's party must be in a room on the other side of the fancy cocktail party.

Oh, well, I wanted to make an entrance, so I guess I'll have to make two. I head back into the room with all the people dressed in black. I don't recognise anyone and heads snap in my direction, so I give a little wave. There's an archway on the other side. That must be it.

Then I see the banner: *The future Mr. and Mrs. Lewis.*

She's taking his name. Interesting. I always thought Presley was going to keep *our* name.

I stride through the archway and my mouth falls open. Presley stands in the middle of the room, surrounded by people. She looks *incredible*. Her hair is pinned up with gold leaf-shaped clasps, and her body is draped in yards of black and gold fabric that shimmers as she moves. She looks like a model in a couture fashion show.

But there's one big fucking problem…she's not in costume.

None of them are.

Presley's eyes widen as she turns in my direction and her smarmy fiancé clamps a hand over his mouth. Shit.

Realisation crashes down on me like an avalanche— Flynn Lewis pulled a fast one. How could he have known about the changes I made? All I'd wanted was to give my sister the kind of party she deserved, a party she would have wanted. Not this…stuffy extravaganza.

Presley rushes forward and the room is filled with tittering and snorts and flashes of *oh, my God.* "What happened?"

"Your future husband's giant pain-in-the-ass best man is what happened." I grit my teeth.

Everybody in the room is looking at me. And I mean literally everybody—even the waiters carrying trays of cocktails around the room with gold swizzle sticks are gaping open-mouthed at me.

"Oh, no." She drops her face into her hands. "This is…unbelievable."

"His assistant stopped taking my calls, so I went ahead and organised a costume party. But it appears they decided to change everything behind my back without telling me." I decide to skip over how it was most likely a retaliation, because that doesn't feel super important to me right now. "I wanted to do something fun for you. I know how much you love dressing up."

Presley hugs me, not seeming to care if she gets white face paint on her cheek. "Can I say I'm glad that I didn't come in costume, because I think you would have kicked my butt. This might be your best work ever."

"Maybe I can pretend to be the entertainment?" I cringe. Out of the corner of my eye, I spot Annaleigh, Sherilee and Pauline. Poor Sherilee looks like she's about to faint. "I don't want to ruin your fancy night. I'll head home and change."

"After you put *all* that effort into your costume? No way!" Sincerity shines out of my sister's eyes—she has something sparkly and gold dusted all over her lids and each time she blinks it's like staring at a cloud of fairy dust. "You look amazing."

"I'm an embarrassment."

"You stand out." She pressed a hand to my cheek. "You have *always* stood out in a way that I could only hope to."

I snort. "Yeah, right."

Mike storms toward us and he looks royally pissed. "What the hell is going on?"

"There was a mix-up," Presley says. "It seems there was a miscommunication with your cousin. Where is he, by the way? I'd like to finally meet him so I can give him a piece of my mind."

"He's running late. Work." Mike rolls his eyes. His face is red and splotchy, like he's battling to hold in what he really wants to say. Seriously, what the hell does my sister see in this guy? "But this is unacceptable."

"Excuse me?" I'm tempted to see how much it will hurt if I swing my chunky, studded boot into his groin. Knowing how much Presley wants to have kids is the only thing that stops me.

"Are you trying to embarrass your sister?" Mike looks at me as though I'm something slimy that he's accidentally stepped on. "You've got quite the reputation for doing that."

"What? I'm not trying to embarrass anybody."

People have gathered closer now to watch the drama unfold. Presley's eyes are shimmering as if she's about to burst into tears and I am one more nasty comment away from punching Mike in the nose.

"No? You fly in and fly out whenever you please, always with a sob story so people pay attention to you." He shakes his head. "You can't even behave like an adult when it comes to your sister's wedding. Oh, no, you have to turn it into a competition by trying to change everything behind my cousin's back."

So he knows. I wonder if my missing invite was an accident after all. Of all the spiteful, nasty things...

Presley looks at me. "Did you do that?"

Shit. "I wouldn't have had to if Flynn—or rather, his assistant—would even listen to a single thing I said. I was trying to give you something that you wanted."

"She didn't want a costume party," Mike spits out at me. "This is another instance of you thinking about yourself."

Of all the things that could possibly hurt me, that statement was at the top of the list. It was a cherished thing between us, harkening back to our childhoods. "Is that true, Pres?"

My twin sister avoids my eyes and it's like a knife to the gut.

"Okay, wow." My face fills with heat, shame burning like a bright flame inside me. "Why didn't you say something?"

"You were so excited." She wrings her hands. "I didn't want to hurt your feelings."

"She's worried you'll go off the rails and leave again if there's an argument." Mike stands close to Presley in a way that makes me want to shove him. But I know that's my own issues rearing their head—I'm jealous of her. I always have been.

But the costume party was something I *genuinely* thought she wanted.

"Can you speak for yourself, Pres?" I ask. The hurt is pouring off me now. "Or are you giving up your voice along with your name?"

Curse my big, bloody filter-less mouth. I regret the words the second they come out of me, because I know they land hard. Her lip quivers and she looks at me like I've kicked her puppy. But Presley doesn't bite back in an argument—she always shuts down when there's conflict. Every single time.

I wonder if it's the same with Mike. Does she let him overpower her in an argument?

I love my sister, but I will *never* be like that with a man. It's why I didn't go back to Vas no matter how many times he called after the breakup. It's why I won't ever get into another relationship with a powerful, strong-willed guy like that ever again.

Presley pulls herself up, straightening her shoulders back and sucks in a breath. "I know you're lashing out because you're hurt. But that was really unkind."

If you ever think being screamed at by someone is humiliating, I can tell you this is worse. My sister's quietly spoken, adult language—that's somehow still full of compassion even as she tells me, rightfully so, what a shit human I am—is much, *much* worse.

Mike steers her away from me and I have this deep, irrational fear that he's going to take her away forever. He doesn't like me—that was clear from the very first time I met him. Fine. The feeling is mutual. But I don't want to lose my sister.

I stand in the middle of the room, watched by all these elegantly dressed people, and I don't think it can get any worse.

Until it does.

A tall, handsome man walks through the doors and Mike immediately rushes over to him. Their eyes drift in my direction, and a smirk tugs at the handsome man's lips. I know that smirk and I instinctively know this man is Flynn Lewis, best man and giant pain in the ass.

Also known as Mr. Suit.

CHAPTER SIXTEEN

Flynn

I SHOULD HAVE known that the maid of honour would throw a spanner in the works. But turning up to a cocktail party in costume, even after receiving the invite with the dress code clearly stated…well, that's plain childish. I should have been more suspicious when I didn't receive a raging email or phone call from her.

Out of nowhere, however, I'm hit with a jolt of lust. The maid of honour is wearing a catsuit so tight it makes her slender legs look like they go on forever. If this *was* a costume competition, then she'd be the front-runner. But we're not at a kid's birthday party. This is a grown-up event, and she looks ridiculous.

Ridiculously hot?

I shake the inappropriate thought off. My cousin Mike is huffing and puffing about how she's ruined his fiancée's night. That she doesn't care about her sister, only being the centre of attention. I place a hand on his shoulder, wordlessly telling him to calm down. I'll smooth things over with the wife-to-be and usher

Gene Simmons outside so everyone can get on with their night.

Before I even have the chance to ask for an introduction, two women storm up to me. For a moment, my heart fails. Blondie is standing in front of me wearing a gold-and-black dress, looking like she's about to cry.

"This is my fiancée, Presley Richardson, soon-to-be Presley Lewis." Mike does his pompous thing and thrusts Blondie toward me. I'm in shock.

How the fuck have I been screwing my cousin's fiancée?

But there's no recognition in her eyes. My head is a spinning top. I'm desperately trying to put the pieces together. Did Drew lie to me? Is this some sick coincidence?

"Nice to meet you, Flynn." She sticks her hand out politely, offering a watery smile that doesn't feel familiar at all. I don't detect any hint of connection with her—so either she's an incredible liar, or I've somehow gotten *very* mixed up.

"Nice to meet you, too." I shake her hand and feel… nothing.

None of the spark I've experienced with Blondie. None of the sizzle and burn.

"We need to talk." Gene Simmons plants her hands on her hips and purses her lips. Her entire face is covered in paint, a perfect replica of the KISS style. But the second she pulls me away from my furious cousin and his bride-to-be, I'm infused with heat and a wild rush of mixed emotions.

"What on earth are you doing?" I say as she drags me out into the foyer and through to a quiet, unused room.

"I'm wearing the costume I designed for the costume party I planned." Steam is practically billowing out of her ears.

"A party you planned behind my back. Unsuccessfully, I might add." Something is ticking in my brain, an uncomfortable feeling that swells the longer I stand in this angry woman's presence. "This isn't my first rodeo, Melanie."

She stares at me for a long, hard second. Then she pulls off the black wig to reveal a shock of platinum white-blond hair. My stomach is roiling. "Actually, my family and friends call me Drew."

Drew. My naughty next-door neighbour. An identical twin.

I don't know whether to feel relieved or sick—at least I didn't accidentally sleep with my cousin's fiancée. But my sexy, mysterious Drew is none other than the thorn in my side? None other than the maid of honour who's been making my life difficult?

"Did you know all along?" I ask, stony-faced. I'm not giving her a damn inch until I know more.

"No! Are you kidding me? *Why* would I sleep with you if I'd known you were Flynn freaking Lewis, the most irritating, stubborn, stuck-up man on earth?" She pretends to stick a finger down her throat.

"Real mature."

"Oh, like how you conveniently forgot to send me

an invite for the party so I would assume my plans had gone ahead? Yeah, that sounds totally mature, asshole."

"Everyone who was on the list *you* provided me received an invite." I fold my arms over my chest. "So if you forgot to put your own damn name on the list, then that sounds like you dug your own grave there, Blondie."

"Don't you *dare* call me that now." Her hands ball up by her sides. "Thanks to you, my sister and I are now having a fight and you've justified why Mike hates me."

"I take no responsibility for the fact that you can't organise yourself." But even as I say the words, I feel a twinge of guilt. My relationship with my brother is the most important one in my life, and I would hunt down anyone who stood in the way of it.

"How am I supposed to organise anything when all my calls go ignored and the replies to my emails are nothing but shitty single-sentence responses that veto every suggestion I have? And that was *before* you fobbed me off onto your assistant."

She looks like she's about to blow a gasket. And I'm in the weird position of being incredibly ticked off and also extremely horny. Seriously, Drew's body was *made* for skin-tight outfits. Her small but perky breasts are encased in faux-leather and the big chunky boots make her look even sleeker. It's totally hot and I should not be thinking about her like that anymore.

It's one thing to sleep with someone you shouldn't by accident, but it's another to make an informed decision to do it again.

"I didn't have time to deal with *War and Peace* every time you emailed me."

She huffs. "Sorry I give a shit about my sister. I'm not sure why I bothered, because apparently I have no idea what she wants anyway."

For a brief second, Drew's tough-girl façade falters. There's genuine hurt there.

"Look, I didn't intend for you to miss getting an invite, okay? I thought you were on the list. It was an honest mistake."

"And switching around my party idea?"

I'm not going to give her an inch there. "That was payback."

Her jaw twitches. She's mega pissed. I'm...*very* unsure what to feel right now. Because my head is telling me one thing, and my dick does *not* agree.

"You look hot," I say.

"Screw you."

"I like it when you're mean." I step forward and she backs up, moving farther into the unused room. Her costume is a stark contrast to the fancy old building with its decorative cornices, gold-patterned wallpaper and polished floorboards. "How do you get in and out of that get-up, anyway?"

"File that under things I'll never tell you." She crosses her arms and all it does is draw my eyes down to where the leather-like fabric stretches over her breasts. "So, Flynn huh? That's kind of an old-timey name."

"Yep. I'm named after Errol Flynn and my brother Gabe is named after Clark Gable." I shrug and the casual gesture makes her jaw twitch. "Our mother was a big movie fan."

"Not exactly living up to your namesake, are you? Wasn't Errol Flynn a massive playboy?"

"And a reported drunk and drug user, neither of which I am."

"Would that make you a 'reported' stick-in-the-mud?" she teases, her tone softening.

"According to some."

"Maybe you need to do something more exciting, Flynn."

"Any ideas?"

Drew's eyes dart to the doorway and that's enough to get my blood thundering and my cock jumping to attention. I can't explain this weird vibe between us—it's equal parts lust and antagonism, but my God it's fun. More fun than I can ever remember having—which, admittedly, is not the highest of bars to clear.

"Once this outfit comes off it's not going back on." Drew nails me with a hard stare.

"It wouldn't be wise to head back into the party wearing it, anyway," I say. "So really, does it matter?"

"If I do that, then what am I going to wear out of here?"

"Tablecloth?" I look to a table that's sitting off to the side of the room. "It's kind of like a bedsheet, and we've established you're already plenty comfortable wearing those."

She snorts and then shakes her head. "Why do I keep wanting to have sex with you? I don't even like you."

"That's a real conundrum." I lean against the wall and fold my arms, not bothering to hide my smirk. "What are you going to do about it?"

"I haven't decided yet." Drew cocks her head. "This could be a good distraction considering I'm pissed at my sister and her fiancé. But I'm *also* pissed at you."

"Ah, but you're pissed at Flynn Lewis, not Mr. Suit."

"True." She nods. "I like that separation."

I suspect she likes separation with a lot of things, because today I saw something real in her. Something vulnerable and hurt. Something I would bet my last dollar that she never wants anyone to see.

I'm officially, deeply and utterly intrigued by Drew Richardson.

But this is bad. She's a wild girl, a loose cannon. And there's no way in hell anonymity will protect us now—her twin sister is becoming part of my family, which means whatever risk-free bliss we've dwelled in previously is gone.

"Want to get out of here, Mr. Suit?" she asks coyly. "I can show you my Gene Simmons tongue action."

"Well, when you put it like that…how could I possibly refuse?"

She walks past me, trailing her hand along the front of my pants, my cock crying out for release. How does she do this to me? Drew takes my restraint and crushes it without effort. I know this isn't a good idea, but I'm like a puppet on strings, driven by my insatiable lust for her.

"You don't want to say goodbye to your sister?" I ask as she heads to the exit.

"I have a feeling she doesn't want to see me right now." The sadness is quickly masked as she crooks her finger, beckoning me outside.

There's no point pretending I'm not going to follow her out there and take her back to my place so we can fuck like bunnies. It's a bad move and for once in my life, I'm happy to knowingly make a mistake.

By midnight we're lying in my bed, satiated. Drew is curled against my side, her cheek resting against my chest and her white-blond hair tumbling all around her. We've showered and she attempted to wash all her face paint off, but there are flecks of black and white in her eyebrows and along the edge of her hairline.

I can't help but smile. I do that a lot around her— even though I *shouldn't* be smiling. I abandoned my best man duties merely seconds after arriving at the party and my phone has been pinging with texts from my cousin all night. I'm *not* that guy who shirks responsibility. I'm not that guy who picks pleasure over duty.

But around Drew... I'm different.

Drew shut her phone off after the fourth call from her sister. I did the same. Now it's blissfully quiet. We're in our own little bubble here, where the outside world doesn't matter and mistakes don't matter and responsibilities don't matter. There's nothing but her smooth skin and hot kisses and the rake of her nails down my chest.

She looks up at me, eyes smudgy and hooded. "Did you have any idea who I was?"

I shake my head. "None at all. In fact, when I first saw your sister tonight I had a heart attack because I thought I'd been screwing my cousin's wife-to-be."

She laughs and presses her face against me. "Oh, man, I wish I'd paid more attention. Part of me had forgotten that you couldn't see my face."

"You might look the same, but I knew she wasn't you the second I shook her hand." I stroke her hair away from her face.

"No crazy vibes?"

"No sizzle."

Drew is naked, the bedsheet draped only over her feet. She's perfectly comfortable in her own skin, more than any other person I've ever met. I could worship her body for hours. In fact, when she sank her nails into the costume as we walked through my front door and tore the damn thing right open, I could have died a very happy man.

"No sizzle, even though we look exactly the same." She ponders this thought for a moment.

"It's not about looks, as much as I *thoroughly* enjoy that part of you." I trace the curve of her shoulder.

"Then what? You like my sparkling personality?" she teases, rolling her eyes. This is Drew's mask. Her self-deprecating "I don't care what anyone thinks of me" front that I bet is entirely bullshit. "My witty repartee."

"I like the fact that you don't try to fit into someone else's box."

"That was bloody obvious tonight, wasn't it?" She lies still while I touch her, taking my time to explore the shape of her. Mostly I'm watching her face—for those small changes of expression, the subtle shift in her eyes. She tries to keep everything she feels far below the surface.

We might seem different—me in my three-piece suits and her in leather and studs—but armour is armour.

"You have a complicated relationship with Presley, don't you?"

Her body shudders a little as she draws in a breath, almost physically resisting my question. But slowly, she looks up at me with clear eyes and a naked expression. "Yeah, kinda."

I want to know more about her. Everything. Anything.

"Why do you ask?" She looks at me with such suspicion I'm almost insulted. Except that I know it's everything to do with her and nothing to do with me.

"I'm curious about you."

"Why?"

I sigh. "Look, you seem to be clinging to this whole mysterious bad girl thing, but I'm interested in *who* you are. You know, as a person."

"That's terribly old-fashioned," she says, but a small smile is creeping across her lips.

"I'm an old man on the inside."

She sucks on her lower lip for a minute, her eye contact intense and unwavering, and I'm lost in their silvery depths. "Presley is the 'good' twin. She was always the better student, the more sociable and popular one. When she was a kid, she was really sick and my mother had to give her everything just to keep her alive. All the love and affection and attention, and sometimes I wonder if that's why she's better at everything now. Better with…people."

"You were left to fend for yourself?"

"All the time. I didn't mind, because she *was* sick and I wanted her to get better more than anything. I love my sister." Drew traces circles on my chest, her eyes following the pattern. "But when we got to school, she shot ahead and now she's always running rings around me. I feel like I can't ever catch her."

"Why do you need to catch her?"

She lets out a soft puff of air. "Just for once I'd like to be the good twin. I'd like to be better at something… I'd like to be ahead."

"Maybe you're going in a different direction." I tilt her face up to mine. "Maybe you're never going to catch her because you're running a different race with a different finish line."

Her eyes search my face, as though she's looking for a sign of insincerity. Or maybe she's looking for something else—a reason not to listen to me. A reason to push me away.

But I won't give her one. I don't want her to go anywhere.

CHAPTER SEVENTEEN

Drew

How is this the same man who's been torturing me by email for the past few weeks? It's not possible that the unexpectedly sweet, incredibly sexy Mr. Suit is Giant Pain in the Ass Flynn Lewis. My brain can't reconcile it.

"You said you had a brother," I say, continuing the discussion against my better judgment. "Clark Gable?"

He laughs. "Yeah, Gabe."

"Who's older?"

"He is."

Why am I asking these questions? This is sex, not a getting-to-know-you session. But tonight I feel like Flynn is the only one who gives a shit about me—the only one who sees past my makeup and prickly attitude and shock value. Presley probably believes I walked into her party dressed differently because I like the attention. Was she cringing the whole time I was trying to plan the costume party?

Good old crazy Drew, at it again.

But Flynn doesn't seem to think there's anything

wrong with me. He's asking me personal questions even when I'm offering what I thought all guys wanted—sex without the need for more. Hell, it's what I thought *I* wanted. But the more time I spend with him, the more he wriggles past my defences.

"Does he also have a stick up his butt?" I'm going for the joking angle, because I'm really worried about how much Flynn is seeing of me now.

"No, I'm the more serious one." He looks up at the ceiling, his long body stretched out on the most massive bed I've ever seen. Flynn's body is incredible—perfectly honed, lean with the right amount of bulk. He's strong without making me feel like I'm hugging a brick wall.

Hugging, huh?

Well, sexy hugging. Not the emotional kind.

"In fact, he told me recently I need to get laid more." Flynn smirks.

"You're welcome."

The grin that splits across his face is cocky and indulgent. "Aren't you a Good Samaritan?"

I poke my tongue out at him. The tension from earlier today has finally left my body and I'm languid and liquid and more relaxed than I've been in months. I reach down for the sheet and drag it up over us, letting Flynn know I'm not going to rush off. "Tell me more about him."

He raises a brow. "He's a good guy. Works for a bank in their technology department. He's got a little girl named Zoe."

"You're an uncle?" I'm surprised for some reason—maybe because I'd put Flynn into this compartment where he was a guy with no family, no real life. He was like a 2-D cutout and now he's transforming into a real person in front of my eyes.

"I sure am." He looks proud as punch and it's the cutest thing ever.

I'm not one of those women who melts for stuff like this…usually.

"Want to see a picture?"

I nod. "Sure."

He reaches for his phone and brings up his home screen—he's in a white shirt and jeans, his reddish hair glowing like embers in the sun, holding a little girl in his arms. Her dark hair is a wild halo around her face and she's grinning like happiness is pouring straight out of her soul.

"This was taken last Christmas," he tells me. "She was four then."

"She's adorable."

He looks at me for a moment, like he wants to say more, but then he tosses his phone to one side and I see the shutters go up. Disappointment stabs me, though I have absolutely no right to feel that way. I was the one who didn't even want to exchange names, so maybe he doesn't want to push this conversation too far.

But now that we've started sharing parts of our lives, I'm kind of glad we're here. Dangerous thoughts for a dangerous situation.

"You know who else is adorable?" He pushes up

and leans over me, sweeping my hair back to expose my breasts.

"If you call me adorable, I'll make sure you regret it."

Flynn chuckles, and the sound is rough-and-tumble sexy. "How about cute?"

"Worse." I wrinkle my nose up. "And don't even start me on sweet."

He pushes me back against the bed and nudges my legs open with his strong, muscular thighs. He's insatiable—how is he hard again? He's like a redheaded sex machine and my body is begging for more.

"What would you prefer me to say?" His lips are at my neck, teeth scraping along my skin and hands skating up my rib cage. "That you're a dirty, rotten scoundrel?"

"Did you just Steve Martin me?" I let my eyes shut as he kisses down my chest. I'm boneless and at his mercy—melting into sensation as he warms me up for round...what is this? Three? Four?

I don't even know. I can't concentrate on his mouth *and* count at the same time, okay?

"Is that *really* the worst thing you can say?" I thread my fingers through his hair and roughly tug him to my breasts. He grunts and gives me what I want—firm, hot lips around my nipple. When he sucks hard, I arch into him.

"You're a dirty girl, Drew. A filthy, sexy, intoxicating, devil of a woman."

Oh, my. I like that.

"More."

He moves to my other breast, kisses trailing over my skin, lighting a fire inside me. "The way you looked with all that smudgy makeup and that dirty mouth, and that fucking obscenely skin-tight outfit tonight…like you want to be used good."

He reaches over to his drawer and pulls another condom out. No scrambling this time. He's prepared for this. And my body is *so* ready for him. I stretch my arms over my head, groaning as he presses against my inner thigh. I'm already sinking into a bliss coma. The way he makes me feel…

"You like my dirty mouth, huh?" I ask.

He rolls the condom down his cock and then leans forward, hands braced on either side of my head as he finds my entrance. I'm tender and a little sore but I don't want to stop. I want to lose myself in him again and again.

"I fucking love it, Blondie."

I roll my hips up and encourage him forward, getting rewarded with a low, rumbling moan in my ear. Flynn's hung. And unlike some hung guys, he doesn't rely on his size. He knows *exactly* what to do—what spots to hit and how to set a good, hard pace. One hand slides up my thigh, lifting my leg up so he can push deeper.

"I love your dirty mouth, your dirty mind, your dirty outfits. That catsuit, my *God*." His mouth covers mine as he drives into me over and over. "It's like you were made to torture me."

I laugh and press my head back into the pillow, the sound turning into a soft moan as he hits a good spot inside me. It's like Flynn knows my body, knows every part of me. He knows how to turn me on, how to make me smile, how to push my buttons.

He doesn't *know you. He knows Blondie.*

My alter ego. The spiced-up, rebellious, armour-wearing version of me.

You're going to get hurt.

"I like you, Blondie." The words are whispered against my ear. "All of you."

"I like you too, Mr. Suit."

He rolls and pulls me on top of him, and I feel powerful and beautiful and free. My head is screaming at me to back away, but I can't. I'm addicted to how he makes me feel. Addicted to the red shade of his hair, addicted to the feel of his hands on my skin, addicted to his half smile and blue eyes and stiff upper lip.

I like him a lot.

It's a rebound, nothing more.

But as he looks up at me, like I matter to him—like this isn't just casual fucking—I'm not so sure I know what this is after all.

The next morning I reach for my phone and turn it on. It immediately lights up with a dozen notifications, texts and voicemail messages. All from Presley.

With a heavy sigh, I get out of bed and reach for Flynn's shirt. My catsuit was…uhh…damaged in its enthusiastic removal last night, so I have nothing to wear and for some reason I don't want to sneak back to my own apartment yet. So I shrug on the shirt and take my phone out into the living area to call my sister back.

She answers on the first ring. "Oh, my God, I was so worried that something had happened to you! You walked out and then you wouldn't respond to my messages and my imagination started spinning and—"

She hiccups and I cringe. "I needed some space to think."

Yeah, "thinking" was exactly what you were doing.

"I'm glad you're okay." She sighs. "About last night—"

"It's fine."

"No, it's *not* fine." Presley sounds like our mother when she gets like this. "We're fighting."

"Are we?" Yeah, I'm being a stubborn bitch. Sue me, I'm hurt.

"Don't be like this, Drew. I want to make sure everything is okay." Her voice wobbles and I feel worse. "You're the only person I really care about having at this wedding."

I snort. "How does Mike feel about that?"

"*Aside* from him. Obviously." She huffs. "But the rest of them could turn up or not, and I honestly couldn't give a shit."

I smirk. "Anne Presley Richardson, I am appalled at your language."

"Says you, potty mouth."

It's weird, but I can hear her smile. Yes, hear. Being twins isn't quite the "psychic connection" that some people claim, but there *is* something special connecting us. Something deeper. I feel her emotions keenly.

Which is annoying when I want to feel angry, but instead I just feel…sad.

"Why didn't you tell me that you didn't want a costume party, Pres? I was only doing it because I thought you loved dressing up and you said a while ago that you never get to do it anymore."

"The Jack and Jill theme had to be a joint decision and Mike didn't like the idea—apparently he told Flynn. So when the invites came through I assumed you'd all sorted it out."

"So it's not that you didn't want the costume party, but that you're letting Mike make the decisions." When did she turn into such a yes-woman?

"Don't say it like that."

"Like what? Like he's calling the shots and you're not standing up for yourself?"

"Marriages are a *partnership*, Drew. Two people. I know you never have to think about anyone but yourself, but it's not like that when you're in a relationship."

I feel like I've been slapped. "I *know* what a partnership looks like, because *we're* a partnership."

"Is this because I'm getting married? Are you worried that Mike is going to take me away from you?"

"I'm worried because he seems to overpower you, and the Presley I know would never let someone treat her like that. Especially not a man."

"You don't understand."

"Why?" I shake my head. "Because I'm so immature than I cannot possibly comprehend what it's like to be in a committed relationship? Newsflash, Pres, I *have* been in a relationship and I know red flags when I see them. If Mike is treating you like this before you get married, do you think he's suddenly going to change after he puts a ring on it?"

The phone goes silent and it takes me a few seconds to figure out that she's hung up. Shit. Why did I have to open my big mouth? Again?

I scrub a hand over my face and turn. Flynn is standing in the doorway, a pair of red checked pyjama bottoms riding low on his hips and his muscled torso gloriously naked. His hair is sticking out in all directions and there's a fine dusting of ginger stubble along his jaw.

Meanwhile, I'm pretty sure I'm still sporting some of my face paint from last night and…oh, no. Tears prick the backs of my eyes, which fill quickly—too quickly.

No. Abort! Abort!

Too late. My tears grow fat and fall onto my cheeks. I can't stop. I'm sobbing like a baby in front of my booty call. What the hell is wrong with me?

He's across the room so quickly I wonder if he has superpowers, and then his arms are around me. My wet cheek presses against his chest and the tears flow harder. I *hate* fighting with my sister. It makes me feel physically ill. And I equally hate crying in front of people. I didn't even cry at my uncle's funeral three years ago. I bottled it all up and then went outside by myself to bawl.

But now I'm a jumble of emotions.

"This is all your fault." I hiccup and he strokes my

hair. "Too many orgasms." Hiccup. "Now I'm emotional from all the endorphins." Hiccup. "And your cousin is a douche canoe."

The stroking motion is soothing. It shouldn't be. I should be alone with a pillow and a bottle of vodka. "I know, Blondie."

"Which part?" I squeeze my eyes shut.

"All of it."

[faint text from previous page bleeding through]

CHAPTER EIGHTEEN

Flynn

I COULD ONLY hear one side of her conversation, but it was enough. Sibling relationships are complicated. I've been in Drew's position. I *know* her pain.

And she's right, my cousin *is* a douche.

The way he talks about his wife-to-be is gross, like she's a check in a box. Like she's an achievement he's unlocked, not a real person. I've stayed out of it, because I've already caused one relationship in my family to fall apart. I didn't want another weighing on my conscience.

I hold Drew close to me, feeling her slender shoulders shudder with each breath. Her hair tumbles messily down the back of the shirt she stole from my bedroom floor. Her hands are tucked between our bodies, as if she's trying to keep some barrier between us. But she's melted into me, her face pressed to my chest and her tears soaking my skin.

"I'm worried she's going to get hurt," Drew says. Her fists finally unfurl, and she relaxes in my arms. "I've been with a guy like that before—they like to control things. They want to have the last word on everything. She won't be happy, because he'll want her to be this quiet, submissive wife. And my sister is sweet and kind, but she's not submissive."

Drew cranes her head up and she's a mess—mottled cheeks, black makeup smudged around her eyes, a dot of blood on her lip where she must have bitten down too hard.

"She always wanted to get married," she continues. "But her first fiancé didn't work out and she left him at the altar—and I'm worried that she thinks because that happened before, she can't do it again. That she can't walk away."

"You can always walk away."

People do it all the time, these days. Hell, it's the reason I barely date—because if I did, I'd want long-term and I know that isn't the way most people operate. Sometimes there's a good reason—like in Presley's case—but sometimes it's pure selfishness, like what happened with my brother's wife.

"What would you do?" Drew's voice wobbles. I'm getting a glimpse of her without her armour now. And the soft, raw vulnerability beneath.

"I've been in your exact situation before," I admit. I guide her down to the couch and pull her against my side. She swings her legs over my lap and rests her head on my shoulder like we've been doing this forever. "My brother was married to a woman who treated him and their daughter like crap. Things started to go bad after Zoe was diagnosed with a rare disease. My brother's wife couldn't cope. She started drinking and partying, and forcing my brother to shoulder all the burden on his own. So I spoke up."

"What did you say?"

"I pulled her aside one night and said that she needed to think about how her behaviour was impacting her husband and her child."

Drew's eyes are wide, red-rimmed. There's not a hint of her defensiveness now, not a shadow of her walls. "And?"

"She walked out on her family and we haven't seen her since."

Drew gasps. "She just…left? That's horrible."

"It's been really hard on Gabe, trying to work while taking care of Zoe's increasing needs. I help them out as best I can." There's a lump in my throat. I *never* talk about this…with anyone. It's not in my nature to open myself up. Especially given my parents' marriage ended the same as Gabe's—my father was saddled with two rambunctious boys after my mother decided she'd prefer to party than deal with her needy children.

He would never understand why Gabe had married a replica of their mother.

"I think you might be a good person under all that frowning." Drew is calming down, and her teasing tone is back. I shoot her an exaggerated frown and she rewards me with a watery laugh. "Do you feel guilty for having that conversation with her?" she asks quietly.

"Yes."

She nods. "I don't know what to do about Presley."

"Lay it all out, but ultimately it's her decision."

"If you had to do it over, would you still have had that conversation with your sister-in-law?"

Was it better for Zoe to have no mother at all than to have one who flitted in and out, paying attention only when she felt like it? I had a mother like that until I was fourteen. I know how much it hurts to see the look of disdain in a parent's eyes. I knew she couldn't stand being a mother, couldn't stand the weight of her responsibilities around her neck.

"Yes, I would still say it all." I sigh. "A leopard doesn't change their spots."

Drew makes a *hmm* noise. "You don't think people can change?"

"Not fundamentally, no." My mother never changed a damn bit until the day she died from an overdose. It made me driven. Made my goals crystallise. Made my understanding of the world and people so sharp it kept me at a distance from almost everyone but my brother and niece. "I think at some point we become set."

"Like concrete?"

I laugh. "Yeah, like concrete."

Silence descends over us and we're lost, but together. Lost in our thoughts, lost in the past. I keep my arm tight around her as if it might stop her running away.

"I don't like people seeing me cry," she says eventually. "It makes me feel weak."

"You're not weak."

"You don't think so?"

"Not even a little bit."

I turn and brush the hair from her face, staring into her beautiful silvery-blue eyes. Her lashes are spiky and stuck together, her skin is ruddy, and she's still the most beautiful woman I've ever seen. Because there's something genuine about her—something that if I'm not careful, I'll fall for.

Would that be the worst thing in the world?

At this point, I'm really not sure.

About an hour later, I'm sitting on the couch with Drew and she's fast asleep. After our talk, she took a shower and I made us eggs for breakfast. Then we decided to chill on the couch and watch a movie. She barely made it past the opening sequence. Now she's hugging a throw cushion and has her face mushed into the soft fabric. Her hair—that glorious, glorious hair—is like a tangled blond cloud around her body. She refused to give up my white shirt and damn if it doesn't look delectable on her. She's on her side, feet in my lap, and her glittery black toenail polish catches my attention.

We barely slept last night, because we couldn't keep our hands off each other. This insatiable desire is new. I'm cool with women—always keeping the upper hand and making sure I get what I want. Only nobody wants to commit to anything these days.

Yeah, yeah. Call me old-fashioned. And while you're at it, get off my lawn.

I reach for the remote and pause the movie before scooping Drew into my arms. She stirs, her eyes creaking open for a second but drooping back down almost immediately. She's exhausted. Wrung out from the emotional argument with her twin sister.

I take her to my bedroom and place her on the mattress. I hadn't even made the bed yet, so the covers are a mess and I pull them up over her. She burrows in deep, wrapping herself up like a sexy blond burrito.

Shaking my head, a big goofy smile on my lips, I walk back out to the main area of my apartment and shut the door quietly. That's when I hear someone outside.

"Drew?" *Knock, knock, knock.* "I know you're in there."

The woman, who I can only assume is Presley, isn't knocking on my door. Shit. I do *not* want to get involved in another family's arguments. I spoke the truth when I said I would have the same conversation with my sister-in-law if I went back in time, but that doesn't mean I want to break Drew's family up, too.

But the knocking continues. Stifling a groan, I head to my front door and yank it open. Presley is in the hallway, her head resting against Drew's front door.

"She's not in there," I say.

Her head snaps toward me, her expression morphing from sad to angry to confused. "Flynn?"

"Yeah, your sister and I are neighbours. Weird co-incidence." I shrug. I'm not sure whether I should tell her Drew is at my place. Our being together—in whatever impossible-to-label thing this is—is supposed to be secret.

Presley looks confused, but she shakes her head in a way that's just like Drew. It's striking how similar they look, even though their vibe is totally different. Presley's in a neat pair of blue jeans and a baby pink jumper with ballet flats and a beige trench coat draped over one arm. She's beautiful, obviously, but in a totally restrained, utterly controlled kind of way.

Nothing like the wild, antagonistic sexiness of Drew.

"What happened to you two last night? You both disappeared and then I called Drew this morning and…" Presley's face crumples. "Oh, God, this is turning into a huge mess. We both said terrible things and then I hung up on her and now I feel sick."

"I brought Drew home last night. She was pretty upset." I'm choosing my words very carefully. "And I suggested that staying at the party in her costume might make things worse."

"Probably. Mike is so angry." Presley sighs. Darkness rings her eyes, and I bet she and my cousin argued well into the night. "He always thinks Drew is trying to steal the spotlight from me. But it's not true…she'd need to be *around* for more than five seconds to do that."

I consider whether I should go and fetch Drew from my bed, but my gut tells me that's a bad idea. "What do you mean?"

"She's a nomad, my sister. Flits from one place to the next, always packing her bags and running away from commitment of any kind." Presley shakes her head. "Every time she moves back home it's only temporary, and she usually leaves earlier than planned. I love her so much, but we're very different, I guess. She's allergic to putting down roots. I don't think she's ever held a relationship for longer than a few months and she *always* leaves first. Even when it comes to her family. She never stays. I know I shouldn't say that, but I just... I really miss her."

The words are a cold fist around my heart. A timely reminder of *why* I can't let Drew get into my head—I've seen one too many free spirits crush those around them with their flightiness and their inability to commit. And I'm Mr. Commitment. I'm committed to my work, to my brother and my niece. To making a difference.

"Why don't I walk you downstairs?" I reach inside the doorway to where a pair of my sneakers sit and I scuff my feet into them. Then I shove my keys and phone into my pocket. "When I see Drew next I'll tell her you came by."

If I fall for a woman like Drew, I'm at risk of repeating the mistakes of my father and brother. And what if I ever introduced her to Zoe...and then she left? I can't have that.

Which means, no matter how drawn I am to Drew, I can't let her get too close. I won't.

CHAPTER NINETEEN

Drew

FLYNN SURE DOES run hot and cold. After he consoled me on Sunday morning, I woke up in his bed, the scent of him on my skin, and yet the man was nowhere to be found. He totally ghosted me.

There was a text on my phone in Flynn's usual spare tone:

Sorry. Had to go to the office.

Was it an emergency? Did the amazing sex give him a sudden burst of inspiration? No idea. But then I put the pieces of the puzzle together. There was another text, one from my sister saying she came by and that I wasn't home, but that she spoke with Flynn.

Given there wasn't any mention of me being in his apartment, I assume he didn't offer up that little fact. Probably for the best. I'm sure Mike would somehow spin it to make it look like I was trying to hurt Presley.

God, I hate that guy.

I know, I know. I should be supportive. My sister loves him, so I should too…or at least tolerate him. But the closer we get to this wedding the less I understand why they're together. If I say anything, my sister will put it down to my history of avoiding relationships. Avoiding being vulnerable with another person.

If only she knew I cried in Flynn's arms this morning.

Not my proudest moment. But it felt…nice. It's been a long time since I let it all out and had someone there to comfort me. My ex certainly wouldn't have tolerated me crying. He told me once that there was nothing more unattractive than a woman who let her emotions run free.

Red flag? Uh, yeah. One of a dozen I ignored because I wanted so badly for our chemistry to mean something beyond sex. More fool me.

And does it mean something beyond sex with Flynn?

I honestly don't know…and I don't know what I want it to mean. Which is why I've been steadfastly ignoring him for the past few days. Only now I need to partner up with him—as maid of honour and best man—to deliver a speech for the rehearsal dinner. We're doing a slide show with funny pictures of Presley and Mike, along with some anecdotes from their childhoods.

Annaleigh told me to "keep it light and funny."

Can do. Keeping it light is my MO—no ties, no commitments, nothing serious.

But now I'm riding the elevator up to Flynn's office with a box of photos from my mother's house and I'm… nervous. I *want* to see him again. I know that because I changed my outfit five times before settling on a black skirt, chunky platform boots and a tight white top over a padded bra that makes my boobs look extra perky. I want to torture him. But I did my makeup so it looks like I'm not wearing any at all—as if I "just woke up like this." I don't want him to think I tried too hard.

Ah, girl logic.

Clutching the box under one arm, I hold my breath while the elevator shoots up to the top floor. Butterflies swirl in my stomach. The anticipation is like a fizzy drink that's been shaken up and is ready to burst.

A soft *ping* announces my arrival and I exit along with two men dressed in business casual. It seems people don't really suit up in this office. Actually, for an office, the place has a nice vibe. It's relaxed, with lots of pale, warm wood and green hanging plants. I don't know much about it, other than it's a medical research firm so I assume they also have labs somewhere. Or perhaps they partner with one of the hospitals? This must be their head office.

A receptionist sits behind a simple wood and silver metal desk. It's very spare and minimalist, a lot like Flynn's apartment.

"Hi." The young guy looks up with a friendly smile. He's wearing a purple-and-white-check shirt, which sits open at the collar. "Can I help you?"

"I'm Drew Richardson. I've got a meeting with Flynn."

"Mr. Lewis?" The guy quirks an eyebrow behind his thick-rimmed glasses as he scans his computer screen.

"Please don't make me call him that." I wrinkle my nose. "He's already got a big enough head."

The guy looks a little shocked by my response. "Right, of course. Sign your name here and then you can head straight through to Francis—her desk has the big yellow flowers in a gold pot. You can't miss it."

"Thanks." I scrawl my name on the electronic signing pad and then follow his directions.

Deeper into the office, I see a small bank of desks where people sit with headsets. There are a few glass-walled offices along one side and a small, open kitchenette in one corner. It's not like any of the cube-farm offices I've seen in movies.

The woman who can only be Francis spots me before I make it to her desk. Her lips are pursed and I'm not sure if it's because she's judging my outfit or if she hates me because of the whole Jack and Jill party thing. Probably both.

"Melanie? Or is it Drew?" Her voice is cold enough to flash-freeze the sun.

"Miss Richardson is fine."

Chances of me getting stabbed with a letter opener? High.

"You can go straight through," she says with an air of reluctance.

Flynn's name is embossed on a silver plate on his office door. I enter and find him standing at the window and looking delectable as ever.

Let me tell you, Mr. Suit is in *fine* form today. His red hair looks brighter with all the sunlight streaming

into his office. And, unlike everyone else here, he's
dressed to kill in a charcoal three-piece suit that's slim-
fitting and obnoxiously hot. Not to mention he smells
like soap and coffee and all good things. It takes every
ounce of my willpower not to launch myself into his
arms.

For a moment we eye one another up, like two territorial animals, neither one willing to make the first move.

I break first. "Hey."

"Hey."

More awkward silence. Wow. It feels like the only
time we communicate clearly is when our clothes are
flying off. Truth be told, I wouldn't mind peeling him
out of that suit right now. "Do you want to do this standing, or should I sit?"

It comes off a little snappier than I want.

"Testy." His lip quirks.

"Annoying." I shoot him a withering glare before I
breeze toward his desk and plonk myself down into a
leather chair, noting the way his gaze glides all over me.
I can't explain the energy between us—it's crackling
and tense and so damn addictive it should come with a
substance abuse warning label.

"So what's the plan?" I ask, dumping my box of photos on his desk.

"I thought you might have one."

I snort. "Why would I bother? You'd just thwart it
like you did last time."

"Still bitter about that, huh?" He lowers himself into
his chair, popping the button on his jacket. His suit is

perfectly fitted to his muscular body and it highlights his broad shoulders and chest.

"I'm not bitter, you're just a poor sport."

"I don't like to lose."

"You play dirty."

"So do you." He shrugs in a way that makes me want to wipe that self-satisfied expression off his face. Yet, despite the smirk, his eyes are like twin blue flames.

Where was this heat when he ghosted on the weekend? He left me alone while the sheets cooled around me. Left me alone after he saw me in my most vulnerable state. I remember that feeling—my ex walked away more than once to keep me in place.

To remind me that *he* had the upper hand.

"I was thinking we could do a timeline of their lives, and maybe share a story from childhood, one from their teenage years and one from adulthood." I keep my mind focused on the task in front of me. Flipping the lid off the box of photos, I pull some pictures out. "We can figure out how to tie the stories to opposite parts of their personalities, to show how they complement one another."

I'm really hoping he'll have something good to say about Mike…because I sure as hell don't.

Flynn is still and silent as a mountain, watching me with focus and intensity. It's unnerving. Unsettling. And yet a delicious heat blooms deep in my belly, fanning through me like rays of sunshine.

Focus, you idiot. You need to stop *falling for guys like him.*

"Did you bring your photos along? You said we could scan them all here." I'm clutching desperately for something safe to talk about. Something neutral.

But he continues to watch me.

"I've actually got a funny story about this one." I hold up a picture of Presley and me. We're both covered from head to toe in red cake and pink buttercream and wearing giant smiles. "We ended up having a food fight, because my mother only baked one birthday cake and we didn't want to blow the candles out together. I started it…"

I'd *always* started it, as a kid. I was a firecracker and Presley was a calm blue ocean.

"I took a fist-full of cake and mushed it into her hair. My mother was horrified, but then Presley turned around and did the same thing to me." I laugh at the memory. "We went through the whole cake in minutes and the food dye tinted our hair pink."

Flynn's lip twitches. But still nothing.

Am I going to have to carry this entire conversation? If I had some cake in front of me right now, I'd definitely mush some in his hair.

"Will you fucking say something?" I slap the photos down on his desk. "I'm not going to play whatever power game you're getting off on right now."

He looks me dead in the eye. "Did you get that top in the kids' section?"

I want to slap him and kiss him at the same time, but I can't really complain. I *did* choose this outfit with every intention of showing him what he can't have—

except I know I'll fold like a bad hand of poker the second he asks me for anything.

Because as much as I want to lump him in with my ex, I can't. Vas would *never* have held me while I cried. He would never have told me a personal story so I knew I wasn't alone. He would never have tucked me into bed after letting me fall asleep on his couch.

Hell, *no*. My ex would have sent one of his staff in to deal with me and he would have extracted himself with all the precision of a practised playboy. But Flynn is…different.

"Did you get that suit in the Obnoxious Asshole department?" I retort.

"I did actually." He runs his hands down his chest, grinning like a sexy villain. "It's my favourite area of the Rich Dickheads Department Store."

I burst out laughing. "I really want to hate you, you know that?"

"Same." Something hot and warning flashes across his face. "It's most annoying."

"Why did you leave the other day?" The question rushes out of me before I have a chance to even *think* about holding it back. Dammit, why do I get like this around him? He doesn't owe me anything and I like it that way because it means *I* don't owe *him*.

He sighs and for a minute I think he's going to give me his "I had to work" bullshit. But he leans back in his chair and knots his hands in front of him. "I felt like I was getting too close."

"Really?" I'm not sure what else to say and I don't

know whether it's comforting or terrifying that he feels the same as I do.

"Yeah. There's something…addictive about you."

I sigh at his word choice. "Funny, that's exactly what I've been thinking about you."

"I don't understand it." He rakes a hand through his hair. "We want opposite things and I promised myself I wasn't going to compromise. I *don't* compromise for anyone else."

But he has for me. It fills my heart, smooths over all the dents and cracks. And truthfully, I'm different around him, too. I'd never let any other man comfort me the way he did on the weekend—I'd make damn sure I was nowhere near anyone before I let it all out. But around Flynn I feel…safe.

"Your sister tells me you can't stay in one place for long," he adds. "She called you a nomad."

It's true. But besides Presley, I've never had anyone who *wants* me to stay and my relationship with my twin is complicated. I've never really belonged anywhere, so I keep moving. "I haven't tried to hide that part of me."

"I know, but the reminder was something I needed to hear."

From where I sit, facing his desk, I can see the back of a photo frame. I reach for it and Flynn doesn't stop me—the picture is of him, Zoe and another man I assume is his brother. They both share the same blue eyes and red hair. The little girl is laughing with her whole body, and the love on Flynn's face is so genuine my heart wants to break.

"She was diagnosed with Batten disease two years ago," he says. Now there's no teasing in his expression, no joy.

I trace a finger over the little girl's sweet face. "Will she be okay?"

"Most people with Batten disease die in their teens or early twenties."

It's not the response I'm expecting, and the information socks me in the chest.

"Her vision is already deteriorating and there's a strong chance she'll start to experience seizures in the next few years. Among other things." Flynn's voice is thick and I suck on my lower lip to stem my tears. I won't cry in front of him again, but hearing the raw pain in his voice—no matter how well he tries to hide it—is killing me. "There's no cure, as yet. *This* is why I work as hard as I do. My company is trying to find a way to slow these symptoms, to give these wonderful people and their families more time together."

"That's why you don't do casual, because of her."

"I had a mother who refused to put her children before her own hedonistic needs. Zoe's mother did the same…she abandoned her the way my mother abandoned Gabe and me." He reaches for the photo and places it back on his desk. "But I'm not going anywhere. I'm going to be a source of stability for her because I know what it's like to be treated as a temporary, disposable thing."

Oh, God. Listening to this big, sexy man open up like this…

I know what he means. My mother wasn't as bad as his, by the sounds of it, but I never felt like I mattered. And in similar situations, Flynn and I have become polar opposites. He's dug his heels into the ground, becoming a pillar of strength and stability.

And I've given stability the middle finger.

Similar circumstances have forced us in opposite directions, as if we're two identical poles on a magnet repelling each other. Pushing away. And yet…

I still want him. I can't stop thinking about him. I'm drawn to him even though I know I won't allow myself to commit. Every other time I've done it I've ended up with my heart bruised and bleeding. Feeling unworthy. *Being* unworthy.

"We're totally wrong for each other, aren't we?" I say.

"Wholly and categorically." He stares at me with those bluer-than-blue eyes, with his sexy half-smirk. "We want opposite things."

"Do we? Because it sounds like we actually want the same thing, we're simply going about it in different ways. I run from commitment to avoid getting hurt and you set the bar of commitment so high that nobody will ever meet your standards." I cock my head. "End result is the same, though—we're both alone."

And miserable.

I won't admit that aloud, but it's true. I'm sick of living a meaningless life without real relationships—romantic or platonic. It's so bloody lonely. But I'm afraid to let another person change me, to convince me to want more.

I won't let myself be vulnerable to that kind of rejection. Because what if I change, what if I become someone new, and I'm *still* not enough?

CHAPTER TWENTY

Flynn

EVERY BRAIN CELL I have is firmly telling me to walk away from Drew—she's the highest kind of flight risk. A nomadic wild child who lives by her own rules and doesn't let obligation ground her. If anyone is going to walk away when things get tough, it'll be her.

You're underestimating her.

That niggling voice is getting louder—telling me that I'm holding myself back from something important. I keep reasoning that it's chemistry. Sexual tension. Good old-fashioned sheet-burning compatibility. Our bodies are well suited…but our minds?

You want more with her.

I do. I want to explore this unexpected thing and see where it goes. And I am not a man who explores. I decide. I act. And other people fall into line.

But not her.

"You think I have high standards?" I watch her expression—it's guarded. But I'm slowly learning her tells.

"Impossible standards," she corrects. "I picked that up about you the moment we met."

It feels like years ago the night I went into her apartment, accepting a drink and declining her invitation for more. Then she wore me down and I loved every second of it. "You said my employees hated me."

"I said they left." She narrows her eyes. "But I didn't guess that you'd expect them to leave."

Francis accused me once of putting people through their paces too hard when I first hire them. It's true, I guess. I expect a lot and I want to see if people are going to fold easily, because I refuse to waste my time on people who don't have tenacity and drive.

Drew hasn't folded.

She's incredibly strong—and I don't mean the tough chick attitude and provocative outfits. She's strong where it counts. Inside.

"When was the last time you dated someone?" she asks.

I opt for the comfortable territory of smartassery. "Does this count?"

"No." She rolls her eyes.

"Why not? We're having sex and arguing—sounds like a relationship to me."

"You're dodging the question." Drew folds her arms over the front of her obscenely tight top, pushing her breasts up higher. It's all I can do not to weep for how perfect they are.

"I'm distracted."

She shoots me a look. Dammit, I'm not getting out of this one.

"Two years ago, around the time Zoe was diagnosed."

I'd decided in my spiral of guilt and pain that I would do things "perfectly," as if it might bring some karmic redemption. I'd quit my job not a month after making partner, dumped the woman I'd been seeing, started my company and poured everything into my work, hoping—praying—that I might be able to salvage things.

"Before me, when was the last time you had sex?"

I don't even need to think about it. "Two years ago."

"Why break your rules for me?" She's looking at me with those ethereal, silvery eyes like she can see right past my bullshit and self-preservation.

"You reminded me what I was missing."

"Ah, the peep show." She looks almost...disappointed.

"I meant excitement. Anticipation." I won't dare say it, but she made me realise I was missing out on living. Being something other than my work. Being something other than a desperate uncle and brother. "I didn't expect you to ask that question."

"I didn't expect you to answer honestly," she admits.

Whatever this thing is between us—it's not casual. I wouldn't have left her in my bed because I needed space to think if it was casual. And casual sex sure as hell doesn't involve getting to know one another, talking about pasts and wounds and the way we protect ourselves. It involves fucking. Maybe dinner.

This is so much more than fucking and dinner.

"I was dating someone up until about a month ago," she says quietly. I don't want to imagine it—another man's hands on her body. Another man cradling her the way I did when she cried. "I thought it meant something. I thought he cared about me as a person."

"Give me a name."

She laughs and shakes her head. "He's not worth your time. Or mine."

"He was an idiot if he didn't see how amazing you are."

"You don't know me, Mr. Suit."

"No? I know you care about your sister more than anyone else on earth. I know you have good taste in music and you don't let people tell you how to act and you're not the kind of woman to give a shit if someone judges you for the way you dress. In fact, you welcome a bit of judgment because it means you can keep your distance more easily."

Her nostrils twitch. "Maybe I just like black."

"I'm sure you do, Blondie." I meet her stare.

"I never wanted to get entangled with you." She bites her lip. The second she walked into my office, my pulse jacked and my hands got twitchy and my mind started circling—that's what she does to me.

I meant every word of what I said: before her, I'd forgotten how to be excited.

"I never wanted this to be more than some mutual pleasure," she adds.

"You're lying to yourself if you think this is only a booty call."

"I thought it was a meeting to discuss the rehearsal dinner presentation." Her innocent tone is betrayed by the cheeky sparkle in her eye. "We are in a very esteemed, professional office, after all."

Is that a challenge? This woman puts fire in my blood like I have never experienced before. It's like she's taken a greyscale world and flooded it with colour. *My* greyscale world, which has been devoid of laughter and light for so long I had forgotten how it felt not to be wearing a boulder around my neck 24/7.

But I can't lie to myself or to her.

"I like you, Drew. But if you're simply looking for a warm body then you should leave."

She pushes up from the chair and I'm given a glorious view of her long, slim legs. For a minute, I'm sure she's about to go. But then she winks at me. "I don't need a warm body. I've got a handheld device that does the job and doesn't give me any smartass comebacks."

I can't help but laugh. "I *do* bring the smartass comebacks."

She saunters over to my door and flicks the lock. The sound is like a gunshot in my quiet office and I'm immediately tense in the best way possible. Electricity filters through me, crackling and hissing until my body is a livewire.

She knows where I stand—this *isn't* meaningless sex. I don't know what is beyond that, but I know I want more. From her, from myself. From life. I want to start living again.

Maybe my brother was right all along—I needed to get laid.

"How soundproof are these walls?" she asks.

"Not soundproof enough." I yank at the knot of my tie, loosening it so I can slide the silk from under my collar. "Come here."

Her eyes grow dark and her skin is flushed the prettiest shade of pink, but she complies. With each step, her chunky platform boots knock against the floor. And then she's in front of me, leaning against my desk.

I shove my laptop back and it pushes into the box of photos, sending them skittering to the ground. Then I hoist Drew up so her bare ass is on my desk. That's right—*bare* ass. No underwear in sight.

"You knew exactly what you were doing when you came in here." I pull the tie taut in my hands and press it against her mouth. She opens, a willing accomplice to this sexy game, her eyes glittering with power. I knot the tie behind her head, not even caring that the silk will be ruined, because the sight of that slash of red between her lips is startlingly erotic. "You wanted me hard as fucking stone, didn't you?"

She nods.

"You wanted me horny and frustrated and staring at your incredible legs so you could pay me back for walking out."

She nods again. Defiant, even if she's speechless.

"You know I like to rise to the challenge, right?" I tilt

her face up to mine to show her I mean business. I've *never* had sex in my office before—never even fantasised about it because work is my sacred space. But for her, I'll bend all my rules.

She reaches for my belt, her deft fingers pulling leather through metal, and with the soft sound of a zipper being lowered, her palm is wrapped around me. I'm so hard it's like I haven't come in a decade.

She takes her thumb and rubs it over the pearly liquid beading at the tip of my cock. I stifle a moan—maybe I should have saved the tie for myself.

"You want to be fucked, Drew?" I whisper in her ear. I'm letting go of her nickname now, because Blondie is a figment of my imagination. And I won't let her hide behind nicknames.

She nods and makes a muffled sound of encouragement. Her hand tightens around my cock, stroking me harder. It's the hottest thing I've ever seen—her legs spread, pussy on display, laid out like a feast over my smooth pine desk. Just the thought of her walking here from 21 Love Street, bare beneath her clothes, one gust of a breeze away from showing the world what she was bringing to me...

I want her more than I've ever wanted anyone.

"I don't have a condom." Of *course* I don't keep one in my desk...why would I?

Her eyes drop down to my cock, and then back up to me. She looks so disappointed it's almost comical.

"I'm clean, though. I get checked and it's been so

long…" And I've always been a safe sex kinda guy—goes with the rest of my control freak personality.

She tries to speak, but it comes out a muffled, jumbled mess. So I hook my finger into the tie keeping her mute and pull it down to her chin. "I am, too. I'm on the pill and I've always used protection. After the last… shitstorm, I made sure I got checked out."

The statement punches me in the gut. So not only was the guy a dick, but he was sleeping around on her?

"I won't ever do that to you," I promise, bringing my mouth down to hers. She moans softly into the kiss and pulls me closer.

"I want to feel you, Flynn. All of you."

I pull the tie up so she's gagged again and I slide my arms around her back, dragging her to the edge of the desk. For a moment, I get a flash of guilt that I'm supposed to be working, but I can't force myself away from Drew. I can't resist her.

The head of my cock rubs against her, and she's soaking. I glide through her sex, coating myself in her and she moans, though it's muffled by her gag. Her hands curl into my shirt and her head rolls back.

How did I stumble across this goddess?

The feel of being bare with her is incredible, and I want to drown in it. I slide back and forth, rubbing myself through those slick folds without giving either one of us what we want. She squirms against me, tilting her hips to try to encourage me to plunge deep. But I hold myself back for a moment, enough to have us balancing on the edge of something incredible.

The head of my cock bumps her clit with each stroke and she's panting, her eyes wide and pleading and face tilted up to me like I'm a god. That's the biggest lie of it all—because she's the one with the power. She's the one who can bring me to my knees.

I grind against her, holding her hips in place so I can torture us both.

"*Fphhrn prrrss.*" Her lashes are fluttering, her eyes rolling back. "*Awwmmmgddd.*"

Then she's quaking. Splintering. Shuddering and gasping behind her gag. I reach down between us and find her clit with my fingers, rubbing around and around, taking her pleasure and forcing it to a head. There's a rush of moisture at her entrance and I push in at that moment, while she's still pulsing.

It feels like heaven and I almost explode on the spot. But I don't know how much time I have with Drew— even if I know I want whatever she'll give. *More* than she'll give. I push all the way inside her until I bottom out.

Our rhythm is a dirty grind, slow and deep and unforgiving. Her nails dig into my ass through my suit pants and I don't care if she rips the damn things to shreds.

As I fuck her, she presses her face to my chest, muffled pleasure sounds pushing me close and closer toward the edge. And it's when she leans back, arching so I can see between us—the sight of my throbbing dick sliding in and out of that glistening pussy, that I know hanging on is not an option. Without taking her eyes off me, she reaches a hand down and circles herself, her swollen clit peeking out from its hood.

Her finger is a blur back and forth, around and around, and the second she breaks, so do I. I plunge deep, emptying myself inside her, and drawing her to me so close that I wonder if anything could possibly break us apart.

CHAPTER TWENTY-ONE

Drew

FOR THE NEXT forty-eight hours after possibly the hottest sex of my entire life, Flynn and I are almost joined at the hip…well, whenever he's not at work. He works harder and has more conviction than anyone else I've ever known. But I'm happy to be a night owl, napping on his couch until he gets home while spending my days exhausted and blissed out.

We've talked over wine, over coffee, over ice cream. I've learned about his family, about the places he's been in the world and the dreams he'd held dear as a child. And in turn, I've let him in by telling him about my life with Presley when we were kids—how my relationship with my mother is remote, how Vas totally broke me.

I trust him with it all.

For the sake of not trying to steal Presley and Mike's thunder, we decide to keep our being together a secret. It's a convenient excuse, really…because we don't know how to label this thing. It walks a fine line between real and imagined, between meaningful and not.

I don't know if I'm ready to hope again…

I twist the printout of my flight details in my hands. I'm due to leave the day after the wedding—what I'd thought would be not a moment too soon—for the sun and lushness of Fiji. I've been longing for a date with the sandy beaches and blue water and endless sunshine and fruity cocktails.

That means I have less than three days with Flynn. *You could cancel the flight. The apartment is free for another month.*

My friend *did* say I could stay as long as I need to until she got back from her whirlwind European adventure. I could have more time with Flynn to decide how I feel. But I'm being forced to make the decision too soon—I'm not ready. I like him a lot, but I don't *know* in my gut what this is.

I thought I knew with Vas and now I don't trust my instincts.

A sharp knock at the front door makes me leap out of my skin. Still unsure what to do, I fold the printout in half and toss it on my nightstand. It's time for the rehearsal dinner—I've barely spoken to Presley since our argument. We've texted but I've been so wrapped up with Flynn, and I've been using our time as an excuse to not deal with the troubles between my sister and me.

But tonight I'll clear the air.

I still think Mike is wrong for her, but Presley can make her own decisions and I'm going to support her. I'm going to give a great presentation and show her how much I care, even if I haven't been around much in the past couple of years.

I will not let a man come between us.

I rush to the door, holding the length of my dress in one hand so I don't trip. "Coming!"

When I yank the door open, Flynn's eyes almost pop out of his head. "I was going to make a dirty joke about how I love when you scream that but…"

I blush. "But?"

"That dress is no laughing matter." He pulls me toward him, bringing his lips down to mine, not caring that they're covered in lip gloss. I melt into his kiss, my body lining his. Neither one of us care if the neighbours see. "You look incredible."

"This old thing?" I try to shrug it off, but the compliment makes me feel like a million bucks.

I've ditched my usual denim and chunky boots for something a bit more sophisticated, but still me. The dress is fitted and made of inky black velvet that seems to shimmer and shift in the light. It wraps around my waist, and flares out over my nonexistent hips, faking an hourglass curve. A line of gothic-style black lace trims the hem and it gives me total Morticia Addams vibes, which I love.

It's the dress I wear when I want to feel beautiful and powerful. It's the dress I wore the night I told my ex I wouldn't let him string me along and now I want to give it better memories. Happier memories.

"This old thing," he mocks me. "Like you don't know

that every man you walk past tonight is going to end up with whiplash."

I slide my hands into his, intertwining our fingers, and he looks at me with smouldering eyes. They promise me everything. Later, he's going to slip this dress from my body and whisper things into my ear. He's going to worship me, and I'll do the same to him.

What he doesn't know is that I have a special treat planned for him.

By the time we make it to the restaurant for the rehearsal dinner—which is some insanely exclusive place with low-hanging lights and gold-trimmed everything—we're having a hard time keeping our hands to ourselves. As the maître d' leads us through the private dining room at the back, I walk ahead of Flynn. His hand finds my ass and I shoot him a look over one shoulder. He's unrepentant and I love it.

How are we going to get through the dinner tonight without giving our secret up?

Halfway through the night, it's time for our presentation. Flynn and I stand at the front of the room, trying not to look at one another lest we give the game away. We've got a portable projector that displays the images we chose onto the wall behind us—including the one of Presley and I with our faces covered in cake and buttercream.

"Having a twin is a complicated thing," I say. "It's impossible for people not to compare you and when your twin is the girl who could do it all..."

Presley watches me, a little wrinkle between her

brows. Tonight she's wearing a silky dress in pale gold, with her hair in big, bouncy curls. But she looks at me like no one else in the room matters. She only wants to hear what I have to say.

"It was hard, being compared to someone like her. But you see, it's impossible not to like Presley as I'm sure you're all aware. She's generous—with her time and her affection and her advice. She's kind, thoughtful. She's a good friend." I smile at her across the table. "She's also got a terrible sense of humour that revolves entirely around puns so bad they make Dad jokes look cool."

The table titters and Presley's grin grows even wider.

"She's also incredibly forgiving. God only knows she's had a lot of practise, because this…" I point to the picture of us with pink hair and wide smiles and messy faces. "Was totally my fault."

"It was!" She laughs and points at me.

"But you see, Presley doesn't hold a grudge. No matter how many times I left, no matter how many we fought or sniped at one another or stole each other's shoes, she would always forgive me." I swallow back a surprising lump of emotion in my throat. "And so when I think about being compared to someone like her, I feel…proud. Proud to call her my sister and proud to have grown up with such a strong yet gentle woman. People don't think those two traits go together, but if you're with Presley for more than five minutes you'll see that they do."

Her eyes shimmer, and she swipes a tear from her cheek. Mike sits beside her, looking stony-faced, not even trying to appear like he's interested in what I have to say. When I falter, Flynn pushes a hand against my lower back, as if to steady me. His presence gives me power to stand up in front of this room and share my feelings—something I have never done before.

With him by my side, I feel like I can tackle anything.

After the dinner is over, Presley pulls me to one side and tackle hugs me. "Easy, Care Bear," I say.

"I hate it when we fight." She looks at me with glimmering eyes. "I know you and Mike don't get along—"

"I shouldn't have been so vocal about it." I shake my head. "He's going to be your husband and you're a grown woman. It's your decision, so I shouldn't have said anything."

"I want you to feel like you can talk to me. About anything."

"There's talking and there's…judging." I bob my head. "I crossed the line, Pres. I'm sorry."

She looks like she wants to say something else, but instead she sucks on her lower lip. The truth is, I *don't* like Mike. I think he'll be bad for her—not in the way Flynn is bad for me, but properly bad.

However, I can't complain about people judging me and then turn around and do exactly the same thing to Presley. I'd promised myself I wouldn't ruin her big day. I need to stick by that, enjoy the time I have with her.

"So we're not fighting anymore?" she asks.

"No, we're not fighting." I sling an arm around her shoulders and rest my head against hers.

Across the room, Flynn catches my eye and the corner of his lip lifts automatically, before he sharply looks away.

"Now, what is *that* about?" Presley asks.

"Subtle as a sledgehammer, he is." I roll my eyes.

"Are you two…?" She shakes her head. "No, I'm imagining things."

The cheeky grin that emerges, despite me knowing we've agreed to keep things quiet, totally betrays us.

"You are!"

"Shh." I pull her farther away from the event. "It's nothing, we're just…"

I can't even explain it to myself.

"A redhead, huh? He's cute." She smiles, clearly chuffed to be in on the secret. "Are you happy?"

"Yeah, I am." For the first time in months I am truly, blissfully, categorically happy. "I really am."

"Then that's all that matters."

Is it? I've always felt like being happy wasn't something to be trusted—because it could be taken away from you at any moment. Happiness was something to ration, to protect. But in protecting myself I'd been happier less and less. I'd forgotten how to let people in.

Until him.

I watch him across the room and my whole body glows with something warm and fuzzy—something precious. Flynn makes me happy. I might not know how to label it, or predict where it's going, but I know that much at least.

I like him and he makes me happy.

CHAPTER TWENTY-TWO

Flynn

DREW WAS MAGNIFICENT TONIGHT—the way she had the audience held in complete rapture, the way she showed her love for her sister…all of it. I'm enamoured. Smitten. We could barely keep our hands off each other in the taxi on the way home and now we're stumbling through her front door, hands wandering and lips kissing and bodies on fire.

"Stop," she says breathlessly, laughter making her voice sound like bubbles. "I'm having a shower before we go any further. My legs are still sticky from when your brother opened that bottle of champagne all over me."

"Oh, Gabe." I shake my head. "He doesn't get out much these days and he's a total lightweight."

"He's really sweet, even if he is a sloppy drunk." Drew grins. "I like him."

"I think the feeling is mutual. He was hinting that maybe I should ask you out."

She giggles, her eyes a little glassy from all the celebratory drinks we've consumed. We're both a little drunk and a lot horny. "What did you say?"

"That I'd take it under advisement."

She drapes her arms around my neck, swaying on her stilettos. "You didn't tell him we're already screwing like bunnies?"

"I didn't think that would be appropriate."

"So serious, Mr. Suit."

"It's for the best." I squeeze her butt. "Now go and have that shower before I haul you over my shoulder and take you to bed."

"Very caveman, I love it." She totters off toward the bathroom. "We're going back to your place, by the way. No boinking on my friend's bed."

I watch as she disappears into the bathroom. "Got it."

The sound of water rushing fills the apartment and steam billows out of the crack where the door sits ajar. I want to join her, but she made it clear before we even got home that she was going to shower alone. I don't question these things—maybe she has something planned. Maybe it's a girl thing. Who knows?

I wait around, letting my imagination swirl. Letting my arousal build. The sound of running water cuts off but sounds continue to come from the bathroom. Not wanting to rush her, I pull out my phone and as if by some weird snap of cosmic timing, my brother's face flashes up on the screen. I answer the call.

"Hey, man." It's not like Gabe to call so late; he should be home with Zoe by now. "Everything okay?"

"Flynn, I need you to come over…fuck." Gabe sounds ruined.

"What's going on?" My eyes dart to the shower. I don't want Drew to suddenly come out of the bathroom and give our secret away, so I duck into the only other room in her friend's apartment—the bedroom.

This apartment is a typical city shoebox, and about a third the size of mine. It's cute but cramped. The bedroom has a double bed, which is unmade and strewn with clothes. There's makeup scattered across a small vanity unit. Typical Drew.

"It's Monique." Gabe sounds like he's about to lose it. "She turned up at the house and the babysitter didn't know what to do. She's been…here. With Zoe. All night."

On the surface, it mightn't sound bad, but I know why Gabe is furious. Zoe was distraught after her mother left, and reopening that wound is only going to add stress in a time when they already have enough to deal with.

"Have you heard from her recently or did she turn up without warning?" I rake a hand through my hair.

"She left a voicemail a few days ago, but I'm not taking her calls. Why would I? She left us and doesn't even call for Zoe's birthday. Now she's saying she wants another chance and I'm…" His voice wavers. "What if she tries to fight me for custody?"

"That *won't* happen. We won't let it."

"I need to talk to her and set things straight, but it's late and I can't leave Zoe alone in the house. The babysitter is already gone."

"This isn't a conversation to have while you're inebriated."

"Maybe this is *exactly* why I should have it now. I can be brutally honest."

"Mate, don't do it. You'll regret it in the morning." I sigh. "Don't go anywhere, I'll get a taxi over now and we can sort this out together."

I hang up and let the gravity of the situation filter through me. I know I need to come clean with Gabe about the conversation I had with Monique—I should have told him before this point, but I'm afraid he'll never forgive me and I'll lose him and Zoe forever.

I sink down on the bed for a minute and drop my head in my hands. My poor brother—he shouldn't be going through all this turmoil. Monique will only stay long enough to get Zoe's hopes up before she takes off again, leaving emotional destruction behind her.

It's a pattern well-worn by our mother and I don't want Zoe to know that pain.

So much for a night of sheet-burning sex. I glance at the door and there's still no sign of Drew, but as I'm about to stand I notice a piece of paper folded on the nightstand. I wouldn't have given it a second thought if I hadn't caught sight of a familiar logo—QANTAS Airways.

I usually wouldn't read someone else's papers, I swear. But between the anguish over my brother's plight and the endless wine and champagne top-ups at the rehearsal dinner…my mind is foggy. And my moral centre is a little muddled. I snatch the paper up and feel the air leave my lungs. Drew has a one-way flight to Nadi Airport in Fiji the day after the wedding.

One. Way.

The knowledge is like an iron fist around my heart. I should have known she wasn't planning to stay—her sister warned me.

She's a nomad, my sister. Flits from one place to the next, always packing her bags and running away from commitment of any kind.

Hell, Drew herself warned me. Didn't she say that she never made an attempt to hide who she was? To hide that part of herself? I place the paper back where it was. I don't have time to think about Drew now because my family is hurting. I need to be there for them. I need to support Gabe and Zoe.

I walk out of the bedroom and grab my coat from the back of a chair. At that moment Drew comes out of the bathroom, looking every bit the unattainable fantasy she is.

"I wanted to surprise you," she says. Her body is draped in a sheer black dressing gown that shows every beautiful part of her—from her perfect breasts to her slim waist and long legs. Underneath she wears a short corset in black and thigh-high stockings with a suspender belt and no underwear. "Do you like it?"

For a full minute, I am utterly speechless. My mind is a lawn mower failing to start, no matter how hard I yank the cord.

"Flynn?" Her face creases with concern. "Are you okay?"

"I have to go." I can barely get the words out. Dammit, couldn't I have reserved a little bit of blood for my brain? I hold up my phone as if that might explain things. "I got a call from Gabe, he needs me."

"Oh, my God, it's not Zoe, is it?" Her worry is so genuine it makes me want to roar. Why does she care if she's planning on leaving?

"She's okay, but I need to watch her while he deals with something," I say tightly.

"I'll come."

"No!" The word shoots out of me so harshly that she reels, her eyes wide and unblinking.

I need to get some space and think about everything that's going on—unlike Gabe, I *don't* want to have an important conversation while I'm still feeling the lip-loosening effects of our celebratory drinks. More important, I refuse to let anyone into Zoe's orbit who isn't a permanent fixture in my life.

And I know my niece will fall head over heels for Drew the way I have.

The way you have? Head over heels is some serious shit.

I'm in deep and being punished because I broke my own rules. I *will* talk to Drew about the plane ticket, because I'm an adult and I'm not going to vanish without giving her a chance to explain—but that conversation cannot happen right now. Not when I'm full of frustrating thoughts and worries. Not when I know I'll speak before my brain has a chance to catch up.

I need a day or two to find my equilibrium before I go there with her.

Drew hugs her arms around herself and looks at me with closed-off eyes. "Okay, well… I hope everything is all right."

She's shutting down. Putting up the walls I'd managed to break through. But I can't worry about that now.

"When will I see you next?" she asks.

"Tomorrow is the buck's and hen's parties and then I'm offsite for a work thing…so it'll be the day after that."

Wedding day.

We'll be dressed up, standing on opposite sides of Mike and Presley while they take their vows. Then she'll be gone. The knowledge wrenches in my chest. This would be the chance for her to tell me she's planning on leaving, to tell me she has a flight booked. To say, *Hey, let's talk about this,* but Drew is silent.

It's for the best.

The robe swirls like a black cloud around her as she heads back into the bathroom, giving me the signal that I can see myself out. I don't want this magic thing between us to be over, but I have a feeling I'm witnessing the beginning of the end.

CHAPTER TWENTY-THREE

Drew

THE WEDDING IS here far quicker than I want it to be. I've been a sad sack the past few days, miserable about the weird tension between Flynn and me. Hurt by the way he so clearly didn't want me to meet his niece.

Hurt also by the fact that my texts and calls have gone mostly unanswered, except for one that said, We'll talk in person. I don't do text chat.

Typical Mr. Stick Up His Butt. The guy has a rule for everything. Maybe *I* should be setting rules and restrictions of my own, rather than jumping through his hoops.

I'd had a whole night of fun planned out for after the rehearsal dinner, including that sexy black outfit. I'd put a container of goodies together—whipped cream and strawberries and chocolate sauce—and I'd planned to seduce him in the kitchen first before we moved the party to his place for the rest of the night.

I ended up sitting on the couch in my sloppy track pants, eating the cream straight from the tub while wondering *just* how much of a cliché I was: brokenhearted girl consumes the weight of her emotions in sugar and fat.

"Drew?" Presley waves me over. "Can you help me? I think one of the buttons is in the wrong hole at the back. Mum wanted to do it, but you know what her eyesight is like."

We're in a waiting room at the wedding venue—a beautiful old Victorian house settled among trees and surrounded by a stunning garden of white and yellow roses. The ceremony will take place in a courtyard decked with white pews and a trellis arch adorned with small white flowers. It's not long to go now. From the sound of it outside, the men have arrived and Flynn's laugh is a lance right through my heart.

Presley catches my eyes in the mirror, frowning. She senses my turmoil but I busy myself undoing my mother's poor handiwork and fixing the line of buttons that run from Presley's middle-back all the way to her butt. Each one is small and fiddly, like a little satin-covered pebble.

The dress is incredible—simple and yet eye-catching. Strapless with a fitted bodice and nipped-in waist and a sleek skirt with a touch of lace that manages to avoid "cake topper" territory all together.

"What's going on, Drew?" She turns around when I'm done and touches my arm.

I catch a glance of myself in the mirror and I don't look like me. Between my uber-girlie bridesmaid dress and the softly curled hairstyle and the pretty, minimal makeup… I look like a carbon copy of my sister.

"I don't know who I am anymore." There's a lump at the back of my throat. "I don't know if I ever knew who I was."

"Don't say that." Presley pulls me in for a hug. "Of course you know who you are. You're a fearless traveller and an incredible costume-maker and you're independent and outgoing and you make friends wherever you go. People love you."

"They don't know me."

It's because I do the same thing every damn time— I hold people at a distance. I put a fence around myself in relationships to avoid the pain of being let down, of finding out I'm never going to be someone's number one.

"I feel like I'm floating through life without any idea where I'm going." I feel tears rush to my eyes but I blink them back. I will *not* ruin a hundred-dollar makeup job. "I don't trust myself to make decisions about people anymore."

Presley sighs and pulls back. She smells like my mother today—like roses and violet candies—because a bottle of YSL Paris that my mother only wears on the most special of occasions was her "something borrowed."

"Can I tell you something?" she says, walking over to one of the big windows overlooking a strip of garden toward the front of the property. It's open, letting in a cool, flower-scented spring breeze and the sound of birds chirping. "I don't trust myself with that, either."

"Really?" I almost can't believe it.

"After the last…debacle, I thought I'd never try to get married ever again. I couldn't believe I got it *so* wrong that I could hurt someone the way I did, by walking out at the last minute. Mike proposed three times before I said yes."

"I had no idea." I shake my head. "We have the opposite problem—you're getting too many proposals and I'm not 'marriage material.'"

"There's no such thing as marriage material, Drew. Because no one is qualified to get married. No one is automatically going to be a good husband or wife based on some arbitrary personality traits. I know you've been hurt badly, but one man's refusal to commit is *not* a reflection on who you are. That's on him and only on him."

"How do you have it all together?" We're separated by mere minutes in reality, but often it feels like a chasm of years. Presley is mature, centred. She's kind and calm and good in a crisis.

"I don't," she whispers. "I have no idea what the future holds with Mike or with anything else. But I'm willing to try."

"I'm supposed to be leaving tomorrow and Flynn's gone cold again, just like Vas did. I'm…scared."

"Because you like him?"

"Yes." The word comes quicker and more freely than I ever thought it would. I *do* like Flynn, a heck of a lot. But enough that I want to stay and put my heart in harm's way again?

"Do you have to go to Fiji right away?"

I shake my head. "I don't have to go anywhere, technically."

"Is it going to sound selfishly motivated if I suggest that you stay awhile and see where it goes?"

I laugh. "Yes, but that's okay."

"Drew, you're a good person. Sure, you don't tick everyone's boxes...but none of us do. We're not made to appeal to the masses." She smiles. "And here's the thing—*nothing* is permanent."

It all sounds so manageable when she says it like that—like I'm not risking having Flynn's well-heeled shoe grinding my heart into the ground.

"Talk to him," she urges. "We've got a few minutes before the ceremony starts, and this thing isn't happening until I give the go-ahead anyway."

Talk to him? What the hell am I supposed to say?

Hey, Flynn, guy I've barely known a few weeks. I'm thinking about cancelling my trip to Fiji so I can see if we're good outside the bedroom as well as in it. Can we maybe continue fucking but also do other nice things, too?

I suck at this stuff so hard.

"Stop thinking and go." Presley comes over to me and gives me a literal shove toward the door.

"I love you," I say, stopping to give her a quick squeeze. I'm so nervous I want to puke, but she's right...we don't know what the future holds. Nothing can protect us, except eternal isolation. And I'm starting to think that's not what I want. "I've missed you a lot."

"Tell him that if he can convince you to stay then he'll be in my good books forever." Her eyes shimmer.

"Don't cry. Mum will *kill* me for ruining everything." I shoot her a look before darting out of the room. Hopefully the men aren't already in the courtyard because I really don't want to do this with an audience.

The old building has a lot of rooms and none of them are marked. I try to listen for the smooth, deep sound of Flynn's voice—a sound I've grown to crave. To need. Classical music floats in through open doors that lead out to the courtyard where my sister will be married. I peek out and spot Annaleigh, Pauline and Sherilee doing their thing, entertaining the guests and smiling. Being perfect.

I continue down the hallway, holding the frothy pink lengths of my bridesmaid dress in one hand so I don't trip. With each step, I'm losing my nerve. The tug of the old way—the runaway, shields up way—pulls me back.

But then I see him. He's coming out of another door, looking sharp as ever in a black tux. It suits him, being buttoned up. And it suits me, because I know that he's at his best when the buttons are popped and skittering across the floor, when he's coming undone. Coming alive and shedding his rules and restrictions like a man undergoing transformation.

"Hey." I hold up a hand, tentative. Anticipating the sting of his rejection and, on some level, craving it so I can go back to how I've always been. A drifter. A wanderer. My protective side wants to use him as an excuse not to grow.

But at the same time, there's a tiny sprout of hope in the barren wasteland of my dating experience.

"Blondie." His lip quirks but it isn't quite a smile. He's playing my game, putting up barriers. "Who are you looking for?"

"An uptight redhead with a penchant for nice suits and dirty talk." I might be trying to change, but I *am* still me. "Know where I could find a guy like that?"

"I'm not sure, but I *can* offer you a guy who's good at judging people and not very good at answering his phone."

Okay, so he's meeting me halfway. That's a positive sign.

"Can we talk?" I say. "I know you've been busy, but I need to get this off my chest and I'm worried it's going to burst out of me in the middle of the ceremony if I don't say something now."

"We can't have that." He stares me down and I have to resist the urge to push him up against a wall. Why does sex come easier to me than talking?

"The last thing I need is to draw *more* attention to myself in this hideous dress." I wrinkle my nose and now the smile comes. "I feel like I did something wrong and I don't know what it is or how to fix it. Everything has been going great and then all of a sudden you're… avoiding me again and it's like I've been doused with ice water."

"Are you leaving tomorrow?" His question is free

of bullshit and pretence, cutting right through me. The ticket… "When Gabe called, I went into your bedroom because we were supposed to be keeping our 'thing' secret and I didn't want him to hear your voice in the background."

Ah.

"I have a flight booked," I admit.

"One-way."

"Yes, it's one-way." Honesty is the best policy, right? If I can't lay it all on the line now, then there's no chance anything real could ever happen between us. "I wasn't planning on coming back."

"Where are you going to live?"

"Somewhere." I can tell my answer doesn't sit right with him—the guy who's always planning his life three steps in advance. He probably knows what suit he's going to wear next Thursday. "I've always been able to pick up a job, no matter where I go. My old boss is now based in Singapore working for an airline there, and she'd have me back in a heartbeat. Or I could go back to London, Dubai… Maybe Canada—I know some-one there, too."

"You know people everywhere," he says with a nod. "But do you know anyone well?"

"No." I've got an army of acquaintances formed of colleagues and roommates and neighbours and light-weight friends. I collect contacts with each move, adding them to the list of people I sometimes text if I happen to be in town.

But when I broke up with Vas and I was crying my heart and soul out, that list didn't help me.

"Don't you want more?" He looks at me like I'm lost, and it hurts.

"What's more, Flynn? People who walk out without a word, who won't let you help when there's a crisis?"

"That's fair." He shakes his head. "It wasn't my finest moment."

"We never set any boundaries, or had a plan for where this might be going. We don't have any rules of operation." Normally those things would irk me: they would make me want to find loopholes and workarounds. I don't like to be confined. "So, I can't really be angry when we'd never made a commitment. But if we're being honest, your reaction to the thought of me meeting Zoe…it made me feel like shit."

The fact that I can even say this to Flynn is telling. I'm like an armadillo with my feelings—when it gets too much, I curl inward, hard stuff on the outside, soft, squishy stuff protected. That last night with my ex, I totally shut down. Because when I tried to be open, he went straight for my weak spot.

Flynn isn't like that. Sure, he's gruff and a little rigid and a total workaholic and yeah, a control freak. But he's kind. Loving. He's generous and sweet and wonderful…

He's everything I've secretly wanted while telling the world I didn't need a man. And I don't need a man.

But I do *want* Flynn.

Not *want* in the sense of mind-blowing sex and can't-keep-our-hands-off-one-another anticipation, although

I thoroughly enjoy that. But I want him for his teasing smile and sweet breakfast deliveries and the way he wakes me up after I've fallen asleep on the couch with coaxing kisses and wandering hands and the most indulgent look in his eyes. I want him for how much he cares about his family and his work, for the difference he wants to make in this world. For his loyalty and ethics and his strong-minded, goal-setting nature.

I want him. Not just now. Not just tomorrow.

Forever is too terrifying to think about, but… I can see us there.

"I know how much she means to you and then you were repulsed by the idea of me meeting her." I resist the urge to wring my hands, because even though I'm showing him my weak spots I need to remain strong. I need to go in knowing this might be the end.

"I wasn't repulsed by the idea, Drew. It's…complicated."

"That's not an answer."

His blue eyes are like an interrogation spotlight, and I can't hide. I can't squirm or move away. He sees everything.

"After her mother left, Zoe struggled with abandonment issues. She would cry hysterically whenever her father left her anywhere and anytime I came over, she'd cling to my leg when it was time to leave." Pain flashes across his face like lightning. "Whenever an adult woman came to the house, Zoe would imprint herself like a duckling. She's extremely sensitive to the idea that people are going to leave her. It's…something I'm very familiar with."

Oh, Flynn.

I want to hold him close and soothe that pain, but my instincts tell me there's more to come.

"Gabe and I agreed that we would avoid bringing people to the house and introducing Zoe unless it was either A, vitally necessary, or B, the relationship was well established, and we could minimise the chance of Zoe growing attached only to feel disappointed again. It's the whole reason I don't date casually, because my family is everything to me and I knew this conversation would come up."

The reality of what he's saying is like a trickle of ice water down my back. "So you don't want me to meet Zoe because you're confident I'll leave and she'll end up feeling abandoned."

I can see the confirmation all over his face. I'm not surprised, but no matter how much I anticipate what he really thinks of me, the truth is still like an ice pick to my ever-tender heart.

"A lot of men would keep their dating life separate, but I'm an all-in kind of guy. If I'm dating someone, I don't want to live two separate lives."

"Did you ever consider what the other person might want?"

His Adam's apple bobs. "Is that what you're really asking?"

"Why didn't you give me a chance?" It hurts to say that kind of question aloud, no matter how many times

I've asked it in my head—to my mother, to boys I dated when I was younger, to everyone who underestimated me.

"You live your life with one foot out the door." He rakes a hand through his hair, disturbing the neat style. "And I don't take chances."

There's a lump in my throat as big as a boulder. I was supposed to tell him how I feel, to tell him that this time I *could* stay...but it feels so fraught. So risky. What if I offer and he says no?

"I like you, Drew. It's been so long since I even considered breaking my rules about dating, and I'm totally and utterly enamoured by you. But that doesn't change my circumstances and finding that ticket, it just...it solidified why this won't work."

The words twist in my chest, cutting and slicing me up. "You've already written me off."

"I've written *us* off, because we're not compatible. I want long-term and you crave adventure. I've set down roots and you want to see the world."

But I don't. I mean, *sure*, I love to travel and that desire won't ever go away. It's part of the reason I wanted to be a flight attendant, but I've been running. Not searching. Not seeking. Not exploring.

Running.

"I like you so much I know it will kill me when you leave."

"*When*, not *if*." His choice of words tells me everything.

Flynn's face is a slipping mask, his emotions finally revealed for their raw reality. He's hurting, and so am I.

Because we don't trust one another yet. There's something here, something special and good, but neither one of us are brave enough to nurture it.

"You said it yourself," he says, his voice thick. "You never tried to hide that you live a different life. That you want different things. Fuck, you didn't even want me to know your name."

"Because this wasn't supposed to go anywhere." Tears are threatening again, but I will not let him see me cry. Never, ever again. "I guess…it *hasn't* gone anywhere."

"I didn't want to hurt you." He looks anguished, guilty. There's a deep crease between his brows, but as I'm about to walk away, there's a blur of colour. Pink. And highlighted hair.

"Drew!" Annaleigh's frantic voice cuts through the heavy tension simmering between Flynn and I. "Have you seen her?"

"What?" I whirl around. "Who?"

"Presley." Annaleigh's eyes are wide. "She's gone."

CHAPTER TWENTY-FOUR

Flynn

HALF AN HOUR LATER, the bride is nowhere to be found. If I needed a more dramatic representation of why I never let people get close, this is it. The groom's side of the bridal party is sitting in a parlour room, dumbfounded that the day's festivities aren't going ahead. My cousin is spouting off in fist-shaking fury, vowing to drag Presley back here to save face.

I doubt that's going to work. I also doubt a marriage that started off in such a fashion would be destined to last.

"I can't fucking believe it," Mike rages. "She was supposed to be the reliable one—it's her sister that's the attention-seeking hot mess. I bet she got in her ear about me."

"Don't drag Drew into this," I growl.

My brother shoots me an arched-brow look across the room. His bow tie is hanging loose around his neck and his hair is askew. The two other groomsmen, friends of Mike, attempt—unsuccessfully—to calm him down.

"How could she *do* this me?" He white-knuckles a crystal glass and when it looks like he's about to hurl it across the room, one of the groomsmen pulls it out of his hand.

"Why don't you take a walk, blow off some steam?" I suggest. "Because if Presley *does* call and you're in this mood, it's not likely you'll entice her back."

Mike looks at me with daggers and then storms out, his two minions following with identical strained expressions. I slump down into a chair and drop my head into my hands.

"What a clusterfuck."

Gabe laughs and shakes his head. "Mate, I think we passed clusterfuck about a half hour ago. This is a shitpocalypse."

I snort. "What happened? A bride doesn't suddenly run away on her wedding day without *some* kind of red flag."

"I have no idea." Gabe shakes his head. "Although I'm clearly not the best judge of who to marry, so what the hell can I say? To be honest, what Mike was saying about Presley... I'm not sure I disagree with her actions."

I frown. "What do you mean?"

"He was talking shit about how the marriage would bolster his chances of taking over the family business." Gabe rolls his eyes. "Dad told me recently that Uncle Pat was thinking about retiring soon, which means someone has to take over. There's one CEO position and two sons, and given I *know* that Uncle Pat has complained about Mike being immature…well, it appears his solution has been to get himself a wife."

I gawk. "Seriously?"

"Disgusting, right?" Gabe shakes his head. "I feel like that poor woman dodged a bullet."

"How are we even related to him?" I cringe. Mike has looked up to Gabe and me ever since we were kids. He never got along with his stepbrother, Sebastian. But Mike was always the kind of kid to take the easy route in life rather than putting in the hard work. "I'm here out of obligation and because Uncle Pat was always kind to us…but that's it."

"Same."

"Do you think Presley overheard something?"

Gabe shrugs. "It's possible, if she came past the room. Mike loves the sound of his own voice and he talks loud enough to wake the dead."

"Imagine saying that on his wedding day." It's low, even for Mike.

"And don't think I missed how you jumped to Drew's defence, either."

"He shouldn't have said that. Drew wants Presley to be happy." Even as I reply, I know I'm giving too much away—but the conversation from earlier is still fresh. Still weighing on me.

Truth is, I feel miserable for how I barked at her when she offered to help with Zoe, and for doubting her. Mostly, I feel miserable because I know she's leaving tomorrow.

I don't want her to go.

"You like her," Gabe says, watching me the way only a big brother can. Like he knows all my secrets and he's ready to call me on any bullshit. "You like her *a lot*."

"Yeah, I do."

"So that whole time at the rehearsal dinner, while I thought I was playing wise matchmaker…"

"I was already seeing her."

Gabe snorts. "I should have known. You're such a dark horse with that stuff. Why were you keeping it a secret? She's great."

"She's leaving." I ball and flex my hands—it's a habit that's stuck from all the dark times after my mother left our family. "Tomorrow. One-way ticket to Fiji."

"Did she tell you?"

"I saw the ticket."

"Ouch." My brother nods, but I know better than to assume he'll take my side for the sake of brotherly camaraderie. Gabe doesn't play like that. "I assume you stormed out without giving her a chance to explain."

"I didn't *storm* out," I reply. "I swiftly exited in a decisive manner."

"You're so full of shit."

"It was the day you called about Monique turning up. Drew asked if she could come and help with Zoe and I kind of…well, I made it clear she wasn't welcome."

"Because of that agreement we made about introducing people to Zoe?"

"Yeah."

Gabe watches me for a moment, his expression guarded. When we play poker, the game seems to go on forever because we're two stone pillars. Hiding our emotions is what we're good at. "I've decided to let Monique have partial custody of Zoe."

"What?" If my eyes were any wider they would pop straight out of my skull. "Have you forgotten what she did?"

Gabe holds his hand up in a gesture that is such a "dad" thing to do. "Zoe's life is different to lots of other kids', and that means I need to be a different father for her than I would be for another child. She doesn't have time for grudges or fear or regrets, because we won't have four or five decades with her. We won't have years to change our minds and find forgiveness. I have to be a better person *now*. Because now is what matters to her, so it's what has to matter to me."

Watching Gabe talk about his daughter always chokes me up, but I'm holding it all in. Being silent as the dead of night. Even though I want to shake him and tell him that Monique is poison and that she'll only leave again.

"What if she can't handle it?" I ask.

"That's a possibility. She might leave," Gabe admits. "She might decide again that it's all too hard. But she might not. She might stay and give Zoe a chance to have a mother who cares about her. I can't control any of that."

"Aren't you worried?"

"Of course I'm fucking worried." Gabe laughs. "I'm shitting bricks at the thought of my little girl getting hurt. But I sat Zoe down and talked to her. I told her that I'd love her no matter what, that I will always be there for her. But sometimes people do bad things because they're frightened or because they're trying to protect themselves. She looked at me dead in the eye and asked me if we were giving her mother a second chance."

"Where did she get that from?"

"Disney, probably." He crosses his legs and bounces his foot. "But I said yes, we're giving her mother a second chance. I almost can't believe it—I never thought I'd see Monique again. I could be making the biggest mistake of my life, letting her back in."

"But?"

"But it's a risk I'm willing to take, because the potential payoff could be that Zoe has both parents in her life. Here's the thing—the whole risk-reward equation isn't set up to tell us to *always* avoid risk. It's to help us figure out if a risk is worth it. If the potential payoff is worth it."

In some areas, risk is where I excel. I quit a job that would have set me up for life to pour all my money into research knowing the chances of finding something in Zoe's lifetime are not in our favour.

But that risk *is* worth it. The chance—no matter how minuscule—that I might be able to help her is worth it. Because that little girl is the light of my life and I'd do anything for her.

But being with Drew isn't worth the risk?

Can I imagine my life with her in it?

Yes.

The answer comes so quickly and without hesitation that it takes my breath away. I *can* imagine my life with her. I can imagine us being old and still crazy hot for one another. I can imagine her sleepy, sooty eyes being the first thing I see in the morning. I can imagine her leaving me dirty notes in my laptop bag and sending me naughty texts while I'm at work. And I can imagine *me* counting down every second of every workday until it's time to see her again.

I've never imagined that before.

"People can always walk away, Flynn. The second we stop trying to control that, the happier we'll all be." My brother knows my mind is drifting. He's always been able to sense when I'm grappling with an issue—big brother magic, perhaps.

"I don't like not being able to control things."

My brother shakes his head. "People aren't things, Flynn."

"You're such a smartass."

But he's right—people have their own minds and make their own decisions. I could never imagine trying to water down a woman like Drew by controlling her decisions. And I guess that's the scariest part—trust. I need to trust that she'll stay if I ask her to, that we'll both be equally invested in making things work. That this heat won't burn itself out.

You know it won't.

Because the fact that Drew has even gotten this far under my skin is telling. I never let people slip past my defences. Ever. I never give people a chance to know me. To see me beyond my fancy suits and my stoic expression. I know there's something between us, something that could be everything.

The question is, can I take that risk?

Outside the room, I hear arguing. A second later one of the bridesmaids bursts in, still clutching her bouquet and holding the length of her pink dress in one hand. Two other identically dressed women stand in the entrance, watching with twin frowns.

"We have to let people know what's going on," Sherilee says. "They're getting restless. Drew *finally* got through to Presley and they're speaking now but…"

I raise a brow. "But?"

"She's not coming back."

Shit. I stand and suck in a deep breath—this is going to be awkward as fuck. I've never been at a wedding where someone's been jilted before. All the failed marriages I know dissolved *after* the vows.

"Where's Mike?" Gabe asks, standing and coming to my side.

"He's outside in one of the private gardens with his parents. They're trying to calm him down." She toys with her earring. "But he's yelling a lot. People can hear."

"Okay, we need to shut this down now." I head out of the room, and the rest of the bridal party follows me. The two other groomsmen are waiting in the hallway and Drew is walking toward us, phone in hand.

I meet her eyes and she gives me a resigned nod. It's over and we need to let the guests know. I hold out my hand and she lifts her silvery-blue eyes to mine for a second before taking it. For now, we're a team.

And after this is all done, I'm going to ask that we remain a team.

CHAPTER TWENTY-FIVE

Drew

THAT WAS LITERALLY the most awkward thing I have ever done in all my life. Having all those faces gaping like stunned fish while I tried to tactfully say that my sister had decided not to go ahead with her wedding…

Yeah. *Major* awkward turtle.

Now the courtyard is empty, save for the celebrant who stands talking to my mother. After the guests were all ushered out, Sherilee, Annaleigh and Pauline hung around for a while, looking a little dazed and confused. The day ended up *not* being capital *P* Perfect.

Luckily for me, that's the story of my life. I have *plenty* of experience with shit not going according to plan.

But I'd be lying if I said I wasn't grateful to have Flynn by my side as we addressed the crowd—he held my hand through the entire thing, letting me speak first and supporting what I had to say. He then took charge of thanking everyone for coming and helping the venue coordinator guide the guests of this ill-fated event out to the car park.

My mother demanded to know where Presley had gone and why she called the wedding off—but my sister made me swear not to say. So I didn't. It's her information to share.

Still, I'm reeling.

She's supposed to be the strong one. The stable one. The one who gets married and has babies and does the family proud. Maybe us Richardsons are not destined for the white-picket-fence life—it never worked out for my mother, and it hasn't worked out for Presley. If my sister can't make it happen, then what hope in hell do I have?

The celebrant looks over in my direction and gives a wave before heading inside. My mother follows her without so much as glancing in my direction. That's okay, let her be angry at me for not spilling the beans. If it keeps the heat off Presley, then I'm okay with that. I can't even imagine what she's going through right now.

I guess all this has done is prove Flynn right. People *do* leave. Even the ones we don't expect.

Thoughts of him are like a knife twisting in my stomach. No matter how much I reason with myself that it's not meant to be, my stubborn heart won't take no for an answer.

If he wanted to be with you, he would have asked you to stay.

I toy with my phone, turning it over and over, mimicking the whirring going on in my head. I swipe across the screen and bring up my inbox, looking at the handy little reminder that the airline emailed me today. I'm less than twenty-four hours away from sand, sun and cocktail-drenched solitude. Less than twenty-four hours away from paradise.

But is it?

I'd wanted to go somewhere beautiful to get my head straight and think about what my next steps should be. Which country would I run to next? What person was I going to be when I got there?

But the more important question is: What kind of person do I want to be *now*?

The answer comes to me swiftly. I don't want to be the person who runs forever.

I call the booking number and when the call centre operator answers, I blurt, "I need to cancel my flight."

My voice shakes as I give her my details, letting go of my escape hatch plans. In two minutes, it's done. I don't know what I'm going to do for work or a place to live or anything else…but I'm staying.

I'm going to ask *myself* to stay.

Because the fact is, I've missed my sister. I've missed belonging and having a place that felt like something more than temporary. I've missed building friendships with the hope that they would last a lifetime. I've missed the Aussie weather and Tim Tams and footy and walking along the Yarra in the sunshine.

I've missed my home.

I push up from where I've been sitting on the raised platform where my sister was supposed to be married, and I dust the dirt from my dress. My bouquet lies on the ground, the delicate white flowers surrounded by a spray of green fronds and leaves. Like everything that my sister chose, it's classy. Elegant.

And now it means nothing.

My heart aches, not because I think she made the wrong decision—I definitely don't—but because I know she's hurting. I want to be here for her. But in order for me to do that, I first need to be here for myself. I need to be enough for myself, before I can be anything for her. Anything for others.

I take a fortifying breath, smelling the jasmine and rich white roses around me, feeling the sunshine on my face. It's not going to be an easy road, but I feel freer than I would have with sand beneath my toes and a lonely future stretched out in front of me.

The sound of my name roots me to the ground. Flynn. Sunlight bounces off his reddish hair, making his eyes look wild and blue as the open ocean.

"Where to now?" His intense stare is hot enough to melt an iceberg.

"My maid of honour duties have officially ended, which means I'm going home to get out of this fairy floss monstrosity." I try to keep things light—try to show him that he didn't shatter my heart. Because really, I have Flynn to thank for a lot. If not for him, I might not have realised how much I'd missed being connected to people. How much I've been suffering because I shut people out. "I would say you can get out of your tux, but I imagine you sleep in your suits."

"You *know* that's not true."

No. He sleeps completely naked and it's glorious.

"You really should wear something when you sleep. It's good to support your junk."

"I'm not going to ask how this conversation so quickly devolved to us discussing my 'junk', but here we are." His lip quirks.

"Is everyone gone?"

"Yeah." Flynn nods. "I called Francis and she arranged for a private car service to collect the bridal party and take them home. My uncle and aunt took Mike."

"Good." This house is gorgeous, but it's in the middle of nowhere. We're surrounded by beautiful Australian native trees as far as the eye can see. "I'm hoping you saved one of those cars for me. It's a long hike to the main road in heels."

"As if I would leave you stranded." He shoves his hands into his pockets, not looking like he's in any hurry to leave. "Actually, I wanted to talk before we go."

"I thought we'd said everything there was to say." My heart thuds, hope filtering through my veins even as my mind shouts at me to retreat. I know this dance well, and I usually listen to my head. But not anymore.

I want to stay. I want to hope.

"I need to set the record straight." He squares his shoulders and the action makes him look even bigger and stronger. Even more beautiful. "When I came across that piece of paper with your flight details, I was devastated. Because despite the fact that we kept telling one another that we were a bad match… I don't *feel* that way. Being with you doesn't feel wrong. In fact, it's the rightest thing I've felt for as long as I can remember."

My knees tremble beneath me. Am I imagining this? Have I fainted from sun stroke and now my brain is playing merciless tricks on me?

"What felt wrong was my assumption that leaving was the end, because I understand now that nothing is permanent. Decisions can be changed and…" Something flicks over his face, an emotion I can't quite read. "What matters is *now*. Not what happened before, not what might happen tomorrow. Now. I like you a hell of a lot, Blondie. I like how strong you are, I like your humour and your smile and those killer legs. I like how much you care about your sister and how you're always up for an adventure. I like that you do your own thing, regardless of what people say. I like that you're bold and decisive and daring. I like it all."

I can't speak. The words won't form on my tongue as my breath stutters.

"I know you're leaving tomorrow and that's your decision. But the ticket is one-way, right? What if you came back after your trip?" His eyes shine and he steps forward, gently pulling me close. I'm unable to express the swirl of emotion dancing like a tornado inside me. "What if you came home?"

He's asking me to stay. No, he's doing something even better. He's giving me the freedom to leave and the option to come back. The option for me to have what I want. Because Flynn isn't a person who clips people's wings. Rigid as he might be, this is his way of showing me he's changed. That he wants to make it work.

The biggest question is: Can I trust him?

CHAPTER TWENTY-SIX

Flynn

I WANT TO rough up Drew's hair. Smudge her makeup. Tear the hem of her dress. Take this polished image and bring the *real* Drew back out. The real woman who has totally and utterly claimed my heart.

For a man of rules and principles, the most telling thing is that I keep bending for her. I'm becoming flexible. I compromise. I say "just once more" knowing deep in my heart I'll never say no. Because Drew is everything I never knew I needed—a woman strong enough to change me, to ground me. To give me hope.

In all other cases a one-way ticket would be a closed case. Relationship null and void! But with her... I can't let go.

"I don't want to walk away from this," I say. My voice doesn't even sound like my own—I'm broken down. Ruined. Emotional roadkill. "What we have... I don't have a name for it, because I've never experienced anything like this before. This is unchartered territory. It's new and..."

"Terrifying?" she supplies, her big, silvery eyes looking up at me. "Petrifying? Something no smart person would ever willingly do?"

"I'm pouring my heart out and you're being a smartass." I can't help but smile as I shake my head. "Really?"

"It's a defence mechanism," she admits sheepishly, pressing a hand to my chest. "I'm much better at being a smartass than I am at dealing with feelings."

"I would never have guessed that," I deadpan.

"It's...how I've learned to protect myself. I keep being told that something about me isn't right, that I need to change, that I'm not...forever material." There's a slight tremble in her lip that makes me want to roar at the sky for the people who made her feel this way. But I know that means facing the way *I've* treated her, too. "So I leaned into it. That way it feels like I'm not forever material because I don't want to be, instead of being rejected when I'm trying. But... I'm not happy pretending to be something I'm not."

"So don't pretend."

"I'm not going to anymore." I know this new sincerity is precious. Something she doesn't hand out easily. "Doesn't mean I'll stop being a smartass, though, because that *is* really who I am."

"And I love it. Your humour is one of the best parts of you." A breeze pushes past us and it whips a stray platinum curl across her face. With a heart that's almost bursting for how beautiful she is, I tuck it behind her ear. "I was wondering if there's something you could do for me tonight."

"What's that?"

This part is the most terrifying piece of all. "Gabe and Zoe are back at my place now, and I'd like to introduce you to her."

She blinks, her eyes glimmering. "Why?"

"Because I realise I've been using her as an excuse not to get close to people. I let my family be a barrier to me finding someone, because I've spent my whole life assuming people would leave anyway. And that's a disservice to Zoe, because I should have been introducing her to strong, amazing women who could inspire her."

"I don't know what to say." Her voice wobbles and tears fill her eyes.

"Say yes, you'll come for a drink."

"Just a drink?" she asks with a watery laugh. "Because we both know what happened the last time it was supposed to be 'just a drink.'"

"Come for a drink, meet my family properly and then I'll kick them out so I can have my wicked way with you." I thumb the edge of her full lips and she shivers in response. "Then I'll help you pack in the morning."

"Why would you do that?"

"Because I really hope you'll come back to me, Blondie. I don't want to wake up in ten years' time regretting that I didn't tell you how incredible I thought you were, because I know nobody else will even come close to you. I don't want to fuck this up by hiding behind my rules."

A fat tear plops onto her cheek and she swipes at it

with the back of her hand. "Dammit! I promised myself I wouldn't let you see me cry a second time."

"What do you say, huh?" I kiss the shimmering trail left by her tears and taste the salt on her skin. "Come home with me, spend the night in my bed. Have your holiday and then give us a chance."

"I cancelled it." Her tears are flowing more freely now, welling and dropping and smudging her mascara.

"Cancelled what?"

"My flight." Her voice is tight, full of emotion. "I cancelled it because I don't want to keep running."

Relief rushes through me like a wave seeking the shoreline and it almost bowls me over. "You're staying?"

"Uh-huh." She nods. "I'm done pretending. Done running."

"I'm *that* persuasive?" I tease.

She tries to swat me, but I capture her wrists. "Nice try, taking credit for my decision."

"Blondie, if you tell me you're staying then I don't care who helped you come to that conclusion. I owe them everything." I lower my forehead to hers and her hands curl into my shirt. "Second chances aren't really my thing. When I screw up, it tends to be permanent."

"You didn't screw up. You were protecting your heart," she says softly, her lips finding mine. She tastes like fruity lip gloss and tears and hope and something that's a whole lot like love. "We're two damaged people trying to find our way in the world."

"I'm so glad you're staying," I whisper against her

neck. I'm a little overcome, and it's a new feeling. A terrifying feeling. But I'd rather be scared and working toward something great than hiding like I have been.

"I'm excited to meet Zoe," she says. "I know what a big deal it is to you and I'm honoured."

"She's the best part of our family, trust me." My heart is so full it wants to burst. "Not like her cranky old uncle."

"I imagine you're not the kind of man who inspires halfway feelings with anyone you come across. People will either love you or hate you." Drew sucks in a breath. "And I don't feel halfway about you. Not at all."

"How *do* you feel about me?"

For a moment she says nothing—she simply draws her lower lip between her teeth and looks at me with such a penetrating stare it's like she can see right into my heart. Past all the defences I've spent years fortifying. Past all my baggage. Past the lies I tell myself. Right through to the little boy I promised I would protect forever against abandonment and pain.

The part of me I've exposed now.

"I feel like this could be it." She swallows. "Like it could be everything."

"Then let's not waste a minute." I kiss her hard and deep, sliding my hands down her spine to cup the sweet curve of her backside, holding her hard against me.

"You can't even wait until we get home?" She tosses her head back and laughs, her eyes sparkling with mischief like they did the very first night I met her. The moment I was changed forever.

"I almost threw everything away," I say, kissing her neck and sliding my hand up her thigh. The moment she melts against me I feel like a king. "I've got to make sure we don't waste a minute."

"Don't worry, Mr. Suit." She loops her arms around my neck. "Forever is *almost* enough time for me to do everything I want to do with you."

"Almost?" I chuckle. "What did I ever do to deserve you?"

EPILOGUE

Drew
One year later...

I'VE FINALLY CONVINCED Flynn to take a week off. It's only taken me booking and rescheduling this holiday four times to get to this point, but I don't care. He's dedicated to his work, to making a difference in people's lives. And the latest trials have kept him in the office for long, long hours. But there's hope, progress. My man won't stop until he's done everything in his power to help people.

My man. Some days I still don't believe that I get to say that.

And, to soften the blow, we're flying first class, in one of those pods that is *definitely* going to aid my "lifetime fantasy" checklist. Mile-high club, here I come! Good thing I don't know anyone who works for this airline. It was one of the reasons I declined the uber-cheap standby tickets my boss offered me.

I look over my suitcase, trying to think of anything I might have forgotten. Toothbrush, wide-tooth comb to get all the saltwater tangles out of my hair, Kindle stuffed full of smutty novels to give me some ideas for other things to add to our list.

Then I squint. Something looks amiss. I swear I had my lacy white beach cover-up sitting on top of my jean shorts. But now it sits in a neat little roll that has *all* the hallmarks of my type A "life is better with packing cubes" boyfriend.

"Flynn!" I crouch down and roll my eyes. "Stop repacking my suitcase!"

He does it all the time with my clothing. I toss a bunch of stuff into one of *my* drawers and he'll go through and fold everything. Seriously, I wonder sometimes if he came out of the womb folding T-shirts.

Marie Kondo has *nothing* on Flynn.

Grumbling to myself, I reach for the neatly rolled piece of white fabric. I'll pack my suitcase however the hell I please, thank you very much. But the second I unroll it, a little blue box pops out and I freeze. Holy shit. Is that what I think it is?

For a moment I can't breathe. In the sunshine streaming through the bedroom window, the velvet shimmers as though it's beckoning me. I reach out and brush my fingertip over the surface, feeling the pile soften under my touch.

Flynn hasn't responded to my yelling, so I grab the box, debating whether or not to open it. Part of me knows a good partner would stash it back in its place and attempt to roll the beach cover-up as neatly as him. While I've been changed by loving him with my whole heart for the past twelve months, I'm still *that* person who tries to sneak a look at Christmas presents under the tree and ferrets out all his hiding spots in the week before my birthday.

Biting my lip, I open the box and gasp. The ring nestled inside features a huge stone, black as the ink Flynn uses with his fancy fountain pen. It's an oval shape and the band has a collection of glittering diamonds hammered into it.

"I *knew* you would open it." His amused voice sounds behind me and I jump so hard, I almost yelp. "Gabe tried to tell me it was dangerous to leave something in the suitcase because it might end up getting checked without you noticing. But I told him, 'Don't worry. I know my Drew—she'll *definitely* find it.'"

"As if I would roll my clothes like that." I sniff. But my false annoyance doesn't mask the fact that I'm reeling. It's a stunning ring in a velvet box and we're going away on our first proper trip together…

"I guess I may as well do it now." Flynn saunters toward me, his hips rolling in that way that still makes me weak at the knees. That I know will make me weak at the knees until the day I die. He drops down in front of me, bending one knee. "Melanie Drew Richardson, the last year has been the happiest of my life. You make me grow every day."

"That's what she said," I say, but my words are choked up.

"Can we pause the sex jokes while I propose to you?" He grins, and I nod, my hands shaking so hard I have to white-knuckle the box so I don't drop it. "I want to marry you, Drew. I want to listen to your dirty jokes every day. I want to tell the whole world that you make me a better man. Because waking up next to you is the best part of my day, followed by feeling your body next to mine at night."

My heart flutters like a bird beating its wings against a cage. I knew things were going well, but this…it's more than I could have hoped for.

"I love you, Drew. I love how you drive me crazy by making a mess. I love how you always wait up for me no matter how late I work. I love that you excite and surprise me every single day. I want to make it official." He holds his hand out and I place the box in his palm. When he slips the ring onto my finger, the fit is so perfect I sigh. "Do you want to do this forever?"

I nod.

"Will you be my wife, Drew? Until we're old and wrinkly and still so hot for each other?"

"Yes!" I push him to the floor, straddling him next to my suitcase. The box skitters across the bedroom floor and my ring glints as if in satisfaction. "I want to marry you, Flynn. I want us to be a family. And I want to be there when you turn into a silver fox."

Flynn laughs and pulls my face down to his. "A silver fox, huh? Would you like me with grey hair?"

"I'll like you at every stage of life." I pepper kisses along his jaw. "You make me so happy."

"You make me happy too, Blondie. More than I ever thought possible." He looks up at me and I feel his love running through my veins. "So we're doing this thing?"

"Hell, yeah." I bring my lips down to his, rubbing my body over his in that way that makes him growl in my ear. It's a sound I want to hear for the rest of my days. "You're mine forever."

* * * * *

COMING SOON!

LET'S TALK
Romance

For exclusive extracts, competitions
and special offers, find us online:

- **f** facebook.com/millsandboon
- **🐦** @MillsandBoon
- **📷** @MillsandBoonUK

Get in touch on 01413 063232

For all the latest titles coming soon, visit
millsandboon.co.uk/nextmonth

MILLS & BOON

MODERN

Power and Passion

Prepare to be swept off your feet by sophisticated, sexy and seductive heroes, in some of the world's most glamourous and romantic locations, where power and passion collide.